W9-AKW-035

My name is Tad. I am twelve years old and a seventh grader at Lakeville Middle School.

Starting this blog is one of my five New Year's resolutions. The other four are:

1. finish seventh grade
2. figure out how to do a kickflip on my skateboard
3. get girls to notice me
4. finally start shaving

So: One down, four to go!

PLANET TAD

TIM CARVELL
Illustrated by Doug Holgate

MAD

HARPER
An Imprint of HarperCollinsPublishers

A portion of the text from this book
was originally published in *MAD* magazine.

Planet Tad

Copyright 2012 by E.C. Publications, Inc. All rights reserved.
MAD MAGAZINE and all related characters and elements are
trademarks of and © E.C. Publications, Inc.

(s14)

Printed in the United States of America.

No part of this book may be used or reproduced in any manner whatsoever
without written permission except in the case of brief quotations embodied
in critical articles and reviews. For information address HarperCollins
Children's Books, a division of HarperCollins Publishers,
195 Broadway, New York, NY 10007.
www.harpercollinschildrens.com

Library of Congress Cataloging-in-Publication Data
Carvell, Tim.
    Planet Tad / Tim Carvell ; illustrated by Doug Holgate.
        pages   cm.
    Summary: "Twelve-year-old Tad navigates a year filled with girl
problems, school antics, and the worst summer job in history, all told in the
form of illustrated blog entries"— Provided by publisher.
    ISBN 978-0-06-193438-4 (pbk.)
    [1. Middle schools—Fiction. 2. Schools—Fiction. 3. Blogs—Fiction. 4.
Humorous stories.]
PZ7.C2537Pl   2012
[Fic]   2011052412
                                                                    CIP
                                                                     AC

Typography by Erin Fitzsimmons
Illustrations by Doug Holgate
Emoticons by Robert Brook Allen
14 15 16 17 18   OPM   10 9 8 7 6 5 4 3 2 1

❖

First paperback edition, 2014

For my mom and dad

January

Hello, world!

My name is Tad. I am twelve years old and a seventh grader at Lakeville Middle School. This is my school:

This is our mascot:

We're the Lakeville Middle School Pirates. I guess because of the "LAKEville." Although, come to think of it, you find pirates in the ocean, not in lakes. Our mascot's, like, some kind of a lame lake pirate.

The more I think about it, the more I realize that our mascot sucks.

Anyway, this is my new blog, which I am starting today, on the new computer I got for Christmas. (It's actually my dad's old computer—he got a new computer and let me have his old one. Not that I'm complaining. There are some things you can't use and then give someone else—like underwear or toothbrushes—but I don't think computers are one of them.)

I've decided to start a blog because I have a lot of important thoughts to share with the world, and also to try and get Natalie Portman to go out with me.

I'm just kidding about that last part. Although if you are Natalie Portman, and you're reading this— like, if you Googled yourself or something—hi.

I live in Lakeville with my parents and my little sister, Sophie. She's seven years old. She's OK, even though she's not as good at sneaking up on me as she thinks she is. For instance, right now, I can tell she's STANDING RIGHT BEHIND ME READING

OVER MY SHOULDER. HI, SOPHIE!

(Just heard her trip over something as she ran out of my room. Awesome.)

Starting this blog is one of my five New Year's resolutions. The other four are:

1. finish seventh grade
2. figure out how to do a kickflip on my skateboard
3. get girls to notice me
4. finally start shaving

So: One down, four to go!

Ugh. I can't concentrate. Sophie's in her room, practicing for her oboe recital Friday night. She's been playing the same five-minute song over and over for an hour, and it's not even a good song.

Actually, on second thought, I don't think there's such a thing as a good oboe song.

3 ⇨

My best friend, Chuck, came over tonight to hang out. He saw that I got a new computer, and asked me what games I have. We poked around on it, but because it's my dad's computer, it doesn't really have any games on it. Still, it's got Photoshop, so we spent a little while playing around with that. For instance, this is what Sophie would look like if she had the head of a dinosaur:

I call her Sophie Rex. I think it's an improvement.

Bad news: Sophie found a printout of Sophie Rex and showed it to my parents. They say that I'm not allowed to Photoshop pictures of Sophie anymore.

Of course, they didn't say anything about Photoshopping pictures of THEM:

They looked really beautiful on their wedding day.

I wonder if spiders have their own version of Spider-Man, where a spider gets bitten by a radioactive human and winds up being able to read and balance his checkbook.

THE AMAZING
MAN
SPIDER
1

Tonight, my parents made me go to Sophie's oboe recital. On our way in, I picked up a program and saw that Sophie would be playing "My Heart Will Go On" from *Titanic*. I looked at my parents and whispered, "Did you know that's the song she's been practicing for the last month?" My dad said, "Nope!" and my mom said, "Never would've guessed it in a million years." And then they made me promise to tell Sophie that she'd done a great job.

Afterward, we went out to dinner, and my dad ordered the spaghetti and meatballs, and I ordered the same thing. The waitress said, "All right. You'll have the pasketti and meatballs." And I said, "No. Spaghetti." And she said, "You're thirteen and under, right?" And I said, "I'm twelve." And she said, "Well, if you're thirteen and under, you can order from the children's menu, where it's spelled 'pasketti.'" And then she whispered, "Look: If you say 'pasketti,' it's three dollars cheaper." And I said, "I'm not going to mispronounce 'spaghetti' on purpose." And my dad said, "Come on, Tad." And I said, "I'm ordering the spaghetti and meatballs for you. If it's worth three dollars to you to have to say 'pasketti and meatballs,' you can order it for me." And my dad thought about it for a second, and then he said, "We'll have two orders of spaghetti and meatballs, please."

JANUARY 8 [mood: embarrassed]

I've been doing the Sudoku puzzle in our newspaper for a year now, and I just found out that *Sudoku* is a Japanese word. Which made me feel stupid, because for all this time, I've thought the puzzles were called Sudoku because they were made by a woman named Sue Doku. I even imagined what she looks like: She's sixty and lives alone with a whole lot of cats, and she spends her days filling in grids of numbers, then erasing almost all of them.

When Chuck came to school today, he asked me, "So, you notice anything different?" I looked at him for a while, and the only thing I noticed was that he was a little more dandruffy than usual, but that didn't seem like the right thing to say. And then he said, "I shaved!" Which makes it official: I am the last guy in the seventh grade to shave. Well, second-to-last. There's Dan Cramer, but he skipped two grades and is, like, ten, so he doesn't count.

I don't know why it's taking me so long—there are girls in my class with more hair on their faces than me. (Not that I envy them that, either. But still.)

[mood: bored] JANUARY 10

In English today, Mr. Parker had us spend the whole class diagramming sentences at the blackboard. Diagramming sentences is like a

So we've been assigned *Watership Down* in Mr. Parker's English class. We've been reading it for a few weeks now, and during today's class, Doug Spivak raised his hand and said, "Hey, wait a minute: This is about rabbits, isn't it?"

I don't know why this is even surprising. Doug's repeated seventh grade twice, and is the guy who, until he was ten, thought the International House of Pancakes restaurants were actually all made out of pancakes. He's not the sharpest knife in the drawer. In fact, he's more like a spoon or something, sharpness-wise.

[mood: curious] ## JANUARY 14

My dad's taking fish oil to lower his cholesterol. Whenever I see the bottle, it cracks me up, because I like to imagine it's supposed to be squirted into squeaky fish.

Today in health class, Mrs. Lewis told us that we needed to learn about what it would be like to be a parent. So she paired us off and gave every pair an egg to take care of, like it's a baby and we're its parents. One of us has to keep it with us at all times until Friday, and if it breaks, we get an F for the project. I got paired with Laurie Watson, the co-captain of the field hockey team. It could've been worse—Chuck got paired up with Sam Turner, the defensive tackle for our football team. When Chuck and Sam asked why, Mrs. Lewis said, "Families come in all different configurations. Plus, we have more boys than girls in this class."

After we got our egg, Laurie asked me what we should name the baby. She said she was thinking of maybe naming it Katherine, "but we'll call her Kate or Katie

Baby Katherine

for short." I just stared at her and said, "Laurie, it's an egg." And she said, "Oh, okay. Fine. Be like that. But I'm calling it Katherine." And then she ignored me for the rest of class. I feel like our egg baby is going to have a lot of trouble at home.

Meanwhile, Chuck was fighting with Sam over their egg. Chuck wanted to name it Chuck Jr., while Sam wanted to name it Sam Jr. If they'd asked me, I would've suggested compromising and calling their baby Suck.

It's probably a good thing they didn't ask me.

JANUARY 17 [mood: irritated]

Man. Only a day into parenting this egg, and Laurie and I have already had our first big fight. I took the egg home last night, because Laurie had field hockey practice, and I realized pretty quickly that it was going to be hard to keep the egg from breaking. So I had what I thought was a pretty good idea: I boiled it.

I was kind of proud of myself, but when I gave it back to Laurie before homeroom, she said, "Something doesn't feel right about Katie." So I told her what I'd done, and she said "You boiled our baby?" so loud that everyone in the hallway turned and stared. I pointed out that at least I didn't poach or scramble our baby, but that didn't seem to make things any better.

Later, Laurie came up to me at lunch and said that she was thinking of asking Mrs. Lewis to let her have sole custody of the egg, with me only allowed supervised visits, but then she realized that really wouldn't be much of a punishment for me, and besides, she needed me to look after the egg during her violin lessons.

JANUARY 18 [mood: Jedi-ish]

Is Jabba a common name throughout the *Star Wars* universe? And does each planet have only one of them? Because it seems odd to me that you'd need to go by "Jabba the Hutt." It makes me wonder if he had one too

many phone calls that went like this:

"Hey, it's me, Jabba."

"Jabba the Ewok?"

"No, the other one."

"Jabba the Gungan?"

"No."

"Jabba the Dagoban?"

"No. C'mon, man. It's me, Jabba! Jabba the Hutt!"

"Oh! Jabba the Hutt! Why didn't you say so?"

JANUARY 19 [mood: anxious]

During health class today, Mrs. Lewis announced that, so far, four out of the twelve couples in our class have broken their egg babies. Then she said that any couple who kept their egg intact would get a bonus A for the semester, and Sam got so excited, he accidentally high-fived Chuck with his egg-holding hand, and Sam Jr. went everywhere. Chuck didn't seem too upset about it, though. He said that he and Sam had been fighting a lot about how to take care of the egg, and he was kind of glad to have that over with.

Well, today was the final day for the egg-baby experiment, and I'm really happy, because I was sick of taking care of my stupid egg. In class, when it came time for us to give our eggs back to Mrs. Lewis, Laurie and I were one of only three couples who'd kept their eggs intact all week long, and she said she was very proud of us. Then she leaned on her desk a little, and our egg rolled off and fell on the floor. That's when Mrs. Lewis realized ours had been boiled. She told us she was very, very disappointed in us, and hoped that we didn't have a baby for many, many years. I told her that made two of us.

Chuck and I were debating: If a fast-food mascot were making your food, which one would you go with—Ronald McDonald, the Burger King, Wendy, or the Arby's hat? We both agreed that we wouldn't choose the hat, but after that, it got harder. I said

I'd go with the King, but Chuck pointed out that a
king probably has people preparing food for him,
so he'd be unfamiliar with proper cooking techniques and wouldn't know how to cook your food to
the proper internal temperature. (Chuck had food
poisoning once, and ever since, he's been terrified
of it. I once saw him ask a lunch lady to reheat his
pudding cup to kill any bacteria.) Chuck said he'd
go with Wendy, but I said that she was even less
likely to know anything about preventing food
poisoning. Plus, I know how gross my little sister,
Sophie, is, and I wouldn't trust anything she prepared. So that left Ronald McDonald, and we both

agreed that if we had to choose between a burger made by a clown and nothing, we'd pick nothing.

I was hanging out at Chuck's place last night, and his older sister, Tracy, had rented *Twilight: New Moon*, so we watched it with her. I have to give it credit: I never knew a movie about a vampire fighting a were-wolf could be so boring.

Sophie came home from school today all excited because she got cast in the school play as Gretel in *Hansel and Gretel*. She was super super happy, because she'd beaten out Sara Cambert, her big rival. Sophie kept talking about how crushed Sara was. Sara's been in a local furniture commercial and was sure that she was going to be picked for the role, but instead, she's going to have to play a bush, "and not even one of the good bushes." Finally, my mom said, "Well, it's going to be a lot of work. You'll have to learn your lines." And Sophie said, "What lines?" My mom explained that if you're in a play, you have to know what to say and do, so Sophie would have to practice her lines every night instead of watching TV, and my dad said it would be a good lesson in the value of hard work. Then Sophie got super quiet and just kept muttering about how Sara Cambert had "won this round."

JANUARY 24 [mood: excited]

After dinner tonight, my sister said that she'd asked her teacher about learning her lines, and "Mrs. McKenna told me that I should practice them with someone. She said it'd be easy for me to remember my lines if I just spent an hour or two every night with my parents going through the script. It'll be a good lesson in the value of hard work, right?" My dad looked at my mom, and my mom looked at my dad, and then they both looked at me. And my mom said, "Tad, you know how you've been asking for a new skateboard?" And that is how I wound up helping Sophie learn her lines for her play.

JANUARY 25 [mood: frustrated]

Argh. I've been going through the *Hansel and Gretel* script every night with Sophie, and it's really no fun. The whole play's written in rhyme, so all of her lines rhyme with the one that came right before, and she still can't remember them. I'll read Hansel's part and say something like, "Look at that house! It's so fine and so dandy!" and then I'll look at her and she'll just be like, "I don't know." And so I'll give her part of her line: "It looks delicious, like it's made out of . . . ?" And she'll still be like, "What? I don't know. Bricks?"

[mood: not good] JANUARY 26

I hate helping Sophie—it's a big waste of time.
And the worst part is, I'm now thinking in rhyme.

Just three more days till I get my reward.

This is too much work for a stupid skateboard.

JANUARY 27 [mood: exhausted]

Well, Sophie's getting a little better at learning her lines. Tonight, for the first time, I said Hansel's line, "Now's your chance, Gretel, start doing some shovin'!" and she said, "Something something something, something something oven?" It's a start.

[mood: relieved] JANUARY 28

Sophie's big show is tomorrow, and I'm glad I'm finally done helping her. I think she'll actually do OK—it took a while, but she learned all her lines, more or less. I'm just happy I never have to think about the story of Hansel and Gretel ever again. It's a weird story. Like, why would anyone want to eat a candy house? Wouldn't it be kind of dirty and sticky?

Just got back from Sophie's big play. It was a little ... weird. We got there, and Mrs. McKenna was all panicked, and told my parents the show might not happen because Jerry Moynihan, who played Hansel, was out sick with the stomach flu. And then Sophie said, "My brother, Tad, knows all the lines! He learned them all when he was helping me!" And Mrs. McKenna said, "Oh, that's wonderful! If Tad can play Hansel, the show can go on!" And Mrs. McKenna and Sophie and my parents and all the other kids were looking at me, and just before I could say, "No way," my mom leaned over and whispered in my ear, "*Lord of the Rings* trilogy DVD boxed set." And I said, "Extended versions?" And she said, "Sure."

So at the age of twelve, I just

starred in an elementary-school production of *Hansel and Gretel*. It was fun right up until the moment I noticed Bill Gilbert in the audience—he's in my class, and I guess his younger brother's in Sophie's class. I think I'd better get ready to be called Hansel at school for the next month or so.

Still, it was pretty nice to help Sophie out. She seemed really happy afterward. I asked her why, and she said, "Did you see how sad Sara Cambert looked in her bush costume?" And then she just laughed and kept imitating her, going "I'm Sara Cambert! I'm a bush! I only have one line!"

Sophie scares me sometimes.

JANUARY 30 [mood: amused]

We have a new exchange student in our class— Claudine Moreau from France. I felt kind of bad for her, because in social studies, Mrs. Wexler said, "Well, class, I think it's exciting to have someone from another country here! Would anyone like to ask Claudine anything about France?" And everyone just kind of sat there feeling embarrassed for her, until Doug Spivak raised his hand and said,

"What do your toasters look like?" And Mrs. Wexler said, "Why would you ask that, of all things?" And Doug said, "Well, I've always wondered how the French make French toast. Like, do you pour the egg and milk into the toaster, or what? It seems messy and dangerous." And Mrs. Wexler said, "Does anyone *else* have anything to ask?"

After class, I saw Doug asking Claudine about French onions, and whether they come out of the ground covered in melted cheese. She looked really confused.

JANUARY 31 [mood: nauseated]

I think the most upsetting nursery rhyme has to be "Pop Goes the Weasel," what with the whole exploding-weasel thing.

February

I would be writing this on the computer in the family room, but Sophie's in there right now, watching reruns of *Hannah Montana*. I still can't believe there's a show where the whole plot is that nobody can tell that Hannah Montana is Miley Cyrus in a wig. The kids in

I mean, come on, guys, really?!

her school make Clark Kent's coworkers look like brain surgeons.

The only way that show would make sense would be if there were a title card at the beginning of every episode that said, "Everyone in this town has had the exact same kind of brain injury that destroys your ability to recognize things, even if those things look exactly alike."

FEBRUARY 2 [mood: groundhoggy]

This morning in homeroom, Mrs. Coleman wished us all a happy Groundhog Day. Then our exchange student, Claudine Moreau, raised her hand and asked, "What is a groundhog day?" So Mrs. Coleman tried to explain it to her, and Claudine asked a lot of questions, like, "How does anyone know if the groundhog actually sees its shadow or not?" But finally, she said she understood: "You Americans believe a rodent controls the weather. In France, we have—how you say?—meteorologists?"

When she put it like that, it did sound kind of stupid.

Went to the mall with my parents today. Sophie and I stopped by the pet store, which is sort of like going to a crappy, free zoo. They had a whole litter of Dalmatian puppies there, and they were pretty cute. Although seeing Dalmatian puppies up close, I didn't understand why Cruella De Vil thought she needed 101 of them to make a coat. I feel like you could make a really nice coat with six or seven of them. Which, it turns out, isn't the sort of thing you're supposed to say out loud in a pet store, because the clerk kind of asked us to leave.

Werewolves are badly named. They're not people who *were* wolves. They're people who *are* wolves. They should be called arewolves. (Or, if you're going to be super accurate, aresometimeswolves.)

At school today, the signs went up for the after-school Valentine's Day dance. I really want to ask Katie Zembla from my geometry class.

She seems super friendly and pretty, and she's always really nice to me after I let her copy my homework.

I tried asking Katie to the dance today, but I got all nervous and wound up asking to borrow her eraser instead. And then I had to erase some stuff so it wouldn't look weird, which meant that I wound up erasing a couple of answers on my homework right before I had to hand it in.

I tried asking Katie again, but I wound up asking to borrow her protractor. It's getting embarrassing.

Good news! I finally asked her, and she said she'd go with me! Well, actually, she said she'd go if this person she's waiting to ask her doesn't by tomorrow. So I'm her second choice!

FEBRUARY 10 [mood: impatient]

It's Friday, and I caught up with Katie after class. She said her first choice still hadn't asked her, but she wanted to give him until the end of the day, so she said she'd call me tomorrow.

[mood: very very very very happy] FEBRUARY 11

Hooray! I just called Katie, and she said she'd go with me! The dance is three days away, so I have until then to find out stuff like what to wear and how to dance.

FEBRUARY 12 [mood: tired]

Mom took me to the mall today to look for a new tie. I like the one I have, but she says girls don't like boys who wear ties that look like fish.

Tomorrow's the big dance! I went to the Dollar Depot today and bought some cK One cologne. Well, actually, it's called dB Two, but it smells just like cK One, and it only costs a buck! It's pretty good—my dad noticed it right when he came home, and I was all the way up in my room. He asked how much I paid for it, and when I told him, he said, "That's a bargain for cologne that strong!" And then he opened all the windows.

[mood: itchy] **FEBRUARY 14**

Ugh. I didn't wind up going to the dance after all. I woke up this morning covered in hives.

Mom took me to Dr. Bauer, who tested me and told me that I'm allergic to the artificial musk in the dB Two, which I guess is good to know. He gave me some Benadryl, and I spent the day at home, recovering. So instead of going to the dance, I stayed home and watched TV with my parents. They tried to be nice about it, but every once in a while, my dad would look at me and start laughing, and then he'd try to pretend that he was laughing at the TV, but we were watching reruns of *Law & Order: SVU*, which isn't really all that funny.

FEBRUARY 15 [mood: ill]

At the grocery store tonight, they were giving away boxes of those Valentine's candy hearts for free because, as the cashier said, "It's not like anyone's going to buy them the day after Valentine's Day." I just ate a few of them and then threw them away. Valentine's hearts are the worst candy on earth. They're, like, made of sugar, soap, and chalk dust.

The family went out to dinner tonight to Chili's, and in the restroom, they had this sign:

It made me wonder if any customer has ever wound up just standing there in front of the sink, waiting for an employee to come wash his hands for him.

[mood: excited] FEBRUARY 20

So I just got back from brushing my teeth, and when I was done, I noticed something: I've got a little bit of hair growing in on my upper lip. At first I thought it was a shadow, but I looked closer and it's definitely a mustache. I may finally be ready to start shaving. I considered asking my parents to get me a razor, but then I decided that I'd let it go for a while and see how long it takes for anyone to notice.

FEBRUARY 21 [mood: mature]

Today was the first day for my new mustache. There's something about having a mustache that makes you feel automatically more mature. I spent the whole day feeling like Johnny Depp in *Pirates of the Caribbean*—holding doors for girls and trying to come up with clever, Jack Sparrow-y things to say to them. When Julie Underhill asked me in class today if she could borrow a pen, I said, "You can borrow anything you like." And she said, "Oh. Um. Well, can I borrow a pen?" And then I realized that I didn't have any pens to loan her. But still—it sounded really cool.

I'm kind of surprised my parents haven't noticed my mustache yet. I feel like it's pretty noticeable—it's the only thing I can see when I look in the mirror. At dinner tonight, whenever my parents asked me anything, I'd pause and think about it while stroking my mustache with my thumb and forefinger. But after I did that when Sophie asked me to pass the turnips, my mom said, "Are you feeling OK? Are you sick? Come over here!" and took my temperature by pressing her lips to my forehead, which I don't think is the sort of thing you do to someone who has a mustache.

[mood: embarrassed] **FEBRUARY 23**

So today at school, Señora Lutz asked me why I was late to Spanish class, and I said, "Wouldn't you like to know?" And she said, "Yes I would. And I'd appreciate it if you didn't take that tone with me." Maybe the light was too low in the room for her to see my mustache. After class, Chuck said, "Why've you been talking weird lately?" And I said, "I can't imagine what you're talking about." And he said, "You've got, like, this weird British accent all of a sudden. You sound like a drunk Mary Poppins."

FEBRUARY 24 [mood: annoyed]

Well, today, I got tired of waiting for my parents to mention my mustache. So when my mom said she was going to the store and asked if I needed anything, I just said, "Maybe some razors?" And she said, "Why?" And I said, "Isn't it obvious?" And she said, "No. Not really." And I said, "My mustache!" And then she walked over and looked at my face really closely and said, "Eh. I don't see it."

[mood: shorn] FEBRUARY 25

Since my mom wouldn't get me any razors, I decided to shave using one of my dad's disposable razors this morning. I couldn't find any shaving cream, so I used some of my mom's hairstyling foam. It turns out that styling foam is super sticky, and razors are a lot sharper than you'd expect. So I came down to breakfast with a Band-Aid across my upper lip and another one on my chin. (I wasn't even growing any hair there, but I figured it'd be good to practice shaving my whole face.)

My dad saw me and said, "Whoa! Tad—what happened to your fa—" But then my mom kicked him under the table and he quieted down. Neither of them said anything about it for the rest of the day, but just now, when I came upstairs to the bathroom to brush my teeth, there was a new electric razor there. I can't wait to use it the next time my mustache grows in. Hopefully, by then my face scars will have healed. And if anyone at school asks, I'm telling them I got into a fight.

From boy...

...to man!

I never understand why *Jeopardy!* does that whole weird "You have to phrase your answers in the form of a question" thing. But I think I've figured out a loophole: If I ever wind up on *Jeopardy!*, I'll buzz in every time and ask the question, "What is an answer in this episode of *Jeopardy!*?" And they'd have to let me win, because that is technically right.

I can't believe nobody else has thought of this.

Today in science, we learned that monkeys and apes are different species: Monkeys have tails, while apes don't. So a marmoset, for instance, is a monkey, while a chimpanzee is an ape.

Doug Spivak raised his hand and asked, "What if you cut the tail off a marmoset? Does it become an ape? And what if you attach that tail to a chimpanzee? Does it become a monkey?" We never found out the answer, because Mr. Parker just put his head down on his desk and made a noise like he was either laughing or crying—it was hard to tell.

Today's Leap Day—the day that comes only once every four years. I feel like whoever came up with Leap Day should go down to the hospital and apologize to all the babies that were born today, because thanks to that person, they're in for a long life of explaining their birthday to people.

March

MARCH 1 [mood: sleepy]

Overslept this morning and missed the school bus, so my mom had to drive me to school. I blame my alarm clock. Why do they even put a Snooze button on there? They might as well just call it an Oversleep button.

[mood: pity] MARCH 2

In my science textbook, I read that even blind chameleons change color to match their surroundings.

I asked my dad how they figured that out, and he said, "Well, I guess they did a study where they blinded some chameleons and then saw what happened."

I think it's weird that somewhere out there in the world, there's a guy whose job title is Chameleon Blinder.

I've been thinking about it, and if I ever have a band, it will be called Chameleon Blinder.

Getting a little excited for my birthday—it's in three days. I'm not having a big party or anything—my parents are going to take Chuck and Kevin and Jake bowling with me, and then out for pizza at Pizza Land.

I told my mom I want a GamePort XL game system for my birthday. Chuck got one for Christmas, and he brought it to school last week. He let me see it. That's all he let me do, though—see it. He wouldn't let me hold it because, he said, "My mom said I can't let people play with it, because they might break it. Plus, it's flu season, so it's better not to touch things other people have touched." (Chuck's a nice guy, but his mom's super nervous about everything, and as a result, so's he. Until he was in sixth grade, his mom made Chuck wear a helmet on the school bus.)

The GamePort XL is pretty cool—there's a game that makes it look like it's got a puppy inside it, and you can make it fetch and stay and stuff. Chuck really likes it because his mom won't let him have a dog, because she's afraid it might one day go crazy and kill him just like this dog she saw on the news. I told Chuck that if I get that game, I'm naming my puppy "Chuckbiter."

I really need a GamePort XL. In study hall today, Chuck and Kevin both spent the whole time playing with their imaginary dogs.

I had nothing to do but draw pictures of blind chameleons:

At breakfast, I reminded my mom and dad that I want a GamePort XL for my birthday, and my mom said, "Well, maybe if you're good, you'll get that GigaPet 9000 you want." And I got all worried and said, "No! I want a GamePort XL! Why did you think I wanted a GigaPet? Those are for seven-year-old girls!" And she said, "Oh, a GamePort? Well, it's probably too late to get you one of those." And then she smiled at my dad. So I think they're just messing with my head. Which isn't very nice.

Awesome!

Not awesome!

Today was my birthday. Bowling and dinner were a lot of fun. (Well, there were two bad parts: First, even though I told him not to do it, my dad told the people at Pizza Land that it was my birthday, so all the waiters and the Pizza Badger came over and sang "Happy Birthday" to me, which would've been fun when I was, like, nine, but I'm thirteen now. And then the fact that I was being serenaded by the Pizza Badger made Kevin laugh so loud, he sprayed soda through his nose and onto my cake. We had to eat around that part.)

Hey, hey, HEY! Party dudes!

Let's pizza PARTY!

When we got home, my parents gave me my present: a Game-Port XL! So I can't blog now—I'm teaching Chuckbiter to fetch.

Bad news. I went over to Chuck's today, and Kevin came over, and we were all playing with our

GamePorts. And then I put mine on the floor and went to the kitchen to get a soda, and then, when I came back, I stepped on it and broke it.

I don't even know what was worse—breaking my GamePort or having Chuck's mom come in the room immediately afterward and say, "You see, Chuck? That's why you shouldn't let Tad touch your things."

I bet that if all the animal mascots for products got together for a convention—like, if the Trix rabbit and the Cocoa Puffs cuckoo and Elsie the cow all got together—I kind of think that everyone would make a point of avoiding the Charmin toilet-paper bears. Seriously. As best I can tell, those bears would talk about nothing but toilet paper, and everyone else would be like, "Hey, we're trying to eat over here."

For vocab in English, we have to learn the word *disgruntled*. It means "unhappy." Weirdly, there's no such word as *gruntled*, meaning "happy." I'm going to try and make it a word, though. I'm just going to start using it in conversation, and hopefully it'll catch on.

[mood: not gruntled] **MARCH 12**

Well, after one day, I'm giving up on making *gruntled* a word. I told my mom that I was gruntled with dinner last night, and she said if I didn't like it, I didn't have to eat it. I told Mr. Parker today that I was feeling gruntled, and he said, "If you need to go to the bathroom, just ask to be excused." And then I told one of the lunch ladies today that the food was very gruntling, and she said she'd had enough abuse from us kids.

Making words catch on is a lot harder than I'd thought. It gave me a whole new respect for Merriam and Webster.

Today at school, we all pretty much wasted a whole period of social studies. Mrs. Wexler was explaining how the United States engages in trade with other countries, like Mexico and Canada. Doug Spivak raised his hand and said, "I'm sorry, Mrs. Wexler? But Canada's a state." And Mrs. Wexler said, "No, Doug, actually, Canada is a whole separate country." But Doug said, "No, it's a state. States have their names on quarters, right?" And then he reached into his pocket and held up a quarter and said, "I got this Canadian quarter a little while ago, and it says 'Canada' on it. So they must be a state. A state full of stupid people who don't know how to make quarters that work in vending machines."

So then Mrs. Wexler spent a while explaining that while Canada uses dollars and quarters, that doesn't make them a state. And Doug said, "But they speak English! That means they must be American!" And she said, "Just because they

49 ⇨

speak English somewhere doesn't mean it's part of America. I mean, Great Britain's not part of America, is it?" And he said, "It's not?" And things went on like that for another half hour.

I bet Doug Spivak's going to get held back again this year. It's too bad. He kind of makes every class more interesting.

MARCH 17   [mood: green]

Today is St. Patrick's Day. Supposedly, St. Patrick's the guy who got all the snakes out of Ireland. I dunno—that doesn't seem like a sainthood-worthy achievement. I mean, committing reptile genocide is really hard to do, but it doesn't seem like it makes you a saint so much as it makes you a really, really good exterminator.

Sophie and I played Monopoly tonight. I'm not sure how that game ever got made. Like, did someone go into Parker Brothers and say, "I have an idea for a game: A dog, a flat iron, a shoe, and a hat are all buying streets. Sometimes, one of them will go to jail for no good reason. Plus, there's an old man with a bag full of money who sometimes wins beauty pageants, there are some railroads, and it never ends and there's no way to tell who won."

It's like a board game based on someone's nightmare.

[mood: excited]   MARCH 19

Today in science class, Mr. Parker said that anyone who enters the science fair this year will get extra credit—and whoever wins will get an A for the semester. I went home and looked on the internet for science fair project ideas, and I found one that looks unbeatable: You can make a volcano out of clay, and put baking soda, vinegar, and red food coloring inside it to make "lava" flow out of it. I don't know what the big science lesson is supposed to be from that, because I'm pretty sure that's not how real volcanoes work.

Then again, I don't really care what the lesson's supposed to be. I just like the idea of making something that explodes.

MARCH 20 [mood: competitive]

So I asked Chuck today if he was making a science fair project, and he said that he was. And I asked him what it was, and he said he was keeping it a secret, because his was so awesome, he didn't want anyone to steal it. Then he asked me what I was making, and I told him that I wasn't going to tell him, but that it was even awesomer than his. So we made a bet. Whichever one of us wins the science fair will pay the other one ten bucks. I'm already making plans on what to do with my winnings. Like maybe getting a shirt that says "I Won Ten Bucks from Chuck."

Here are some things I learned today while doing my science project:

- If you're going to make a volcano, don't make it out of your sister's old Play-Doh on your kitchen table. Because if you do, when you pour baking soda and vinegar in it, it might start to leak all over the kitchen floor.
- Also, don't use a whole bottle of red food coloring, because the giant puddle on your floor will be super red.
- Also, don't run when you're getting the paper towels to clean up the table and the floor, because you'll just slip and fall and get it all over you.
- Also, try not to time the whole thing to the moment your mom comes home from work. Because it turns out that if your mom walks in the door and finds you under the kitchen table, in the middle of a giant

red puddle, and covered with red liquid,
she'll scream really, really loud, in a way
that you've never heard her scream before.

That is what I have learned about volcanoes
so far.

At lunch today, Susan Meyers asked me if I was
doing a science fair project. I told her I was, but
that it was top secret. She said, "Oh, I'm doing one
on optimizing the uses of activated charcoal in a
water-filtration system."

I'm not even sure what that means, but I know
this much: It's no match for a tiny volcano. I'm *so*
going to win.

 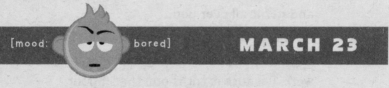

In order to do some research on volcanoes, I went
to the library and got a whole bunch of books on
them. I also rented the movies *Volcano* and *Dante's*

Peak. Applying the scientific method, I now have a hypothesis that all movies about volcanoes suck.

MARCH 24   [mood: nervous]

Well, I got the volcano done in time for tomorrow's science fair. I think it looks OK, even though I kind of screwed up in painting it—it was supposed to look gray, but when I put the paint on the clay, it wound up looking dark brown. Sophie kept saying it looks like "a pile of poop," and then laughing, until my mom told her to stop.

I also made a posterboard display covered with facts about volcanoes. For instance, did you know that "Volcano" is the nickname for rugby player Lesley Vainikolo? Wikipedia is awesome.

You know, SCIENCE!

Tonight was the school science fair. My parents helped me bring my volcano in and set it up. Then Chuck got there with his parents and his science project: a volcano that erupts baking soda and vinegar. And then other kids started coming in, and it turns out that, like, twelve guys from my class all made volcanoes. I guess we all went to the same website and got the same idea. Three other kids even had pictures of Lesley Vainikolo as part of their displays. Stupid Wikipedia.

So I'm not getting an A in science after all. In fact, Mr. Parker seemed so unimpressed that by the time he got to me, he said, "Don't even bother pouring the vinegar in. I get it. It's a volcano."

Susan Meyers won the science fair. I was pretty sad about it, until Mr. Parker told her that she'd have to compete in the regional science fair, which takes place during our spring vacation. Chuck and I agreed: We were glad we hadn't won.

Afterward, I took my volcano over to Chuck's house and we put some of his little brother's Lego men in front of both of them, poured vinegar in them, and videotaped the whole thing. It was sort of like *Dante's Peak* meets *Volcano*, but with better acting.

MARCH 26 [mood: hungry]

I've never understood why it's such a big deal in *Green Eggs and Ham* that Sam won't eat green eggs and ham. Not eating green eggs and ham seems like a really good policy to me.

[mood: denial] **MARCH 29**

Oh, man. So I came down to breakfast this morning, and my mom looked really sad, and my dad said: "Your great-aunt Sophie died yesterday." And I said, "Which one was she?" And my dad said, "She was your mother's father's sister." And I said, "The one with the bright-red hair?" And my mom said, "No. That's your great-aunt Katie. Sophie's the one with the cane." And I said, "Oh! You mean the mean one who always picked her terrier up by the neck? Wasn't she dead already?" And my dad gave me a look that told me that was the wrong thing to say.

Great-Aunt Sophie (R.I.P.) Great-Aunt Katie (not dead)

My little sister Sophie's pretty upset—she was named for our great-aunt Sophie. She came into my room tonight and said, "Where do you think Aunt Sophie went?" And I gave her the same answer my parents gave me when our golden retriever died: Great-Aunt Sophie was taken to a farm where she gets to spend all day chasing rabbits and playing with other great-aunts.

That seemed to make her happy.

MARCH 30   [mood: slightly irregular]

After school today, Mom took me to the outlet mall to buy a new suit for Great-Aunt Sophie's funeral, because I outgrew my last one. Mom always takes me to the outlet mall to get clothes. One day, when I'm older, I want to wear clothes with labels that don't have the words SLIGHTLY IRREGULAR stamped on them. I wanted to get a suit with big pinstripes, like Jay-Z would wear, but Mom wouldn't let me—she made me get a really boring black one instead. When I got it home and showed my dad, he said, "Are you leaning over to your left?" And I said, "No." That's when we realized that the right arm was a lot shorter than the left one. Stupid irregular suit. Now I'm going to have to spend all day Saturday leaning slightly to the right, to compensate.

MARCH 31   [mood: relieved]

Well, today was the funeral. Everyone said nice things about Great-Aunt Sophie, but the truth is, she smoked nonstop and hit her terrier with her cane and was super mean. She wasn't a nice lady. But I guess you can't say that at a funeral. So everyone pretended to be really sad. Except for her terrier. He looked happier than I'd ever seen him.

April

[mood: irked]

Attention, friends of Tad!

If you go onto Facebook and find <u>this profile</u>  with my name on it, please be aware that IT IS NOT my profile! It is a fake profile that my friend Chuck put up as a stupid April Fools'

facebook

Name: Tad
Age: 12
Interests: nose-picking, butt-scratching, playing classical banjo, and dressing up like a girl.

joke. He thought it would be funny. But if I had a Facebook profile, I wouldn't list my interests as "nose-picking, butt-scratching, playing classical banjo, and dressing up like a girl." I don't even like the banjo.

However, rest assured that <u>this profile</u> of Chuck is the real one. Honestly, I'm as surprised as anyone to find out that Chuck cried at the end of *Titanic* and still wets the bed, but if that's what his profile says, then it must be true.

APRIL 2   [mood: annoyed]

When I was at Great-Aunt Sophie's funeral, I saw my uncle Scott, and he taught me a new joke. When he saw me, he said, "Hey, how've you been? Do you want a henway?" And I said, "What's a henway?" And he said, "Oh, about three pounds."

Get it? Because it sounds like I was asking, "What's a hen weigh?"

So I tried telling the joke today. First I tried it on Chuck—he asked how my trip to Great-Aunt Sophie's funeral was, and I said, "It was good, except I lost my henway." And he said, "A henway?

I don't know what a henway is." Then I tried it on Señora Lutz, when she asked where my Spanish book was, and I said, "I must've left it in my locker next to my henway," and she just sighed and said, "Well, run back and get it." Finally I tried it on Doug Spivak in social studies—I asked him if he'd remembered to bring his henway. And he said, "What's a henway?" And I said, "Oh, about three pounds." And he thought about it for a few seconds, and then he said, "I don't get it."

I don't care. I still think it's an awesome joke.

APRIL 3

[mood: excited]

Hooray! I've been practicing for weeks, and I finally figured out how to do a kickflip on my skateboard! Well, sort of—I can jump up and flip the skateboard beneath me, but I haven't figured out how to actually land on anything other than my face. Still, though, the first half looks pretty great. And besides, landing isn't important. The important thing is, I can take a picture of me in midair and put it on my Facebook page, and it'll look awesome.

Gaaaargh! Chuck and I spent all afternoon in his driveway, trying to get a picture of me doing my kickflip, but my dad's digital camera really sucks. Here are some of the photos we took:

This one was taken, like, a second too soon.

This one was taken a second too late.

This one is of Chuck's finger. He's not a very good photographer.

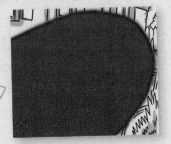

Anyway. We're going to try again next weekend.

Hopefully, by then the swelling in my face will have gone down.

Easter Sunday's in a few days, and Sophie's been talking a lot about the Easter Bunny lately. All through dinner, she kept saying stuff like, "I hope the Easter bunny brings me lots of Cadbury Creme Eggs!" or "Does the Easter Bunny know I don't like licorice jelly beans?" I asked her how the Easter Bunny makes Peeps, and she explained about the Easter Bunny's Peep factory, and my parents just sort of nudged each other and smiled.

What they don't know is that back when she was six, Sophie told me that she'd figured out that the Easter Bunny doesn't exist. But she'd also figured out that Mom and Dad really like pretending to be the Easter Bunny, and that they probably give her more candy than they would if they knew that she knew that they were the ones leaving it. And since they have to give me the same amount of stuff they give Sophie, I've realized that it's in my best interest to keep my parents believing in Sophie's belief in the Easter Bunny. So we both put on this little show for my parents. It's actually sort of cute how excited they get about it. I mean, I know that it can't go on forever, but it's sort of fun while it lasts.

APRIL 6 [mood: happy]

Good news! I was talking to Chuck and Kevin today, and Chuck mentioned how we're trying to take the skateboard picture. It turns out, Kevin's dad has a really nice high-speed digital camera that's amazing at taking action shots. Kevin said he could sneak it out and let us borrow it, but that we'd have to be super careful, 'cause it's a nice camera and really expensive. And then he mentioned it again. And then he mentioned it a third time.

   Kevin worries a lot.

[mood: hungry] **APRIL 7**

Tonight at the grocery store, my mom sent me off to buy Easter candy while she distracted Sophie.

I bought a bunch of chocolate stuff and some Peeps. Did you know that the official name of Peeps is "Marshmallow Peeps"?

Why would you bother putting the word *Marshmallow* on there? It's not like there are other kinds of Peeps, and you have to call them Marshmallow Peeps to prevent people from confusing them with Cheese Peeps or Meat Peeps.

APRIL 8 [mood: hyper]

Well, today was Easter, so I woke up to the sound of Sophie running around the living room screaming at the top of her lungs. I came downstairs and found out that she'd already eaten the ears off her chocolate rabbit, a Cadbury Creme Egg, and a whole box of Peeps, and my mom had taken her Easter basket away from her. Sophie really can't handle her candy.

Then we had breakfast, and my mom told the same story she tells every year, about how when I was five, we went to a petting zoo on Easter to see the rabbits, and my parents told me, "Look! It's the Easter Bunny!" and I ate some of what I thought were tiny chocolate eggs that the Easter Bunny had laid. Sophie loves hearing that story, but I still don't see what's so funny about it.

APRIL 9 [mood: scared]

Ohhhhhh crap. Kevin gave me his dad's camera today, and I put it in my backpack. But when I got home, I kind of forgot the camera was in there, so I did what I usually do with my backpack, which is throw it into the corner of my room. That's when I heard a noise. A bad noise, like someone else's dad's camera breaking. And sure enough, when I took it out and turned it on, the camera just made this weird whining noise.

Oh crap oh crap oh crap.

Oh crap.

APRIL 10 [mood: terrified]

I took Kevin's dad's camera to the camera store today, to ask about how to fix it. I was sort of hoping they'd tell me that it just, like, needed a new battery or something. But instead, the creepy guy at the camera store who looks sort of like Elmer Fudd told me that I'd knocked the lens out of alignment. I asked him what that means, and he told me it means that I need to pay him $300. I told him I'd just try and fix it myself, then. That's when he told me that just having had him look at the camera would cost me $50. I told him I didn't have $50. He said he'd keep the camera until I did.

Great. All I wanted was a picture of me doing my kickflip. Now Kevin's dad's camera is broken and being held for ransom by Elmer Fudd.

[mood: depressed]

I did some looking on the internet. It turns out you really can't repair a digital camera by yourself. So I need $350.

I gathered together all my money today, and went through all the sofa cushions in the house, twice. You know, just in case someone had dropped 1,400 quarters in there lately. Nobody had. In total, I have $37. That's $313 less than I need. I'm too embarrassed to ask my mom and dad, which means I need to figure out a way to get that much money, and fast. There is one option, but it's too scary to even think about.

I tried to avoid Kevin all day at school today, but he cornered me at lunch and asked me where his dad's camera was. I lied and told him I'd left it at home. He said to be sure to bring it in tomorrow, because his dad was looking for it.

So I had no choice: I borrowed money from Sophie. She's kept every penny anyone ever gave her—all her allowances and birthday checks and even her money from the Tooth Fairy. I asked

if I could borrow the money, and pay her back with my summer job money. She told me she'd loan me the $313, but only if I paid her back $375 in three months. Also, she told me that I might owe even more money, if something called the "prime lending rate" goes up.

Sophie is the scariest seven-year-old in the universe.

So I went to the store, and Elmer Fudd fixed the camera. I paid him the money and went to Kevin's house and gave him the camera. I don't know how I'm going to pay back Sophie, but at least everything's over.

Scariest seven-year-old in the universe!!

So Kevin came up to me at lunch today and said, "Hey, what did you do to my dad's camera?" I almost puked up my ravioli, but instead I just said, "Nothing. I didn't do anything." Then he said, "Are you sure?" And I said, "Yeah." And that's when he told me that the weirdest thing had happened. His dad told him he'd dropped the camera a few weeks ago, and it had stopped working. That's why he'd been looking for it—to take it in for repairs—but now it was working fine again. Kevin shrugged and said, "Funny, huh?"

Yeah. It's funny. It's frickin' hilarious.

If the Mario Brothers were real people, I bet Luigi would constantly be wondering, "Just once, why can't we be referred to as the Luigi Brothers?"

Do Chinese people have Scrabble?

Today in social studies class, we learned about the Donner Party, which is nowhere near as much fun as the word *party* makes it sound. They were a group of pioneers who were going across the country and ran out of food, so they wound up eating each other. I think there was more to the story, but I spent the rest of the period distracted by trying to figure out how that worked—like, did they cook the people they ate? Or eat them raw? How did they decide who'd get eaten and who'd be doing the eating? Did they just start with the fat guys? Or what?

I looked through my textbook for more information, but they didn't have anything—not even a recipe. I hate textbooks. They always leave out the most important parts.

I also think that the Donner Party's situation would have made for the best episode ever of *Little House on the Prairie.*

So in all my classes, we're getting ready for the statewide standardized tests we have to take at the end of the month. Anyone who scores above a 90% on an exam will automatically get an A in that subject for the semester.

Today in social studies, Mrs. Wexler made us all take practice evaluation tests, so we'll be used to them by the time we have to take the real ones. It took a while, though, because every time she started to say that we needed to use a number two pencil, Doug Spivak laughed uncontrollably about the words *number two*.

[mood: embarrassed] **APRIL 18**

Today was a very bad day. My math teacher, Ms. Bolton, came in with a Band-Aid on her cheek, and Chuck passed me a note that said, "What's with the Band-Aid?" And I wrote a note back that said, "I don't know. Maybe she cut herself shaving?" But as I passed it to him, Wendy Gilman (who's been mad at Chuck ever since he accidentally gave her a bloody nose in a kickball game) grabbed it and raised her hand and said, "Ms. Bolton! Tad and Chuck were passing this note!" So Ms. Bolton took it and read it, and then she got really quiet, and her mustache got a little quivery, and then she said that she was done teaching our class for the day and we should quietly read our math books for the rest of the period.

I think it would probably be a really good idea if Chuck and I did well on the standardized test, because I don't think we're getting good grades in math this semester.

Ms. Bolton

Ms. Bolton gave everyone an oral pop quiz today. She asked most people what 2 plus 3 is, or what the square root of 9 is. She asked Chuck to explain the proof of Fermat's Last Theorem. She asked me for *pi* to 25 digits.

Yep. We're in trouble.

Ugh. I spent last night working on practice problems, trying to get ready for the math exam. On the plus side, if I ever find myself on a train heading east at 90 miles an hour, and learn that there's a train 500 miles away, heading directly toward me at 75 miles an hour, I'll know exactly how much time I have left to live. So that's nice.

I wonder how it is that the X-Men all got their names. Like, did they get to pick their own? I'm sure that Storm wasn't named "Storm" by her parents, and, coincidentally, wound up being able to control the weather. I bet there was some time for all of them where they tried out different names to see if they would fit. Like, for a couple of weeks, Cyclops had everyone calling him "Bright Eyes," and Wolverine went around practicing signing his name as "Slicey-Hands," just to see if that seemed like a good fit for him.

APRIL 22 [mood: bored]

I think a better show than *Deal or No Deal* would be *Deal, No Deal, or Eels*, where one of the briefcases is full of angry eels.

If sphere n has a radius of 2 inches and is placed within cube z, which measures 4 inches on each side, who will care?

A) Tad

B) None of the above

(Answer: B)

 [mood: adventurous] **APRIL 24**

Here's what I wonder about the Legend of Zelda: Every time they come out with a new game, it's all about how Zelda got kidnapped again, or frozen, or sent back in time, or whatever. And I'm beginning to think that, at a certain point, she should rescue her own dang self. It's not like I don't enjoy the games. It's just that I think that there should be a button you can push so that, when you reach the end of a game and she's thanking you, you can go, "What's your problem? Seriously—getting kidnapped once or twice, I can understand. But I'm beginning to think you just like having people rescue you."

Oh for the love of . . . She cannot be serious!

Oops!

You guessed it...kidnapped again! (Can you believe it? *giggle*)

Rescue, please! The Princess

APRIL 25 [mood: hopeful]

Well, today was the big math exam. I don't want to get my hopes up, but I think I did really well. (If nothing else, I did better than Doug Spivak, who got really angry when he found out that, while it was multiple-choice format, the test wasn't like *Who Wants to Be a Millionaire*, and he wouldn't be allowed to phone a friend on any questions.) After the exam, I talked to Todd Ross, who's the biggest math geek in our class, and he and I had the same answers for almost everything. So I think I might actually do okay this semester. Which is good, 'cause I can't wait to forget all the stupid math I just had to learn.

This morning in homeroom, while pledging allegiance to the flag, I had an awesome idea for a horror movie: What if a flag became possessed with the soul of a serial killer? And then all these kids pledged allegiance to it, so they had to do whatever the flag told them to do? It'd be sort of like *Children of the Corn*, only with a flag. It would be called *Pledge of Darkness*.

OK, now that I've written it out, it looks sort of stupid. But I swear, it seemed like a really good idea this morning.

PLEDGE OF DARKNESS!

YOU WILL OBEY!

I've been thinking more about the pledge. I think a really good prank a country could pull on America would be changing its name to Forwichistan, because then it'd sound like kids were saying, "I pledge allegiance to the flag of the United States of America, and to the republic Forwichistan." If I were the president of, like, Luxembourg, I'd totally do that.

My results from the standardized tests came back today. The good news is, I did OK in most subjects. The bad news is, I got only 18% of the questions right on the math test. Ms. Bolton gave us back our answer sheets, so we could check them against the actual answers and figure out what we did wrong. And that's when I saw that I'd accidentally started filling in ovals on the second question, so all my answers were off by one.

And if that weren't bad enough, Ms. Bolton

announced to the class that everyone did OK on the tests, except for one student, who finished in the "dull-normal range," who did "worse than a monkey filling out the form randomly," and who

was, according to the exam, "brain damaged." And then she stared right at me.

After class, Doug Spivak came up to me and said, "Don't feel so bad, man. 'Dull-normal' is still half-normal, right?" It was nice of him to try and make me feel better. But I wish he hadn't.

May

MAY 1   [mood: annoyed]

Sophie's reading *The House at Pooh Corner* right now. I liked those books when I was a kid, even though it bothered me that they never explained what two kangaroos were doing in the middle of England. Did they escape from a zoo? Are they runaway circus animals? I always sort of wished there was a whole book just about how Kanga and Roo got to the Hundred Acre Wood.

OK, this is weird. After math today, I came back to my locker and found this note had been stuck in it:

I have a secret admirer! Which is kind of cool, and kind of creepy. I don't know who it could be. I showed it to Kevin and Chuck. Kevin wants to be a forensic investigator like on *CSI*, and he suggested that we put it under a black light or dust it for finger-prints. But I don't have a black light, or fingerprint dust. (We tried rubbing regular dust on it, but it just got all smudgy.) Then Kevin said it was too bad the note wasn't written in blood, 'cause then we could do a DNA match. I pointed out that we don't have a DNA-matching machine, either. Also, as Chuck said, it's probably a good thing that my secret admirer doesn't write her notes to me in blood.

Today I found another note stuck in my locker:

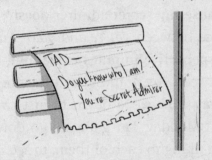

TAD —
Do you know who I am?
— You're Secret Admirer

I showed it to Kevin. He asked if he could see the first note, and he looked at them side by side for a while, then said, "I think it's definitely from the same person who sent you the first note."

Kevin can be a little slow sometimes.

[mood: intrigued] **MAY 4**

At lunch today, Kevin actually had a good idea: He'd brought in last year's yearbook, and we went through our class and crossed out every girl who'd ever told me she didn't like me, or that I was grossing her out, or to stop talking to her. That got rid of a lot of them. Then we crossed out every girl who already was dating somebody, which got rid of a lot more. And Chuck pointed out that we could also cross off every girl in an advanced English class, 'cause my secret admirer doesn't know the difference between *you're* and *your*. And then he had to spend five minutes explaining the difference between *you're* and *your* to Kevin.

Anyway, now we're down to just twenty-eight girls. On Monday, I'm going to go down the list and try talking to each of them, to see if I can figure out which one it is.

MAY 5

[mood: muggle-ish]

My parents just started reading the *Harry Potter* books to Sophie—last night, I heard them reading the beginning of the first book to her. Here's what I don't understand about Hogwarts: Okay, so the school has a sorting hat that can figure out each student's true nature, and assign him or her to the appropriate house, right? But there are four houses. Three of them—Gryffindor, Hufflepuff, and Ravenclaw—are full of normal people. And then there's Slytherin, which has NOTHING BUT EVIL PEOPLE. If I ran Hogwarts, when the sorting hat assigned a student to Slytherin, I'd send him home, or maybe to, like, wizard reform school. I mean, duh.

Ugh. So today I managed to talk to six of the girls on my list. I don't think any of them are the one. I asked Julie Kahn how she was doing and she said, "Who wants to know?" I asked Samantha Scanlon if I could borrow a pen, and she sighed and made

me give her a dollar as a deposit, so she could be sure to get it back. Three different girls, when they saw me coming, pretended their cell phone had just rung and they had to answer it, which was really obvious when Violet Paterson did it, because she doesn't even own a cell phone, so she used her calculator instead. And Nina Liu was really friendly to me, which I took as a good sign, until she

asked me, "Do you think your friend Kevin likes me?" Which is good news for Kevin, I guess, but doesn't help me.

[mood: discouraged]

OK. I give up. I tried talking to three more of the girls on my list. I asked Kate McLean, "How's it going?" and she told me, "None of your business." When I asked Sara Jacobsen what time it was, she said, "Time for you to stop bothering me." And Deb Chang just stared at me as I talked to her, then turned to one of her friends and said, "Did you hear something? It's like someone was speaking, but I didn't see anyone."

That's it. I'm done trying to figure out who it is. I'm going to spend my time doing other stuff. Like figuring out what you call a Hot Pocket when it gets cold. Is it a cold Hot Pocket? Or just a Cold Pocket?

Well, the secret admirer mystery's solved. I got another note in my locker today:

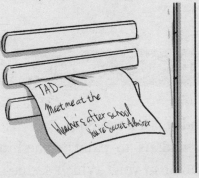

TAD—
Meet me at the bleachers after school
Your Secret Admirer

So I went down to the bleachers, and I waited, and I waited, and I waited, but nobody showed up—the only person there was Stu Lawrence, who also seemed to be just waiting around. So we started talking, and he asked me why I was hanging around, and so I told him about my secret admirer. And he got sort of pale and asked to see the note, so I showed it to him. And he said, "Is your locker near Tara-Ann Dillon's?" And I told him, yeah, I had the locker next to hers. And he said, "Aw, crap," and he turned super bright red.

And then neither of us said anything, but he just took the note out of my hand.

So I guess Stu Lawrence was accidentally my secret admirer. He asked me not to tell anyone about the whole thing. I told him that'd be fine by me.

In art today, Mrs. Sweeney gave us each a canvas and told us to paint "something that feels very familiar to you." Which seemed like kind of a dumb assignment, because why would anyone want a picture of something they see every day? "Boy, it's a good thing I painted that picture of my shoes! It saves me the trouble of looking down!" But Mrs. Sweeney's kind of weird and artsy like that. (She's a sculptor, and I remember one time, she showed us one of her sculptures and said it was called "Reclining Woman," but to all of us, it just looked like a pile of rusty metal. Chuck leaned over and said, "If she's in there, I hope that woman has a tetanus shot.")

Anyway, I decided to paint a picture of our fridge

at home, and I'd gotten pretty far along when Chuck looked over at it and said, "Why are you painting a robot?" Once he'd pointed it out, I realized he was right: It totally looked like a robot. In fact, it looked a lot more like a robot than a fridge.

So I tried starting over, and painted over it with white paint, but everything started smearing and running together and turning gray. I was worried I'd have to ask for another canvas, until I had a great idea: I'd paint over it with black paint, and put a yellow line down the middle of it, and then paint in a dead opossum. Which is totally familiar to me, because it's something I see from the school bus all the time. I'd painted it black and was just adding the yellow line for the divider when Mrs. Sweeney came by and said, "My, Tad! This looks interesting! What're you painting?" And I said, "The dividing line." And she said, "A dividing line? That feels familiar to you?" And I said, "Um, yeah." Then she got excited and said, "You feel divided? Torn? Ambivalent? Torn between two worlds?"

I could tell from the tone of her voice that there was only one right answer. So I said, "Yes. That is exactly what I feel." She got even more excited, and said, "This painting is the only one that truly fulfills the assignment!" Which is weird, because it just looks like this:

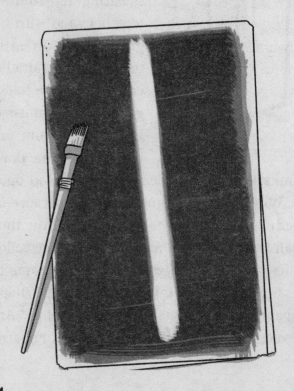

I still think it'd look a thousand times better with a dead opossum in the middle of it.

We went to the grocery store tonight, and I saw a little kid riding around in the shopping cart, in the backward-facing seat near the handle. I don't even remember the last time I sat in one of those. I mean, I know that there was a time when I was really little, and I used to sit in there and just chill out for the whole shopping trip. Then there was a time when I stopped, and I had to walk all the way around the store while my mom tried to figure out which of her coupons hadn't expired yet.

I kind of wish my mom had told me when I was taking my last ride in that shopping-cart seat. I think I would've enjoyed it more.

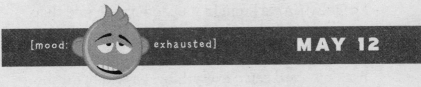

Tomorrow is Mother's Day, so Chuck and I went to the mall to find presents for our moms. I found a really good book for her, called *Drop 15 Pounds in 30 Days!*, because she's always talking about how much she wants to lose weight. But I showed it to my dad when I got home, and he took me back to the bookstore to exchange it. I asked him what I should exchange it for, and he said, "Anything else."

MAY 13   [mood: happy]

Today was Mother's Day. Sophie and I got up early to make my mom breakfast in bed. We decided to make her French toast, and I think we did OK. I mean, the only bread we had left in the house was rye bread, so we had to use that. And we were out of milk, so we just mixed together some some non-dairy creamer and water. And we didn't have any vanilla, so Sophie crumbled up some Nilla Wafers and stirred them in. But my mom seemed to really like it—when we brought it up to her, she said that she wanted more maple syrup, and by the time we'd gone downstairs and gotten it and brought it back up, she'd eaten everything. I asked her if she wanted us to make some more, but she said no, she was full.

Big news: Chuck and I were walking home from school this afternoon when this dog started following us home. (Well, I guess it didn't start following us until Chuck gave it some of his leftover nachos.) Anyway, after we got to my house, the dog kept sitting outside and whining. At first, my mom said to leave it outside, and it'd get bored and find its way home. But it just sat there whining, and my mom said to let it in, because it was really distracting her from watching *So You Think You Can Dance* (which, by the way, is a stupid name for a show. It's like if, instead of *American Idol*, they'd called it *Nice Singing, Jerkface*).

Tomorrow, we're going to put up signs saying that we found the dog, to see if we can track down its owner. But if we can't, my mom said maybe we might keep it. I might have a dog! Here is a picture of it:

His name is Rex. It's short for Dogasaurus Rex.

Here is the first thing I have learned about having a dog in your house: Don't feed them nachos. Not ever.

Anyway. After spending the morning cleaning the living room rug, my dad and I went to the store and put up signs with a picture of Rex on it. I really hope nobody calls. (I tried leaving one digit off our phone number, but my dad noticed.)

[mood: thoughtful] **MAY 17**

You know what I bet would suck? If you died and went to heaven, but really hated harp music.

Well, it's been five days, and nobody's called to claim Rex. I think my parents are growing to like him, too. We've figured out that he knows how to fetch, sit, roll over, and stay. My mom says that means he probably has an owner, but I think it just means he's a really smart dog.

[mood: excited] **MAY 21**

This morning was a little exciting. We got a brand-new school bus for our ride to school. Rocky, our school bus driver, was super psyched about it. He said, "I've been asking the district for a new school bus for three years now." And then he whispered, "I wasn't supposed to say anything, but the brakes on our old bus were shot. It was just a rolling death trap."

I kind of wish he hadn't told me that.

Anyway, it's nice having a brand-new bus. It's the first time I've ever been in a school bus that didn't smell just a little bit like vomit mixed with orange-scented disinfectant. I wonder how long it'll last.

Rocky the bus driver

MAY 22 [mood: disappointed]

Well, this afternoon, I got an answer to my question. A school bus can go approximately thirty-one hours without smelling like vomit. Becky Keeton had a bad tuna-fish sandwich at lunch, and lost it just before my stop. When I was getting off the bus, Rocky was sadly getting out the paper towels

and the sawdust and the disinfectant. I looked at him and said, "It was nice while it lasted," and he sort of smiled and said, "Yeah, it was."

Hooray! Rex has been with us for eleven days now, and nobody's claimed him, so my parents said we're gonna keep him! Tomorrow, we're going to take him to the Lakeville Cat & Dog Hospital to get him checked out. Sophie got really excited about the idea that we were going to the Cat & Dog Hospital, until my mom explained that that just means "veterinary clinic," and not "a hospital where all the doctors are cats and dogs."

Great news about Rex: The vet said the dog seems healthy, he just needs to be fixed. (Sophie asked what *fixed* means. My mom said it means a dog needs to be repaired. I said, "Yeah, repaired by cutting off his—" but then my mom asked me whether I liked having my Wii, and whether I'd like to have it taken away for a month, and I stopped talking.)

MAY 28 [mood: happier]

Well, Rex is back from the vet. It's probably a good thing he doesn't know how stupid he looks with this cone on:

Sophie asked why he has to wear the cone. I told her it was so he could pick up satellite radio.

Ugh. Bad news. We got a call today. Turns out, Rex has an owner. Also, his name isn't Rex. It's Mr. Kensington. I guess his owners were off on a cruise for the past three weeks, and their dog-sitter didn't want to ruin their vacation, so she didn't call to tell them he was missing. The owners were super grateful—apparently, Rex is a purebred German Spitz, and he's, like, won prizes at dog shows. They said it was a good thing we found him, because they're planning on making a lot of money by breeding him. My parents just kind of looked at each other, and then my mom said, "Good luck with that."

I don't get the plot of *Jurassic Park*. Like, if you're bringing back dinosaurs from the dead

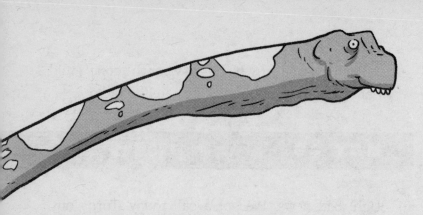

for a theme park, why not just bring back a few brontosauruses? Why would you bring back the velociraptors and the tyrannosauruses? Are there that many people who, when they find out there's an island full of dinosaurs back from the dead, are going to go, "Which ones? Because if it's just the vegetarians, I'm not interested"?

June

[mood: excited]

Just one more week left of school before summer. I can't wait for vacation to start. Our teachers seem even more excited than we are—Mr. Parker was walking around the class whistling and humming today. And our principal, Dr. Evans, stopped Doug Spivak in the hallway to tell him that he'd managed to get a D-plus average, so he'd be going on to eighth grade. "Do you know what that means? We're almost done with you!" she said, and they both started jumping up and down happily. I guess it's nice that she cares so much about Doug.

Oof. This morning, we found out that the seventh graders are all going to have to sing a song at the eighth graders' graduation on Friday afternoon. I guess it was an idea dreamed up by the chorus teacher, Mrs. Valeri, who's super mean—like, even the other teachers are afraid of her.

So we're all supposed to sing "I Believe I Can Fly." Which is just stupid—I thought the idea was, we were done with school for the year, so we didn't have to do what our teachers said anymore.

And if we have to sing a song, why does it have to be some lame song about some stupid guy who thinks he can fly? And worst of all, we have to rehearse it every day with Mrs. Valeri during our lunch period. I can't wait till I'm out of middle school and people can't force me to do stupid stuff I don't want to do ever again.

JUNE 5 [mood: even more annoyed]

We rehearsed our stupid song today at lunch. Mrs. Valeri kept getting angry at us because we weren't singing it right. She kept saying, "You're all off-key!" and I kept thinking: If we're all off-key, then isn't it possible that the key we're singing it in is the key that it should be in?

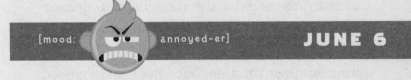

[mood: annoyed-er] JUNE 6

Today in rehearsal for the graduation song, Mrs. Valeri got really mad at Charlotte Regan for being "pitchy" and "sounding like a bag full of cats," until Charlotte started crying and left the room.

Mrs. Valeri said, "I'm sorry, but I just want to make sure the eighth graders have a good time at their graduation." I guess she doesn't care if anyone else has a good time at their graduation.

JUNE 7

[mood: even more annoyed-er]

Rehearsal today was even worse than yesterday. Mrs. Valeri shouted at Chuck and me and said we were "ruining the song on purpose," and then said that anyone who she thought was "deliberately singing poorly" during graduation would get detention. I'm not even sure how you get detention during summer vacation, but Chuck and I agreed that we weren't going to take that risk. So tomorrow during the song, we're just going to mouth the lyrics.

Well, I'm now officially an eighth grader! We sang at graduation tonight, and we're done.

But that wasn't even the best part. The best part was, at lunch, Chuck told some other people at our table about our plan to mouth the words. And I guess they told some other people, and they told some other people, and everyone agreed that it was a really good idea. Because tonight, at the graduation ceremony, when it came time for all of us to sing, every single kid in our class just mouthed the words to the song. All you could hear was Mrs. Valeri playing the piano, and this slight smacking sound of everyone's mouths opening and closing.

My dad said it was the funniest thing he'd ever seen. Mrs. Valeri ran after everyone afterward, threatening to keep them in summer school, until our principal, Dr. Evans, put her hand on Mrs. Valeri's shoulder and said, "Give it a rest, Constance."

It was a good day.

JUNE 9   [mood:  free!]

Yesterday was the last day of school! Yeeeeeeeeeeeeeeeeeeeeeeeee-ha! Summer!!!!! This is going to be the best summer ever!

I spent the day doing nothing but watching TV and playing video games. I could get used to three months of this.

Another day just sitting on the couch doing nothing. Watched *The Shawshank Redemption* on TNT twice in a row. I think *The Shawshank Redemption* may be the only movie they own.

Today, my dad came home while I was watching *The Shawshank Redemption* for the fourth time and said, "How'd you enjoy your weekend off?" And I was like, "Huh?" And he said, "Well, you know that you're getting a summer job, right? We're not going to just let you sit here and rot your brain for three months. Besides, working teaches you valuable lessons." I told him that I'd been working really hard for nine months straight, and didn't I deserve three months off to recover? He just laughed and laughed and laughed, and when Mom came home, he made me repeat it to her, and then they both laughed together for a really long time.

Well, I went to the local newspaper today to see if they needed anyone to deliver papers for them. The woman there gave me an application to fill

out, and so I did. And then she asked me whether I had a bike, and where I went to school, and what my favorite subjects were, and what hours I was available to work. And then she told me that they weren't hiring anybody, because they had all the paperboys they needed. I asked her why she'd gone to the trouble of asking me all those questions. She just shrugged and said, "Nobody ever comes to visit me in the circulation department."

Father's Day is tomorrow. I never know what to get my dad. Today while he was watching a baseball game, I went in to ask him what he wanted, and he said, "Just a little peace and quiet."

Which seemed like an odd thing to ask for as a present, but I went to the store and bought him five sets of earplugs.

Father's Day is today. My dad really seemed to like the gift I'd gotten him—he said to my mom, "I can use these when we visit your family!" She didn't seem to think that was funny at all.

Today, I noticed something weird on a dollar bill: Next to George Washington's picture, there's a tiny signature. But it's not George Washington's signature—it's the Secretary of the Treasury's, whoever that is.

As best I can tell, his name is Hnnnny Nnn Pnnlnjn.

Being Secretary of the Treasury seems like a pretty cool job—you get to sign all the money. I wonder if part of the job requirement is that you have a good, official-looking signature. Like, I bet Traci Williams from my class could never be Secretary of the Treasury, because she dots the *i*'s in

her name with hearts. Nobody would trust money
with this on it:

JUNE 22 [mood: frustrated-er]

I went to the food court at the mall today, where
the Cinnabon manager told me I was too young for
them to hire. Stupid Cinna-
bon. I'm glad they didn't
hire me. If the manager's
any indication, every-
one who works there
winds up fat, covered
with zits, and reeking
of cinnamon.

[mood:  excited]

Great news! I got a job at the Hot Dog Pound! They're that hot-dog place up by the interstate, and I went in today because they had a "Help Wanted" sign, and they had an opening! I asked if I was too young, and the guy behind the counter said, "You're sixteen, right?" And I said, "No, I'm thirteen." And he said, "What's that? You said you're sixteen?" in a way that sort of suggested that that was the right answer. So I told him yes. The only weird part is, he asked me how tall I was. When I told him, "I'm five-four and a half," he said, "Perfect. Try not to grow before tomorrow." Who knew hot-dog restaurants had height requirements?

[mood: exhausted] **JUNE 24**

So I went to work today. I wore a pair of khakis and a button-down shirt, because Mom said it would impress the boss. But I shouldn't have bothered dressing up, because I spent the day wearing a hot-dog costume.

Let me say that again: I spent the day *wearing a hot-dog costume.*

It turns out that was the job—to stand out in front of the restaurant as their mascot and wave at cars as they drive by. I can understand why the last guy to have this job quit: The costume is cramped and hot and hard to see out of, and it smells like someone else's feet. Plus, in case I didn't mention this: It's a giant hot dog.

This is way worse than Cinnabon could ever be.

[mood: exhausted]   **JUNE 25**

Today, during my fifteen-minute lunch break, Pam from the drive-thru told me what really happened to the guy who was in the suit before me: He didn't quit—he passed out from heatstroke. She said he just kind of weaved all over the parking lot and then fell down with his legs in the air. "It was really funny," she

said, and then realized who she was talking to and was all, "Oh, but I'm sure it wouldn't be funny if it happened to you."

I'm trying to drink lots of fluids so I don't get heatstroke, but the restaurant makes us pay for the drinks we buy—even water! And since I'm only making 7 bucks an hour—5 bucks after taxes—and a drink is $1.75, I think I could wind up losing money this summer. Dad's right: A summer job *does* teach valuable lessons. Like, for instance: Work sucks.

JUNE 26 [mood: humiliated]

My manager, Sean, came out today and told me to wave and dance more. "Nobody wants to eat at a place where the food looks depressed," he said. "Look happy!" I pointed out that if I were really a hot dog, I wouldn't be happy to stand and wave in front of a restaurant where my fellow frankfurters were being eaten. And he said, "Maybe you're a really dumb hot dog, and you haven't figured it out yet." Great. I'm going to spend the summer not just being a hot dog, but being a really stupid hot dog.

Sophie left for camp today. This is her first time going to sleepaway camp, and she was afraid of being homesick. I told her that homesickness was nothing to worry about, and that what she should really be afraid of are the Forest Strangler and the Summer Camp Claw-Handed Serial Killer and the Feral Wombats Who Are Able to Open Doors. I think her first night at sleepaway camp's gonna be great.

JUNE 28

So I haven't told any of my friends what I'm doing for a summer job, and today, Chuck and Kevin came to the Hot Dog Pound for lunch. I could see them through the peephole in my costume, but they couldn't see me. And I could hear them pretending to sneeze and saying "Wiener! Wiener!" behind my back. I don't know which is worse: that they did that to me, or that, if I weren't inside the stupid costume, I'd probably be with them doing the exact same thing.

[mood: irritated]

JUNE 29

I got a reprimand at work today. I don't think I was doing anything too wrong, but Sean said that I couldn't whisper to customers as they entered the restaurant, "You're eating my babies." I considered suggesting that, instead, I could yell "Bite me!" at people, but he seemed pretty annoyed with me already.

Well, this was my last day at the Hot Dog Pound. Apparently, I passed out in the parking lot and Pam dragged me inside. It turns out I was horribly dehydrated. Sean promised to give me two weeks' pay if I didn't sue, and my dad said, "Don't worry, we won't make you find another job." Which made me really happy, until he said, "There's a lot of chores that need doing around the house, anyway." So . . . I'll still be working, just not getting paid. Great.

July

[mood: pensive]

Spent today drinking Gatorade and recovering from yesterday's dehydration incident. Watched a double feature of *Night at the Museum* and *Night at the Museum 2* on TV, then fell asleep and had a weird dream about a movie called *Night at the Zoo*, where Ben Stiller's a security guard at a zoo where, at night, all the animals magically turn into stuffed dioramas. It was kind of a boring dream, actually.

SIGH

JULY 4

Today's the Fourth of July. My dad asked me how I was feeling, and I said, "Pretty good," and he said, "Great! You can go clean the gutters!" I told him that, in the spirit of Independence Day, I shouldn't have to do anything I didn't want to. He said that that would only be true if he were forcing me to pay taxes without representation, or quartering soldiers in my room.

JULY 6

Hooray! I was out mowing our lawn today, and some woman was driving by and asked me how much I charge per lawn. I guess she thought I was some sort of lawn-mowing service. I tried to think fast, and told her $15. She said, "Wow! $15? That's so cheap!" And then she hired me to mow her lawn.

So the good news is, someone's going to pay me for the chores my parents have been making me do for free.

Although the bad news is, I really, really wish I'd said $25.

I mowed that lady's lawn today, and she seemed pretty happy with it. She said she had some other friends who need yard work done, and she asked if she could give them my number. I told her yes. Then I started thinking that I could turn this into an actual business, so I took the money she paid me, went to Kinko's, and made some signs to advertise my service. It took a few tries:

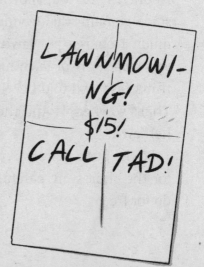

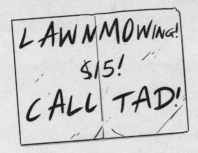

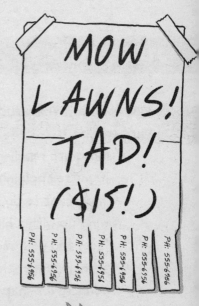

Lawnmowing is really a much longer word than you would think it is.

My arms are sore. I spent the whole afternoon mowing the lawn and trimming hedges for our neighbor Mrs. Graham. I think hedges are stupid— I told Mrs. Graham that when I have a house, I'll have a yard full of cactuses. And she said, "Cacti. The plural is cacti." And I told her that if that were the case, then wouldn't more than one waitress be a group of waitri? She muttered, "Smart-ass," and paid me.

Here's what I've learned after three days of doing yard work:

- Mosquito repellent doesn't work.
- If you're applying sunscreen, it's really important to do it evenly. Otherwise, you'll wind up with a big red splotch on your face, and your mom and dad will spend a whole dinner trying to figure out what country it's shaped like, no matter how many times you ask them to stop.

- Mowing lawns makes your back super sore.
- Some people have much bigger lawns than others, so it's really, really stupid to charge a flat rate.
- Tylenol, sunscreen, mosquito repellent, and gasoline all cost a lot of money, which eats into your profits.

JULY 11 [mood: cranky]

I just got back from putting up some more of my flyers at the supermarket. On the way home, I saw a new person out in front of the Hot Dog Pound in the hot-dog suit. I wonder how many employees they go through in a summer.

[mood: sore] JULY 12

Argh. I was supposed to go to Six Flags with Chuck today, but this morning I woke up too sore to even move. So instead, I stayed home and sat on the couch all day, taking Tylenol and watching TV. At one point, I dropped the remote behind the couch and it hurt too much to get up and reach for it, so I wound up having to sit there, watching all of *The Lake House* and half of *The Sisterhood of the Traveling Pants*, before my parents came home.

I kind of miss just going to school.

I went down to the supermarket today to put up more of my flyers, and just as I got there, I saw a guy pulling down the ones I put up two days ago. I told him to stop, and he seemed sort of embarrassed, and said he was sorry, but he runs a lawn-mowing service, and I was really cutting into his business. I guess I charge only, like, one-quarter of what he does, so a lot of his

Frank's
Lawn Care *now only three and a half times the price of that one kid!*

customers went over to me.

I felt kind of bad for him, and then I thought of an idea: I don't like mowing lawns, and he doesn't like losing customers. So I told him that I'd give up my lawnmowing business if he'd agree to pay me $7.50 for every lawn I didn't mow. He said that sounded fair to him. So now I work for Frank's Lawn Care as a lawn nonmower.

I may have the best summer job ever.

JULY 14 [mood: frantic]

So tonight was kind of crazy. I was sitting around watching TV when my dad came home to find that Sophie had mailed a big envelope home from camp. He opened it up, and it was a construction-paper card that said "Happy Birthday, Mom!!!" That's when both my dad and I realized that we'd forgotten my mom's birthday, so he grabbed his car keys and we went to the mall—he found her some perfume and a Michael Bublé CD, and I found a kiosk called "The Perfect Gift! Your Astrological Sign on a Mug!" I told the guy there that my mom's birthday was today, and he gave me a box. It wasn't until my mom opened it up that I realized that not all astrological signs look good on mugs.

Why would you even sell that?

[mood: queasy]

Sophie's been at camp for two weeks now, and I have to say, I'm beginning to miss having her around. Not so much because I miss having her annoy me, but because she always ate all the strawberry in the Neapolitan ice cream. With her gone, my mom's saying, "I refuse to throw away perfectly good ice cream," so my dad and I have to eat our way through the strawberry before my mom will buy a new carton of it.

I was over at Chuck's house tonight. His older brother, Sid, is home for the summer from college— he's a professional amateur skateboarder, but in the meantime, he's working as a busboy at Applebee's. He showed us the tattoo that he got of the Tony Hawk company logo on his bicep. It looks really cool, and we all agreed it sucks that his manager at Applebee's makes him wear long-sleeved shirts to cover it up whenever he's working.

So sullen!

Coolest guy EVER?!
I say yes!

When I got home, I asked my mom when I could get a tattoo, and she said, "When I've been dead at least five years."

That seems like a really long time to wait.

Sophie got back from camp today. We went to pick her up at the elementary-school parking lot, where the bus dropped her off. She ran over and hugged my mom and dad and said, "I missed you guys soooooo much!" Then she turned to me and whispered, "Hi, Tad. Do you have the $375 you owe me?"

I'd kind of forgotten that today was the due date to repay my loan from Sophie. I went to my room and collected all my earnings from this summer so far: I had just enough to pay back Sophie, with $8.27 left over. Sophie took it and said, "A pleasure doing business with you."

I really hope that when Sophie grows up, she uses her powers for good and not for evil.

[mood: pain]   **JULY 18**

I went to the dentist today for a checkup. I don't think my dentist likes me very much. It's partly my fault. I called him "Mr. Park." And he said, "It's

Dr. Park. I'm a doctor." And I said, "Really? Dentists are doctors?" And he said, "Yes, we are." And I said, "But you just deal with teeth." And he said, "Teeth are part of your body. We're doctors," and seemed kind of mad. Afterward, he told me I had two cavities, and added, "So I guess you'll be back at this doctor's office soon, for a doctor's appointment, with me, your doctor."

I'm realizing that it might not have been a good idea to annoy the guy who's going to be drilling into my teeth.

It's raining out, so there's nothing to do. Sophie and I spent a little while playing Hangman. Hangman's sort of a strange game, if you think about it. Supposedly, the idea is to avoid having your little stick-figure guy get hanged, right? But pretty much as soon as you've gotten even one letter wrong, you're not just dead—you're decapitated.

I feel like once your head's been hung, it really doesn't matter if they hang the rest of you.

Another rainy day. Watched *The Wizard of Oz* with Sophie. There's all sorts of stuff I don't understand about that movie. Like for instance:

When Dorothy lands in Oz, three members of the Lollipop Guild show up right away to welcome her, and they're like, "We represent the Lollipop Guild, and on behalf of the Lollipop Guild, we welcome you to Munchkinland." How did the Lollipop Guild decide so quickly who would represent them? Like, somehow, within seconds of a house landing in their town, did they have a meeting to vote on who should go welcome the person in the house? Or does the Lollipop Guild have a standing committee on People-in-Flying-House-Welcoming?

Also, why doesn't the Wicked Witch of the West put diapers on her flying monkeys? As Mrs. Shelton learned the hard way during our fifth-grade field trip to the zoo, monkeys like to fling their poop at people. And flying monkeys would probably just poop all over everything. Sure, the Wicked Witch's monkeys seem pretty well trained. But if I had a flying-monkey army, I'd make sure to keep them all diapered, just in case.

And also: If having water thrown on you were going to make you melt, wouldn't you be a little more careful about leaving buckets of water lying around?

Aside from that, though, it's a pretty good movie.

I wonder: Is there any law against changing your first name to "Doctor"? Because it seems like there should be.

I wonder when chickens figure out that they can't fly. Like, does every chicken go through a period of looking at ducks and going, "One day, that'll be me," before eventually realizing that, nope, it's never going to happen for them?

I bet chickens get angry at birds who *can* fly but who choose to walk.

Really? Really, this is how it's going to be?

JULY 25 [mood: puzzled]

If breakfast cereal is so popular, how come nobody makes dinner cereal? I'd eat it.

[mood: happy] JULY 28

Today, Chuck and I invented a fun new game called Guitar Villain. You play Guitar Hero, but instead of trying to get the highest possible score, you see if you can get the lowest possible score. If you play it just right, a song will sound like "SQUONK SQUONK SQUONK SQUONK SQUONK" for three straight minutes. We played it for about half an

hour before my mom came downstairs and told us that if we didn't stop making that awful noise, she'd make us go outside to get some fresh air.

JULY 30   [mood: pensive]

Dog the Bounty Hunter is an interesting show, but it'd be ten times more interesting if it were about a bounty-hunting dog.

August

[mood: curious]

Today on TV, I saw a guy say that a goldfish has a memory span of seven seconds. It made me feel kind of sorry for them, because I bet the only thing that ever goes through their mind is, "Oh my God, I'm drowning! No, wait, I have gills. Oh my God, I'm drowning! No, wait, I have gills. Oh my God, I'm drowning! No, wait, I have gills."

Sophie has her best friend, Amy, over for a sleepover tonight—they're both sleeping in a tent in the living room. Originally, they were planning on going camping in our backyard, but then Amy said she was too scared to do it, because she might get bitten by a rattlesnake. My dad tried to talk her out of it by pointing out that rattlesnakes don't even live in our area, and besides, "You're twenty times likelier to be hit by lightning than bit by a rattlesnake." And the good news is, Amy's not afraid of rattlesnakes anymore. The bad news is, she's now completely terrified of getting hit by lightning. Seriously. She may never leave our house.

I've been watching a lot of *Battlestar Galactica* reruns lately. If you've never seen it, *Battlestar Galactica* is about people from a planet millions of miles away from Earth, and they have pretty much the same clothes, language, appliances, and expressions as we do. The only differences are that they use a made-up swear word that you can say on television, and the shape of the paper they use is different.

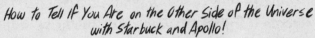

How to Tell If You Are on the Other Side of the Universe with Starbuck and Apollo!

On the other side of the universe paper!

Our paper!

I wonder what that show's fan conventions are like. Does everyone just show up carrying around a piece of paper with the corners cut off, so that people know they're dressed up as characters from the show?

I went to the mall with my mom today to finally buy my summer reading books, *Animal Farm* and *The Great Gatsby*. My mom also dragged me along to Bed Bath & Beyond, which is such a stupid name for a store. The "Beyond" part makes it sound like they sell, like, tickets to Narnia or something, but it turns out, "Beyond" just means "forks and scented candles."

I rented season one of *24* yesterday to see if I could watch it all in a day. It doesn't take a full 24 hours—it turns out that each hour is only around forty minutes, because the episodes on the DVDs don't have commercials. Which is sort of weird, since the show's supposed to take place in real time. I wonder what the characters do for those extra twenty minutes of every hour. Maybe that's when Jack Bauer gets to pee.

I had to hide what I was doing from my mom and dad, 'cause I knew they wouldn't approve. So I spent most of the day in my room watching the DVDs on my computer. But I took a quick break for dinner, and asked my sister for the salt by saying, "Quick—the salt—send it over here! There's no time to lose! Pass the salt! PASS THE SALT NOW!" That's when my parents searched my room to see if I was on drugs, found the *24* episodes, and confiscated them.

AUGUST 7 [mood: bored]

Thirty pages into *The Great Gatsby*, and I'm still waiting for him to do something great. He just seems like a boring rich guy to me.

[mood: sleepy] AUGUST 8

Bad news: Sophie found my copy of *Animal Farm*, thought the cover was cute, and read it. (She's Gifted and Talented, and reads at a ninth-grade level. I know this because she keeps telling everyone she meets.) Now she keeps waking everyone up with nightmares about how the evil pigs killed Boxer the horse.

There is one bright side, though. I got her to tell me everything that happened in the book, and now I don't have to read it. I tried to get her interested in *The Great Gatsby* by telling her it was about animals, too, but she didn't believe me when I told her everyone in it was a weasel.

My family's leaving on vacation today. We're going to spend a week in Florida, visiting my Grandma Judy in her new retirement home. Well, actually, just five days with Grandma Judy—it's a twelve-hour, two-day drive each way. My dad's excited about it, because Grandma Judy's his mom. And Sophie's excited about it, because my grandma takes her shopping and they sit together at night and watch home-makeover shows and eat ice cream together. My mom and I are less excited about it. I hate going shopping, and I hate home-makeover shows, and my grandma always calls me "Taddy," which I used to be called back when I was, like, five, but nobody calls me anymore. And my mom doesn't like my grandma. She never says so, but I can tell that she doesn't, through little hints she drops, like asking my dad, "Why do we have to go visit her?" and always sighing heavily halfway through my Grandma Judy's name, so it comes out as "Grandma . . . (sigh) . . . Judy." I'm good at picking up on small clues like that.

OK. My mom just came into my room and asked,

"Are you packed yet for the trip to Grandma . . . (sigh) . . . Judy's?" So I guess I should go pack. I'm packing my swim trunks—the one nice thing about going to Grandma Judy's is at least I'll get to go to the beach. It'll be fun to go swimming. Plus, I'm super pale, so it'll be a chance to maybe get a tan just in time for school.

AUGUST 10 [mood: exhausted]

Uuuuuuugh. Today was a looooooooong day of driving. The first few hours of the trip were OK, because Sophie was watching a DVD of *The Little Mermaid* and I was playing on my GamePort XL. But a few hours in, the batteries died on my sister's DVD player. My sister started whining, and my mom said to my dad, "I thought I told you to recharge them!" But my dad was like, "No, that was your job! My job was to drive to my mother's!" My mom was like, "Well, it was your idea to go visit her!" and my sister just kept whining because the movie had stopped before the ending. I said, "You've seen the movie, like, fifty times. Did you forget how it ends? She gets legs." And my mom snapped, "Tad! Be nice to your sister!" which I thought was really strange, because I was the only one in the car not whining or shouting at anyone.

So then my mom told me to let Sophie play with my GamePort, but Sophie didn't want to play with it, because it didn't have any games involving princesses or cake, which are the only kinds of games that Sophie likes to play. And so my dad announced that we'd be entertaining ourselves the way that he did on car trips when he was a kid, by competing to see who could count more cows on their side of the car. Which is a stupid game, because winning and losing really depends on how many cows there happen to be on the side of the road. Sophie was cheating, which made me really angry, until I remembered that I didn't actually care who won the game.

Anyway. We just stopped at a motel for the night. It's the second motel we stopped at. We checked into the first one, and Sophie got all excited because there were machines on the beds that made them vibrate if you put in a quarter, and my mom just picked up our bags, went to the car, and told my dad, "Find another motel." I don't know why. I think vibrating beds sound like fun.

AUGUST 11 [mood: bored]

Well, this morning, we drove the rest of the way to Grandma Judy's place. She seemed really happy to see us. Or happy to see my dad and my sister, anyway. She gave my dad a big hug, and turned to Sophie and said, "Sophie! You've grown so much! You're such the little lady! I've got a whole *Trading*

Spaces marathon saved up for us to watch, and a carton of Neapolitan with your name on it!" Then she turned to me and said, "Taddy, it's nice to see you," and to my mom she said, "Well, you've certainly put on some weight!" My mom was still trying to think of a response when Grandma Judy started carrying Sophie's suitcase up to her room.

After all that, by the time we got all settled in, it was too late to go to the beach. But my mom said we can go tomorrow.

AUGUST 12 [mood: bored to death]

Man, this trip sucks. It rained today, so we wound up skipping the beach. But Grandma Judy turned to Sophie and said, "You know what the rain is good for?" And Sophie said, "Outlet shopping!" So we went shopping at the outlet mall. Outlet malls are like regular malls, only bigger, and without the only stuff that makes malls bearable, like food courts or bookstores where you can look through comic books.

I was getting really hungry, so I was happy when Grandma Judy said that we would stop at the Cheesecake Factory on the way home. But it wasn't the Cheesecake Factory restaurant, it was an outlet store for a factory that makes cheesecakes. Grandma Judy bought two, but wouldn't let me eat any, because she was going to freeze them "for when company came." Anyway, the weather guy on TV said that it'd be sunny tomorrow, and my mom promised that, no matter what, we'd go to the beach.

Argh. Today we were supposed to go to the beach, but instead, Grandma Judy said she had a surprise for us: She wanted us to meet her friend William. He's also super old, and he lives down the hall from her in the retirement home. He seemed OK, even though he did try playing "I've got your nose!" with Sophie and me, and pulling quarters out of our ears, which even Sophie's too old for. I kept thinking that it would be funny to grab his dentures and go, "I've got your teeth!" but I knew everyone would be mad.

Also, I didn't want to

Got yer nose!

No you don't.

touch his dentures.

Anyway, hanging out with William was fine. The only weird thing was that my dad kept saying over and over, "You never mentioned that you'd made a friend," which I thought was strange, because why would Grandma Judy call my dad every time she makes a friend?

AUGUST 14 [mood: happy]

Well, we finally went to the beach today. We just got back, and it was a lot of fun—I went swimming, and helped Sophie build a sand castle, and we picked up, like, fifty shells. The only downside is, I didn't get a tan at all—which is weird, because I wasn't even wearing any sunscreen. (I knew I didn't have much time to get tan, so I figured I'd wait till I was a little brown, and then put the sunscreen on.) I just stayed super white all day long. Anyway, I'm going to go ask Grandma Judy to turn up the air-conditioning, because for some reason, it suddenly feels really hot in here.

Owwwwwwwwwwwwwwwwwwwwwwwwwwwww.

I am covered in a giant, awful sunburn. Turns out, it takes a few hours for the sun to really change your skin's color, so last night, my whole body turned from white, to pink, to red, to redder. Sophie spent a while last night trying to decide what color I was, and finally chose "Kool-Aid Man."

We were going to go back to the beach today, but it hurts whenever the sun touches my skin, so instead, I'm spending the day indoors, covered in Noxzema, sitting in the living room in a lawn chair because Grandma Judy doesn't want the Noxzema getting on her furniture's plastic coverings. I've been stuck here all day, watching TLC home-renovation shows with Sophie and Grandma Judy—I keep dozing off, and then waking up to them squealing any time someone sponge-paints a wall or adds a sconce.

This is officially the worst vacation ever.

AUGUST 16 [mood:  miserable]

Spent the day driving back from Grandma Judy's place. We're halfway home now. Nothing to report, except that there are 78 cows on the left side of the car on the way home and—according to Sophie—394 cows on the right side.

Oh, and my sunburn is now peeling super badly. It's itchy, but I'm trying not to touch it, in order to see if I can just slip out of a Tad-shaped skin husk, like a snake.

 [mood: relieved] ## AUGUST 17

Sooo nice to be home again. Crawled into bed and slept for twelve hours. Never want to see a home-decorating show, ice cream, or the sun ever again.

AUGUST 18 [mood: annoyed]

Ugh. Our neighbor Dawn is here, hanging out with my mom, so I'm hiding up in my room. I don't like

Dawn. For one thing, she smokes, which is just gross. My mom will usually hang out with her on the back porch, so that our whole house doesn't wind up smelling all Dawn-y. But the main reason I don't like her is that she begins, like, half her sentences by saying "Frankly" or "To be perfectly honest" or "Truthfully," which just weirds me out, because it always gives you the sense that, whenever she *doesn't* begin a sentence that way, then she's just totally lying.

AUGUST 19 [mood: curious]

Sophie's been reading a book all about unicorns, but it doesn't answer my big question about them: Why'd we stop at one horn? If you're going to make up a mythical animal, why not make up bicorns, tricorns, quadricorns, and so on? I think that the octocorn would actually be kind of a cool animal.

Today was Sophie's birthday. She's having a party this weekend, but for her actual birthday, we went out to dinner to her favorite restaurant: Red Lobster. I don't get the restaurant name Red Lobster. Aren't all lobsters red? It's not like they have a rival called Green Lobster.

Actually, on second thought, I bet the way Red Lobster happened was, the founder originally was going to call his restaurant Lobster. And so he painted it on the sign, and realized that the word *Lobster* looked kind of stupid up there all alone—like, it didn't look like it was a sign for a restaurant that served lobster, it just looked like a sign a lobster would put on his house. But there wasn't a lot of room to add anything, so he just squeezed the word *Red* above it.

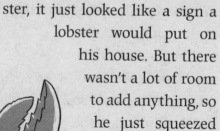

My mom's running around getting ready for Sophie's eighth birthday. She's having a Barbie-themed party. That was her third choice. Her first choice was to have a princess-themed party, but then my mom told her that if that was the theme of the party, it couldn't just be HER being a princess—she had to let the other girls be princesses, too. Her second choice was a Lady GaGa–themed party, and both my mom and dad told her absolutely not. So it's a Barbie-themed party. I'm going to try to be out of the house as long as I can.

[mood: curious] **AUGUST 25**

I bet the hardest part about being Bruce Banner isn't the moment when you turn into the Hulk. It's when you're done being angry, and you calm down, and suddenly you're naked in the middle of a whole lot of rubble, and someone's looking at you like, "Um, that's my car you just threw." I bet that part never gets any easier.

Well, today was Sophie's party. I went to the mall and managed to miss almost the whole thing— only one of Sophie's friends was still there when I got home, Brenda Winters, who was waiting for her mom to pick her up. She'd had too much cake and ice cream and kept saying, over and over, "I think I'm gonna throw up!" My mom looked really nervous, because Brenda was sitting on the couch that's not Scotchgarded.

Anyway, for her birthday, my parents got Sophie a hamster, which is totally unfair, because they never let me have a pet. This is what her hamster looks like:

Mr. Squeakers

His name is Thunderclaw. Sophie calls him Mr. Squeakers, but he and I both know his name is Thunderclaw.

Thunderclaw!

Chuck came over today, and we sneaked into Sophie's room to play with Thunderclaw when she was out at her oboe lesson. I think he's a really smart hamster, because Chuck made a little maze out of Legos, and Thunderclaw figured out how to get through it in no time. Chuck's coming over tomorrow, when Sophie and my parents are at her oboe recital, and we're going to build a hamster-size obstacle course to test Thunderclaw's strength and agility.

Oh, man. Today was a long day. Chuck and I were putting Thunderclaw through the obstacle course, and he'd already finished the swimming portion in the bathroom sink, and the ice-skating portion inside a carton of sherbet we found in the back of the freezer. But then, during the Road Rally, when we had him in my radio-controlled car, Chuck took a turn too hard and it slammed into the coffee table. Thunderclaw went flying off somewhere in the direction of the sofa, and we couldn't find him, despite spending a long time diagramming where he could have landed:

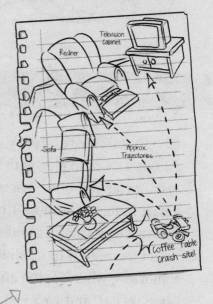

Finally, we gave up on finding him, and ran down to Pets-a-Million to find a replacement for

Thunderclaw before Sophie got home. I think the one we found looks a lot like him, especially after we added some spots with a brown magic marker:

Mr. Squeakers II

Gotta go—I hear Sophie and my folks getting home.

AUGUST 29 [mood: relieved]

Good news! Sophie thinks Thunderclaw II is her original hamster! Although she did tell Mom and Dad that Mr. Squeakers is suddenly "a whole lot bitey-er."

[mood: guilty] AUGUST 30

Um. Well. Today brought good news and bad news. The good news is, we found Thunderclaw I. The bad news is, he was in my mom's Rice Krispies.

I guess, after we lost him, he ran into the kitchen

and climbed into a cereal box for some food, and then he couldn't climb out again. So this morning Mom was pouring herself some cereal, and suddenly she screamed, because there in the bowl, with his four tiny paws in the air, was the lifeless body of Thunderclaw I. Sophie started crying and

ran to her room, and then a minute later, she came back down to tell us that it couldn't be Thunderclaw, because he was still in his cage. And mom said, "Well, how did a hamster that looks just like him wind up in my cereal?" I tried to suggest that maybe it was a prize—like, they were giving away one free dead hamster in every box of Rice Krispies.

Mom stared at me for a really long time, and then she asked, "Is there something you want to tell us?"

And I answered honestly: No. There was absolutely nothing I wanted to tell her.

September

School starts on Tuesday, so today I had to go back-to-school shopping with my mom. (She won't let me go on my own. Apparently, you buy one "I'm with Stupid" T-shirt and suddenly you're not allowed to buy clothes by yourself anymore.)

We spent the whole day going from store to store, and she made me try stuff on, then come out of the changing room to show her. The worst moment came at Marshalls, when I tried on some jeans and she announced, "Those look like they're too tight in the crotch!" That's when I looked up and saw that April Dawson was shopping nearby, and she was trying hard not to crack up. And then I realized April was with her mom, and her mom was *also* trying not to crack up.

It's too late for me to change schools this year. I checked. But I told my mom that I'm not going shopping with her ever again.

Well, today I found out what's worse than going shopping with my mom: not going shopping with her. She brought home a bunch of clothes from TJ Maxx and said, "I bought you some school clothes!

I'll return whatever doesn't fit!" Some of the stuff was OK, but some of it was really ugly. She bought me a purple sweater-vest, and I told her I didn't like it and wanted her to return it, but she insisted that I keep it, because, she said, "It makes you look so handsome."

I don't even understand sweater-vests. Like, are they sweaters for people whose arms don't get cold?

I've hidden it in the back of my closet. Hopefully, she'll forget she bought it.

SEPTEMBER 3 [mood:  sad]

Today's Labor Day, so my parents have the day off work. I'm not sure why. It's Labor Day, so shouldn't they have to work extra-hard instead?

Unless maybe it's called Labor Day in salute to anyone who's ever gone through labor.

No, wait. That's what Mother's Day is for.

(I'm spending my time thinking about stuff like this to try and distract myself from the fact that summer is over, and it's my first day of eighth grade tomorrow. It's not working.)

Today was my first day of eighth grade. It's cool to finally be the oldest kids in school—we get to use the eighth-grade lockers, which are over by the lunchroom. But for fun, Chuck and I walked by the hallway where the sixth graders have their lockers, just to watch them wandering around looking lost, or running to get Mr. Fox, the custodian, to open their lockers because they forgot the combination. Speaking of which: Chuck taught me a neat trick to remember your locker combination. You can hide it in your math notebook by putting it into a fake equation. Like, if your combination is 9-30-6, just write in your notebook "9 + 30 = 6." That way, if anyone finds your notebook, they won't

Sigh. Every year . . .

figure out that's your locker combination—they'll just think that you're sort of dumb and not very good at math.

SEPTEMBER 5 [mood: frustrated]

Arrrgh. Today I figured out the problem with Chuck's math-notebook method for holding on to your locker combination: It doesn't work if your math notebook is inside your locker.

[mood: excited] SEPTEMBER 6

The big news at school is that there's a new girl in our class. In homeroom, Mrs. DeWitt said, "I want you all to give a big Lakeville Pirates welcome to Jenny Bachman. Her family just moved here from Idaho, so she's starting school a little late. Welcome, Jenny!"

After homeroom, I said to Jenny, "So what's Idaho like?" And she said, "Actually, I'm from Ohio. Mrs. DeWitt got it wrong, but I didn't want to correct her." And I said, "Oh," and then there was an awkward pause, and I was about to say, "What's Ohio like?" but then Mark O'Keefe came over and said hi, and she said, "Hi! I like your Iron Man shirt. He's my favorite superhero. Well, Marvel superhero, anyway." And they walked off together talking about comic books.

So: She's cute, she's nice, she likes comic books. And I wasted my chance to talk to her, all because Mrs. DeWitt confuses Idaho with Ohio. Stupid geography.

Jenny Bachman (!!!)

Not from Idaho!

Cute!

Loves comics

SEPTEMBER 7 [mood: smitten]

Chuck and I spent a long time at lunch today arguing about which of the X-Men has a lamer superpower, Storm or Iceman. Afterward, Jenny Bachman came up to us and said, "I'm sorry—I couldn't help overhearing. Clearly, it's Iceman. Storm can at least control the weather. What can Iceman do? Make your drink cold? Still, nobody's as lame as Gambit. What kind of superhero has playing cards as a weapon? If you wanted to kill him, all you'd have to do is attack him with fifty-three guys."

Then she walked away. Chuck and I are both totally in love.

SEPTEMBER 10 [mood:  dread]

This morning, I was heading out the door to school, and my mom said, "You know what would look nice with that shirt? That sweater-vest I got you. Why don't you go put it on?"

I told her I was late for school, so I couldn't change. But now I know: My mom hasn't forgotten the sweater-vest. She's going to make me wear it. It's only a matter of time.

Tonight, at dinner, my mom said, "You know what I hear is really 'in' this season? Sweater-vests. All the big celebrities are wearing them now." And I said, "But I don't want to wear a sweater-vest," and she said, "Trust me on this, you'll look really cute in it. The girls will like it!"

After dinner, my dad took me aside and said, "Don't even try fighting her on this." He's got a point: My mom thinks she knows a lot about fashion, so she can get really obsessed with how we dress. She once wrestled Sophie for ten minutes to get her into a yellow polka-dotted dress for Easter. (Although, to be fair, Sophie did look nice in it.)

Well, today it happened: I was running late for school, so my mom had to drive me. And before we left, she said, "It's getting cold out. Go put on another layer." So I went back to my room, and found that all my sweaters and sweatshirts were gone, except for the purple sweater-vest.

So I put it on, and planned to take it off as soon as I got to school.

Then, on the way into the school, I saw Jenny Bachman. I tried to hide so she wouldn't see me, but she looked over and said, "Hey! Nice sweater-vest!"

Argh. The only thing I hate more than when my mom forces me to wear stuff is when she's right.

SEPTEMBER 16 [mood: radioactive]

The Teenage Mutant Ninja Turtles are fun, but I bet that if you exposed turtles to radiation, they wouldn't suddenly gain a whole lot of martial-arts abilities. I bet they'd just get, like, covered with blisters and die.

Leonardo leads...

Donatello does machines...

Raphael is cool but crude...

Michelangelo is a party dude!

In bio class, we're learning about bacteria. On Thursday, Mr. Hamilton ran a swab across Leanne Chu's desk and then swiped it on a petri dish. Friday, he showed us all the bacteria that had grown on the dish overnight. It was pretty cool, but it totally freaked Leanne out. She showed up today

with a big bottle of Purell, and kept squirting it on her hands and staring at her desk like it was gonna attack her. Mr. Hamilton tried to calm her down and told her that there's bacteria on everything—even the food we eat. I don't think it worked, though. I saw her in the cafeteria later, closely examining a fish stick like she was looking for germs.

So today at school, Chuck was talking about this online game he's found, "Sword of the Valkyries." He says it's great—you can roam around ancient

Norway as a Viking and fight, like, other Vikings and dragons and stuff. So I just went on and created a new character for myself. I was going to just call him "Tad," but the name "Tad" was taken, and so was "Tadd." And so was "Ttad." And so was "Ttadd." So I wound up going with

"ViciousVikingSlayerTad3." ("ViciousVikingSlayer-Tad" and "ViciousVikingSlayerTad2" were taken.) I'm about to start playing—wish me luck!

Man, I'm tired. I started playing "Sword of the Valkyries" last night, and wound up joining a guild and going on a dungeon run. We found a baby

dragon, and all the other guild members already had one, so they let me keep him! I named him Fritz. Anyway, by the time it was all done, I looked up and it was two in the morning. Totally exhausted now. Going online to feed Fritz, then to sleep.

Soooooooooooo tired. When I went online to feed Fritz, some of the guild members asked if I wanted to go on a quest to get an immunity amulet, which I could totally use, because I keep getting killed whenever someone throws a cup of mead at me. (There's a lot of dangerous mead-throwing in "Sword of the Valkyries.")

So we went off and got one, and then the guild members said that since they'd helped me on my quest, I should help them go fight this wizard who's been harassing them. And I couldn't really say no, after they'd helped me get my amulet. So I'm not sure when I got to sleep, but I think the sun was rising. Just going to check in on the game now, and then I'm going to collapse.

Ugh. I'm in so much trouble right now. I stayed up till four last night playing "Sword of the Valkyries," and I really didn't feel like waking up and going to school this morning. So I told my folks I had a sore throat and a fever, and needed to sleep, and they let me stay home.

That would've worked out great, except that, when Sophie came home, she found me playing the game. The good news is, I convinced her not to tell Mom and Dad. The bad news is, in return, now I have to do pretty much whatever she says. I just spent an hour playing Uno with her, and in a few minutes, I have to go play Sorry! I also have to figure out a way to let her win, 'cause she gets mean when she loses.

My life officially sucks.

[mood: aggravated] SEPTEMBER 22

Grrr. ViciousVikingSlayerTad3 is dead. I was just about to go into battle when Sophie called me in to look under her bed for monsters, and by the time I was done, my character had been slain with a lightning bolt. So my guild kicked me out, on account of deadness. And then Sophie made me come into her room and kill a spider.

SEPTEMBER 23 [mood: annoyed]

If anyone reading this saw tonight's episode of *CSI*, could you please email me and let me know how it all turned out? Just before the episode ended, Sophie changed the channel to watch *SpongeBob SquarePants.* I was all ready to complain to Mom and Dad, but then Sophie said, "Are you sure you want to do that?"

So instead, I just went up to my room and drew pictures of SpongeBob being used as a sponge.

So last night, Sophie made me clean out her hamster's cage, and now, no matter how much I scrub, I smell like hamster. I thought it was just my imagination, but this morning in homeroom, Julie Underhill sniffed the air and said, "Ew . . . I smell something hamstery. I think it's Tad. Mrs. DeWitt, can I move?"

[mood: stressed] SEPTEMBER 25

7:04 p.m.:
I didn't think things could get worse, but now—BRB

7:06 p.m.:
they have, because—BRB

7:09 p.m.:
Sophie's got a little bell she rings whenever she—BRB

7:11 p.m.:
wants an Eskimo pie or a Fruit Roll-Up, which is surprisingly—BRB

7:14 p.m.:
often.

SEPTEMBER 26 [mood:  relieved]

Today I had to give up going over to Chuck's house because Sophie insisted that I come to the tea party she was having with her stuffed animals. Which was bad enough, but then, when I got there, I found out that I wasn't even a guest—I was their waiter. So I had to keep on pouring fake tea for her teddy bear and elephant and

Robo Sapien, and Sophie kept complaining loudly to them that I was a really awful waiter, and saying that she wasn't going to tip me a dime.

After a half hour of this, I finally put the teapot down and went downstairs to Mom and Dad and told them that I'd faked being sick. I was expecting them to get mad and ground me or something, but instead, my dad just laughed and said, "We were wondering how much longer you could last." I guess my folks figured it out last week. As my mom put it, "We thought that having to be bossed around by Sophie was far worse than anything we could have done."

Anyway. I've got to go. I need to go tell Sophie about all the new monsters I've noticed under her bed.

SEPTEMBER 27 [mood:  surly]

I just got back from Best Buy, where they were selling a Special Edition DVD of *X-Men Origins: Wolverine*, with director's commentary. I think the only commentary I'd want to hear during *X-Men Origins: Wolverine* would be the director being poked with a stick, over and over, until he apologized for making a really crappy Wolverine movie.

SEPTEMBER 28 [mood: grossed out]

I don't get why some people think it's OK to leave their chewed-up gum in the drain of water fountains. It's really gross to have to stare at their gum when you're getting a drink of water. You know where I bet that doesn't happen? At the offices on *CSI*. I bet if someone did that at a CSI lab, they could examine the bite marks in the gum and then use dental records to match them up to the person who chewed it, and then force them to put it back in their mouth. At least, that's what I would do if I worked at a CSI lab.

October

[mood: sleepy]

Our whole family went to the zoo yesterday. And then, for Sophie, we went to the Children's Zoo. I don't understand the Children's Zoo. Like, isn't the whole zoo for children? It's not like the rest of the zoo is the Adult Zoo, where the bears swear and the giraffes smoke and the chimps serve hard liquor.

Anyway, Sophie really enjoyed the Children's Zoo, because they have machines where you can buy food and give it to the animals. She was having a lot of fun, feeding the pigs corn and giving

each of them names like "Mr. Pigglesworth" and
"Dr. Piggington." (Sophie's not very good at coming up with names.) And then my dad said to my
mom, "Oh! This reminds me: When we get home,
I've got to remember to defrost the pork chops for
dinner." And Sophie said, "Why would a pig remind
you to defrost pork chops?" And my dad kind of
froze up and said, "Um, I don't know," which is
weird, because the answer's pretty
obvious. So I told Sophie, "Duh!
Pork chops come from pigs."
And then she screamed,
and all the animals
ran away, and she
started crying,
and we had to
go home.

At dinner,
Sophie refused
to eat her pork
chop. She just
kept poking
it with her
fork and say-
ing, "Poor Dr.

Piggington." I felt a little bad for her, but on the other hand: more pork chops for me.

Oh boy. Today, Sophie announced that she was going to be a vegetarian. She's not going to eat anything made from animals—no hamburgers, no steaks, no pork chops, no bacon. She's just going to eat chicken nuggets and vegetables. And then my mom pointed out that chicken nuggets are made from chickens, and Sophie kind of paused, but then she said, "OK, fine. I won't eat chicken nuggets, either, then." So tonight, we all had steak, and Sophie had cheese ravioli. She kept looking at us as we ate and saying "Moo" until my mom made her stop.

"Moo.."

For dinner tonight, my mom made turkey meat-loaf, and just as we were all getting ready to eat it, Sophie said, "I'm not eating turkey!" And my mom sighed and said, "Oh! You're still doing that?" And she had to get up and make Sophie some mac-and-cheese. Which would've been fine, but every once in a while, under her breath, Sophie would whisper, "Gobble-gobblegobblegobble." It sort of ruined dinner.

[mood: stuffed] **OCTOBER 4**

It was nice out tonight, so my dad grilled hot dogs and hamburgers for dinner, except for Sophie, who got a veggie burger and a Tofu Pup. She let me try a bite of each of them, and the nicest thing I can say about them is, size- and shape-wise, they're just like hot dogs and hamburgers. Taste-, texture-, and everything-else-wise, they're pretty much like kitchen sponges. Sophie tried to make us feel guilty while she was eating, by saying "Woof!" and "Oink!"—which confused my parents for a little while. But then they explained to her that hot dogs and hamburgers don't have any dogs or ham in them, and she started mooing.

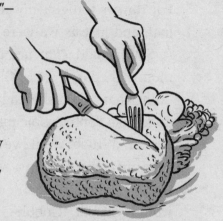

OCTOBER 5 [mood: fishy]

Sophie's vegetarianism is beginning to annoy everyone. I could tell, because my mom made fish for dinner, and as she served it, she announced, "You know what noise a fish makes? None. Fish don't make any noise at all." Then she gave Sophie some beans and rice. But I'll give Sophie credit: She ate her dinner really fast, then said, "May I be excused?" and went into the family room to watch

Finding Nemo with the volume turned all the way up. My mom just rolled her eyes and said, "We've got to do something about this."

OCTOBER 6   [mood: glad]

This morning, there was a nice surprise for breakfast: My mom made bacon for everyone. We all had some, except for Sophie, who got cold cereal. Which was too bad for her, because she looooooooves bacon. And then my mom said, "Oh! I accidentally made enough for four of us by mistake! I'll just put the extra over here," and put it down next to Sophie. I could see her looking at it all through breakfast, and it was driving her nuts. And finally, she said, "You know what? I bet not all pigs are nice. Maybe some pigs are really mean. And maybe some pigs deserve to die." And then she started shoving the bacon in her mouth.

Afterward, my mom and dad and I all agreed that it was a little scary and a little creepy. But, on the plus side, she's not going to be mooing or oinking during dinner anymore, and that's a really good thing.

OCTOBER 7 [mood: confused]

Went to the mall today and walked by the Build-a-Bear Workshop. I don't understand why anyone goes there. The mall has, like, three toy stores in it, where you can buy bears that've already been built.

[mood: nervous] OCTOBER 8

In homeroom this morning, Jerry Baxter leaned over and told me the big news: His older sister is friends with Megan March's older sister, and his sister told him that Megan March had a sleepover at her place, and all the girls who were there made a list, grading all the eighth-grade boys on cuteness, from A to F. Jerry said that he got an A-minus, which isn't too bad. I asked him where I was ranked, and he said he didn't know—all he knows is that he got an A-minus.

I told Chuck about the list, and he started telling other people, and by lunchtime,

A-the list was pretty much the only thing anyone was talking about. Ryan Pendleton finally said, "This is stupid—we don't even know if there is a list or not." And then he walked over to Megan and said, "So Jerry Baxter gets an A-minus, huh?" And she said, "I don't know what you're talking about." And he said, "The list you made at your sleepover? Grading boys on cuteness?" And she said, "We never made a list. And also: Jerry Baxter didn't get an A-minus."

So there's definitely a list. Now I just need to find out where I am on it.

WHAT?

Not yet rated!

OCTOBER 9   [mood: curious]

Today, we all spent another day just trying to find out where we stand on the list. Chuck says that he spent a while talking to Ingrid Grant, who was at the sleepover, and she told him that he got a B-plus, but that she'd wanted to give him an A. I asked him if he found out what I got, but he said that he was a little too distracted.

On the bus ride home today, Doug Spivak leaned over and told me that someone had posted the grade list on the wall of the girls' bathroom. I asked him if he'd seen what my grade was, and he said he hadn't, but that he'd gotten a C-plus. And I was about to say something like, "Well, look, it's just a stupid list," when he said, "Pretty sweet, right? It's the best grade I've ever gotten in anything."

I guess, in some ways, it must be nice to be Doug Spivak.

Before school today, I tried to go into the girls' bathroom, but it was never empty. And I tried again at lunch, and the same thing happened. That's when I realized that I couldn't go in there when everyone else was out and around in the hallways, which left me with only one option. During English, I went up to Mrs. White and whispered, "I have diarrhea," and she let me go to the bathroom during class. So I sneaked into the girls' bathroom and took a look at the list.

And my name's not on it.

Billy Maguire

NO WAY!

B-Minus!

I checked and double-checked, and it's not there. Every other guy in our class is on the list. Billy Maguire is on the list, and he moved away two years ago! But I'm not on there, and I don't know why. Is it because I'm too ugly to grade? Because they're angry with me for some reason? It's driving me crazy—I'd almost rather have a bad grade than no grade at all.

Well, this morning, before class, I went over to Megan's locker and asked, as casually as I could, "Hey, Megan: I know there's a list. I saw it in the girls' bathroom. Why am I not on it?" And she said the worst three words she could possibly say:

"Who are you?"

And I said, "I'm Tad." And she said, "Oh. Right! Tad. Yeah, sorry. We just forgot about you."

I've gone to school with Megan since kindergarten. We were paired up in the "buddy system" for a full day for our class trip to the state capitol in sixth grade. I can't believe I was forgotten.

I'm going to have to try and be more memorable.

I've come up with a great plan to get more people to remember who I am. I realized that I need something to make me stand out, so I've decided that I'm going to start wearing a hat all the time. I'm going to be the hat-wearing guy. Maybe I'll even get a nickname, like "Cap Boy" or something. I'm trying it out tomorrow—wish me luck!

Bad news: Turns out, it's against the school rules to wear a hat all the time.

But tomorrow, I've got a great plan: I'm going to be the kid who always wears funny buttons to school. I got one that says VISUALIZE WHIRLED PEAS, and I'm going to wear it all day tomorrow.

Guess what? It's also against the rules to wear buttons to school.

But I'm not giving up. Now I've got a foolproof plan: I'm going to wear sunglasses everywhere. I've even figured out what my nickname should be: "Shades." This has got to work.

Well, it turns out that it's really hard to see indoors when you're wearing sunglasses—so for instance, you might not see the door to the faculty lounge opening until it hits you in the face. I got a bloody nose, and my sunglasses broke. Dr. Evans said she was really sorry, but I should know better than to wear sunglasses indoors.

After school, Chuck told me that it might be time to stop trying to come up with ways to be memorable. As he said, "Right now, you're going to

ow...

be remembered as the guy who keeps getting in trouble for wearing things." He had a point.

OCTOBER 19 [mood: confused]

I've never understood why Batman has villains named the Joker *and* the Riddler—there's not a huge difference between a joke and a riddle. I bet they both would get super sensitive if you pointed out the similarities, though. I bet if you brought up the Riddler around the Joker, he'd be like, "No, no, we're totally different! Sure, we both hate Batman. But he only uses the kind of humor that's question-and-answer-based, and mine is more of a prank-type thing!"

[mood: disgusted] OCTOBER 22

In bio class today, Mr. Hamilton made us dissect mice. Seema Gupta refused to do it, because she said that she had a mouse at home named Buttons and she wouldn't be able to dissect a mouse without thinking of him. But Mr. Hamilton said that if she refused, she'd get an F on the assignment. That's when Seema suddenly remembered that Buttons was a gerbil, not a mouse, and so she'd have no problem doing the assignment.

Mr. Hamilton kept walking around the room, saying things like, "See if you can find the squeaky part" and "Save the tail—it's a delicacy!" At one point, he held up two of the dead mice like they were puppets and pretended they were talking to each other.

I used to wonder why whenever our family went out to dinner at Applebee's, I'd always see

Mr. Hamilton there, eating alone. But I think I've figured out why.

Today at lunch, Jenny Bachman came over to my table and invited me to her Halloween party! Actually, she invited everyone at the table. I think she invited everyone in our class. But still: I got invited to a party at Jenny Bachman's house! And it's a costume party, so I have to come up with something that'll impress her.

I told my parents about the party at dinner, and my mom was like, "Oooh, a Halloween party! Why don't you just reuse one of your old costumes? We have some makeup—you could go as a clown! You did that in third grade, and you were so cute! Or a cat—remember the year you went as a cat? I think we still have your ears!" And I said, "Mom! It's a party at a girl's house!" And then she said, "Oh! Right. So I guess you don't want to go as Cookie Monster again, either, huh?"

Chuck and I spent most of lunch today trying to think of a good costume. It needs to be cool and creative, and it can't have a mask, because I want Jenny to be able to see my face. And it has to be something we both can do, so that if people think it's stupid, there's at least one other person at the party who's dressed equally stupidly. We finally decided that we'd both go as vampires, because girls seem to really, really like vampires. But Chuck just called me and said that his mom won't let him go as a vampire, because she's afraid he could swallow his vampire teeth and choke.

It's not easy being Chuck.

[mood:  happy] **OCTOBER 25**

Chuck had an awesome idea today: He's got a black suit from his Bar Mitzvah, and I've got the one we bought when Great-Aunt Sophie died. We just need to wear black ties and sunglasses, and we can be Men in Black! Chuck is a genius.

I got in trouble tonight at dinner, and I'm still not sure why. Sophie went to the mall with my parents today and picked out her Halloween costume— she's going as Sleeping Beauty. And all I said was, "Y'know, I don't understand why the prince would want to kiss Sleeping Beauty, because she's been lying there for a really long time, so I bet she stinks. I mean, there's no way that, after lying there for all that time, she hasn't peed herself." And Sophie started to cry and say that she didn't want to be the princess who smelled like pee, and that she wanted a different costume, and my mom announced that I wouldn't be allowed to watch TV tonight.

[mood: annoyed] OCTOBER 27

In trouble again. My parents went to the mall and got Sophie a Little Mermaid costume, and all I said was, "You won't be able to say 'Trick or treat.' The Little Mermaid gave away her voice in order to get legs, remember?" And Sophie said that she didn't want to go the whole night without speaking, so she'd have to get a different costume, and I had my Wii taken away.

[mood: careful]   **OCTOBER 29**

Sorry I didn't write yesterday. My parents took my computer away after they came back with a third costume for Sophie, a Cinderella costume, and I said that it was a really pretty dress, given that it had been sewn together by mice and rats.

I need to learn to keep my mouth shut.

OCTOBER 30   [mood: pensive]

Sophie's getting ready for Halloween—she's been practicing saying "Trick or treat!" really loud. I don't understand why we still say "Trick or treat."

Nobody actually bothers to trick the people who don't give them candy, so the whole "trick" part of "Trick or treat" is just an empty threat, and everyone knows it. I think the "trick" part is just there because it makes it sound like you're offering people an option—it just seems rude to knock on people's doors and shout, "Treat!"

 [mood: blue] **OCTOBER 31**

6:15 p.m.

Jenny's party is two hours away, and I can't get in touch with Chuck. He wasn't in school today, and he's not answering his phone. Meanwhile, my mom and dad just took Sophie trick-or-treating. Sophie finally settled on going as an angel, and Mom and Dad got kind of mad at me when I looked at her costume and said, "You know, another way of looking at it is that you're going as a dead kid," and Sophie started to cry. My mom and dad only got her to stop by promising to take her trick-or-treating over in the super-rich neighborhood where people give out full-size candy bars.

6:37 p.m.

Just got a text message from Chuck. He's got strep throat, so he won't be able to be the other Man in Black. Which kind of ruins the whole plan, because the Men in Black thing only works if there's more than one of you. If it's just you, you look like a funeral director. Now I don't have anything to wear to Jenny's party.

7:21 p.m.

I just had a great idea! I remembered Jenny saying once how much she loved the movie *Avatar*, and how she thought the guy from it was really cute! I dug around in the attic and found the blue makeup from when I was Cookie Monster. I covered my face and arms in blue makeup and put some yellow dots on it, and I borrowed the wig that Sophie wore when she went as Hannah Montana two years ago—it's not bad, if I do say so myself. I'm off to the party now—wish me luck!

9:40 p.m.

Ugh. Bad night. I got to Jenny Bachman's house, and she seemed sort of startled when she opened the door and I was standing there. She was like, "Are you a Smurf?" And I said, "No! I'm a Na'vi! Like from one of your favorite movies, *Avatar*?" And she said, "Oh! Right!" And then her mom saw me and said, "That's blue makeup?" And I said, "Yep!" And her mom said, "I'm sorry, but please don't sit on any of our furniture. Or touch our walls. OK?"

So I stood around for a few minutes near the punch bowl, and saw what everyone else had come as—a lot of people weren't even wearing costumes, and the ones who were, were wearing really simple ones, like the guy who'd stapled some socks to himself and come as Static Cling.

And then it got even worse: I saw Mark O'Keefe, who was there dressed as Wolverine, with his arm around Jenny Bachman.

After that, I decided I didn't want to stick around anymore, and I

started walking home. I was halfway home when my parents drove by, and my mom rolled down the window and said, "Tad? Is that you?" And I said, "Yeah." And my dad said, "Weren't you going as one of the Men in Black?" And I said, "Chuck got sick." And then my sister said, "Is that my Hannah Montana wig?" And I said, "Maybe." My mom said, "We'd offer you a ride home, but . . . you know . . . the car's upholstery." So I walked the rest of the way home.

Now I'm in my room. I washed as much of the blue off as I could, but I keep finding more, like in my ears or on my neck. Sophie just came to the door and said, "Tad? I'm sorry you had a bad time at your party. You can have one of my Snickerses if you want." Which was really nice of her. I mean, she's allergic to peanuts, so I'm not sure why she didn't let me have all the Snickers. But still . . . it was nice of her.

November

Well, there's good news and bad news: The good news is, I'm now very memorable—everyone in school knows who I am, and I even have a nickname.

The bad news is, the nickname is "Smurf."

I guess everybody found out about my *Avatar* costume from the other night. I can even hear people whispering "Smurf" when I walk down the hallway. The only nice part about the whole day was when Jenny Bachman came over to me and said, "Tad! I'm sorry you didn't stick around the other night. I don't care what anyone else says—I thought your costume was really cool." Which was really nice of her, and almost made up for the fact that our conversation ended with Mark O'Keefe coming over, saying, "Let's go!" and then, as they walked away, adding, "Later, Smurf."

NOVEMBER 3 [mood: confused]

Sophie just got back from her best friend Stacy's birthday party at Chuck E. Cheese. I wonder what the meeting was like where they decided on that restaurant's mascot. Like, did anyone pipe up and go, "Hey, maybe we shouldn't have our mascot be a six-foot-tall rat"? Or was everyone just OK with it?

[mood: happy] **NOVEMBER 4**

Today's the end of Daylight Savings Time, and like I do every year, I accidentally set my watch forward, instead of backward, so I spent most of the day two hours off. I always get that "Spring forward, fall back" thing wrong, because it seems like, if you've just sprung forward, then you're more likely to fall forward. Go ahead—try it. Jump forward and see which way you fall.

See?

That's why I've been trying to come up with my own way to remember how Daylight Savings works. Here's one:

"Coiled springs hold lots of power, go ahead and add an hour.

When you fall, you'll hurt your back, so an hour you should subtract."

I realize that one's a little long, though. Here's a shorter one I came up with:

"Spring flowers? Add an hour.

Fall snacks? An hour back."

I know that the "snacks" part doesn't make sense. I'm still working on it.

NOVEMBER 5 [mood: thoughtful]

We're studying Greek myths in class now. Today, we learned about Medusa, whose face could turn anyone who looked at it into stone. What I can't figure out is how everyone discovered that fact.

It's not like you could *see* Medusa turn some-one into stone—if you were there, then you were turned into stone, too. And if you weren't there, and showed up later, how would you be able to figure out that the reason all your friends were now statues was that they'd looked at Medusa? I guess maybe, one time, someone was in the next room when his friends went in to see Medusa, and his friends shouted something like, "Here comes Medusa! She's coming this way! She's rounding the corner! We're just about to see her! Oh, wow, she's hideou—" And then the guy figured out, after the fact, "Oh, looking at Medusa turns you into stone."

Yeah. That must be what happened.

NOVEMBER 7 [mood: absentminded]

My dad's been teaching me to play chess. It's a strange game. I kind of can't concentrate on playing it, because I just keep picturing this weird kingdom where castles keep moving sideways, bishops are always walking diagonally, and horses can only gallop in L-shapes.

[mood: bored] NOVEMBER 8

I was flipping around on cable today and caught a bit of *Star Trek: The Next Generation* and then some of the last movie they did, and y'know what? That robot got old.

Then
(Such technology!)

Now
(Robotic wonder!)

Today in class, they passed out the order forms for school pictures. I brought it home, and my mom said, "Well, Tad, you want to give it another try this year?"

I have a bad history with school pictures. I've never gotten a good one. In first grade, I got distracted by a noise when the picture was taken, so it's just a blurry picture of the back of my head. In second grade, I was chewing on my pen that morning and it burst open, so my face is covered with a big ink blot. In third grade, I sneezed right when the camera went off. In fourth grade, I wore a shirt the same color as the background, so it looks like a picture of a floating head. In fifth grade, I had the hiccups when the picture was taken, so I'm all blurry. In sixth grade, I had an allergic reaction to the free comb the photographer gave everyone, and my eyes got so puffy, I could barely see. In seventh grade, I had a bloody nose earlier that day, so my shirt is covered in blood. (My dad calls the photo "your mug shot.") So at this point, my mom just checks the box for the smallest package of photos they offer—one 5 x 3 photo and four wallet-sized photos. "If they're good, we'll order more," she said.

But this is going to be the year I have a good school picture. I can just feel it. I'm going to get a haircut this weekend, and it's going to look great.

First Grade   Second Grade   Third Grade

Fourth Grade   Fifth Grade   Sixth Grade

Seventh Grade

Stupid Supercuts. I went to get my hair cut today, and at first it was really nice, 'cause there was a TV above the barber's chair, so I could watch it while my barber cut my hair. It was only toward the end of the haircut that I realized my barber was watching the TV, too. So instead of what I asked for—which was short on the sides and long on top—I got a haircut that was short on the left side and long on the right. It made my head look lopsided. It was so bad, the only thing I could do was ask the barber to take the clippers and make it short all over. I also asked him to turn off the TV while he did it.

Anyway. Now I have a buzz cut. It's OK, though— I'll just wear a hat in my photo.

[mood: embarrassed] NOVEMBER 13

Well, there are two bad things about my new haircut: One, my head is really, really cold. And two, as June Chen pointed out in front of everyone today at lunch, without much hair on my head, you can totally see that I have a huge unibrow. She said I look like Bert from *Sesame Street*, which would be mean if it weren't kind of true.

I've got to fix this before Friday.

NOVEMBER 14 [mood: embarrassed-er]

Here is some advice: If you are going to try to get rid of a unibrow, don't just take a razor and shave down the middle of it, because you'll probably cut

off more than you mean to, and then you'll try to even it up on one side, and then you'll realize you cut too much on that side and need to even it up on the other side, and one thing will lead to another and then you'll have no eyebrows.

Here is some more advice: If you've semi-accidentally shaved your eyebrows off, don't try to draw them on with a Sharpie, because even if you do a really good job, people will notice and make fun of you. Also, it takes forever to wash your fake eyebrows off.

So today was picture day, and I showed up wearing a baseball cap and sunglasses. The photographer told me I wasn't allowed to wear them in the picture, so I took them off. And then he looked at me and said, "Do you have some sort of a disease?" And I said, "No. I have a bad haircut and I shaved off my eyebrows sort of by accident." And he leaned over and whispered, "Um . . . do you want me to accidentally leave the lens cap on for your photo?" And I said, "That'd be great." So here's how I'll look in this year's yearbook:

Eighth Grade

The sad thing is, I think it may be my best school photo ever.

"Two scoops of raisins" sounds really impressive until you realize that they never say how big the scoops are. What if the scoops are super tiny, and only hold one raisin each?

In biology today, we learned that raccoons are nocturnal animals, so if you see one in daylight, it probably has rabies. Then, when I got home, Sophie was watching *Pocahontas*. It really changes that movie if, the whole time, you keep thinking, "Man, that raccoon's *totally* going to bite her face off any second now."

You know who I feel bad for? The second-to-last airbender. Because I bet he was probably really good at bending air, and nobody ever even talks about him.

I wonder how seals got to be named "seals," while sea lions got the name "sea lion." "Sea lion" is such a better name than "seal." I like to imagine that when all the animals were picking out names, the seals went first, and they said, "We want to be called seals!" And they were pretty happy with

that, until the sea lions' turn came, and they were like, "We're going with 'sea lions'!" And the seals were all like, "Wait: You can do that? Just choose a

219 ⇨

cool animal and put 'sea' in front of it? Can we be sea eagles?" But the animal-naming committee was like, "It's too late, we've moved on to these guys over here. What do you want to be called?" And the sea horses were like, "Sea horses!"

Today was Thanksgiving, and I'm stuffed with turkey. Dinner was good: My aunt Pam and uncle Owen came over, and my mom made turkey and cranberry sauce and stuffing and green-bean casserole and sweet potatoes, all of which I hate eating on any day of the year but Thanksgiving. I guess Thanksgiving's supposed to be just like the first meal the Pilgrims ate with the Native Americans, but I'm not sure whether the Pilgrims or the Native Americans brought the marshmallows for the sweet potatoes or the canned onions for the green-bean casserole.

After dinner, my uncle Owen said, "Do you want to play a little football?" So I went into the living room, turned on the Wii, and put in Madden NFL, but it turned out, he wanted to play real football, with, like, a ball in the yard. I'd never really thrown a football around much before. It's kind of hard, and boring, and there are no cheat codes to help you throw it better. I don't get the point of it.

NOVEMBER 24 [mood: irritable]

I don't get why they're Alvin and the Chipmunks. Alvin *is* a chipmunk. It should be Alvin and the Two Other Chipmunks. Or maybe The Three Chipmunks.

(I know it's not the biggest logical problem in a movie about three singing chipmunks. But still, it bothers me.)

[mood: thirsty] **NOVEMBER 26**

Today, I got into an argument with Chuck about how to pronounce "Minute Maid," as in "Minute Maid orange juice." I said it's pronounced "min-itt," as in, the thing that there are sixty of in an hour, and he said it's pronounced "mih-nyoot," as in, something that's really tiny. I told him that was stupid, and why would anyone name their orange juice for a tiny cleaning woman? And he said, well, if it's pronounced "minute" as in "a minute of time," then what's a "minute maid"? Someone who cleans up after you, but only for sixty seconds?

I hate to admit it, but he sort of had a point.

NOVEMBER 28 [mood: cold]

This morning, I saw my neighbor Mr. Baxter packing up his car for a trip. He said he was going to drive up to the lake this weekend to go ice fishing, which is weird, because it's pretty easy to make ice at home.

December

There's a weekend-long James Bond marathon on TV, and I watched some of it with my dad today. Here's what I wonder about James Bond: I get that he has a license to kill. But what do you have to go through to get it? I like to think that first, you have to have a learner's permit to kill. Like, you can go around killing people, but your mom or dad have to come with you. And then maybe there's a written portion, where you have to answer a lot of multiple-choice questions about when it is and isn't okay to kill. And if they catch you killing while you're drunk, they can take away your license, and then you have to ask a friend to do all your killing for you. That must suck.

I watched a little more James Bond with my dad. It cracks me up that one of the villains is this guy:

SNIFF
SNIFF

Because if he's got a cat on his lap, that means that somewhere nearby in his evil lair, there's got to be a litter box.

In social studies, we're learning about how America got started from thirteen colonies. I can't believe anyone would start a country with thirteen of anything— it's just unlucky. If you ask me, they should've either added a colony or kicked one of them out—probably Delaware.

[mood:  fidgety] DECEMBER 7

Today in social studies, Mr. Rao started off by telling us that today is the sixty-fifth anniversary of Pearl Harbor. Doug Spivak raised his hand and said that *Pearl Harbor* came out in the summer, but Mr. Rao explained that he was talking about the actual attack on Pearl Harbor, not the movie. And then Doug said, "Wait: The stuff in *Pearl*

Harbor really happened?" And Mr. Rao said yes, it really happened. And Doug said, "Well, what about *Armageddon*? Did that really happen, too?" And Mr. Rao said no, that one was fake.

And so then for about five minutes, Doug listed movies, and Mr. Rao told him whether the stuff in them really happened or not. (*Zorro*: No. *The Alamo*: Yes. *Saving Private Ryan*: Yes and no. *Pirates of the Caribbean*: No. *Dodgeball*: No. *National Treasure*: No.) When Doug asked about *Raiders of the Lost Ark*, Mr. Rao refused to answer any more questions.

DECEMBER 8 [mood:  grossed out]

If you think about it, *tater tot* is a bad name for a food, because it suggests that you're eating potato babies.

[mood: inquisitive] DECEMBER 9

It's a Wonderful Life is on TV today. If it's true that every time a bell rings, an angel gets its wings, then I don't understand why Clarence goes to so much trouble to help Jimmy Stewart. It seems like he could just as easily get his wings the next time a handbell choir performs.

DECEMBER 11 [mood: puzzled]

I really don't understand why any baseball team would choose to name themselves the Anaheim Angels. That's like calling yourself "the Anaheim Dead People."

There was an assembly today where we all had to listen to the kids in the choir sing Christmas songs, plus one Hanukkah song and one song about Kwanzaa. They sang "Rudolph, the Red-Nosed Reindeer," and I started thinking about the reindeer games they wouldn't let Rudolph play. What kind of games would reindeer play? They walk around on all four of their limbs, so it's not like they can catch or throw anything. And they certainly can't play tag, because their antlers are so pointy. I suppose they could play board games or something, so long as they could pick up their playing pieces with their mouths and maybe throw the dice by rolling them around in their mouths and spitting them out. If that's what they were doing,

I don't feel all that sorry for Rudolph, because board games are kind of lame.

DECEMBER 13 [mood: nauseated]

In English class, we read the story "The Gift of the Magi," which is about this woman who sells her hair to buy her husband a watch chain for Christmas—only he's sold his watch to buy her combs for her hair. And the moral of the story is that it's better to give than to receive, although to me, the bigger news in the story is, some people buy hair. That's so weird.

[mood: sleepy] **DECEMBER 14**

I've been thinking about it, and I think a good story would be "The Birthday Gift of the Magi." It's about a woman who sells her hair to buy her husband a watch chain, and he's like, "Oh, hey . . . thanks,"

Good grief, she's bald!

and then he doesn't give her anything, because it's not her birthday. And they both just sort of sit there, feeling kind of awkward.

We're doing Secret Santa in my homeroom. We picked names yesterday, and I got Aaron Reynolds, who used to beat me up and give me wedgies in elementary school. Luckily, Chuck got Patricia Ortiz, who I've kind of liked since sixth grade, and he agreed to swap names with me. So now I have to figure out what to get Patricia that:

A) she'll really like, and

B) costs under $10, 'cause that's the limit they set.

Which sucks, 'cause you can't really get anyone anything good for ten bucks. Chuck pointed out that you can get ten small chilis at Wendy's for $10, but I don't think that's the sort of thing you want to unwrap from your Secret Santa.

Chuck's mom took us to the mall today so we could find our Secret Santa stuff. I was thinking of getting Patricia a tiny bottle of perfume or something, but I couldn't find any bottles that didn't cost, like, eight times what we're allowed to spend. Also, the salespeople at JCPenney were spraying samples on people, and Chuck kept getting hit by them, so he really wanted to leave. I can't blame

him. He was beginning to smell like one of my mom's magazines.

We went through the rest of the mall and didn't find anything for Patricia, but at Best Buy, Chuck found a discount bin of $10 DVDs, so we tried to find the one Aaron Reynolds was least likely to want. I hope he enjoys *Legally Blonde 2: Red, White and Blonde.*

DECEMBER 18 [mood: nervous]

After school, Chuck and I went downtown to do more shopping. We didn't find anything for Patricia, and we looked everywhere—even Victoria's Secret. Actually, we didn't really think we'd find anything for Patricia there—we just liked having an excuse to see what the inside of the store was like.

I asked if they could help me find something for one of my classmates, and the saleslady said, "Is this your girlfriend?" and I said, "No, just a girl in my class." And the saleslady said, "There is nothing here you should buy for her."

So tomorrow's the Secret Santa exchange, and I really needed to buy Patricia's gift today, so Chuck and I had his older sister take us to the super-nice mall on the other side of town. I wound up getting her present at the Godiva chocolate place. The smallest box they had was $15, but it looked tiny and only had, like, three chocolates in it, so I wound up getting her the one that costs $30. It's more than I'm spending on any member of my family, but then again, I don't really want to ask any of them out.

[mood: annoyed] DECEMBER 20

Today was the big gift exchange. We all dropped our presents in a box, and then they were handed out. Chuck got a copy of the third Harry Potter book, which had clearly been read by whoever gave it to him. I got a note saying that my Santa didn't have time to buy anything, and that he'd give me $10 later. Meanwhile, Patricia opened up her present and was all like, "Oh, chocolate! Great! Someone's trying to make me break out and get fat." So Aaron offered to swap his DVD with her. And she was all, "Oh, that's so sweet of you! I love this movie! Thank you so so so so much!" And then it came time for everyone to tell each other who their Secret Santa was, and I told Patricia, and she kind of said, "Uh-huh," and went back to talking to Aaron.

And as if that weren't depressing enough, after homeroom, I walked by Jenny Bachman's locker, and she was showing off the necklace that Mark O'Keefe had gotten her.

One of these days, I'm going to write a

story called "The Gift of the Tadi." It's about how it's better to give than to receive, but sometimes, it just sucks all around.

DECEMBER 21 [mood: happy]

Great news! Jenny Bachman broke up with Mark O'Keefe!

I guess she was wearing her necklace at the mall, and then she saw, like, two girls from other middle schools wearing the exact same necklace, and she asked them where they'd gotten it, and all three of them thought they were dating Mark!

This may be the best Christmas gift I've ever gotten.

[mood: humbug] **DECEMBER 23**

OK, I realize it's not the point of the story, but still: If I were Scrooge, and I got to see Christmas Future, I'd try and snag a newspaper while I was there so I could place bets on sports and win a lot of money.

DECEMBER 24 [mood: excited]

It's Christmas Eve. My mom and dad just gave Sophie and me our night-before-Christmas presents, which are—as always—pajamas. My pajamas have pockets in the pants. I'm not sure why. I guess so I have someplace to put whatever I pick up in my dreams?

[mood: merry] DECEMBER 25

Christmas was fun. My parents got me some aftershave and some books and video games and a new sweater-vest, and Grandma Judy sent me some Lego blocks, I guess because she still thinks of me as being seven years old. Sophie got some accounting software and a real grown-up accounts-receivable ledger, which is exactly what she wanted. She also put on a really good show of pretending to be excited because Santa had come for a visit, which made my parents happy.

DECEMBER 26 [mood:  sleepy]

According to the calendar, today is something called "Boxing Day" in England. I hoped that meant that the whole country took part in a big fistfight, but apparently, it's just what they call the day after Christmas there.

[mood: disgusted] DECEMBER 27

It snowed yesterday, so Sophie and I went to the park and made a snowman. Here is some advice, if you're thinking about making a snowman: Make sure you don't do it in the part of the park where dogs tend to poop a lot. We got about halfway through rolling one big snowball when we figured out why our snowman smelled so bad.

DECEMBER 30  [mood: annoyed]

Tonight, my mom made me sit down and write a thank-you note to Grandma Judy for the Legos she sent me. I felt stupid writing out the words "Thanks for the Legos—I look forward to playing with them," but my mom insisted it was the polite thing to do. But when I asked if she was going to send a thank-you note for the talking bathroom scale that Grandma Judy got for her, she said, "None of your business."

[mood: delighted] DECEMBER 31

Well, it's the last day of the year, which always makes me a little sad. Looking back on the past year, it was pretty OK. I got most of my New Year's resolutions done: I created my blog, I started shaving, I learned how to do at least half a kickflip, and I technically *did* get some girls to notice me, even if it was just to call me "Smurf."

And next year might be a good year. I went down to the mall today to exchange the Lego blocks for a Wii game, and I ran into Jenny Bachman. I told her I was sorry to hear that she and Mark O'Keefe had broken up, and she said it was OK, she didn't have much in common with him anyway. Then she asked if maybe I wanted to go ice-skating with her sometime, and I said sure. So we made a plan for next Saturday.

So things might be looking up for me. I feel like good things might be about to happen. I'm excited, I'm hopeful, and I'm very very nervous.

Because I have no idea how to ice-skate.

Tim Carvell is the former head writer for *The Daily Show with Jon Stewart*, for which he won six Emmys. He has also served as a writer and editor at *Fortune*, *Sports Illustrated Women*, and *Entertainment Weekly*. His work has also appeared in *New York* magazine, the *New York Times*, *Esquire*, *Slate*, and *McSweeney's*; the *Daily Show* books *America: The Book* and *Earth: The Book*; and the anthologies *More Mirth of a Nation*, *Created in Darkness by Troubled Americans*, and *The McSweeney's Joke Book of Joke Books*. He lives in New York with his partner, Tom Keeton.

For exclusive information on your favorite authors and artists, visit www.authortracker.com.

Also available as an ebook.

EVERYONE IS MAD FOR TAD!

Follow the laugh-out-loud adventures of Tad's year-in-the-blog

PRAISE FOR *PLANET TAD*:

"This book will make you laugh. If you're not into that sort of thing, consider yourself warned." —Stephen Colbert

"Hilarious to anyone who ever went through, is currently in, might go to, or flunked out of middle school." —Jon Stewart

"Tad is the rapid-fire, pop-culture-referencing, actually funny stand-up-comic-in-waiting that I wanted to be in middle school!" —Tom Angleberger, author of the *New York Times* bestseller *The Strange Case of Origami Yoda*

Join the fun at www.facebook.com/planettadbook!

MAD

HARPER
An Imprint of HarperCollinsPublishers

PLANET TAD is based on a blog of the same name in MAD MAGAZINE.
™ and © E.C. Publications. (s14)

Want More
PLANET TAD?
Subscribe to

© E. C. Publications, Inc.

New Episodes in Every Issue!

Go to **madmagazine.com**
or call **1-800-4madmag**

MODERN PHEASANT HUNTING

Steve Grooms

Foreword by Richard E. McCabe

EAU CLAIRE DISTRICT LIBRARY

STACKPOLE BOOKS

90460

Modern Pheasant Hunting

Copyright © 1982 by Steve Grooms

Published by
STACKPOLE BOOKS
Cameron and Kelker Streets
P.O. Box 1831
Harrisburg, PA. 17105

First printing, April 1982
Second printing (paperback), *July 1984*

All rights reserved, including the right to reproduce this book or portions thereof in any form or by any means, electronic or mechanical, including photocopying, recording, or by any information storage and retrieval system, without permission in writing from the publisher. All inquiries should be addressed to Stackpole Books, Cameron and Kelker Streets, P.O. Box 1831, Harrisburg, Pennsylvania 17105.

Cover art by Robert K. Halladay

Printed in the U.S.A.

Library of Congress Cataloging in Publication Data

Grooms, Steve.
    Modern pheasant hunting.

    Includes index.
    1. Pheasant shooting. I. Title.
SK325.P5G7   799.2'48617   81-18372 (pbk.)
ISBN 0-8117-2208-2   AACR2

Dedication

To the memory of Butch and Gary, who made so much of the few pheasant seasons they were given to hunt, and to the still-lively spirit of Brandy.

Contents

Foreword

It was six years ago that Steve Grooms invited me to join him on a pheasant hunt. Although we hunted together that autumn for ruffed grouse, woodcock, and Canada geese, we had only one opportunity to share pursuit of ringnecks.

My records show that on that occasion we were accompanied by Steve's springer spaniel, Brandy, and my yellow Labrador, Mac—two very special friends. The ledger also tells that we hunted for seven hours over most of two and a half quarter sections of chopped corn, soybeans, and alfalfa in southern Minnesota. A brief notation at the margin indicates that it was about twenty degrees that November day, with a fifteen-to-twenty-mile-an-hour wind. Intermittently, snow fell, and I recall it came down at a forty-five-degree angle, its flakes ricochetting off our exposed faces with the impact of tenpenny nails. Eight pheasants were seen, the entry concludes, of which five were hens. Two shots were fired at two of the three roosters; two birds were bagged, both by Steve.

My records do not indicate that this was an unusual hunt, yet it certainly was. Every pheasant hunt is an exciting event; in the company of Steve Grooms, it is also high adventure. Few of the very many with whom I have hunted equal Steve's enthusiasm for, or skill in hunting pheasant, or have his sense of respect and appreciation for the ring-necks' craft, tenacity, and beauty. One succeeds when hunting with Steve Grooms, regardless of the bag.

But this book is not about Steve. It's about the ringneck pheasant—its deserved niche in croplands, marshes, and glens across the North American landscape, and its coveted place in the hearts of dedicated sportsmen. The following pages do not contain the idle musings of a writer who happens to be a hunter. Instead, they represent a rich trove of experiences, insightful reflections, and sensitivities of a hunter who happens to be a writer.

So now it's my turn. Let me invite you, through the chapters of this book, to join Steve Grooms on a pheasant hunt. Whether a beginning hunter, a veteran gunner or someone who simply would enjoy learning more about ringneck habits, habitats, and other mysteries, be assured that you will find it an entertaining and rewarding experience.

Wildlife Management Institute   Richard E. McCabe

Preface

I love pheasants. I love the way they look. The forward half of a rooster, with its riot of improbable colors—the irridescent purple and green, pure scarlet, stark white, and shimmering copper—is a perfect reflection of the brassy, cocky side of the bird's personality. And yet, the rear half—with those muted tans, the surprisingly effective camouflage barring, and that whimsical touch of effeminate blue—reflects the wily, elusive side of the pheasant's nature. Here is a bird which might boil out of the grass between your legs, hurling curses and dropping whitewash as it sails down the wind. Or it might clamp head and tail to the ground and vanish mysteriously from a tiny chunk of cover tightly surrounded by men and dogs. The rooster pheasant is a riverboat gambler all decked out in show-off finery; his flamboyant exterior belies the icy cool tactician lurking within.

I love the fiercely independent spirit of the bird. There never was a tame pheasant. Oh sure, a cock pheasant will sleep in a shelterbelt

EAU CLAIRE DISTRICT LIBRARY

just yards from a farmhouse; he will help himself freely to the farmer's grain; and he will even indulge in some sexual indiscretions with barnyard poultry. But while the pheasant accepts or steals whatever he pleases from mankind, he is absolutely his own bird. Tame a pheasant? You might as well try taming a scorpion!

I admire the courage and awesome tenacity of pheasants. On many occasions I have seen a rooster take a heavy load of shot, a hit which spun the bird in the air or knocked it sideways; and yet the valiant bird kept flying. I remember one big cock that ran thirty yards after being downed, fought an even match with a Labrador, and was still flashing its spurs when I got to it to administer the coup de grace. I later found that bird had a broken thigh, two broken wings, and five pellets in its vital area. My father used to express his respect for the vitality of roosters by removing the head from each bird he shot and then hiding it. If roosters grew a few pounds heavier they would probably hunt people. And knowing what I do about the strategic shrewdness of pheasants in field maneuvers, I would sure hate to have one on my trail.

I stand in awe of the resourcefulness of gun-wise pheasants. I cannot count the times I have seen roosters dematerialize and escape from traps that would have held Houdini. Last fall I had the chance to observe a big flock of pheasants which had been pressured hard for five days. In the five days our party hunted them I never saw a rooster make a poor decision about the best way to escape the hunters. Time and again, foolproof strategies were spoiled when the cocks broke out of the cover by the only route which could take them to safety out of range of the guns. The hunters had the advantage of advance planning, the assistance of dogs, the unfair edge afforded by firearms technology, and (presumably) superior intelligence. All the pheasants had was their ability to make instant decisions to run, hide, sneak, or flush. And, by any fair scorekeeping, you would have to say the pheasants won nearly every round.

I was raised hunting pheasants, have hunted them almost all my life, and hope to hunt them for many more years to come until I can no longer totter through the cover with a gun. I think I understand them, and they consistently behave as if they understand me. When hunting ringnecks I try my damndest to be like them; I emulate their unlikely combination of Apache warrior and chess master.

If a fairy godmother ever appears to offer me three wishes, I already know what I will ask for first. Just once, for one exhilarating day, I would love to be a springer spaniel smashing through a deep marsh filled with tricky roosters. Just imagine it: running flat out through a shifting screen of cattail stalks with only inches of visibility; sucking in the maddening scent of nearby cock birds; and coming at last face-to-face with the cacophonous eruption of a flushing rooster whose streaming tail would just elude my snapping jaws. And would I hunt obediently under control, staying in range of the guns? Hell, no!

Surely this is a bird which deserves the highest regard of the modern hunter. And yet, that measure of respect is rarely extended to the pheasant. Quail hunters are apt to look down their noses at the pheasant because he is not enough of a gentleman to squat stupidly in front of a locked-up pointer until some hunter saunters in to shoot him. Grouse and woodcock hunters are apt to adopt superior airs around lowly pheasant hunters, rather like opera-goers who sniff at bowlers. Yet, their beloved birds have none of the tenacity or strategic sophistication of the ringneck. Duck and goose hunters speak reverently of the sagacity of waterfowl, but can you imagine an experienced rooster flying to his doom because he was fooled by some plastic decoys and beguiling talk on a little wooden horn? Fat chance.

It is no wonder that dedicated pheasant hunters get a little testy and defensive at times. They might even be tempted to defend the ringneck by punching holes in the reputations of other gamebirds. But, speaking as one such dedicated pheasant hunter, I love all those other birds and would not care to speak against them. I only wish other hunters were not so quick to mock pheasants. Without discrediting quail, I might point out that my friends and I sometimes hunt them as a way of taking a rest from the wars with mean cover and too-smart roosters. I enjoy grouse hunting partly because it is such a simple-minded physical activity, calling for none of the nerve-wracking stratagems of pheasant hunting. It is the cover, not the birds, which makes grouse hunting difficult: a fact easily appreciated by anyone who has spent as much time as I have trying to get a shot at roosters in alder tangles that would be grouse cover if they were a little farther north.

Yet, pheasants are widely dismissed as dumb, slow, and easy. Why? Perhaps it is because so many hunters encounter pheasants only on the season opener, in that brief moment when the birds of the year do not yet understand that they should not escape hunters by flying away from them as if they were any other land-based predator. These young birds, just a few months out of their eggs, cannot fairly be expected to understand the long-range killing potential of a load of chilled sixes—and they don't. What amazes me, though, is the way so many of them seem to acquire that wisdom, for within hours after the guns first begin to boom in the cover, you suddenly find pheasants behaving as if they knew exactly what a shotgun can and cannot do. Still, those callow roosters of opening day are so easy to hunt that they foster the notion that pheasants are the one gamebird any neophyte can find and shoot.

Perhaps the reputation of pheasants still suffers from the memories many hunters have of the halcyon days of the 1940s, when a short walk in any cornfield would send clouds of birds roaring up, and any half-competent shooter could quickly knock down a five-bird daily limit. Today the legends of those awesome flocks are hard to believe, and it is easy to see how few hunters would acquire a high regard for a bird so easily hunted.

Yet, it seems to be a universal law of human nature that we perversely assign value to objects in direct proportion to their elusiveness. And the modern pheasant is amazingly elusive. Because of this, the contemporary upland hunter is coming at last to value the pheasant as the wonderful gamebird it has always been. Thus, we have the irony of declining pheasant populations giving rise to a new breed of pheasant hunter.

He puts far more into his sport than did hunters of those days when the ringneck was the undisputed king of the uplands. And, except in terms of pounds of meat, he gets far more from his sport. He walks long miles in frostbite weather, wades into horrible swamps and jungles of horse weeds, and cuts his flesh on all varieties of nasty brush; all this in hopes of flushing a rooster in range. In view of the low number of birds, and especially in view of the wily nature of the survivors, the modern pheasant hunter knows he has no guarantee of gunplay on his hunts. Yet he hunts, and you can bet that when he succeeds in bringing a lustrous cockbird to bag, he will pause for a moment to admire it. Today's pheasant is a splendid gamebird, and the modern pheasant hunter knows it. Out of my fond respect for this hunter and his grand quarry, this book was written.

1

The Challenge

Let's follow a pheasant hunt. Imagine we, like Superman, can see right through the weeds, allowing us to understand everything that will happen on this hunt.

A Typical Hunt

A station wagon rolls along a gravel road early in the morning and crunches to a stop near a marshy wildlife management area a few minutes before legal shooting hours begin. The center of the area is too wet to walk in, but this area has a fat fringe of marshy weeds all around it. The four hunters now clambering out of the car figure they can conduct a drive around the edge of the marsh. It is the fifth day of the season, so the pheasants have not been subjected to their second weekend of gunning pressure. The hunters have no dogs. They do not know what you and I know, but there are five roosters in the weeds which the hunters plan to drive. The hunters stretch, load up, and check their watches. Okay, time to go!

The last man to get his shotgun loaded bangs the tailgate of the wagon to shut it as he hurries to catch up with his three partners. Almost a hundred yards away from the road you and I can see an old rooster, a veteran of last year's season. He hears the slamming station wagon door. While the hunters are climbing off the elevated road and getting lined up, that rooster breaks into a dead run and never slows up once. By the time the hunters have covered a few yards, the old rooster is out of the management area and running hell for leather through a field of cut corn. They will never see him.

The party has covered less than fifty yards when they get close to the second rooster. Hearing them approach, he sneaks nervously ahead and to the right of the oncoming line. He pauses from time to time, listening carefully; then he squirts through the weeds again, always drifting ahead and to the right of the drive. Finally he senses he has successfully outflanked the fellow on the far right side of the driving line. The line plows ahead, not guessing that two roosters have already slipped away to safety.

The third cock is a young of-the-year bird who has been lucky enough to be somewhere else this year when hunters stomped through the cover. The approaching danger alarms him. He ducks into a heavy clump of canary grass to hide. Finally he decides the hunters are too close for comfort so he takes to his wings. There is a shout and two guns boom. The young rooster falls. Someone yells, "Looks like the opening day crowds didn't get 'em all!"

They move again. Soon the fourth rooster perceives the danger. This bird has come to associate safety with the wet part of the marsh; so that is where he heads, darting quickly through the undergrowth until he nears the standing water. The man on the far left hand side of the drive is unusually determined to let no pheasants escape the hunt on his flank, so he is sloshing along in water ankle deep. The cock is surprised to hear a predator coming at him in the water, but he responds quickly by swimming for several yards until he can clamber up on a little island of vegetation surrounded by water. The hunters never guess they have walked close to them.

The fifth rooster decides to play it cool. He slinks into a tight pocket of cattails and grass and freezes while he waits for danger to pass. The line does pass him, even though the nearest hunter comes within a few feet of stepping on the skulking bird. Right after that, however, the group stops because this same hunter is having problems with all the coffee he drank on the road. He lays his gun aside, unzips, and seeks relief. The rooster, having decided it has been spotted, takes two running steps out of the hiding spot, leaps, and emerges noisily from the cattails. The unzipped hunter is in no position to shoot, so the pheasant reaches the safety of a draw in an adjoining field. Everyone in the party laughs; then someone exclaims, "Shoot, I'll bet we've been walking by roosters all morning."

They haven't, actually, though you and I can see how they got that impression. Thanks to our special insight, we now understand that roosters have at least five different ways of avoiding hunters: they can flush, run wildly, sit tight, sneak, or even swim away from trouble. Five ways...and from your point of view as a hunter, only one of them —flushing—suits your purposes.

So how can anyone hunt such a contrary bird? Basically, you have to keep in mind all the escape tactics available to roosters, then conduct a hunt in such a way that you eliminate all the options except flushing at close range. All of which is easier said than done! If you are one man alone with no canine assistance, the odds are stacked heavily against you. If you hunt with a gang, you will succeed more often in trapping cocks in places they have to flush from; but the party we just watched had about as much luck as they could expect, seeing only two of five cocks and bagging only one. If you hunt with dogs, you'll do far better. With two good dogs, the hunt we have just watched would have probably collected four of the five roosters in the cover if the hunters had shot well.

That is pheasant hunting, and it still beats me why some hunters claim it is so easy. One of the fascinating problems in pheasant hunting arises from the fact that cocks can elude you in two entirely different ways, sitting tight or running. The more you try to cut off one of those options the more you leave yourself open to being beaten by the second. I always compare that situation with the problem of a batter facing a great pitcher. Most Hall of Fame quality pitchers have at least two completely dissimilar pitches: usually a fast ball that can be heard but not seen, and a slow curve that "drops off the table" when it breaks. That's just like the bag of tricks used by experienced roosters. No wonder hunters strike out so often.

The Bird We Hunt

Talk to a biologist about the pheasant and one of the first things he is apt to mention is that the ringneck is an "exotic." I would hasten to agree, except I fear biologists mean something rather different than I do when I call the bird exotic. Indeed, you will sometimes detect a slight sniff of disapproval in their use of the phrase, as if the pheasant had stowed away from its Asian fatherland and slipped past customs into the New World with the aid of a phoney passport.

While I will grant that the ringneck is the most exotic element in a sere November prairie landscape, I am not about to admit that he is an alien who is allowed to stay because of some dubious squatter's rights. The pheasant is as American as you or I. Like us, he is a transplant from another continent who has had to scratch hard to make a go of it in his adopted country. Like us, he represents the culmination of many decades of genetic melting pot mixing. We could even argue that the pheasant has a better claim to citizenhood than we do, since he has been on American soil for 100 generations (though those generations are admittedly short ones). And while the ringneck cannot claim to have "come over on the Mayflower," the second pheasant stocker in American history was no less a figure than George Washington, who released several birds at Mount Vernon during his first presidency. Friend, those are mighty impressive credentials. If the pheasant has not earned the right to call himself American, I do not know who has.

I am going to resist the temptation to ascribe qualities of the American personality to the pheasant, though some other writers have shown less restraint. Yes, the bird has an undeniable cheekiness, a sort of cocksure American common man's bearing. More democrat than patrician, he is not one to play the game of survival by gentlemen's rules. But the comparison quickly falls apart. When hunters march in file to pin a rooster in a sure trap, only to have the bird calculate the only way out of trouble with an icy nerve and shrewd grasp of the situation, I am more inclined to compare him with a Russian chess master than anything American. Then, too, I think about that rooster who survived his fourth gun season in heavily hunted country in spite of having only one leg. Now I ask you: is that kind of indomitable toughness typical of the American spirit? Alas, I fear that to call the pheasant typical of the American spirit is to flatter ourselves immodestly.

Today's pheasant is actually a culmination of years of breeding by many different strains. (Photo by Minnesota Department of Natural Resources)

The pheasant, of course, was not originally American. The bird comes to us from Asia, although by some roundabout routes. While the bird is still often referred to as the "Chinese" ringneck, that strain is just one of many which produced the modern American gamebird we know. The first successful stock of pheasants, those famous thirty-eight birds stocked into Oregon's Willamette Valley in 1881, came from China. But much of the stocking in New England involved the dark-necked English pheasant. Those birds have a fascinating history. Legend has it that the Argonauts introduced pheasants from near the Black Sea to Europe about 1000 B.C. during their quest for the Golden Fleece. From there, according to other legends, the pheasant crossed the channel to England with Julius Caesar and his Roman legions in the first century B.C.

Though it would be fun to point to ancestry to explain the color variations often found in today's pheasant, we would be on shaky biological grounds. The pheasant we hunt today is the mongrel end product of a bewildering number of genetic strains. In addition to the English and Chinese types, the Japanese and Mongolian are considered most important. By some accounts, no less than forty-two Asian and two European species of pheasants may have contributed to our pheasant. When word spread of the incredible success of the Oregon stocking effort, sportsmen's clubs and state game agencies across the land rushed to establish huntable populations in their areas. Roosters and hens from different species did not hesitate to mix with each other at courtship time in the spring.

Thus, the modern American pheasant is truly that: a bird whose confused genetic heritage has been tested for many generations against the harsh demands of survival in his adopted land. We cannot, therefore, explain the presence of an especially dark bird by referring to English ancestry. Color variations are, after all, common in game birds. Witness the wide range of color found among ruffed grouse. In spite of the many bloodstocks that were mixed to form the modern pheasant, he is said to look very much like the original Chinese ringneck.

Pheasants are the second largest gamebird hunted by flushing. Sage grouse can approach seven pounds of body weight, but very few hunters pursue them. Turkeys, even larger, are usually ambushed on the ground. That means that the pheasant is the "big game" for the great majority of American upland hunters. Roosters usually weigh just a little less than three pounds, with hens weighing about half a pound less. A four-pound bird is big, indeed, though there are records of cocks scaling five pounds. If I saw a five-pound rooster in the field I would probably run the other way.

Pheasants are about three feet long, though to my eye a cock flushing at close range seems much larger than that. Thousands of disgusted hunters have emptied their guns in the general direction of flushing roosters, only to ask themselves afterward how they possibly could miss a three-foot-long bird five times at a distance of twenty yards. A common explanation is that two-thirds of what they were shooting at was only tail feathers, and you have to do a lot worse to a cock than shred his tail if you mean to eat him.

Pheasants are not especially fast. Their average flying speed is thirty-five to forty miles an hour. Still, that is fast enough to cover the distance from you to the outer range of your shotgun's reach in a little over a second. Occasionally a cock will get his flying equipment so wet he can barely fly at all. Then too, quite often the birds will catch a stiff prairie wind and hit top speeds that just about singe the tips of their feathers.

It is relatively easy to distinguish between a young bird of the year and a cock that survived his first season. On the other hand, you can never be sure about differentiating between a second-year bird and one of those rare greybeards that has made it to his third fall. Three years ago I shot two roosters in a ten-minute hunt. The smaller one was clearly a second-year bird, and the larger bird was considerably bigger in body size, tail length, and spur length. I wanted to call that one a third-year bird, but better-informed biologist friends tell me he was just as likely a jumbo second-year rooster. Only about 5 percent of a year's crop of roosters will live into a third hunting season, so the odds of any of us shooting a rooster three or four years old are very long.

Strategies

Recall my earlier description of a typical pheasant hunt. Now let's analyze the birds' escape options a little more before talking about ways to beat them. Naive birds are apt to sit tight until trouble gets too close, at which time they burst into flight until they reach safety.

Flying at thirty-five to forty miles an hour, pheasants can move out of range before many hunters get more than a shot at tail feathers.

Hunters are apt to call these "dumb" pheasants, yet they are nothing of the sort. Most pheasants encountered by hunters are only five or six months old, hardly out of their chick down. They have already learned they can escape land-based predators by a combination of freezing and flying. We should hardly mock a young bird for not being born understanding the lethal potential of a shotgun at forty-five yards.

One of the birds in our story, the most experienced, ran wildly at the first indication hunters were around. Pheasants can cover ground quickly, even when they run with heads and tails held close to the ground to avoid being spotted. When they do not care about secrecy they carry their heads and tails high, and then they move even faster. A pheasant hunter I recently met insists that the human being cannot outrun a pheasant, but I know a slim and persistent hunter who has run down several cocks which were wounded but fully capable of running. Put it this way: when a sprinting rooster is matched against

Note the differences here between two first-year birds, one evidently being the product of a much earlier nesting.

a hunter wearing boots and toting a gun, the pheasant nearly always wins.

Pheasants that learn to run wildly at the first sign of trouble rarely end up in roasting pans. This is the one rooster escape tactic which you can do little to beat. Sometimes you can anticipate the situation and set up one or more of your party to block the logical escape route. Sometimes these birds can be marked down after they have flushed wildly. Then they can be rehunted—maybe even twice—until they get in a spot where you can flush them in range. Or sometimes you can pursue wildly running roosters in dense cover, using a flushing dog to trail them, until the birds decide running isn't working and try to fly instead. Usually, though, wildly running roosters are safe roosters. They are the ones you see posing so proudly along the roadsides with their harems each spring.

I have noted that pheasants also sit tight to let danger pass by. Until you have seen it a few times, you would not believe the way a gaily colored cock with a body three feet long can make himself invisible in a worthless bit of grass that presumably would not conceal a meadow mouse. When a pheasant decides this is the best trick for eluding you, the true cool nerve of the riverboat gambler in him takes control. All pheasant hunters have stories to back this up. I remember a cock that sat in a tiny clump of weeds out in an open area for half an hour while hunters laughed and ate lunch just a few feet away. When the wind shifted, one of the Brittanys suddenly jumped to its feet and went on point. Of course, no one believed the dog, and of course that bird made a spectacular exit to safety.

Yet, roosters sit tight less frequently than most hunters believe. Hens do it all the time, and every pointing dog fan has had occasion to curse the fact he has to hunt those blankety-blank footloose cocks instead of the cooperative hens. Early season roosters in lightly hunted country are far more likely to sit tight than old birds or birds of the year which have been pressured. We overestimate the number of skulking roosters partly because those occasions we catch them at it are so memorable. I have had roosters explode out of places so unlikely that I could not have been more surprised if they had flown out of my hat.

You counter skulking roosters in three ways. First, it helps to simply move slowly. When hunters walk quickly and evenly—as opposed to slowly and deliberately—cocks are much more likely to sit down to let them pass. It also helps to move with an uneven pace and to stop frequently. Experienced hunters have learned that this stop-and-go tactic unnerves the birds. Cocks are content to sit tight as long as they think the tactic is working. When you stop and they can no longer tell where you are, they might lose their cool. Or they might not, which is why the use of a dog is absolutely the best way to make flushers out of skulkers. The value of a dog is easily seen here. Skulkers are one of the biggest problems for dogless hunters, while they are the easiest bird for hunters with dogs to bag.

In the hunt I described earlier, remember that one of the roosters sneaked his way to safety. Though hunters complain often about "running" roosters, most of those pheasants are actually sneaking away. Sneaking is probably the preferred escape tactic of the great majority of roosters. It is a more deliberate, controlled evasive maneuver which lets the bird keep track of his pursuers.

Since most birds are sneakers, what should hunters do about them? Most of the popular pheasant hunting tactics are designed to deal with sneaking birds. The best example is the classic drive, a sort of dragnet operation. Some drives, like the one I described, involve a single row of hunters sweeping in a line through cover. In more open cover (such as cornfields) a better drive will have part of the party lined up at the opposite end of the cover to "block" or "mousetrap" the sneaking birds. Whenever a sneaking rooster finds his escape route sealed off he is apt to sit tight. Then, if danger gets too close, he will fly. And that is what you want.

You should work sneaking cocks as carefully as possible. If you charge at them too hard they will turn into runners, often runners that flush far out of range. Work them slowly, though, and they may sit for a close flush. Smart hunters also use the lay of the cover to encourage sneakers to turn into close flushers. In heavy cover it is smart to work the birds away from the center of cover toward the fringes. When cocks run out of good cover, they might sit down for a close flush. One of the best tactics is to drive the birds up into a point of cover which extends away from the center. Expect your flushes right at the point when you move out to pin the birds against the margins of the cover. Interestingly, another smart strategy seems to be exactly the reverse of this one: drive the birds away from thin cover into heavy cover. This works when you are in cover too thin to encourage the birds to sit down, such as a typically sterile modern cornfield. If you push the

Work pheasants slowly toward the edge of the cover for a close flush within range. (Photo by Jim Layton)

pheasants toward a bit of thick cover nearby, however, you may find them willing to sit tight until you move in to force a flush.

It all seems to come down to this: you trap cocks by either surrounding them, pinning them up against the edge of cover, or pursuing them with a dog into a place where they think they can beat you by skulking.

But hey, what about that bird that got away from the hunters in the story by swimming? What should a hunter do about roosters that pull that stunt? I am not sure, just as I am not sure about how to outfox a cock which slips into a groundhog den, or walks into a creek until only his head sticks up above the waterline, or spends his daylight hours strutting around with barnyard fowl, or . . .

2

Pheasant Dogs

It is almost impossible to exaggerate the value of a good dog to the modern pheasant hunter. Nothing will help the dogless pheasant hunter so much as enlisting the assistance of a four-footed hunting pal. While there are times and places where hunters without dogs will score as well as hunters with dogs, they are rare and becoming more so. I am convinced that a dog can triple the bag of most hunters. But to say that is to miss the point. Quite apart from the number of birds brought to hand, dogs can more than triple the pleasure of your hunts. If you have never watched a dog happily attacking pheasant cover, drinking in scent and puzzling out the strategies of wily cocks, you just do not know what you have missed.

Dogs can help hunters in four ways. First, they help find birds. Since modern pheasant hunting typically involves low bird populations, you face the problem of finding the few birds which reside in a large area. The foot speed and keen nose of a good dog can cut that problem

A good bird dog helps the hunter in four ways: finding pheasants; successfully working even the most elusive roosters; teaching the hunter new ways of outsmarting the birds; and reducing cripple losses.

down to a manageable level. Second, dogs help you work the birds you find. Simply getting near a rooster usually does you little good, since pheasants have so many ways of eluding hunters. But a good dog can trump just about any card a tricky rooster plays; so more of the birds you get near will become flushers. Third, a dog will teach you more about pheasant hunting than any book or veteran hunter ever could. A dog can even make a positive experience of those times when birds bamboozle you. Finally, dogs will reduce cripple losses, which makes your game bag heavier and your heart lighter.

The research I have read on the value of dogs seems misleading to me. Field studies indicate that dogs will allow you to bag twice as many birds as you would get without them. But those figures are based on raw averages; and since at least a third of the dogs you will see in the pheasant fields are worthless or worse, I persist in believing a good dog will at least triple your bag. As an example, research shows it takes the average hunter anywhere from four to ten hours to put a rooster in his game bag. But in the first years of Brandy's career she and I took little more than two hours to collect a cock, and by now we have worked that average down considerably. I never want to hunt pheasants without a dog again.

Oh sure, there are dogs which do more harm than good. All the truly godawful hunts I have experienced have been distinguished by particularly bad dog work. You know, like those times when the whole hunt comes to a shuddering halt while someone's pooch chases a deer into the next county. I have had hunts soured by companions who kicked their dogs, and I have stood by in misery while an uncontrolled dog reamed out all the birds from the country we were about to hunt as their owners (I won't call them "handlers") brayed blue oaths at them. It happens.

But a good dog is an invaluable asset. To get a good one, remember that a competent pheasant hunting dog is a fifty-fifty product: 50 percent good breeding and 50 percent sound training. It is a waste of time to try training a palooka, just as it is foolish to think you can simply buy a dog with a fancy pedigree and have it hunt without being trained. I will not discuss training here, as the topic has been thoroughly covered in several specialized books, but never forget that pheasants are tricky birds which can challenge the best of dogs. You are doing yourself and your dog a great disservice if you do not train him thoroughly. As I have got some reservations about advice in other books about *buying* a pheasant dog, I would like to discuss that in a little more detail.

First let's deal with the thorny issue of whether or not pointing dogs can be good pheasant dogs. You will read that roosters will "ruin" a pointer by skipping out from under points. Yet, pointing dogs are preferred by many good ringneck hunters. Certainly, the first decision faced by a puppy shopper is whether he wants a pointer or a flusher.

Can pointers handle pheasants? There is, in fact, no simple answer. If you could shoot hens the story would be different because they often hold beautifully for a point. Roosters usually do not. That still does not mean a pointer cannot hunt pheasants, for the hunter who reads his dog and gets into position can even get shots on cocks which are sneaking or running away from a pointer. Many pointing dog hunters, in moments of candor, admit that half the cocks they take are not shot over firm points. Still, the dog was a great help in finding and trapping the birds.

You can express the "pointability" of pheasants in terms of percentages. On opening weekend you'll get a high percentage, perhaps well over half, of your birds over solid points. Two weeks later you might be doing well to get points on one rooster in five, and things just get worse from then on. Finally, toward the shank of the season, some lucky hunters get afield right after a snowfall and take nearly all their roosters over classic points.

That seems to argue that pointers do not get to do their thing much of the time and so flushers must be better. I come close to agreeing . . . yet cannot quite. The difficulty is that we should never forget that we are not just hunting birds. The pleasures of pheasant hunting include companionship, the joy of exercise, the challenges of shooting, and, to a large degree, the thrill of watching your dog. Each of us has to decide how much value to assign to these aspects of the hunt, especially whether you are mostly interested in results or in the processes by which they are achieved. The pointing dog lover can draw more pleasure from a single productive point than some hunters get from a quick daily limit. And please understand. In such matters neither hunter is

Pointing dogs such as these often find it difficult to hold firm points as the birds sneak or run away. (Photo by Jim Layton)

"right" or "wrong." You simply need to acknowledge that many pointer men get a bigger kick from points than bagged birds, while the flushing dog hunter usually has his eye on the results. It is a highly personal decision.

While it is fun to debate the strengths of different breeds, as I will do here in a moment, the plain truth is that there are remarkable differences among different litters or breeding programs within any given breed. Most literature on hunting dogs is misleading in this area because it overemphasizes the distinctions among breeds and understates the potency of particular breeding practices. For example, there are soft, wimpy Brittanys, and there are Brits that are harder than railroad spikes. Some retrieve with gusto, while others will not retrieve no matter how long you thump on them. Some will dog your heels, while others scour the horizons. It is mostly a matter of how they were bred. Other breeds display the same range of variation.

When you have chosen a breed, you've only gone part way toward finding the right dog. The really critical step is to find the right litter; that bunch of pups whose parents blessed them with exactly the right genetic heritage for your hunting style and personal taste. It is always

It is a good rule of thumb, when selecting a puppy, to look for the most active and curious members of the litter. (Photo by Mike Rahn)

fun to buy a dog with a blue ribbon pedigree, yet do not be dazzled by those champion dogs which cling precariously to remote branches of the family tree. What really counts is the quality of the sire and dam, not what their great-great-grandpappies did.

All pheasant hunters occasionally need the help of a dog to retrieve a cripple (some more than others). You can get by with a half-hearted retriever if you mostly hunt in small draws in picked fields. But if you share my passion for routing roosters out of heavy marshes, you will be sorely disappointed with any dog which is not a whiz at chasing down running cripples in the thick stuff. Maybe you never scratch down a cock with a weak hit, but I do, and so, I put a high premium on retrieving ability when considering pheasant dog breeds.

Labrador Retriever

Labs are probably the best bet for most pheasant hunters. You just cannot fault them. They make excellent pets, whether kenneled or kept in the home, and they are wonderful with children. Labs are so highly trainable that they are frequently chosen for specialized obedience, guide dog, and performing dog use. The buoyant spirit of a Lab will not be crushed by heavy-handed training tactics. And of all dog breeds, none other is more likely to train itself to hunt pheasants with "on the job" unprofessional training.

Physically, too, Labs seem ideal for pheasant hunting duty. Their more deliberate speed is better suited to working pheasants than the fiery pace of some dogs. Labs are big enough to feel at home in heavy cover. Unless you buy a dog with hip dysplasia (a fairly common problem), you will find there is nothing delicate or prone to break on a Lab. Their coats are thick enough to protect the dog, oily enough to shed mud, and short enough to turn away most burs. While many breeds require careful combing or other fussy maintenance, if you put a little food near the head end of a Lab you can just about forget about doing much else.

No breed beats a Lab at coming up with running cripples in touchy situations. A typical performance was turned in one afternoon by Pawnee, Gary Crawford's superb Lab. Gary wing-tipped a rooster on a day when gusty winds were whipping scent every which way. Pawnee tracked the bird patiently across open country for twenty minutes before scooting down a fence line and disappearing. Our party stood around for several long minutes before Pawnee finally appeared on the horizon, proudly bearing the pheasant. That retrieve had to have been half a mile long.

Springer Spaniel

More than any other breed, springers have been bred to hunt ringnecks, and what wonderful pheasant dogs they are. There is no happier sight in the world than a merry springer bombing around in birdy cover. With their tails buzzing and their ears streaming out, springers are a joy to take afield. And they do the job. Whether a bird sits, sneaks, or runs, the springer will hang in on the trail, until the cock is bounced out of cover, and you can bet that dog's jaws will be snapping just behind the bird's tail. Then it is up to the guns, and if they fail to do their job, the springer will display almost as much skill and persistence in the retrieve of a cripple as the very best Labs. In addition, they have loads of personality. There is something impish in the spaniel character which makes him resent doing a task when

Springer spaniels excel at flushing roosters, but because of their build, they are often considered too small for very rugged cover.

This picture captures the passion with which Brandy hunts and her determination to follow the birds. (Photo by Larry Brown)

he does not see the point of it. While Labs will execute complicated commands as faithfully as a robot, a springer is apt to retrieve a bird just close enough so you can take a step or two to claim it. Careful training will correct this; I mention it as an insight into the breed's nature. Springers will hunt their hearts out for you, but they are inclined to think they know more about the sport than their masters. Often they do.

Springers quickly learn to quarter to the gun and most of them naturally work in range. Nevertheless, their aim is always to bust into a bird as soon as possible. If you have no control over your springer, the dog will boost a rooster into the air before you are ready. The challenge of training a springer is to get some control over the dog when it is on a hot trail.

Springers are about as small as a dog can be to still attack heavy rooster cover well. I have read they are too small for all-day hunting in rugged cover. My pal Brandy, however, has bombed around in the worst cover imaginable for five days in a row. She sure would not want me to report here that her breed cannot handle any cover a rooster can handle. Springers are a nice size for living in a home. They do not do well in kennels, as they are very people-dependent.

Springers are as affectionate as any dog breed in dogdom, and you can count on them to lick the hand of any burglar who enters your home. They have a remarkable "Jekyll-Hyde" split personality. The same sappy lap dog which sighs while you rub its ears will assault hellholes of thorny cover like a banshee. Brandy hates being left out of the action so much that she has taught herself to scale barbed wire fences by going up rung by rung until she flops over at the top. That stunt has frequently left her badly cut up, but Brandy has never encountered pain serious enough to distract her from her passion for pheasant hunting.

Brittany Spaniel

The Brit is probably the best choice for the hunter buying his first pointing dog. Brits reflect their spaniel heritage in several ways. They have that "I'll do it my own way" characteristic. Like springers, they are very curious, which causes them to poke around in any little hidey-hole they encounter. Brits are also highly affectionate—perhaps slightly less gushy than springers—and very loving. Like springers, they are nicely sized for living with the family.

Recent American breeding practices have made it hard to describe the way Brits hunt. The first of these dogs to come to this country were generally dismissed as unstylish plodders. When more and more American breeders tried to produce a Brit which could compete in field trials, the little spaniels began to strike out and cover more ground. As I said earlier, the breed varies considerably on this point. Many Brits retrieve, and many do not. If you look hard enough, you will find a Brittany that works a good pattern for the walking hunter and also retrieves. Just do not take these qualities for granted.

A good Brittany is a helluva fine hunting dog. They seem to adapt to different terrain and different species of game better than many breeds. Outdoor writer Charley Waterman's pal Kelly pointed eighteen species of upland game in his distinguished career. I am also impressed by the number of Brittanys I have seen that taught themselves to hunt with very little help from their owners. They seem to have the right

The Brittany is the easiest all-around dog to hunt with, often teaching himself to hunt, enthusiastic in any terrain. (Photo by Bob Prchal)

blend of instinct, intelligence, and eagerness to please needed to make neophyte trainers look like experts. Of course, that may be reflected by the fact that Brits are rarely bred for anything but hunting. They are generally conceded to be one of the least beautiful of hunting dogs, with their wedgey heads and scrimpy tails. I am sure selective breeding could produce a small Brittany which would look as noble as any English setter, but (thank God) most people who judge dogs only by their looks have lavished their attention on other breeds.

Some folks have called the Brit the "upland hunter's beagle," meaning the breed appeals strongly to the average hunter. With no pretensions of being a polished trainer, this hunter simply wants a dog that loves to hunt. The friendly, adaptable, good-natured Brit is a top choice for the modern pheasant hunter.

German Shorthair

Much the same can be said about the shorthair. Like the Brittany, this versatile pointing breed is currently riding a wave of popularity with practical hunters. Also like the Brittany, shorthairs are being bred in this country with the intention of producing a faster and more stylish trial dog. That is a controversial trend, but most authorities agree

American breeding has given the breed some zip and range which the earliest imports sadly lacked.

A friend has described the shorthair as the natural first pointing breed for the hunter who has hunted behind a Lab but now wants a dog which stands still instead of running when it is close to a rooster. Shorthairs have the same general size and muscular build of Labs. Like Labs, they have abundant hunting desire and forgiving natures, two qualities which endear them to amateur trainers.

Shorthairs tend to hit cover in a methodical, uninspired, but steady way. They would rather trot than run and are more apt to bull through cover than leap over it. When skittish roosters sashay out from under points, shorthairs do not throw tantrums or quit. They just point again. They have been called "meat dogs," which is either criticism or praise, depending on your priorities. They are the dog most often seen on

Steady nature, methodical pace, and muscular build make the German shorthair reliable and popular especially with amateur trainers.

commercial hunting preserves, which says something about their ability to perform steadily.

Of all the pointing breeds, shorthairs are probably the most proficient retrievers. Some authorities speculate the breed has a little bloodhound in it from way back in the days the Germans first developed the breed. At least shorthairs act as if they were part bloodhound, paying more attention to foot scent than most pointing breeds do. The heavy cover hunter who favors pointing breeds often hunts with a shorthair.

But shorthairs are not quite as easy to appreciate as some breeds because they tend to reserve their affection for their immediate families. They often seem aloof to strangers. This makes them better guard dogs, though they are plenty affectionate and playful with people they trust.

German Wirehair

Of all the breeds discussed here, the wirehair (or Drahthaar) is the least common. Yet, it is rapidly gaining a reputation as an excellent pheasant dog. The wirehair is firmly established as the top dog in Germany, a country where dog training and breeding are considered far in advance of those activities here. Wirehairs are versatile hunting dogs that work pheasants exceptionally well.

Wirehairs are much like shorthairs. In fact, they are a related breed, but they have an additional measure of high spirit and a bouncy gait. Wirehairs hop lightly over brush a shorthair might plow through; they seem to have the legs of a kangaroo. Some people also feel wirehairs have more of a sense of humor than their short-coated cousins.

The coarse, shaggy coat adds both a comic touch and a measure of practicality to the wirehair. The bristly hair fends off burs and keeps the dog warm in winter weather. Like shorthairs, wirehairs have a lot of natural desire to retrieve. Some hunters favor wirehairs simply because they are more purely the product of strict German breeding practices. The dogs have not been altered to suit the American field trial ideal (which seems to assume we all hunt quail from horseback on huge plantations). The wirehairs I have seen have been remarkably comfortable dogs to walk behind. They stay in range, hunt restricted areas thoroughly, and are easily called in with a whistle toot. They hunt under control, yet with a bouncy enthusiasm. You can expect to see more of them in pheasant cover.

Related to the shorthair, the German wirehair has a natural desire to retrieve. Their rough coats protect them well and give them a distinctive appearance.

Other Breeds

The dogs discussed so far are more likely to give you a fine pheasant dog than others, yet training and individual breeding practices can make an enormous difference. Let's at least acknowledge some of the other breeds which hunt pheasants well.

Chesapeakes have worked nicely as pheasant dogs for many rough cover hunters. They are extremely strong and are superb retrievers. Their bodies are more adapted to water work than upland hunting. Some hunters find Chessies a challenge to train. The good ones are so good that many folks are happy they tried them.

English pointers are considered by some dog men to be absolutely tops on pheasants in situations where the birds are widely scattered. In such places the raw intensity and great range of a pointer can be a godsend. On the other hand, bitter late season weather can dampen their appetites for hunting. These tough, fiery dogs work beautifully for the accomplished trainer, though they do their best work on birds other than pheasants.

All of the other so-called continental breeds are capable of excellent work on ringnecks. The vizsla, weimaraner, griffon and pudelpointer all have their fans.

I also owe a few roosters to the help of golden retrievers. As intelligent and trainable as the Labs, goldens have suffered from breeding based on good looks instead of performance. But there are plenty of dandy goldens around. Their coats attract burs and they have no strong advantages over Labs. Yet, I would hate to think pheasant hunting was such a serious business that there was no place in it for decisions of the heart, and the golden is a beautiful pet who can hunt roosters with the best flushing breeds.

Finally, let's admit that the odd mongrel will also do creditable work on pheasants. A good friend actually owned a Lab/pointer cross which pointed like a pointer and retrieved like a Lab. Often, these crossbreeds do not work so well (they point like a Lab and retrieve like a pointer). The most amazing pointing breed performance I ever heard about was turned in by a dog that wandered out of a farmyard and volunteered to join a party which had several highly trained purebred pointers. Soon the purebreds were all in the car because the barnyard dog was finding all the birds. What kind of dog was it? If you tried hard to pin down its ancestry, the best you could say was that it was a "brown" dog.

Teams

Serious pheasant hunters often have more than one dog. A pair of hunters I know will carry six or seven dogs along on some hunting trips. Among them are a pair of "racehorses" that are rarely seen once released and a pair of plodders who check out each side of each blade of grass to see if there is a pheasant underneath.

Carrying more than the minimum number of dogs makes sense in view of their importance in modern pheasant hunting. You can put down a fresh pooch when the first dog is all fagged out. Or if a dog is injured you will be grateful you have a backup. Once Brandy jumped into a muskrat trap set in a drainage ditch and injured her toes. She wanted to hunt on three legs but I could not let her, and I would not hunt without her, so I suffered through several days of inactivity that I had set aside for pheasant hunting.

Hunters with several dogs can "fine-tune" their canine corps to suit prevailing conditions. Faced with wide expanses of thin cover, they can put down a brace of big-running dogs. Faced with roosters sitting tightly under dense multiflora, they can hunt behind a slow older dog with a vacuum cleaner nose. At times they might turn loose two, three, or more dogs. Can you imagine hunting in the wake of six dogs? I have been told it is not as crazy as it sounds.

3

Guns and Ammo

It is a great comfort, when you miss a pheasant, to blame your gun. That simultaneously excuses your bad shooting and prepares a case for buying a new gun. Most hunters live with the soothing delusion that they are actually far better shots than they have so far shown in the field. If they could just buy the right gun, they think, all that bottled up skill would reveal itself like a genie released from a bottle!

This can strain a marriage. When I met Kathe, I was shooting a 12-bore Browning Light Auto 5 with a Poly Choke mounted on a barrel cut back to twenty-three inches. It looked like a prison guard's gun, but I shot a lot of pheasants with it. Then one day I shot behind a streaking right-to-left crossing cock, so that night I told Kathe I needed a new double-barrel because "the old auto has just never swung right for me." The Browning B-SS that replaced the old humpbacked auto was pure poison on roosters when I did not forget how to shoot. But when I muffed a shot on a rooster that made a fast exit downwind one day, I explained to Kathe that this proved "I need a lighter gun which handles quicker." So the 12-gauge was traded in for a B-SS 20-gauge, and it was a great pheasant gun when I let it be. Then came the day I almost stepped on a rooster the size of a young turkey. In my excitement I dumped both barrels before the old cock had barely cleared the tops of the canary grass. Naturally, I turned to Kathe and pointed

Autoloaders such as this one make fine pheasant guns. The lighter models especially are excellent for prolonging a hunter's endurance.

out how this proved I needed a new gun because "you need more firepower than this to hunt pheasants." So I bought (of all things) a five-shot 12-gauge Browning auto, very much like my first repeater.

Yet there is an epilogue to the story. I carried that gun all season before its extra firepower did me any good at all. Early on in the season I realized that if I missed a cock with the first three shots I was darn well going to miss it with the fourth and fifth shells as well. By stuffing five hulls in the magazine, I was lining the pockets of the ammunition companies and indulging my own bad habits. So I inserted the "duck plug" in the forearm to reduce the gun to a three-shot, which made the gun nicer to carry and less expensive to feed. But since I always seemed to kill my pheasants with the first two shots, or missed with all three, it dawned on me that I might as well be carrying a double after all. Finally, on the last day of the season, Brandy bounced up a big cock in an isolated terrace in an Iowa cornfield; and it was my third shell which brought it down. I have always thought of that bird as the "$300 rooster," since that is what the gun cost. He was, and is, the only pheasant I have claimed with the third shell from that gun.

One reason for that is that these days I do almost all my hunting with a new gun, an SKB 600 over/under. I have shot so well with it that even I cannot use my misses as an excuse to buy something newer. The gun suits me. I have total confidence in it. If I do my part, it will do its part—which was true of all the other guns I have owned, too!

With that tale as background, perhaps you will understand why I now find it hard to participate enthusiastically in elaborate debates about the perfect pheasant gun. If you can find a scattergun which is pleasant to carry and which reliably will deliver two or three quick shots through a moderately choked barrel, you have got a pheasant gun. If you hit well with that gun and trust it, you have a wonderful hunting partner that should be treasured, no matter how much or little you paid for it.

Firepower

Let's return to that seductive notion of firepower. It is easy enough to agree that the modern pheasant hunter almost never truly needs the fourth or fifth shell many magazine shotguns make available. When a single bird flushes, you are going to get him with the first three shots or you are not going to get him. If you have three shells you can miss with one and still collect a double, should the chance arise. Our fathers might have hunted in a time when clouds of roosters gave them the chance to blaze away until their guns got hot, but the modern hunter who does more walking and less shooting will not be disadvantaged if he's got only three shells. That is enough.

It is not so easy to dismiss the need for the third shell. Many hunters routinely waste the first shot. When that happens to a double-gun hunter who then makes a weak hit with the second barrel, he then suffers the misery of watching the cripple fly on while it is still in range of his empty gun.

Nevertheless, experience and common sense keep telling me that two shells are really all I need. The first gun I owned was a nifty little Savage hammerless 20-bore single-shot, a dandy youngster's gun unfortunately no longer made. With it I occasionally had the sweet pleasure of tumbling roosters from in front of my father and his much heavier 12-gauge pump. I traded in the Savage to get the Browning autoloader mentioned earlier. But as soon as I had the five-shooter in my hands, the first shell might as well have been a blank for all the good it did me. I began to think of my first shot as a preliminary to real shooting. I bagged a slightly higher percentage of roosters with the auto than I had with the single shot, but not many.

So what is the lesson? It is this: the more quick shots you have, the less care you will take with each one. Just knowing you can miss once and still have four more "at bats" is an encouragement for sloppy shooting. The next time you get in a shooting slump, try loading a single shell in your gun. It sure improves your concentration on the first shot!

It is hard to find fault with the pheasant hunter's traditional favorite, the 12-gauge. The other two sound choices are the 20- and 16-gauges: both of them so close to the 12-gauge in effectiveness that it does not make sense to debate the point at length. You are never undergunned with a 16, and very rarely with a 20. But anyone buying a gun primarily for pheasants should have a good reason for bypassing the 12-gauge. The size and tenacity of a rooster allow him to take a heavy dose of shot and keep flying. I have always felt I owed it to the birds to carry enough gun to do the job right. The 12 can deliver a slightly heavier load of shot at full velocity than either the 16 or 20, though the difference is slight. Those 12-gauge guns that are not overly heavy are automatically top choices for pheasant hunters.

Handling Qualities and Fit

Weight is increasingly important for modern ringneck hunters. Earlier styles of hunting featured cornfield drives where very little walking resulted in a whole lot of shooting. A piece of ordnance weighing nine pounds when loaded was no great burden then. Today's pheasant chasers walk a whole lot more for less shooting. The modern pheasant hunter is also likely to take on heavy cover where only one hand is free to carry the gun while the other is fighting to part the brush. A gun weighing 6½ to 7½ pounds is about right. My own ideal is a 12-gauge weighing 7 pounds when loaded.

Balance is one of those intangible qualities which all hunters can recognize in a gun but cannot explain. Either a gun seems to swing happily or it does not. Some guns are too heavy at one end or the other, and quite a few are just too heavy overall. Generally speaking, the sweet swinging pieces are those which have their weight concentrated near the center—in the classic phrase, the weight "lies between the hands." Doubles—either side-by-sides or over/unders—are more likely to exhibit this quality than other shotguns; but there are badly balanced doubles just as there are nice handling pumps and autoloaders. This is a subjective matter. The gun that feels like a railroad tie in my hands might be perfect for the guy with arms a lot bigger.

Proper stock fit, like balance, is another will-o'-the-wisp concept. Most shotgunners start by being oblivious to the importance of stock fit and then pass into a troublesome period in which they think it is more crucial than it is. My own experience defies all the rules. My 20-gauge has a stock a gunsmith altered to make it extremely straight. The drop at the comb, which is the most pertinent specification, is only 1⁵⁄₁₆ inch. I have also got a standard autoloader with 1⅝-inch drop at the comb. The difference in comb height between those guns is enormous; yet I can shoot one on Saturday and the other on Sunday without noticing a difference. This is an extreme example of the way we all tend to adapt our shooting style to the gun we are using even though the stock fit deviates from the theoretical ideal. This is not to say that stock fit is unimportant. Most modern shotgunners recognize that stock fit is, in effect, the "sights" of a scattergun. Differences of physique and shooting form make different stock dimensions appropriate for different shooters. But do not fool yourself. I know a few hunters who blame their stocks when they blow a shot; actually, they have never

The best double-barrelled shotguns tend to be more evenly balanced and concentrate their weight near the center.

done enough shooting to acquire competence. Factory issue stocks fit the great majority of hunters. That is truer today than ever before; manufacturers have acknowledged changing tastes by making stocks a little longer and quite a bit straighter than they used to be. Straight stocks shoot high. Since most pheasants are taken on the rise, high shooting guns are best for most shots.

Action Type

Excellent pheasant guns are built in all of the four major types of action. At one time or another I have owned and shot all kinds, and I respect them all. In spite of my great fondness for doubles I see many advantages in the repeaters. They are fine bargains, especially if you buy a second or third barrel to increase their versatility.

Pumps are the best buys of all. They are also lighter and more reliable than autoloaders. I regret the fact I cannot carry them one-handed with my left hand (a pump will not balance well if you hold it by the forearm). That great classic, the Remington 870, weighs just

A pump action shotgun, light enough to carry comfortably in one hand, makes an excellent bird gun. Overall they are lighter than autoloaders but do not carry as conveniently as the double.

what it should in its 12-gauge version. Ithaca's Model 37 is another light, fast-handling pump. A relatively new gun with many fine qualities is the Browning BPS. If you appreciate a beautifully machined and indestructible gun, find a Winchester Model 12 in the 16-gauge version. This is one of the most honest and potent pheasant guns ever built. These and other slide-action shotguns are great pheasant hunting companions.

Public taste seems to be swinging from pumps to autoloaders. It is not that they shoot faster, for they do not; but the styling, automatic functioning, and soft recoil of today's autoloaders are very attractive. Women and young shooters are not the only ones to appreciate the gentle kick of gas-actuated autos. The reliability of any autoloader will suffer if they are not kept clean, though they function well with reasonable care.

There are many good ones. The Remington 1100, extremely popular with waterfowlers, is heavier than it should be for pheasant hunting in its 12-gauge model, though there are some light models in the smaller gauges. Browning's recently introduced B-80 promises to be an exceptional ringneck gun. Their old Auto 5 12-gauge is heavy, though the 20-bore is all it should be. If you turn up an old "Sweet 16" version of this gun in good condition you will have found one of the finest pheasant guns ever made. There is one autoloader which might be too light for some hunters, though it is a great gun. Franchi's recoil-actuated Standard Automatic weighs less than six-and-a-half pounds in its 12-gauge form and only a tad more than five pounds as a 20-gauge. Yes, it kicks, but most pheasant hunters ignore that in the heat of the action. Still, this is one gun I would put a recoil pad on.

Before discussing the doubles, let's consider some of their unique advantages. Because they do not have a long action positioned between the stock and breech, doubles are shorter than magazine-fed shotguns. That may be why they move so nicely. They are distinctly more pleasant to carry because they are lighter and more natural to grip. The tang safety of a double is more convenient than the trigger guard safeties of the repeaters. Only doubles offer the advantage of two chokes, though it's a feature of debatable value. They are more reliable than autos or pumps, a feature of supreme value. Finally, doubles are safer, for it is far too easy to leave a live shell in the action of a repeater when unloading it. With a double you can extend the courtesy to others you meet of cracking the action open. It is a nice way of showing them your gun will not go off while they are near.

Three Iowa roosters that fell victim to Bill Gallea's 20-gauge. The 20 is, for all practical purposes, the smallest gun that can be recommended for pheasants.

All these advantages must be weighed against the high cost of doubles and the fact they hold just two shells. You will notice that many hunters who once owned repeaters will end up shooting a double when they are older, but I do not think this proves that those who shoot pumps or autoloaders are any less mature. Clearly, anyone who buys a double for its imagined snob appeal is less mature than the guy who loves his old 870 with its worn blueing and scarred stock.

The availability of attractively priced and designed doubles seems to vary comparatively with the strength of the dollar against the Japanese yen. The light and reliable SKB guns, the standard 200 and the straight stocked 280 are wonderful ringneck guns when you can buy them. The Browning B-SS, in either the Standard or Sporter model, is a top buy. Though heavy in its 20-bore version, the 12 is just right. I once assumed that the horizontally paired barrels of a double would point less precisely than a single sighting plane. My hunting experience disproved that notion totally.

Many experienced shotgunners prefer the over/under to all other types. Fortunately, there are several highly desirable and fairly priced models to choose from. Browning's Citori, a wee bit heavy in the 12-

gauge form, is one of the leaders. While Ruger's Red Label is heavier than a 20-gauge should be, it is such a beautifully engineered and designed gun that it deserves careful consideration. Several friends claim the Winchester 101 is so good they don't know why everyone does not shoot one. I have heard the same from buddies who shoot Berettas, and Beretta has recently debuted some attractive new models. Finally, I cannot say enough nice things about my SKB over/under. A 12-gauge bored improved and modified, it is a joy to carry and shoot. I am not likely to find a gun which does a better job of executing my intentions when cock birds are airborne.

Choke

Discussions about the ideal choke for pheasants quickly get heated. The bigger the pattern your gun throws the more likely you are to hit birds; but the tighter the pattern, the better your chances are of bagging a bird which only offers a long shot. Caught on the horns of that dilemma, pheasant hunters get pretty frustrated when trying to choose a choke.

This situation encourages the armchair ballistician to expound his pet theories and pound on anyone who does not accept them. I once hunted with a fellow who told me that, unlike my gun, his extra-full choked shotgun would either kill birds cleanly or miss them cleanly. He probably had better luck on other days: the day I hunted with him he fringe-hit two roosters which ended up outrunning the dogs. Those would have been dead birds with modified, improved, or even cylinder choke patterns. I also remember a hunt I took with a friend who had just written a magazine article about how skeet chokes are tops for ringnecks. After dusting a bird or two at long ranges with his open barrel, he went back to the car to borrow my backup 12-gauge with its modified barrel.

Before I get carried away with strong statements about the ideal choke, let me put the matter in perspective. For several reasons it is foolish to get dogmatic about choke. First, you need to recognize that the choke stamped on a gun barrel is only a nominal designation. It is no guarantee that the barrel will deliver patterns with the right amount of constriction with all types of shells. It might not put out its promised pattern with any type of shell. More likely, a barrel which delivers 60-percent patterns with one load might pattern 45 to 70 percent with others. So if you are dissatisfied with your gun's choke, you can often get the desired results by switching shells. A little time spent with patterning sheets will tell you what the shells are doing in your barrel.

Recognize, also, that the ideal choke must be chosen to suit your shooting style. I have hunted pheasants with two converted (but not reformed) grouse hunters who would typically fire their first shot at about the time most flushing roosters had completed their fourth or fifth wing beat. Improved cylinder chokes were tight for them! Yet, there are those rare cool customers who can wait out a close flusher and who love to fire a tightly choked gun like a rifle at distant birds.

Finally, you have to consider the unpredictable nature of the bird. Any discussion of ideal choke must be based on some theory about the range of the bird at the moment of the shot. Early season birds tend to flush at closer ranges than late season birds. But that phrase "tend to" is an admission that you will get fifty-five-yard shots on opening day, while on the last day of the season you might flush a tight sitter which just about flies up your pants leg. And as for the theoretical advantage of a double, with its tighter choke for that longer second shot, you will often get shots at incoming roosters that are reducing the range with each wingbeat. You just do not know what the birds will do. That is pheasant hunting.

Where does that leave you when you choose a choke? The classic debate on pheasant gun choke has been between those who preferred the advantages of large patterns, which hit more close- and medium-range birds even with some shooter error, and those who champion tight chokes, which tend to "overkill" close pheasants but which have the pattern density needed for clean kills at long ranges. Somehow the idea has spread that full chokes offer more killing power, and many folks have convinced themselves that by simply waiting out the close flushers they could kill anything with a tightly choked barrel.

Just about everything in the choke debate has been wrong. Not only have many hunters—including a few who have claims to expertise—been wrong in their conclusions, but they have been asking the wrong questions. Even many of the oft-repeated assertions about shotshell performance and the influence of choke have been mistaken. Recently, with the work of Bob Brister and Tom Roster, these matters have been subjected to a new type of hard-headed analysis. Ah, but the old ideas are going to die hard!

We learn from modern shotshell research that we should seek a gun and shell combination which delivers the highest quality of patterns at the ranges normally encountered in pheasant hunting. That word "quality" means many things. A high quality pattern will have an even dispersal of shot: no big gaps, no tendency to clump shot, and no cripple-producing fliers. A high quality pattern will be efficient, putting a high percentage of the shot in the usable pattern, with as few wasted shot outside as possible. And a high quality pattern will have a short shot string—that neglected third dimension of patterns—so that most of the shot will arrive at the target at about the same time.

I will return to these concepts when I discuss shotshells, but now you have enough background to say that improved cylinder chokes offer the highest quality patterns at pheasant shooting ranges, though modified chokes work almost as well. Full chokes rank a distant third place; they tend to throw uneven patterns with lots of fliers and excessively long shot strings. Pattern sheets show how ragged full choke patterns are, yet they make tight chokes look better than they are because they disguise the effects of shot stringing.

But what about open chokes? Can they truly kill roosters at the usual ranges? They can, indeed. This is partly true thanks to modern shotshell design improvements which make the better of today's shells highly efficient. Recent research has also shown that the shot swarm does not always disperse at an even rate upon leaving the barrel, upsetting another old assumption. Improved cylinder chokes deliver ideal patterns for ringneck hunters. They open up quickly upon leaving the muzzle, and then hold together for a long time in a deadly swarm before finally dispersing too much to be effective. Contrarily, full choke patterns tend to move out in an excessively tight, ragged clump until some point far downrange, when they suddenly open up and then quickly become too loose to kill cleanly. Full chokes are at their best in a tight range from forty to fifty yards, which is to say they are best only in a short distance which is well beyond the range of most shots at pheasants. Modified chokes fall somewhere between improved cylinder and full chokes in their behavior, though showing more of the good qualities of improved chokes than the bad qualities of full chokes.

Almost all pheasants are shot within twenty to forty yards of the shooter; more are shot at twenty yards than at forty. That is almost identical to the range in which improved cylinder chokes throw their best killing patterns (actually, nineteen to thirty-eight yards with some popular 12-gauge loads). That fact clearly establishes improved cylinder as the choke of first choice for most pheasant work. If you are unnerved by the idea of shooting such an open choke late in the season you can switch to premium quality shells with extra-hard-plated shot and get patterns which kill at longer ranges. It is a lot harder to try to make a tight choke shoot open patterns. In view of the range of most pheasant shots and in view of the behavior of patterns, full chokes are the worst choice of all for ringneck hunters. Putting it another way, open chokes are better at medium and long ranges than tight chokes are at closer ranges.

I can sum up the recipe for a great pheasant gun. It will be a fairly light 12-, 16-, or 20-gauge. The action can be a pump, autoloader, side-by-side or over/under—suit yourself. The stock should be rather straight. If a single barrel, the gun should be choked modified or, preferably, improved cylinder. If you choose a double, get an improved cylinder/modified choke pair. Such a gun has always been pure poison for pheasants, and as we go into the modern era of pheasant hunting it is increasingly superior.

Discussions about the ideal pheasant hunting load can quickly become tedious. In any party of four or five hunters, you very likely will find at least one who puts his faith in big shot and at least one who thinks a dense cloud of smaller shot is more lethal. Back and forth they will argue, until you get the impression the whole thing is strictly a matter of personal choice, almost a religious decision. Fortunately, there is a way of breaking the tick-tock rhythm of this debate, for the matter of ideal load is really not as subjective as it seems at first.

Shot Size

I can begin by acknowledging that both sides of the debate have merit. If your shot is too small, it may not have sufficient energy to penetrate feathers, tissue, and bone. I have rolled pheasants at close range with number 8 grouse loads and had them fly on. On the other hand, if your shot size is too large you are apt to have patchy and loose patterns. Even a number 2 pellet will not kill a pheasant cleanly if it fails to hit a vital area.

That seems to thrust us firmly onto the horns of the dilemma. Do you want big, mean pellets or do you want a lot of pellets? What many

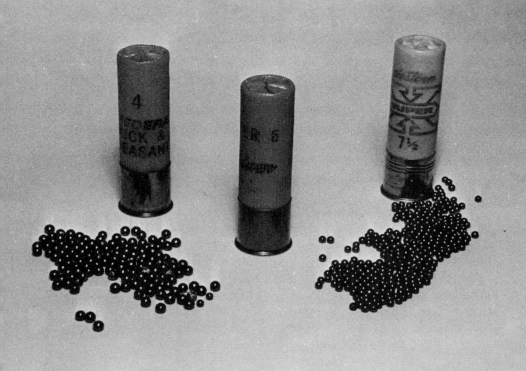

What's better, a smaller number of large shot or a lot of smaller shot? The shell with the load of 6's is the best choice most of the time.

hunters decide is that they want both, and they think they get out of the dilemma by using magnum loads filled with shot. That way, they reason, they can have their cake and eat it too by enjoying both dense patterns and the clout of heavy shot sizes. Well, it does not work that way, as you will see.

Researchers have shown us another way to break out of the debate about shot sizes. I will condense their position here. Briefly, you start with some calculations about how many pellet strikes on the body will be required to kill the bird cleanly. In the case of the pheasant, the minimum number required is three pellets. This must be related to the minimum amount of pellet energy needed for those pellets to penetrate sufficiently the body of the bird and its vital areas. For a bird the size of a pheasant, that amount of pellet energy is 1.75 foot-pounds.

But what do you know when you know that killing a pheasant cleanly requires at least three pellets with at least 1.75 foot-pounds of retained energy? You can get that effect with a close shot with 7½ shot, just as you can get it farther away with larger shot.

The next step is the critical one, at least in terms of choosing shot size. You must decide what range you want as your outside limit for shooting a rooster. What, in other words, is a realistic guess about the longest shot you are apt to attempt? The tables I have seen show forty-five yards as that figure, and it is a distance I can live with. If you think you are apt to shoot at a bird farther away you will need to accept larger shot in order to have enough energy to penetrate a pheasant at those ranges. If you are absolutely sure you can discipline yourself to accept only shorter, say thirty-five-yard, shots, you are justified in choosing a smaller shot size in order to get a denser pattern. If you do accept forty-five yards as the longest shot you are apt to take, the best shot size is number 6 or 5. Number 6 and 5 shot have enough energy at those ranges to do the job, and always your best shot size is the smallest one which has enough authority to penetrate sufficiently, for the smaller shot sizes increase your odds for hitting a vital area.

This rational framework for picking an ideal shot size should end all those hot stove league debates, though I am sure it will not. The key point it makes is that you are handicapping yourself by choosing larger sizes than the recommended ones as long as you observe the maximum range limit. In other words, since number 6 shot has all the energy needed at forty yards, by moving up to size 4 shot you are choosing an inferior shell. I know the idea of "big shot" sounds like you are getting "more" of something; but the plain truth is that the extra penetration power is irrelevant, while the fact you will be sacrificing pattern density is very relevant.

It works the other way, too. If you hunt over a pointing dog and refuse to shoot birds unless the dog holds the bird and it flushes close to you, your best shell is probably one with 7½ shot since that shot size retains plenty of energy for clean kills out to about thirty yards in most loads. As long as you strictly observe a thirty-yard limitation, your best shot size is probably 7½.

To finally choose a shot size, every pheasant hunter must do some soul-searching about this question of range. I know I shoot far more pheasants at twenty-five yards than I do at forty-five yards; yet I have had whole trips where thirty-five- to forty-five-yard shots were the norm. As a modern pheasant hunter, I do not want to pass by the chance to shoot at any bird "in range" because I know there may not be more than one or two birds in range on a given day's hunt. I can happily accept a forty-five-yard range limitation, which means that number 6 shot is best for me, but I would regret the limitation of about thirty yards that I would need to observe if I chose a smaller size.

Is there a place for number 5 shot? The answer is an emphatic "yes." The problem with number 5 shot loads is that they are so hard to find, and I fear one day they may not be available at all. Even today they are not available in many of the higher quality shells. But shells with number 5 shot make sense late in the season, or at any time when hunting pressure has made pheasants flush wild. In the early season it is typical to get a variety of shots on roosters: some going away, some crossing, and some incoming. But when you hunt birds which have been pressured, the typical shot will be fairly long and the bird will often be going directly away from the gun. That is the classic crippling shot because the pellets have the greatest possible amount of material to penetrate before they reach a vital area. That is, the shot must come through the feathers, pass on through the lower body cavity, and penetrate to the chest area. Since many pheasant hunters tend to shoot slightly low on gently rising roosters which jump up at the fringes of shotgun range, this is a situation which unquestionably promotes crippling shots.

By now we have defined appropriate pheasant shot sizes in this manner: short shots, 7½ shot; most shots, 6 shot; and long shots, 5 shot. Does that define the best load? Not quite!

The Efficient Load

You will remember that, in order to kill a pheasant cleanly, I said that a certain minimum number of pellet strikes on a bird were needed. So far, I have discussed that issue as if choice of shot size was the only factor in that issue, but it is not. Choke, shotshell efficiency, shot load, velocity, and gauge all play their role.

At this point it is appropriate to return to the issue of whether or not magnum shells are appropriate for pheasant hunters. Remember, I said that magnum shells seemed to solve the dilemma of dense patterns versus heavy shot by offering lots of shot capacity, so a load of 1⅞ ounce number 4 shot (from a three-inch 12-gauge magnum shell) would seem to give almost as many number 4 pellets to the pattern as the often-recommended 1¼ ounce of number 6 pellets.

Unfortunately, it does not work that way. The biggest myth in American shotgunning is the notion that magnums are the best long-range load. They do have more shot, but no matter how much shot you start out with in the shell, the only relevant number is how many actually get on the distant target. And if you look only at the number of pellets delivered to the target, the more efficient high velocity loads make the magnums look mediocre. Bob Brister reports, for example, that reloads developed by Tom Roster for the 12-gauge which had 1½ ounces of shot, consistently put more shot in the pattern at forty yards than mammoth factory 10-gauge loads with two ounces of shot. Remember: what you start with (in terms of the shot payload) is not what you get where it counts. In fact, evidence shows that the more shot you cram into the limited space of a hull, the *less* efficient that load will be.

The reasons are not hard to find. To varying degrees, all the magnum loads sacrifice certain qualities of good shotshell design in order to fit all that shot in. Typically, the cushioning wads are reduced and the shot protector may be shortened so it no longer protects the whole shot column. Both shortcuts result in shot deformation. In the first case, shot is deformed (mashed out of its original round shape) by inadequate protection from the shock of gas expansion. In the second case, shot lying on the outside of the column is deformed by being scrubbed along the barrel as the wads drive it out. Deformed shot quickly kites out of the pattern and does you no good at all.

Magnum loads look puny in another sense, for they are the slowest loads of all. Most hunters think of magnums as "hard hitting" loads which excel at long range shooting, yet the opposite is true. The low velocity levels of magnum shells mean that the pellets have less impact and take a little longer to arrive at the target. The result of all this is that the best load for pheasant hunting at all ranges is the ordinary "high velocity" load, for it features high impact, high pellet speed, and high quality patterns. In the 12-gauge that load is the 1¼ ounce, 3¾-dram load; in the 16 it is the 1⅛ ounce, 3¾-dram load; and in the 20 it is the 1 ounce, 2¾-dram load. These classic loads are ideal for all but the closest shots on pheasants.

Pellet hardness also has a major impact on shell performance. I have noted before that deformed pellets become fliers which leave the effective pattern. Shot hardness is directly related to how bad this problem is. Lead is soft, so hardening agents are added to it to allow

These two big roosters helped convince the author of the effectiveness of premium shells with copper-plated shot.

the pellets to retain their true shape. Yet, because those hardening agents are much more expensive than lead, manufacturers do not add them to their cheap "duck and pheasant" mass-sale loads. The more expensive loads feature harder shot. Federal has produced loads which feature hard shot which is further plated with copper for greater protection against deformation. They are extremely efficient.

I can vouch for their effectiveness. I have shot nothing but Federal Premium high velocity loads on pheasants in the last three seasons. When I first used them, I bagged forty-five of the forty-seven birds I fired at while hunting in all kinds of weather at all times of the season. Most of them would have fallen to ordinary loads, though I am inclined to credit the shells for a few roosters.

By switching loads and patterning the results, the modern pheasant hunter can get a variety of patterns from the same barrel. If the copper-plated loads have any liability it is that they work too well (they pattern too tightly) in some barrels. Still, they are highly efficient, which is good. It is more effective to shoot these efficient loads through a relatively open choke than to shoot economy loads through a tight barrel.

There is good reason to believe pheasant hunters will be shooting "steel" loads in the future. Now required for much waterfowling, these loads with their soft iron pellets have several advantages over the lead loads most of us shoot today. They are currently more expensive than lead loads, yet the rising price of lead could make the soft iron loads more economical. They work better than you may have heard. Because the soft iron pellets are far harder than even the plated lead pellets, they deform less. That makes steel loads as efficient as even the top quality lead loads. The lighter steel pellets also deliver higher muzzle velocities than lead loads. That should result in shorter leads at the ranges at which most pheasants are shot though most hunters will never see the difference.

Two adjustments need to be made to make steel loads perform well. First, since steel is less dense than lead, you need to choose a larger shot size to retain sufficient pellet energy. Number 4 steel is the equivalent of number 6 lead. Second, since steel loads pattern so tightly, they typically give modified patterns from barrels marked improved cylinder. Thus, skeet or improved cylinder barrels are better than tighter chokes for shooting steel at pheasants.

The effectiveness of steel on pheasants is not simply a matter of theory. Two of my friends have used it extensively, and the stuff is deadly. Federal has an especially lethal three-inch 20-gauge load which will make a potent pheasant gun of any open-choked quail or grouse 20-bore with a 3-inch chamber.

I need to deal with a final issue related to the selection of a good pheasant load. Remember I said earlier that at least three pellet strikes on a pheasant were needed for clean kills, and that for shooting within forty-five yards number 6 pellets had the necessary energy to do the job. You still need to make sure that your loads will have enough pattern density to do the job when fired through the guns you will use. Forget about tables, pattern percentages, nominal choke, and theories. Just take your gun and shells out somewhere where you can do some pattern testing and find out how well your loads work at different ranges.

The testing is simple. Put up a pattern sheet (any large piece of paper), blaze away at it from some measured distance, and then draw a thirty-inch circle around the shot cluster. Count the pellets hitting inside that circle (it helps to draw a slash through each hole with a magic marker as you count it so you do not miss holes or count them twice). As long as you have got a minimum of eighty-five holes in that circle, you have a killing pattern from your barrel using your own hunting loads at that distance. There is no need to do this at forty yards, for that is just an arbitrary distance traditionally used for designating choke. Percentages do not count for this test. All that counts is whether your gun and shells are putting enough shot in that circle at different distances. Most discussions of pheasant loads end, as this one does, by recommending high velocity loads of number 6 shot for most pheasant hunting situations.

4

The Well-Prepared Hunter

Few hunters debate the topic of comfortable, protective clothing with the fervor they reserve for discussions about shot size and the best dog breed. The topic, to be sure, lacks romance; though it hardly lacks importance. I have seen as many hunts wrecked because of poor clothing as for any other reason.

It stands to reason that the comfortable hunter will hunt more effectively and enjoy the experience more than the poor guy who is miserable. If your socks are nagging at you with every step, you are not going to take those extra steps across the bare plowed field to stomp that little patch of foxtail that might hold a rooster. Or if you are so icy cold right down in your bowels that you cannot think of anything else, you might not be able to raise a gun when a cock appears. That's a worse feeling than being bone cold.

There is even a point where discomfort becomes pain, and the bad clothing choice which was taking the fun out of hunting suddenly threatens to take you out of the hunt. A good friend was in so much pain from some ill-fitting boots last fall that he almost quit an important hunt and flew home. Clothing selection obviously is more critical for the hunter who takes a long trip than for the lucky local who can afford to make a mistake because home and a change of clothing are just over the hill.

Hunters, tending as they do to be traditionalists, have not yet caught on to some recent solutions to old clothing discomfort problems. The new breed of young backpackers and cross-country skiers has created a demand for outdoor clothing which is comfortable when worn in active use under all weather conditions. The modern pheasant hunter now has available to him remarkably well-designed and functional clothing.

Each pheasant hunter needs to assemble a system of hunting clothing to suit his needs. This must be highly personal. Differences of cover, hunting styles, prevailing weather, and physique all play an important role. The idea of a "system" of clothing is to put together the right combination of garments to let you hunt in comfort in any circumstances you are likely to meet, with no gaps or duplications. The time-honored layer system permits that sort of flexibility.

Boots and Socks

The most critical component of the system is a good pair of boots. Boots scare me. Almost nothing else except rotten weather has so much potential to spoil a hunt. In fact, the serious hunter needs two pairs of comfortable broken-in boots at any time. Almost any other needed item of clothing can be purchased in a nearby town, but if your boots meet with disaster and you do not have a comfortable backup pair, your hunt may be doomed. It is also nice to have an extra pair if the first becomes soaked.

There is room for much individual preference in boots for pheasant hunting, yet certain qualities are so desirable that all hunters agree on them. Pheasant boots should be flexible, both in the sole and the leather. Most authorities claim that an extra pound of weight on your feet is equivalent to a dozen extra pounds on your back, so pheasant hunters need light boots. But do not get carried away. There are some extremely light and expensive boots on the market. While they would seem to be a dream boot for pheasant hunters, they are so thin that they may not stand up to the abuse many hunters give a boot. I hit barbed wire hard enough and often enough to worry about sinking a fortune into a delicate boot.

Most hunters also like a smooth-soled boot about eight or nine inches high. If your boot tops are too high they will bind your calf muscles. If they are too low they will fail to give your ankles support and will let your socks load up with burs. In some western areas it might help to have the traction of lug-soled boots, such as the popular Vibrams, but all my experience has run the other way. In the muddy farmland where most pheasants are hunted, lugged soles are a great nuisance because they load up with gunk until they are heavy and then they drop that mud all over your vehicle and home. I have never found the need for more traction than that afforded by nearly smooth soles, and if anyone is likely to slip and fall down because of slippery soles, I would have done it by now. If you keep moving as you should, your feet will not get cold in all but the most bitter weather. But older and less active hunters might want to consider insulated boots. Recent improvements have made insulated boots lighter and less liable to become heavy with sweat.

Maine Hunting Shoes. Alternating between two pairs of boots extends the life of the boots by as much as three or four times the life of one pair.

Waterproofness is almost always desirable because pheasants are so often found in and around wet places. Yet, waterproofness is a relative thing. No matter what boot you buy, your socks will get wet from sweat, and unless you treat your boots, they will let water in eventually. Boots which only get wet slowly, by imperceptible degrees, are what most hunters accept as waterproof. Yet, there has been progress. Hunting boots are made from chrome-tanned or oil-tanned leather. The chrome-tanned leather has a dry, light look, while the oil-tanned leather seems shiny and dark. You have to treat both types with waterproofing (two distinctly different types of waterproofing), and until recently the oil-tanned leathers were easier to keep dry. Recent improvements in technology have made some chrome-tanned boots so waterproof they carry a lifetime guarantee. The better chrome-tanned boots shed water while allowing moisture from within to pass out.

The same cannot be said of rubber boots. When you hike any distance in them you will get wet feet from trapped perspiration. Worse, rubber boots do not hug the foot the way they should, and often they seem determined to bend in the wrong places. They chafe, in other words. Still, they have their place. My buddy, Jim Layton, uses rubber boots for hunting in wet snow. As long as you do not hunt too long in them at a time and you remember to change socks frequently, they work well enough.

If you plan to plunge into a deep marsh, however, you need to accept the limitations of rubber. Swamp hunters usually pull on rubber hip boots to wade into wet cover where they can roust out startled cocks. This is hard work. The work is harder if your boots refuse to flex with your feet. It helps to lash them around the ankle and down across the arch to hold them in place. Hip boots are usually so heavy that they add to the fatigue you would normally feel after taking on a swamp for several hours. The best answer may be the new breed of featherweight chest waders sold by Royal Red Ball and Hampshire. These are comfortable, ultralight waders made of a surprisingly tough fabric. They are made only in a stocking foot type of chest wader and they are not cheap. These waders are so light and flexible you can actually forget you have them on. They are a valuable addition to your clothing system.

While all rubber boots do not attract many fans, the rubber bottom/ leather upper shoepack is extremely popular. Best known is the version built by L. L. Bean and sold as its "Maine Hunting Shoe." These

All rubber boots. Note the socks worn by this hunter extend high enough above the top of the boot to prevent uncomfortable sliding down and bunching around the ankles.

boots are about as light and comfortable as bedroom slippers. At less than three pounds a pair they are as light as a boot gets. To improve arch support and protection from rough ground, you will need to add sheepskin-lined steel innersoles. The nice thing about this is you can switch innersoles during the day or after the hunt to help keep your feet dry and comfortable. The rubber bottoms of the Maine Hunting Shoe are waterproof as long as you do not go in water over ankle depth, yet the boots do not have the objectionable qualities of all-rubber boots. As a final treat, this is one of the least expensive pairs of boots you can buy. But the boots aren't terribly tough. I frequently slash up the rubber bottoms on barbed wire before I have worn them two seasons. Smaller tears can be patched as you would patch rubber waders. L. L. Bean will also repair the boots by either sewing on new tops or bottoms, honoring a Maine tradition of thrift. Once this past season I was hunting with four other hard-core pheasant chasers when someone noted, "We look like an advertisement for Bean's." Sure enough, all five of us were wearing Maine Hunting Shoes.

Another perfectly functional hunting boot is the inexpensive waffle-soled "work boot" sold by such companies as Montgomery Ward and Sears. The soles of these boots will be a resilient corrugated-crepe material. The uppers are soft, sewn with a moccasin toe. They usually sell for a third of the price of a premium leather boot. In boots, as in other things, you usually get what you pay for, and these are not very waterproof. But if you find a make which seems right for your feet, buy several pairs and get them coated with a top grade of waterproofing. They will serve you well.

None of this should be taken to mean that a premium boot—Herman's Survivors, Red Wing's Irish Setters or Browning's Featherweights, for example—are poor choices. Many hunters find them comfortable and even a good value. Premium quality boots make more sense for hunters who do not charge into heavy cover as insanely as I do. I should not spend $100 on boots I will slice up in a season or two, but most hunters have more good sense than I.

We all must learn which socks work best by a process of trial and error. Most hunters learn to buy boots on the large side and make up the difference by wearing a pair of socks. I like to wear a light cotton/nylon sock with a heavier wool/nylon sock pulled over it. I can adjust to different weather conditions by changing the thickness of the outer socks. Since I like to change socks during the day I end up wearing four pairs of socks a day, which means I have to pack at least a dozen pairs of socks for a three-day trip. I am comfy in socks which come just to my boot tops or socks which pull up almost to the knee; those socks which fall in between in length have been miserable, always slipping down and bunching up. It is a real luxury to change socks during your noon break. This little trick is worth more in comfort than buying the best boot ever built.

Clothing

Like socks, underwear must be chosen carefully because it has a very high irritation potential. You will probably want something soft between your skin and your rough outer clothing. Long underwear does this beautifully, but it is too warm during much of the season. The Scandanavian cross-country skiers apparently had the same problem, and their answer is a new light polyolefin underwear which wicks moisture away from the skin; it is stretchy, comfortable, and protective without being hot. Another good answer, also from Scandanavia, is the fishnet underwear. Early in the year I like the airy comfort of a fishnet T-shirt under my hunting shirt. When temperatures drop I can get the same comfort from a Duofold underwear top, usually worn under a cotton/polyester turtleneck sweater and a shirt chosen to suit the weather. When the weather is still warm, I like the polyoelfin long underwear bottoms because they protect my skin against the friction of hunting pants working up and down with each step. Later on I will switch to Duofold underwear bottoms. Their cotton/wool two-layer fabric is wonderfully comfortable and sufficiently warm for any winter hunting I do.

The best hunting pants are the double-faced models with poplin fabric protected by nylon facing. Pants are sold with naugahyde and even leather as facing, but they are heavy and hot. Worse, the heavier materials dry out slower, while one of the beauties of the poplin/nylon pants is that they are so quick to dry from your body heat when they get soaked. The slippery poplin/nylon pants also let your legs swing freely in tall grass, reducing friction which would tire you out. Of course, the main function of the facing is to turn brush and brambles without letting your legs get cut up. Hunting pants should be cut full to allow free movement. You should be able to lift your leg high with no hint of resistance. These boxy trousers may look unstylish, but there is no sense at all to fighting your pants all day. Buy hunting pants with short inseams so the cuff does not quite brush the top of your boots. Long pants fray and wear out faster than pants of the right length, though all of them tend to wear out too quickly along the cuff to suit me.

Few hunters fully appreciate the value of good hunting pants. About half the hunters I see afield each year are wearing blue jeans, a type of pant which neatly exemplifies all the wrong qualities for pheasant hunting! On occasion I have had to hunt in other pants when my hunting pants were destroyed. Each time I have immediately noticed that I was afraid to attack cover the way I should because I knew the tops of my legs were vulnerable. If you cannot slash an opening in brush with your legs, you will be a long time picking your way through it. At the same time, I have been impressed to find how much harder I have had to work to move because the other pants' fabrics did not slip as easily through cover as my nylon faced pants. The same point was made again when Kathe finally got some real hunting pants. She immediately began plunging more confidently into heavy cover.

Well-designed pants have other nice touches. A button-down flap over your wallet pocket offers peace of mind. Some pants have facing which does not come up high enough; you want it to reach all the way to the crotch. I might sew a strip of nylon around the cuffs of my next pants, as that is inevitably where they wear out.

These "brush pants" are perfect for rough pheasant country. The front of the legs are protected by heavy nylon facing while the trouser legs remain comfortable and fully breathable.

It is easier to get a good hunting shirt. The trick is to put together the right combination of shirts in your clothing system to meet all degrees of weather severity. Early in the year I hunt in a polyester/cotton shirt of the type sometimes sold as "Safari Cloth." Later, a good chamois cloth or light wool shirt adds welcome warmth and is usually worn over a light turtleneck and some light underwear. Some hunters like to slip on sweaters when temperatures drop, but sweaters attract burs like a magnet, and that is trouble no hunter needs at day's end.

Vests and Coats

Over the shirt I will wear a hunting vest for the first few weeks of the season, and switch to a coat when it is both cold and windy. Vests fit the system concept better, for they can be combined with other clothing items such as down jackets or light nylon rain jackets. In warm early-season weather vests are more comfortable simply because they do not make you stew in your own juices the way a coat will. One of my favorite vests has a nylon mesh back which helps vent heat and perspiration. It is made by Duxbak, a company which produces many sensibly designed garments for hunters. I once hunted in a rainstorm with a friend whose vest was built with several layers of fabric. At the end of the day I was shocked to find out how many pounds of water his vest had soaked up. I like vests made with fluorescent orange cloth. I will say more about that in a moment.

Pheasant hunters need a vest with a large, well-designed game bag. Some vests have wretched little pouches which begin to cramp your swing when you have only one rooster in them. The two vests and the coat I now use all have commodious game bags which can hold three roosters without pinning my arms back as I walk. The better game bags displace outward from your body as their load increases. A good game bag will also have some provision for unfastening at the top where it attaches to the coat or vest. This makes it easy to clean out the bag.

Deep pockets are also important. External shell pockets lead to scratched gunstocks and eventually to lost shells when the elastic ages and relaxes. The same loops, however, are convenient to work with when they are under a flap or in a deep pocket; loops in your pockets help keep shells organized. You will have difficulty walking in rough cover if your pockets bulge outward too much when loaded. You want

This hunting coat is intelligently designed to comfortably carry birds while allowing the hunter adequate swing.

the leading edge of your pockets to offer no surface which will snag on brush. My newest vest, by Bob Allen, has a small pocket with a buttoning flap which is just right for carrying an orienteering compass and pocket knife.

Most of what we said about proper vest design applies equally to hunting coats. I like coats made of light but windproof material which are also roomy enough to allow me to add warming layers underneath. The coat I have used for the last eight years is not much thicker than a dress shirt, yet it cuts the wind and keeps me warm if I keep moving. It is so right for my hunting that I will probably go right on sewing up rips and burst seams in it for several more years. It is a Duxbak, made with what they call Mains'le cloth. Many coats have fabric which is too stiff and bulky. The conventional canvas duck hunting coats are an example. Since many of these coats are built to sell for a price, they often have badly designed shoulder seams which cramp your swing and their game bags are those beastly little things which displace inward when you carry birds. Many coats feature a provision for loading birds into the bag through a slit in front, but if your bag is as big as it should be you will have no trouble dropping a bird in the back pouch directly.

Hats

I cannot imagine hunting without a hat, though people do it all the time and do not seem to feel sorry for themselves. A hat gives your face some protection when you are bucking brambles. More important to me is the fact I can adjust the brim to protect my eyes from the sun, and I will change the attitude of my hat constantly as I change directions. Above all, a fluorescent orange hat is the best insurance against getting shot you can buy. It helps to have fluorescent orange on your body anywhere, but a "Hunter Orange" hat has incredible impact when viewed even from great distances, in heavy cover, or on grey days. It makes sense to put the bright orange on your head since that is the highest part of your body and the part least likely to be totally obscured by brush. All the statistics I've seen corroborate the theory that fluorescent orange clothing protects against shooting accidents.

There is another side to the issue. I consider the wearing of bright clothing to be a courtesy to others in the party. The high visibility of this material, especially when worn on a hat, makes it easy for everyone in the group to keep track of each other. That means you will have less time wasted while everyone stands around bellowing to locate Uncle Frank who has seemingly disappeared. You will also be able to take shots at a higher percentage of flushed roosters because you will not be in doubt about whether one of your partners is in the line of fire. I would buy a dozen of these hats in all sizes to lend to my partners, if only I believed they would wear them!

Winter Wear

Extreme cold weather puts special demands on the pheasant hunter's clothing system. Pheasant hunting is an active sport. The ideal clothing selection for any given day will have you cold for the first half hour until your body's system heats up. It's easy to dress warmly enough for most winter weather by adding layers, yet some states have long seasons which might see you trudging around in high winds and sub-zero weather. Then you are in danger of frostbite if you are not prepared. The coldest weather I recall hunting in was a day featuring a wind chill of 54 degrees below zero. I can honestly report that in weather like that you have to want a pheasant very badly in order to put up with the pain. Yet, the hunting can be great when air temperatures plummet.

Since a large share of your body's heat escapes through your head, the first response to extremely cold weather is to wear a warm cap which will also protect your ears. Balaclava face masks are effective, as are insulated hats with furry ear flaps. Snowmobile masks will keep your face warm while protecting your lungs from the cold air.

The trickiest part of dressing for bitter weather hunting is keeping your hands warm without making it impossible for them to get a shotgun into action. My best answer is to treat each hand as a separate problem. I will wear a warm mitten on the left hand, and put a moderately warm glove on the right hand, which has to work the safety and trigger. Then I will carry a hand warmer in my right hand coat pocket to keep that hand from stiffening up. This works only if you can carry your gun comfortably with your left hand, which is one reason I like a double barrel.

Up to a point you can keep meeting colder air temperatures by adding layers. A down jacket slipped under a hunting coat works fairly well, though it is bulky. A new product, another Scandanavian innovation, which works well is acrylic pile. Acrylic pile keeps its warmth when wet, is flexible enough for the most active hunting, and has a special cushy-soft warmth that cannot be beat. It is porous, so you must wear it under some windproof garment. If I ever again hunt pheasants in minus 54-degree wind chills, I will wear my snowmobile suit. It is bulky, but I have found out in goose hunting that I can still mount a gun when wearing it.

If you get the feeling you would like to change into more comfortable clothing at the end of the day, there is something wrong with your hunting clothes. They should be the most comfortable clothes you own. Still, it is a luxury to pack a change of clothes in the vehicle so you can don something a little lighter and drier at the end of a hard hunt. I carry a pair of wool slippers with leatherette bottoms, like the old "muk-luks," and it is one of the sweetest feelings I have known

*Large hunting coat fits comfortably over the smaller zippered down jacket. Face pro-
tector and cap with earflaps reduce the risk of frostbite on these usually exposed areas.*

to pull them on at the end of a long day and head for home with a tired dog and a few roosters in the back of the car.

More Thoughts on Clothing

Jim Layton, a frequent hunting partner who is as canny about people as he is about ringnecks, has a different perspective on hunting clothing. Jim wears a cheap hat with a hybrid seed corn emblem, the typical farmer's pin-striped bibbers, and a faded hooded sweatshirt. In short, Jim looks like a farmer. When he approaches a farmer he does not know, he will leave his hunting coat in the truck. Then, after talking several minutes about the outrageous price of farm machinery and the equally outrageous weather, Jim offhandedly turns the talk to pheasants. He is not actually trying to pass as a farmer, but he knows it helps to look like someone who knows farming and a farmer's problems. He gets to hunt in places most guys do not.

Hunters have been ribbed about their scruffy appearance for so long that most of us have quit caring what impression we make on others. That is a mistake. To be sure, the first requirement of your clothing is comfort. But too many hunters adopt an attitude of total unconcern for the way others see them. Yet, most pheasant hunting is done on private land, so any hunter who must ask permission to carry a weapon on someone else's property had better think about the impression of his character his clothing gives. Farmers who are asked to trust strangers with guns around their livestock, fences, and buildings are forced to make snap judgements about character. Your clothing will contribute a lot to the first impression you make.

Does that mean you need to go hunting looking like a fashion plate? Absolutely not! In fact, one of the quickest ways to make a bad impression is to look too flashy and well-heeled. If your whole outfit looks brand new, the landowner has cause to wonder how much experience you have. If you drive up in a luxury limousine and step out wearing white hunter's safari garb, he can be expected to feel a little natural resentment towards someone who is so conspicuously wealthy. On the other hand, looking outright slovenly is not likely to make anyone think you are someone they should trust. Hunting clothing which is well used but well cared for will avoid all the pitfalls I have described. There is no need to make major concessions to improve your image, but it is something to think about unless you always hunt on public land.

Strange as it sounds, I am also convinced that hunters should think about the impression they make on the general population, and clothing is one part of that impression. This works both ways. You can contribute to the image of hunters as slobs by such thoughtless measures as wearing a flamboyant hat with rooster tail feathers stuck here and there in the hat band. On the other hand, I darn well want people to know I am a hunter, so I dress like a hunter in public situations, especially when I am spending money. It is one of my private convictions that the general public will care more about pheasant habitat and think more favorably about hunting and hunters if they are aware of the contributions to rural economies that hunters make. This may not seem like an important way to strike a blow for the future of hunting, yet it will probably do more good than all the pro-hunting editorials that appear in magazines only read by avid hunters.

Other Equipment

Pheasant hunting does not require a great deal of equipment. It is, at heart, a simple activity which is not much different from what cave dwellers did millions of years ago. I especially appreciate the fact that high technology has not found a place in pheasant hunting. The equipment we will discuss here is not absolutely necessary, though often nice to have.

Those who hunt with dogs will need a kit for toting canine paraphernalia. A comb will help clear hairy ears of burs. When hunting in dry country you will need to carry water and a dish, though in most pheasant habitat your dog will find water along the way. It is dangerous for your dog to hunt in a choke collar; the best collars have fluorescent orange panels sewn to a durable nylon strap. Some hunters find they need to travel with first aid ointments to reduce irritation in their dogs' ears. And it is only fair to travel with a few doggie treats to reward good performances.

It is also smart to carry a few first aid products for yourself. Most important among them would be moleskin and scissors. I have seen badly blistered hunters return to action after treating their injuries with moleskin and tape. The popularity of running has led to the introduction of a promising new product, called "2nd Skin," for treating blisters.

I intend to carry it. Aspirin and antacid tablets take little room in your personal care kit. Experienced hunters know they should travel with a roll of toilet paper, though the new moist towelettes may work better.

If you are on a longer hunt you may enjoy peace of mind if you carry gun cleaning equipment. I doubt that modern firearms need cleaning after only a few days' use unless they were dirty to begin with, but many of us enjoy the ritual of tending to the guns at day's end.

A few items will help you keep the bagged birds in good condition for the table. I carry birds in plastic garbage bags after field dressing them. Most pheasant hunting takes place in cold weather, so it is no problem to keep the birds cool. Early season hunting can be warm, however, so insulated chests filled with bags of ice are important then. I have kept birds in good condition for six days that way. The plastic bags keep the birds from getting soaked as the ice melts. You will want a sharp knife to aid in field dressing or cleaning. The moist towelettes mentioned before are handy for cleaning your hands after field dressing the pheasants.

Occasionally, it helps to have binoculars in the car. If you hunt in large management areas you can sometimes sit on a high spot before shooting hours start and use the glasses to mark birds down as they return to cover after grabbing breakfast in the fields. When the crops are down you can often spot roosters sneaking around the edges of cover, especially early or late in the day.

Because I am an outdoor writer I always travel with cameras, but I urge all hunters to consider carrying a camera to record memorable events. The smartest camera buy for most hunters will be one of the ultra-compact 35-millimeter rangefinder models. Some have auto-focus, while auto-exposure is standard on most. Automatic wind, a less common feature, is handy. A self-timer will let the cameraman get in his own photos. These little cameras are goof-proof, yet they will produce an excellent image. Many of the pictures in this book were taken with my Olympus XA, a little jewel. I carry it with me in my game bag at all times. It has rewarded me with many precious mementos of my hunts that I would have lost if I had worked with other equipment. I have got a film record of the first solid rooster point made by a friend's young setter, and that picture alone is worth the price of the camera.

Every pheasant hunter is a bit different about what he likes to eat or drink while hunting. I have been with guys who wanted to knock

This 35-millimeter is compact enough to be carried by the fussiest hunters. Total weight: as much as five 12-gauge shells.

off for a full restaurant lunch at noon; whereas I like to eat a big breakfast before shooting hours and then stop for no more than a few minutes all day. A good quick energy booster is the ''gorp'' concoction carried by backpackers. Hard-boiled eggs pack a lot of energy for their size. Coffee is good for waking up before the hunt, but when you work up a good sweat you will want something cool. Having tried just about everything, I have learned that relatively unadulterated fruit juices like apple or grapefruit are the most satisfying. Carry twice as much as you think you will need.

All this accessory equipment can be a hassle to find and pack each time you take a trip, so experienced hunters keep the whole kit together all through the season. It does not hurt to have a checklist to help pull all these items together.

Pheasant hunters must often live for days at a time out of a duffle bag. As nice as duffles are to carry they are hell to find anything in. I am always cussing because I forgot to bring an important coat, only to find when I get home that it was lost in an obscure corner of the duffle all along. Another problem is how you keep fresh clothing separated from what you have worn. After years of smelling my socks each morning to sort them I now carry a plastic garbage bag into which I put all dirty clothes. At the same time I have finally got a duffle with compartments and pockets sewn into it. These two innovations have made life on the road a lot more fun.

Serious hunters usually work from four-wheel-drive vehicles. In the recent past that usually meant a Blazer, Bronco, or Cherokee. High gas prices, however, are forcing many pheasant hunters into compact four-wheel-drive trucks with toppers. Having all four wheels pulling for you can be important when you drive way out in lonely country on muddy roads. Once you have been badly stuck in such a place you will give a lot of thought to getting an unstickable vehicle.

Last season I took a long trip in my station wagon with a compact trailer hitched behind to carry the extra gear. It worked surprisingly well. The little trailer had way more room than we needed to carry equipment; so that left the interior of my compact wagon free to accomodate three hunters and two dogs. Then I could leave the trailer at the motel while our group hunted. We could have had as much room in a full sized four-wheel-drive, but today's hunters often find it too expensive to run such a rig every day just to have enough carrying capacity in the hunting season.

Maps

The biggest aid to the modern pheasant hunter, ranking right after a gun and a good dog, is a set of detailed maps of the country he will be hunting. As suitable habitat disappears each year, it becomes more and more important to pick a place to hunt. And maps can help enormously. The right kind of map can point you toward good country, help you find the right person to talk to once you get there, and help you find your way back to the place on a later hunt. Don't underestimate the importance of that last point. One of the sweetest agonies possible for a pheasant hunter is driving around trying to relocate a farm which has a wonderful bit of cover on it and a friendly farmer. Ah, if only you could find it again!

Not long ago I found maps boring, but today they are scarcely less important to my hunting than shells. I have several rules which I never compromise. First, I will buy, copy, or steal any map of pheasant country that I can get my hands on. Even if other maps seem to be better, I will pick up a new map in the hope it will show something the other maps do not. Second, I never *ever* throw out a map, even though it has been replaced with one that looks better. Third, I will never again loan out a map for which I do not have at least one copy.

This obsession with maps is based on my conviction that no hunter has as many good places to chase pheasants as he ought to. If you ever quit looking for new places to hunt because you have got a few nice farms or management areas which suit your purposes, you can count on heartbreak. Your pet farm is going to fall into new hands, and next thing you know the bulldozers and tiling machines will have wiped out the cover. Even wildlife management areas can go sour if too many other hunters start working them or if some manager decides your favorite marshy ringneck area should be flooded to make a new area for ducks.

The first type of map a pheasant hunter needs is the kind which shows where the wildlife management or public hunting areas are. These are usually state publications, and they vary in quality from state

With a trailer to carry equipment and guns, the hunter spends less money than he would taking a four-wheel-drive vehicle. However, this arrangement somewhat limits access to more remote areas.

to state. But get whatever maps are published and keep looking for newer editions which might have recently purchased areas included. Get multiple copies so you can keep one in your hunting vehicle and at least one at home for more intensive study.

Since every serious hunter is apt to have maps of the state wildlife areas, it is often useful to get the less widely publicized maps to federal waterfowl production areas. In many parts of the country the best pheasant habitat will be areas officially listed as waterfowl production areas. Another category of public lands which can be invaluable for pheasant hunters is the Corps of Engineers holdings along their impoundments. The Corps, mindful of the need for better relations with sportsmen, usually has nice maps of public lands in its control.

Leaving no stone unturned, you might also want to check out "National Grasslands" maps. Such country is not often top pheasant habitat, but it can be. Or, perhaps a careful reading of your state game laws may list certain "wildlife refuges" which are open to public hunting. The refuge title may have been assigned at a time when people believed that such areas would be havens for wildlife which could then repopulate areas devastated by hunters. That outdated thinking has led to the anomaly of lands officially called "refuges" being wide open to public hunting. Even maps of Indian reservation lands might be important to pheasant hunters in some states. Or you might get maps from railroad companies which show the location of lands under their control. In short, any map except a city map is apt to be of interest to the modern pheasant hunter.

Pheasant hunters especially need good county road maps. In many states these can be purchased from the state highway department. Often you will find these highly detailed county maps bound together in a single volume and sold as a "sportsman's atlas" or "guide to fun" in the state. These are invaluable. If the county maps you buy do not have wildlife management areas marked plainly, filling in that information is an excellent project for you in the off-season. If you cannot buy a bound volume of the county maps of the state you hunt in, you should assemble your own book of maps for pheasant range counties and combine them yourself in some protective device.

In each state, "plat" map books list the specific owner of each parcel of land in each county. These have obvious value for hunters. Plat books can save you an awful lot of chasing around, and I would much rather spend my valuable hunting time chasing pheasants instead of chasing down landowners. You will commonly find that one man might own several big pieces of land in a county. With plat maps you can identify and locate him, while without them you probably cannot. Plat maps are not cheap, nor are they always easy to buy since many are sold in county offices only during regular work-week hours, but they are extremely valuable to the modern hunter.

The famous United States Geological Survey topographical maps are also useful. If you want to check out a new hunting area you should study topo maps for a long time before actually arriving in the area to look for a place to hunt. Topo maps show marshy areas, woodlots, ponds, and winding rivers, all land features of great interest to pheasant hunters. You especially want to study topo maps to learn where rough, irregular land lies out of sight of county roads. All the hours you spend poring over maps out of season are positive contributions to your effectiveness as a pheasant hunter and a pleasant extension of the joys of hunting into the closed season.

Every pheasant hunter should keep one master set of maps on which are recorded all the good hunting sites. This master set will usually be a collection of detailed county maps, though plat maps will serve even better. You should keep scrupulously complete records on these maps of places you can hunt and how the cover lies. Never trust your memory. In addition to showing you the way back to good hunting spots these maps can save you the embarrassment of a trespass conviction.

Preseason Scouting

Smart hunters like to scout out new places to hunt during the off-season, usually in spring. It does not make much sense to throw away valuable hunting time in the season doing a job that could have been done better the previous spring. In the off-season you can be more deliberate and experimental, and by working with maps you can pinpoint promising country lying off the beaten path.

What is more, spring is a better time to establish relationships with landowners. Farmers are far less harried in spring than they will be during the fall harvest when most hunters come to ask permission to hunt. And farmers recognize that the fellow who cares enough about his sport to work at it in the spring is unusually dedicated and more likely to be a safe person to allow on his lands. Your spring scouting should concentrate on locating both birds and nesting cover. The best time to count pheasants is early to middle May, preferably on a bright day with winds under ten miles an hour and a heavy dew. Prowl around the country roads at sunrise, and keep track of both the number of birds you see and the number of cock crows you hear. Heavy dew conditions force the birds into open areas where you will more easily spot them. Only by doing this in several areas or one area over a period of years will you get a sense of the strength of the populations. It's a nice way to spend a morning in May.

But even if you do not see birds, the presence of good nesting cover is a good sign. That nesting cover will often be mowed flat when the season starts; so other hunters will not know what the country looked like in spring. The most promising sign of all is a big stand of uncut hay late in June, for that land probably produced a healthy crop of pheasants.

Game agencies know that the most accurate predictor of the fall harvest is the roadside population census conducted in August. These counts are conducted much the way I have described in my comments on spring scouting. Game agencies use data from August counts to make population density maps and, in some cases, to make final decisions on the hunting season. Few hunters know that the data collected in these counts is public information which is made available to hunters with enough industry to make the necessary phone calls.

Enterprising hunters will find other ways to sniff out birdy areas. By chatting with mail carriers, policemen, and the men who travel around cutting hay, you can get a good idea of where the birds are. If you locate an area with tons of birds (although it is not known as prime pheasant country), so much the better!

5

A Place to Hunt

There is an avid pheasant hunter in central Iowa who will probably never buy this book. Ron does not need to read anyone else's thoughts on pheasant behavior or hunting strategy because he already knows everything he needs to know about pheasant hunting. What he already knows is how to win a welcome to hunt farms which are off-limits to other hunters. And friends, when you know how to do that, you can eat pheasant instead of chicken just about all year long.

Farms which are "wide open" to anyone who takes the trouble to ask permission will steadily lose birds throughout the season. But those farms which allow nobody except a special friend or relative to hunt on them will usually offer opening day quality hunting right down to the shank of the season because they keep their roosters and pick up extra birds from surrounding lands that get more pressure.

Now, as far as Ron is concerned, pheasant hunting is pretty easy. He mostly looks for quail and picks up all the roosters the law allows along the way. That is possible, though, only because he has collected quite a number of farms where only he can hunt. He does not even work hard at that. It comes naturally. Ron is the sort of fellow who really enjoys long, relaxed conversations with farmers. He also works for a company which publishes an excellent cookbook, and you can bet he has put copies of that cookbook in the hands of farm wives all over the best pheasant range in Iowa.

Lucky is the pheasant hunter whose daily work naturally has him rubbing elbows with landowners in good pheasant country. I know a fellow who sells those huge and expensive batteries used on modern farm machinery. Every now and then he gets the chance to sell a perfectly good "factory second" battery at a bargain price, and by some coincidence all those bargain batteries end up on farms where hunters—or, rather, other hunters—cannot set foot. Country lawyers and doctors win invitations to hunt on lands closed to the rest of us. My father and I once got to hunt on such a farm, thanks to the influence of our family doctor. We called the farmer just before coming out to hunt and asked if he had some birds on his place. "Do I have pheasants?" he asked in astonishment. "Lookin' out the back winda' I see. . .oh, three, four roosters walkin' round the yard right now!" We had a short, noisy hunt on his place, thanks to our mutual friendship with Doctor George.

Where you hunt is at least as important as how well you hunt. That is why smart pheasant hunters are always working to collect a treasure trove of special farms or ranches where they can get early season hunting right on through the season. Decide for yourself how important it would be to be given the keys to some hunting land locked up against others. Speaking for myself, I would not dream of getting married again unless it would be to the daughter of someone with several thousand heavily posted acres of land in prime pheasant country!

Getting On

Where I grew up, the phrase for securing permission to hunt was "getting on." The art of getting on has many subtleties for those who work at it. I have already mentioned my friend who dons farmerish clothing when he expects to be asking permission. Another guy works in a big city, but when he is standing hat-in-hand at the back door of a farmhouse his accent and demeanor become so Ah-shucks,-ah'm-jus'-a-country-boy that you would have to see the transformation to believe it. I once walked up to the kitchen door with him to try to get on a particularly nice looking farm—("nice looking" meaning this farm had a healthier crop of foxtail and cockleburs than corn). The lady of the house greeted us cautiously, saying her husband was away and he never let anyone hunt on the place anyway. Now, those are the most discouraging words you can hear at such a time, but Larry kept talking and reaching back for all the country boy charm he could muster. I was downright ashamed of him before he was done, but we got the go-ahead to hunt and an invitation to come back again real soon.

Other hunters get so ingenious with their ploys that you could just as fairly call them devious as clever. Most of the time all that foxing around does not make any difference. Most landowners have a policy on hunting requests. And, in fact, most of them grant permission to courteous hunters. Yet in that group of farms which are ordinarily closed to strangers there is a certain number you can get on if you happen to ask in just the right way. And that keeps pheasant hunters thinking about the best way to approach landowners just as some folks rehearse the smooth lines they intend to use in singles bars.

Surprisingly enough, it often is in your favor if you are a nonresident. When a farmer lets a nonresident on his land he is fairly sure he will not see the same guy back with two carloads of friends every weekend through the rest of the season. Farmers are also naturally sympathetic to the hunter who spends a chunk of money and drives long highway miles in hopes of having a little fun. When I am hunting far from home I make a point of telling landowners where I am from. Since areas just across a state border often get inundated with nonresident hunters, nonresidency works against you there.

Many hunters make the mistake of bluntly popping a narrow question: "Can I hunt that slough on the west end of your corn?" You will do better if you greet the landowner by name, give him your name and home town, then say something like: "My friend and I've come down here looking for a few pheasants, and I wonder if you could help me." If he does not want you in the slough by the west end of the corn he at least has the chance now to tell you he owns an "eighty" a few miles to the south which has not been walked since opening weekend.

It is smart and simply more courteous to deal with landowners on a person-to-person basis rather than rushing to settle the legal issue of whether or not you can get on. It can be a mite intimidating to have the whole party standing right by the door when you ask permission, so it is better to send an envoy. But the rest of the group should stand by the car where they can be seen, rather than slinking down in their seats like escaped felons. Large groups, understandably, will be refused far more often than parties of one to four hunters. I often hunt with my wife, and I always bring her along when asking permission. Some farmers are confused and intrigued to see a woman hunting, but when Kathe flashes her smile they at least know we are not likely to walk into their fields and shoot one of the prize heifers.

Freelancing

Freelancing is my name for driving into an area "cold" with no previous contacts. Good hunters never freelance unless they can help it, yet we all must do it from time to time. There are two problems with freelancing. You can waste a great deal of time driving and trying to chase down the right person to ask. When you finally locate a delicious bit of cover, you are apt to find the farmhouse is occupied by an indecisive tenant farmer who is working for an absentee landlord who lives "in town" some forty miles away.

Freelancers also get lean pickings because they automatically choose the same places to hunt that looked good to other freelancers. This especially becomes a problem later in the season, when any good looking cover in sight of a country road has been tramped through by someone just about once a day all season long.

One way to beat this is to only ask to get on farms which are posted with "No Hunting" signs, for those signs scare off many freelancers. Often they have been erected merely to stop strangers from wandering in to hunt without first securing permission. Experienced pheasant hunters recognize different attitudes in different "No Hunting" signs. The "No Hunting Except by Permission" signs are a clear signal that polite requests will usually be honored. Commercially produced "No Hunting" signs which the farmer purchased in a store are often used simply to discourage trespassers. But when you see a series of hand-lettered posters warning "Keep Out!" you know you risk getting chased back to your car by a German shepherd if you knock at the door to try to talk your way on.

It pays to keep a sharp eye on the roadsides and margins of the

There are different kinds of "No Hunting" signs. This one suggests a polite request to hunt will not be refused.

fields as you drive about looking for a place to hunt. While you are basically looking for good cover, the best cover of all is that patch of weeds you actually see two roosters ducking into as you drive by. Few freelancers work at spotting birds as hard as they should. By looking for birds as well as cover, you will discover a few of those birdy farms which have cover not visible from the roads.

Experienced hunters always try to work with maps when free-lancing. Topo maps will tell you which country roads are likely to lead you to marshy or uneven land where not all the cover has been extirpated. Plat maps might save you hours of frustration chasing down absentee landowners, when you could have been chasing roosters instead. Wildlife management area maps guide you to public lands if you grow weary of seeking private lands to hunt. And, at the very least, you should have some good county maps so you can mark down the exact locations of the good farms you turn up. When I try to imagine what Hell will be like I usually think of it as a place where pheasant hunters drive around in circles forever, knowing they are achingly close to a wonderful place to hunt which they forgot to mark down on the maps!

Corn Up, Corn Down

Good pheasant hunters pay close attention to the harvest of such crops as corn and sorghum. The progress of the harvest is especially crucial around the opener, yet even the late season hunter can use information about the harvest to put more cocks in the bag.

Early season hunting can be next to impossible if weather has prevented the harvesting of most of the tall grain. Most farmers do not want heavy-footed hunters stomping around in their valuable crop-fields. Worse, the pheasants will use standing corn or sorghum fields as their primary daytime cover until the fields are harvested. Not only are such fields hard to hunt, if you are allowed to try, but the birds will be widely scattered. When the combines roll through the fields they change the pheasants' world drastically, and send most of the birds into the smaller stands of cover lying around in marginal areas. And you can hunt them there.

That is why good hunters will never make plans for an early season hunt without checking on the progress of the harvest. If even half the corn is standing in an area of high bird populations you are smarter to switch your attention to some area with fewer birds but no standing crops. You will probably have less competition from other hunters, too.

As farm practices have changed over the years, the corn harvest has begun earlier than it used to—about the only new farming practice which has benefited pheasant hunters. Yet some years will see so much fall rain that the harvest may be delayed by weeks. Since standing crops all but kill pheasant hunting, you can enjoy excellent sport late in the season by hunting regions where all the crops were up in the first weeks. When a remarkably wet fall delayed the harvest in Iowa a few years ago, some friends and I found opening day type hunting on Thanksgiving weekend.

Sorghum fields are a prominent feature of the fall landscape in some excellent pheasant regions, and they affect hunting exactly as corn does. If anything, the birds feel safer in sorghum than in corn, though a picked cornfield is a slightly better bet to hunt than a field of cut sorghum. Soybeans, though pheasants eat them with gusto, do not affect your hunting the same way because a rooster feels pretty naked in a bean field even before it is harvested.

You will sometimes hunt an area where the harvest is rapidly being wound up. Obviously, it makes sense to plan your hunts with the harvest in mind. As long as some corn or sorghum is standing it will be loaded with birds. Some of the best hunting you will get comes right after the machines have leveled the crops and the birds are spending their first days in the next best cover available to them. I wish I did not feel compelled to add that it is rude, lazy, and unsafe to stand at the end of a crop field being harvested and have the farm machinery drive birds toward you. Whether such "hunting" is sporting or not may be debatable, but there is no doubt that it sours relations with landowners. The modern pheasant hunter hardly needs more of that.

Marginal Areas

Some of the best hunting is available in regions with no special reputation for producing bumper crops of pheasants. Since every pheasant hunter dreams of working good cover with loads of birds, we all seek out the very best areas to hunt. Many state game agencies help us by printing maps showing relative bird populations, yet even if they did not do this hunters would pull together tips from various sources to get a fix on the area with the greatest number of birds. Inevitably, hunting pressure concentrates disproportionately and centers on a handful of towns to a degree not warranted by any real differences in population levels. If Adams County has twice as many pheasants as Buchanan County, you can bet Adams will get six times the hunter pressure. When this happens the birds in the "good" areas either get quickly shot or become so smart you can not hunt them.

You will enjoy a higher quality hunt if you can find a few farms or a region which has good cover and is surrounded by country that is bare and relatively devoid of birds. Those state pheasant distribution maps are far too crude to reflect these tiny hotspots within marginal areas. These birdy areas may have been created by the caprice of glaciers, so that a small area of rough land might hold weeds and birds in a large area which is flat and sterile. Or regional farming practices can make the difference, as when the tradition of crop rotation persists in a small area surrounded by chemically dependent modern farmers. These small areas are not easy to find; yet they are more than worth the trouble of locating. The average hunter always wants to know where the greatest population of birds is. If you can locate such a gem—closer than the famous but over-hunted pheasant country—so much the better. Let others put expensive hours of driving time in while you slip into your patch of sweet cover in a nearby, unheralded area.

There is a practice in some parts of the pheasant range which I would love to see adopted elsewhere: farm families take in pheasant hunters as paying guests early in the season. They can hunt the land owned by the folks they stay with or they can move around. But it is not the guarantee of a place to hunt which makes this experience so delightful. The real bonus is the wonderful farm cooking and generous hospitality the hunters get. And it does not hurt any city-dwelling hunter to spend a little time with rural people, and to see things through their eyes. All in all, this tradition is a pleasant alternative to the impersonal experience of sleeping in a motel and eating in the car.

The Hunting Party

What has twenty-two legs, eight different ideas of where the pheasants are, four conflicting opinions of who is in charge, and eight incompatible conceptions of what it is, at the moment, doing? Easy! That's just your average pheasant hunting party of five men and three dogs. To the tune of assorted whistle toots and curses, it hacks its way through the fields with all the precision of a train wreck. And everyone usually has a helluva time anyway.

Plenty of pheasant hunters enjoy the Chinese-fire-drill approach to pheasant cover. Whether they get pheasants or not, they would rather hunt in the company of several friends. And if the whole thing makes more noise than sense, well, that suits them to the ground. When such a group manages to shoot three pheasants, there will be on the average about three men claiming to have hit each bird; and so, in a sense, everyone gets to go home thinking he shot a limit.

If that is your favorite way to hunt pheasants you hardly need any advice on how to do it, but it is not my way. I am not as patient as I should be when waiting for Fred to find his dog or Tom to have his

Living with a farm family you not only learn where the pheasants are, but you become acquainted with the "locals" for a total hunting experience. (Photo by Tom Huggler)

cigarette break. And as for the strategy discussions, I can pass them by, too. "Bob and Sam and Sam's kid, now, you all work the cover back while the rest of us post and Mike takes the fence line and we'll all converge." "Whaddaya mean, work it back?" "You work it back, I'm going to post." "What's back?" "You work it back; I'm posting." "But what's back? Where do I go?" And so forth, and so forth!

Elsewhere in this book we have touched on problems with large parties, yet they deserve to be summed up here. Large groups are unpopular with landowners, and I suspect with good cause. It is very difficult to organize big groups, so you end up standing around for a third of your hunting hours while ambitious field maneuvers are debated and never executed as planned. Worse, large parties are far more likely to fire upon themselves in the heat of the moment. Every time you add a hunter to the group you increase the odds that someone in the party will be one of those characters who has his gun trained on a dog or man half the time. I remember quite well the icy terror I felt when I learned that the man who was on my right as we started a cornfield drive held to the theory that "the best safety is a trained trigger-finger" and so walked around with his gun off safe. I do not need to put my life on the line to get a chance at a rooster. Nosiree!

On an entirely different level, large hunting parties make little sense for today's pheasant hunting circumstances. There simply are not enough birds to justify the marshalling up of all that manpower. Let's say a group hunts on three farms or two big management areas in a day. They will be doing pretty well to see a dozen roosters, not all of which will be in range. They will see those dozen roosters whether there are three or eight hunters in the party. Figure it out for yourself. If you are one of the party of eight, you might come home with a bird or two if you're lucky. If you are in the smaller group, you will either have a daily limit or at least enough shooting chances that you could have one. I do not for a moment mean to suggest that shooting a limit is the point of pheasant hunting, but those who hunt with bloated parties should at least recognize that they have chosen the pleasures of hunting in a big gang over the pleasures of actually hunting pheasants.

Is there any place for big groups in these days of sparse pheasant populations? Yes, at least one. Whenever you are faced with a fairly large and complex piece of cover which is loaded with pheasants, the only sensible way to hunt in it is with a sizable group. I have met with only one such situation in recent years. I was with a group which wanted to hunt a big South Dakota farm shelterbelt. Here was cover so light that roosters would not sit in it, and it had many odd projections which would serve as escape routes. Those factors, plus the size of the cover, meant that even ten men converging on the cover could not block all the exits known to the roosters. But, for better or worse, such situations are rare today.

Is there any such thing as an ideal number of hunters in a party? Yes. Either three or four hunters can hunt modern pheasant cover efficiently, especially if they use dogs. Strip cover, like an irrigation ditch, often has two sides which must be carefully worked. Usually you can do that with three hunters, two driving and one posting. If you find a wide strip of cover on each side of the ditch, you might be better off with two men blocking the ends. It is very hard to imagine situations where five hunters will make better use of the cover than three or four, while a good two-man party with dogs will be able to hit the prime cover and get all the action they need in a few hours.

In fact, for much of the season, one man and a good dog are the most efficient party imaginable. If they select their cover carefully and work it well they can put up the two or three cocks they need to call the day a big success. The problem is that a single hunter cannot block the end of strip cover, nor can he cover all the exits when attacking a a patch which has several likely escape outlets. Another problem is presented by strip cover which has a line of screening brush or too much width to be hunted by one man even with a good dog. But until the roosters get extremely evasive, a single hunter and a dog will walk fewer hours for their limit than any other kind of hunting party.

Every pheasant-hunting party needs ground rules. If you are to hunt safely and effectively, everyone needs to know what they should and should not do. And while it might seem slightly unpleasant, someone needs to seize an occasion before the hunting starts to make the whole party understand clearly what the ground rules should be.

First, there should be a clear understanding of when each hunter has the right to shoot at a flushing rooster. Years ago I had an angry dispute with a partner who shot a cock which had flushed right in front of me and was still quite close. Later, after hard feelings had disappeared, I realized he was a grouse hunter who had been taught to keep firing at any bird in sight until it was down. Because pheasants usually flush in the open and offer clear shots, I had been taught as a youngster that nobody fired at a bird except the hunter who was closest to it. That principle worked a little better in the days of pheasant abundance. Today I hunt with people who understand that the first shot belongs to the man closest to the bird. If he misses, anyone else with a safe and in-range shot is free to try for the bird. Adopt any rule you wish. Just make sure everyone knows exactly what it is before there are roosters in the air.

You will also need to make some ruling about shooting at wounded birds on the ground. Let's take for granted the fact that you will not hunt with people who want to pot a sitting or running rooster which has not been shot. But conscientious hunters might differ in their opinions of safety of shooting a wounded bird which is a potential running cripple, so this is one of those details you should work out in advance.

You also need to know ahead of time whether or not each man

shoots his own birds or whether "party shooting" is allowed. If you accept party shooting, the fellow with the hot gun and good dog might kill eight birds of a twelve-bird party limit. For some groups, such conduct is game hoggism of the nth degree; for others, it is the most sensible way to run a successful hunt which allows each hunter to go home with enough birds for a good meal. Most state game agencies regard party shooting as illegal, yet this is one one of those game laws which is violated more often than honored. At the very least, the man who has already limited out owes it to the others to ask whether or not they would regard it as a favor if he took any more shots.

Who's in Charge?

Every hunting party needs one leader. Democracy may be the best way to run a society, but it is a godawful way to run a hunt. Usually, the field captain should be the fellow with the most experience with pheasants. If the most experienced man is on somebody's else's turf, he should give way to the man who knows how the cover lies and what the birds are apt to do in this particular area. But nobody should be in doubt about who is in charge. The bigger your group, the more important this becomes. Large party pheasant drives will go danger-ously wrong unless they are firmly organized by a leather-lunged vet-eran of many hunts who will make himself understood at all times and who is capable of whipping the troops into shape.

In addition to understanding pheasants, field captains must have a clear sense of priorities. The safety of all members has to come before any other consideration. Next, the field captain must work to bring off a successful hunt in which the group works efficiently in a way likely to put pheasants in the air. Finally, the field captain should be aware of who is and is not getting any shooting. If he really knows his pheas-ants, he should be able to juggle things so the prime opportunities on the next maneuver fall to those who have been left out. That can often be accomplished by using those who have missed the early action as blockers. If you are hunting with women, youngsters, or older men, they often appreciate being put on post while the more athletic hunters buck the cover to drive birds their way. Older hunters make the best blockers, combining the virtues of experience with shooting and a sober awareness of the importance of safety.

I recently had the experience of hearing three men describe, separately, a hunt I had had with them. The three stories were so different you would not have known they were describing the same hunt (and I would have told a totally different version of it). That experience underlined for me the importance of being considerate of others in the party. You must try to consider how the experience is working out for each member. Good field captains are aware of how much fun each party member is having, and great field captains know how to ensure each member's fun.

6

Cycles and Pheasant Behavior

If you carefully track the activities of a flock of pheasants you will see they have a daily cycle of activity; they move from spot to spot throughout the day in a predictable way. That would seem to be a terribly important thing for a hunter to know, for by grasping the cycle, he could be in the right place at the right time all day. Alas, things are not quite so simple.

The Daily Cycle

Let's describe the theoretical cycle. The birds are supposed to spend their nights in roosting areas, which can be marshes, grassy areas, or even farm shelter belts where the birds sleep in the safety of the trees. At daybreak the birds often move to the roadsides, where they enjoy the first rays of sunlight and grab a little gravel for their gizzards. Then they jump into the grain fields to feed. After feeding, they spend the middle part of their day in "loafing cover" where they do not do much but loaf. Afternoon brings another trip to the feeding areas to tank up again. After that, the birds will return to their roosting area.

This is a seductive theory. If you believe it, you believe you can keep in hot action by moving with the birds. You start in the roosting areas, switch to the feeding fields, then comb the loafing areas before hitting the feeding areas again, and end up with a glorious shoot in the roosting areas. It sounds like the very best way to hunt pheasants. But it does not work out that neatly. Here is why.

For one thing, pheasants quickly modify their daily cycle in whatever ways they have to in order to avoid hunters in the season. What they do the week before the opener may be nothing like what they do the week after the opener. I have heard of a deer hunter who took up a stand on a wildlife management area which held quite a few pheasants. Just at daybreak he witnessed a mass eruption of birds from the center of a deep marsh. Every pheasant in the area took to the air at once, flying directly to a field of picked corn where they fed frantically for fifteen minutes before flying directly back to the center of the marsh again. All this took place before shooting hours for pheasants had begun. The birds were totally safe in the corn, and just as safe in the marsh, because they were surrounded by four feet of water which lay between the island of floating vegetation they sat on and the fringe of the marsh. Now, I defy you to use the model of the typical daily pheasant cycle to help hunt those birds!

Weather, like hunting pressure, will change the cycle. Pheasants are hardy birds with ample reserves of energy. In nasty weather they can park in the roosting areas for three days at a time. More frequently they will make a single feeding foray instead of two each day. On the other hand, in balmy autumn weather they might jump into the corn at daybreak and not leave until nightfall.

Because mid-day is the hardest time to score on pheasants, the daily cycle theory is particularly tantalizing when it suggests the birds will be locatable in loafing cover around noon. Yet there are problems. First, just try defining "loafing cover," and second, just try hunting in it if you figure out what it is. Loafing cover is usually defined as a spot lying near feeding areas which features light cover. Often, it is on a south-facing slope so the birds can enjoy the late fall sun. Yet pheasants change loafing cover locations throughout the season or even day to day, so that the same rooster might loaf in a brushy fence line at one time and in a shelterbelt next to a farm at another time. A second problem is that the definition of loafing cover applies to too many areas. If the birds are spread out in all the thin cover near food during the middle of the day, they probably have so much of that kind of cover that you are not ahead by knowing that is where they are. Even more discouraging is the fact that pheasants select loafing cover with security considerations in mind. During the season they will tend to loaf in spots which cannot be approached by hunters without the birds knowing about it long in advance. It does you no good at all to know some birds are in loafing cover if you cannot hunt them there. The same thing applies to birds in feeding areas much of the time.

Another problem with the daily cycle theory is that it assumes there is a variety of habitat. When pheasants have the rare good luck of moving between thickets, groves, grain fields, grassy fields, south-facing slopes with light cover, and deep marshes, they probably will exhibit something like the classic daily movement cycle. Yet, modern farming practices have severely cramped the daily cycle. In most areas the birds will be darn lucky to have two kinds of habitat: feeding areas and security areas.

A final problem with the traditional daily cycle theory is that it has little to do with the game laws of this country. Hunting regulations often limit the usefulness of the concept. In some states the legal shooting hours start too late to let you take advantage of early morning roosting area concentrations, while in other states the shooting hours close before many roosters have returned to roosting areas.

Never forget that the point of pheasant hunting is trapping a rooster into flushing at close range. It hardly helps you to know the birds are in the loafing or feeding areas if you cannot hunt them there. No matter what the theoretical daily cycle tells you, the best approach is usually to hunt in the best cover near food, all day long. That is where you will have your best chance of finding a bird you can get up in the air at close range.

Can an awareness of the daily cycle help you? Sure. If the surrounding feeding areas are thick enough or small enough to be huntable, you should hit them at the peak feeding times. If you are hunting early or late in the day, when pheasants move the most, you should favor travel lane type cover (like brushy fence lines) over big, dense blocks of cover. Above all, you should be aware of the preferred roosting

Rather than strictly observing the daily cycle, hunters should hunt the best cover around. These birds were taken in an area open to public hunting. (Photo by South Dakota Game, Fish and Parks Dept.)

areas, for some exciting late-day shooting is possible when hunters close out the day by hunting in roosting spots. Few states allow pheasant hunting early enough in the morning to take advantage of roosting area concentrations then, but it is common for legal shooting to last up to that climatic late movement to roosting areas at dusk.

While you can almost ignore the daily cycle of pheasant movement, you can never ignore the importance of the seasonal cycle. There may be only one pheasant season listed in the hunting regulations, but good hunters know there are at least three different "seasons" within that season. Some would argue there are four. You need to know them.

The Opener

Depending on where you hunt, the opener might last for half a day or as long as a few weeks. This period is typified by the abundance of naive roosters in the population—birds which let you walk right up on them before they flap away. Most areas in good pheasant country see this easy hunting lasting only a day or a day and a half. In lightly hunted country you might find inexperienced cocks even past the second weekend of the season.

Hunting on the opener can be ridiculously easy, and it can be frustratingly difficult. You better know what you are doing. The problem with opening day hunting is that there are too many hunters afield. They provide lots of competition and send sportsmanship to levels lower than you will find in the rest of the year. Many people who lack the skill or will to hunt pheasants later in the year will be out on the opener, taking shots they should not, jumping fences to hunt where they do not belong, and horning in on other folks' hunts. Even if you have got exclusive rights to hunt a good farm, do not be surprised if you spend more time chasing off trespassers than chasing roosters. Public hunting areas frequently feature Coney Island crowds and a boisterous atmosphere in which safe and intelligent hunting is difficult. Unskilled hunters often think of the opener as the only time worth their efforts. Skilled hunters often think of the opener as the only time they would not be caught afield.

Weather can kill the usually easy opening day hunting. An especially heavy dew will make the usual hunting areas so wet that pheasants avoid them. More often, wet fall weather will retard the crop harvest so that standing fields pull in and keep roosters almost all day. The pheasants naturally like the security and food they find in standing cover. Hunting will be very slow in areas where much more than a third of the crops are unharvested.

Early season hunting is often best in short upland grasses, the kind of cover you would write off later as "hen cover." On opening day you can often have excellent hunting in the sort of short cover the hens would have used last spring for nesting. Sure, you can also find birds in the heavy cover, but there will be plenty of time for that later on. The opener is a nice time to hunt because you can take on short cover where it is a joy to watch your dog work.

The key to good hunting early in the year is locating places to hunt ahead of time. It is an enormous waste of precious hunting time to drive around looking for a place to work on the opening weekend. Whether you plan to hunt on public or private land on the first weekend you should make a firm decision in advance about where you'll go and show up early so you do not squander time driving when you should be hunting.

Opening weekend is a good time to work two types of cover often thought to be second-rate later in the year. Public hunting areas, though overrun with clumsy hunters, can still be excellent. Often, the trick is to wait until the first two or three hours of noisy hunting on them are over. Then start your hunt at the time most hunters are leaving. With good dogs you will do well. Roadsides are often so productive early in the year that you will not need to hunt anywhere else. If you see a bird in a ditch early in the season you have a good chance of getting him and maybe others with a relatively simple drive. Check the game laws of the state in which you are hunting, since roadside hunting is subject to very different kinds of laws.

The Middle Season

Now we come to the middle season. It features so many changes that it is tempting to divide it into two seasons: the early middle and late middle. Week by week you will find the hunting tougher as the cocks adjust to hunting pressure by inhabiting unhuntable places or acquiring escape routines which fool hunters. The middle season starts

Smarter and more elusive during middle season, roosters often hide out in timber.

right after the opener and continues right up until the arrival of the first
bitter winter weather.

Lucky is the hunter who can go afield during the week instead of
weekends, right after the opener, for he will enjoy great action. He will
find enough birds to get a few easy chances, and conditions will be
excellent for hunting a few of those roosters that provide more of a
challenge. At least in the early days of this period, you will find birds
in classic pheasant cover unless the crops are still standing. Serious
pheasant hunters treasure the early part of the middle season because
then, as at no other time, there will be the right mix of bird and hunter
populations. You can usually hunt without a lot of outsiders breaking
in to mess up your plans, yet the cover will be sufficiently birdy.

What is tough about the middle season is that the pheasants quickly
decide that avoiding hunters is the top priority in their lives. You can

just about see their skill at avoiding hunters improving day by day. By the end of this period it is easy to get the impression that every cock in the territory has been killed or chased away.

Usually, at this time of year, the pheasants will be hiding in regions of the pheasant range which have "impossible" cover. In my home state of Minnesota the cocks will often hole up in marshes so wet you would need a boat to get at them. But does that mean that roosters automatically resort to "heavy cover" in the middle season? Not at all. They just go where hunters do not go. If there is some godawful cover around, that is where they will be. But in a state like Iowa, which is blessed with plenty of birds but not much rugged cover, the birds are quickly driven away from the heaviest cover. Instead, they will slip into woodlots, plowed fields, and isolated patches of terrace cover far away from heavy weeds. In short, they go where hunters generally do not go. A typical stunt for a mid-season rooster is to spend the whole day in bare fields of picked corn; and, even if you know that is where he is, you do not have much of a chance at him. With every passing day, the roosters learn where they can go without getting harassed by hunters.

What can you do? Early in the middle season you simply hunt as well as you know how. Hit the good cover, and hit it well. But as time goes on, you will need to hunt smarter and harder. More and more you will need to do the difficult and unconventional things, for all the easy and obvious approaches will be a waste of time. Do you have permission to hunt in a gorgeous weedy draw which leads away from a country road? Great. Only now your only chance to get a rooster will be if you work it backwards, from the far end toward the road. If you are lucky the cocks will not expect that and may not have invented a good contingency plan to deal with danger coming at them from the "wrong" side.

In the middle season—especially the latter portion—you will be totally lost without the aid of a good dog. Early in the year it makes some sense to hunt with enough friends to surround the birds or block all the escape routes. But when the number of available roosters drops and the birds get smarter, you will find that large group hunting is far less efficient than hunting with small parties with experienced dogs. A good dog can turn a little cold bird scent into a hot flush often enough to make hunting good at any time of year.

If a good pheasant dog is the middle season hunter's best friend,

This stuff is typical of cover chosen by roosters after they have been pressured. You definitely need a dog here.

his best overall tactic is the classic "block the exits" maneuver. I am inclined to block the exits any time after opening day—even on opening day—yet I get fanatical about the importance of blocking when the early season shades into middle season hunting. Moreover, as time passes you need to get more subtle in your definition of "exits," for the pheasants will learn to favor the less obvious escape routes after they have been pressured a bit. Little fingers of cover which look insignificant will become the primary escape routes later in the year.

Let me offer an embarrassing example. I once set up a "perfect" trap with my friend, Bill Gallea. Bill quietly slipped into position to block the far end of a beautifully weedy ditch that Brandy and I were driving. The ditch was deep, densely weeded and surrounded by cut corn, so I was sure the cocks would have to run right at Bill. Well, they did not. Five hens and three roosters got away from us by slipping out of the ditch and running out a dinky little crease in the ground which had next to no cover in it. Yet it was enough, and since we were hunting in the third week of the season the pheasants knew what would happen if they simply ran down the big ditch to where Bill waited. My mistake was to see the cover only in its most obvious form. To my eyes it was shaped like an "I" while the pheasants knew it was a "Y." That is typical middle season pheasant behavior.

As the middle season progresses you need to keep changing the kind of cover you hunt in. With each passing week of the season the obvious cover visible from the roads will get hit so often that the pheasants will move toward farms posted against hunting, toward odd-ball cover (like a rural cemetery), and toward those small pockets of weeds hidden away from sight of the roads. Remember that weedy creek bed which was so full of birds on opening day? Late in the middle season it probably holds a hen and three cottontails. Meanwhile, there is a scruffy clump of ragweed with no more than six square feet of cover which rings an abandoned hog pen. And that bit of cover might hold three roosters at a given moment. Oh, by the way, you have to cross sixty yards of open field to get to the hog pen cover, so it is a dandy place to hunt if you get a kick out of seeing cocks flushing out of range!

In the middle season it becomes increasingly important to know individual farms and the behavior of particular roosters. If you have never set foot on a farm before you will probably hunt in all the obvious places—the places cleaned out by those who preceded you. It really helps to know the cute tricks preferred by roosters in a particular area, for pheasants are birds of habit who will keep resorting to tactics which worked for them before. When you know what they will do you can prepare countermeasures and, more likely than not, get tricked in a new way. But that is middle season hunting.

One consequence of the nature of middle and late season hunting is that nonresidents do badly. It is not enough to be a good pheasant hunter now; that is less important than who you know, because good hunting late in the middle season is almost always hunting in places others have not been allowed to work. One smart approach is to hunt only on private land which is heavily posted against hunting—having politely asked permission first, of course—because many hunters shy away from farms plastered with "No Hunting" signs. Usually those signs are there just to discourage trespassing. Nothing is more valuable at this time of year than having the right local connections to get on land which has not been worked hard.

I can recall such a place. It is posted, although from the road it shows as much cover as you would find in a tray of kitty litter. Yet the place has a hidden bit of cover on its back side: a steep weedy hillside and several thickly weeded ditches. This place gets better and better as the season progresses because it picks up roosters from the heavily hunted adjacent lands.

The Late Season

Finally we come to the late season. It is special. Most of what I have read about late season pheasant hunting has actually referred to what I would call the tag end of the middle season. There is reason to insist on the distinction, for winter weather changes bird behavior and improves your chances of getting some shooting. Remember that the middle season is defined as the time when roosters put avoiding hunters at the top of their list of priorities. In the true late season, however, the onset of bone-chilling cold weather will force the birds to alter their priorities and concentrate on keeping warm.

Late in the year you will be hunting the same shrewd, resourceful rooster who made you look silly a couple weeks ago. And what a bird this is! A late season cock pheasant has more tricks up his sleeve than a fifteen-year veteran NFL quarterback. Quite often he will be the bird smart enough or lucky enough to find a piece of cover which cannot be approached secretly. Late in the year even the young of the year roosters are sporting long tails and are as elusive as a Confederate light cavalry unit late in the Civil War. Every such rooster you bag is a trophy.

The unpleasant, unavoidable truth about late season hunting is that it is cold. If it is not cold, your odds of scoring are even worse, for that puts you right back into an extremely late middle season situation—the hardest hunting of all. So you must hunt in cold weather—sub-zero weather if at all possible. Yet if cold weather is your ally, it has its drawbacks. Every additional insulating layer of clothing you put on also insulates you against good contact with your shotgun.

Another element of late season hunting is snow. We will discuss it more later on. For now it is enough to know that snow is a mixed blessing. Plowing through high drifts of snow is hard work—almost as hard as slogging over a semifrozen plowed field with a light skiff of snow melting on top. I have had many occasions to regret the way snow slowed down hunters at critical moments. Yet snow has its benefits and its fans. A fresh snow can be a joy to hunt in. Even dogless hunters can tell what the birds are up to, and the pheasants may be reluctant to move much in snow.

To hunt pheasants late in the year you must find those rare concentrations of roosters. Often, birds return to the heavy cover they deserted earlier in the year. While they can run circles around hunters in such thin cover as woodlots, they cannot get shelter from the cruel winds in the trees. So late season birds like densely textured cover, things like thick ragweed stands, cattails, bullrushes, plum thickets with underlying grass, canary grass, and phragmites. Sorghum is excellent winter cover if it has not been cut. The birds will favor dense cover in low-lying areas which do not take the full force of the winds whipping in from the northwest.

To flush birds late in the season you must hunt long and hard. Block all the exits and take special pains to move quietly. In extremely bitter weather you may need to urge the dogs to work cautiously, for the pheasants will often sit tight with their feathers clamped against their bodies in a way that prevents scent from spreading. Remember that late season birds are usually bunched up, often grouped by sex. You can hunt almost all day, and then the next foot you put down can put a day's limit of roosters in the air at once—usually out of range!

It is too easy to get the impression that earlier hunters wiped out the pheasant population, yet in most areas the country will carry almost half as many birds as it did on opening day when hunting seemed so easy.

By and large, late season hunting is a matter of long hours for short wages—*if* you think a pheasant is just a pheasant. But I am one who loves chasing a dog through the drifts of December with a shotgun and a runny nose. I get more satisfaction from a late season cock than from three opening day birds. And on those rare days when you stumble home with a limit of late season pheasants, you will have drunk deeply from one of the sweetest cups of pleasure known to hunters.

7

Weather Factors

For better or worse, weather has a major impact on pheasants, pheasant hunters, and pheasant hunting. Though it will be different depending on time and place, there is good and bad pheasant hunting weather. Often bad weather is good, if you are a serious hunter. Too often, the modern pheasant hunter does not get to pick his weather, for he must make do with what the red gods provide when he makes a major trip. When you hunt in bad weather you might enjoy blowing a little steam with some heart-felt cussing, but it does more good in the long run to make some sensible adaptations in your hunting.

Temperature

Heat is rarely a problem. Pheasant seasons are usually set at times of the year when keeping warm is more of a problem than keeping cool. But not always. South Dakota's season, as one example, falls early enough that sweltering heat on the opener is common. Hunting in heat quickly exhausts dogs and hunters alike. More troublesome is the threat of dehydration. Carry plenty of water for your dogs and yourself. You might even need to carry water—heavy though it is—into the field. Some hunters have learned to take a big drink before setting off on a hunt even though they are not thirsty at the time.

Cold air temperatures, or their absence, make a big difference late in the year. As I just noted in my discussion of late season hunting, bitter weather will concentrate birds in warm, dense vegetation. Conversely, a late winter warm spell is just as deadly to late season hunting as it is to your kids' front lawn snowman.

Humidity and Rain

Humidity levels make or break the hunting for those of us with dogs. We humans seem to have only a primitive grasp of the tricky phenomenon of scent. It is at least clear that some humidity is necessary to make scenting birds possible. Extremely dry air can nearly cancel a dog's sense of smell. My records back this up. There was a severe drought in the Midwest a few years ago. Brandy's effectiveness fell off by about 50 percent that year. Worse, she lost several cripples she would have come up with in a normal year. By working hard in heavy cover Brandy still managed to put up birds for me, yet she acted like a dog whose nose had been surgically removed. About all I could do was make a special effort to pounce on potential cripples because I knew the dog would not do the job unaided.

Rain, a special form of humidity, used to make me miserable until I learned how to adjust to it. Light rains are no problem for dogs or men. You get damp, sure, but that is part of the sport. But heavy, sustained rains are another story. I have yet to hear of the clothing that will keep an active hunter dry then. Yet, the real problem is the effect of rain on the birds. They seem to disappear. When you are manfully struggling in a deluge to salvage a trip, it just adds insult to injury when all the birdy cover you hit is empty.

Pheasants, you see, do not like getting wet. Their long legs and plumage offer protection against light rains, but extended and heavy showers will soak the cover so badly that the birds are forced to change habits. Pheasants with badly soaked feathers can barely get airborne. When you consider how wet your legs get from walking in grassy weeds after a rain you can understand a pheasant's problems. Cover like that transfers water to the birds' bodies, so they move. If you hunt typical cover in a heavy rain you are working just the kind of cover the pheasants desert at such times.

Where do they go? During a rain, every pheasant tries hard to huddle under some kind of overhead protection. That often means they get under trees. Exactly where they go, of course, depends on what their surroundings offer as umbrella cover. Willow stands, honeysuckle hedges, conifers, farm groves, windfallen trees, shelterbelts, dense briar patches, scrub oaks along railways, and even such tall weeds as phragmites can give the birds a bit of relief from the rain.

Since the pheasants will be tightly concentrated in shelter and unwilling to leave it, rainy day hunting can be fast enough to make up for its discomfort. The shots are typically short and easy, though pheasants flying through timber are as tricky to hit as grouse in similar places. The best way to hunt these birds is with a flushing dog which is held at heel until the guns are in position around the umbrella cover. Then the dog is turned loose to stir up the indignant pheasants. Smart hunters learn the spots which offer overhead cover and work only these places. They waste no time on any cover lying in between.

Wind

High winds can be disastrous to a pheasant hunt, and there are no nifty solutions for hunting in a gale. Wind hurts you in several ways. Gusty winds knock the bird scent around so much that the best dogs can lose self-control when they know they are near birds they cannot pin down with scent. Under these circumstances even veteran dogs can go bonkers. Hunters have their problems, too. When a rooster gets up in a wind it will quickly hit speeds most pheasant hunters are not used to, and it can be hard to swing a shotgun fast enough to catch up with a windblown cock. When I hunt in high winds I constantly coach myself to get the gun ahead of the next bird to jump. Then up will come a rooster with flames trailing from its feathers and I will punch two holes in the airspace he has just vacated as he rides the jetstreams to security.

The worst feature of wind is the way it makes pheasants spooky. A good friend recently saw opening day pheasants that looked like shell-shocked veterans, all because of bad winds. Last season I was

It is important in rainy weather to wear not only water repellent outerwear, but lightweight, well-ventilated gear as well. (Photo by Gary Clancy)

flabbergasted to find even the hens so skittish they would dash madly through dense cover before flushing out of range. Pheasants ordinarily hear extremely well, and so they count on their hearing to keep out of predators' jaws. When high winds toss the vegetation about, pheasants know they cannot hear approaching danger. They lose faith in sitting tight or sneaking, so they trust their speed instead.

You can adjust in three ways. First, make every effort to hunt silently. You have to make some noise, but use hand signals instead of curses to control your dog and cut out any unnecessary chatter. Second, hunt the wind-sheltered areas. Low-lying cover like deep ditches will attract birds because the wind does not assault such places nearly as hard. A secretive hunter once told me he did well in windy weather by hunting the extreme downwind edge of standing corn.

Sounds good, doesn't it? Then he added that there was more to his technique than that, but he had already told me more than he wanted to!

The single most important adjustment to bad wind is to hunt into the wind. Now it does not take a genius to see that if you hunt upwind all day you will end up with a mighty long walk back to the car, so compromises must be made. In any hunting country there will be some spots which are far more promising than others. Save those for the upwind work, and come downwind in less promising cover. You will get closer to pheasants when working against the wind because they will not hear you coming as well. Forcing the birds into the wind also puts them at a disadvantage on the flush. They will either have to buck the breezes as they fly straight away from you, or they will turn to go with the wind and come back near you for a close shot. If you must hunt crosswise to the wind it is smart to put the best shooter on the downwind side where the roosters typically go.

Snow

We have briefly mentioned that snow can help or hurt pheasant hunters. I am convinced the birds realize they are easily seen when running in snowy cover. When you hunt old snow which is packed down, that awareness can make cocks wilder than they would otherwise be. But a fresh snow encourages them to sit tight. In very cold weather after a good snow you can find birds literally buried under the mantle of snow like winter grouse. When you step into a winter concentration of roosters hiding under the snow you better have a sound heart.

Dogless hunters get a big thrill out of trailing pheasants in fresh snow. It is not necessarily easy, for a few birds can lay down a lot of tracks in a short time, but we all hunt better when we at least know by fresh tracks that there are birds nearby. Often you can identify the tracks of roosters because their tails will leave distinctive drag marks in fresh snow. Fresh snow also eliminates cripple losses. By watching for the tracks of other hunters you can save yourself the futility of hunting right behind another party.

Yet, I am not overly enthusiastic about snow. As a hunter who works with dogs, I feel that snow does not help me trail birds at all. In fact, snow slows me down, makes me work harder, and does nothing to increase my comfort. The right combination of snow and air tem-

Snow enables dogless hunters to trail birds. In this case, the absence of tail drag marks suggests the bird is a hen.

peratures also causes painful ice balls to build up between the pads of many hunting dogs' feet.

Still, snow changes the game, adds beauty to the landscape, and makes the hunt more interesting. If you have never hunted with a good dog you can begin to see what you have missed by hunting after a fresh snowfall.

8

The Bird's Environment

The average hunter walks about with eyes five feet above the ground. The average rooster walks about with eyes which are about a foot above the ground. The birds see cover differently because of that, as you will quickly find out by flopping down on your belly in heavy pheasant cover. It changes the perspective considerably.

Understanding Cover

It also changes your perspective if you live in the cover all year, as a pheasant does, rather than visiting it briefly for a few hours each fall. A rooster not only lives in his cover, he stays alive by knowing it in intimate detail. He knows just where one vegetation type shades into another. He knows where a clump of horseweed has a little projection which leads away from the center of the cover. He knows where the wet spots are and where the texture of the cover is favorable for keeping his rump warm on a nasty winter day. A pheasant knows his cover well or he does not last long in the pheasant business!

If you, too, lived close to the ground and in complete dependence on your surroundings you would be extremely aware of the stem density of different cover types. The texture, or stem density, of different cover types varies considerably. Pheasants get the greatest warmth from leafy vegetation with high stem density. Other cover types, such as ragweed or willow clumps, are great security cover but worthless to a cold rooster. He needs cover which will cut the wind and trap his body warmth around him. At other times of the year he will favor cover with different characteristics, depending on what is most threatening in his environment.

Hunters rarely see cover as a pheasant sees it. The birds, I am sure, would get a big giggle out of hearing us talk about their environment. Most hunters can deal with two notions of cover: it is "heavy" or it is "light." What they mean by heavy is that they find it unpleasant to walk in. For example, since hunters find walking in alder tangles a wretched experience they will call alders "heavy" cover. But down where the pheasants walk, alders are seen as predator-repellent but rather open areas. If those alders arch over a well-developed understory of grass, the cover will be seen by the pheasants in an entirely different way, though any hunter walking there will just notice how miserable it is to have branches forever in his face.

I have heard that Eskimos have seventeen different words for "snow." They live so closely with the white stuff that they have entirely different names for what you and I would see as slightly different versions of the same thing. I suspect that what you and I call pheasant cover is a complex world for which the pheasants have at least seventeen names. We cannot entirely succeed at seeing cover the way they do, though it sure helps to try.

Fortunately, there is another way of looking at pheasant cover which we can all understand and which will help our hunting. Since our eyes are five feet above ground, we can see the shape of the cover.

They say that the grand old game of chess was invented to duplicate the intricate strategic encounters of armies on the field. As pieces move about the board and chessmen are eliminated, each player continually develops new strategies in order to checkmate his opponent's king. Pheasant hunting is like that. Like a chess player, the pheasant hunter

This cover is difficult for a hunter to walk through, but relatively easy at pheasant-level.

continually evolves new strategies as he moves through cover, always trying to think several moves ahead.

To be sure, there are interesting differences. In chess both parties can see each other's moves, while in pheasant hunting you must proceed on the basis of assumptions you make about the moves of your unseen quarry. But another major difference is that there is no standard "board" on which the game of pheasant hunting is played. Pheasant cover comes in all shapes and sizes, and each has its own impact on your strategy. Things get more complex and fun when one type of cover melds into another type.

Strip Cover

The easiest cover to work is what I call strip cover. Any cover which is long and thin and proportioned like a ribbon qualifies as strip cover. Examples include drainage ditches, long grassy terraces, draws choked with plum thickets, long grassy terraces, corn or sorghum cut in strips, creek beds, waterways, some narrow railroad sidings, and brushy fence lines. The distinctive quality of strip cover is that it is so narrow the pheasants in it cannot slip around you. That removes one of the pheasant's favorite evasive maneuvers, so birds in strip cover will resort to the other tricks in their repertoire. Do not forget this. Since the birds know they cannot outflank you they are all the more likely to run wildly or sit tight to let you rush by.

Strip cover is easily worked by small parties and it is the best cover for the lone or dogless hunter. Depending on the width and thickness of cover, a strip can be worked by from one to four hunters. Unless you think the birds will sit tight, as they will on the opener or during some weather conditions, you should always divide the party and put a blocker at the end of the strip cover. The two big mistakes made by hunters in strip cover are working too fast and failing to block the end of the cover.

I especially enjoy one moment when hunting strip cover alone, a time I think of as "the moment of truth." With no blocker to turn back

When walking strip cover, it is important to work steadily and, if possible, to block both ends.

the birds from the end of the cover, the most critical moment in a strip cover drive is when you are 80 to 40 yards from the end of the cover. You can assume the birds have been sneaking ahead of you as you walked the strip. When you are near the end of the cover but still out of gun range, any flushing bird is lost. But if you cross that all-important stretch from 80 to 40 yards from the end without the birds coming up, you know that either there are no pheasants ahead of you or that you have got them trapped within gun range.

Block Cover

Cover lying in large blocks is the hardest to work because the pheasants have unlimited mobility. Typical examples include wildlife management areas, cornfields, marshes, large weed fields, and big timber stands. The twin challenges of block cover are first, finding a rooster in all that cover, and then trying to trap it into a close range flush when it has an unlimited range of escape routes in the continuous cover.

To find the pheasants, it helps to look for different types of cover within the overall cover. The birds will not often be found randomly spread in large blocks of cover, though until you get out there and start hoofing through the weeds, you will not guess which areas the birds are favoring. For example, in large management areas you often find birds concentrated in draws, in willow stands, and in patches of cattails surrounded by other weeds. It is smart, too, to hunt the perimeter of block cover, especially edges which border on feeding areas.

Dogs really shine in block cover. Since dogless hunters do so badly here, hunters with dogs can get action by specializing in the kind of cover which holds birds but repels hunters. Since any hunter can handle strip cover, it only makes sense for hunters with canine assistance to concentrate on cover unhuntable by most groups without dogs.

You can hunt block cover without dogs if you work with large or even small party drives. Small party drives involve several hunters ambling along, usually with lots of stop-and-go action; they try to drive the birds away from the center of the cover toward the margins where flushes will more likely come. In heavy block cover it does not often pay to split the party into blockers and drivers since the pheasants will just squirt out the sides of the drive anyway. In cornfields, the most common block cover hunting situation, it works well to split the party

Dogs in block cover compensate for the pheasants' increased mobility.

into drivers and blockers since the birds naturally run the length of the planted rows.

Patch Cover

Patch cover, the third type, is any clump of cover standing by itself. It ranges from tiny patches of grass surrounded by fall-plowed fields to big shelterbelts. Other examples include grassy terraces in the middle of cut corn, stands of willows or alders, odd weedy corners farmers cannot get their machinery into, brush piles left after clearing operations, clumps of snowberry standing in sparse prairie vegetation, or some abandoned farm structure such as a delapidated windmill which has some weeds at its base. Any isolated patch of cover up to about half an acre fits my definition; anything much larger should be considered block cover. Put another way, patch cover is cover your party can comfortably surround.

A bird caught in an isolated patch of cover would seem to be easy to bag since he is trapped in a small area with no escape route but the skies. Since that is so, however, hunters get sloppy and pheasants get tricky.

Hunters often blow chances by strolling up to patch cover casually, intending to split up to work it once they get there. Since the birds know they are caught in an isolated spot, though, they will often rocket wildly out the back side of the patch if you are not careful. The proper approach to patch cover is to have the party split before getting near it. Then each hunter comes in toward the patch from a different direction, converging at the same time. If you are too lazy to do this you will get plenty of chances to ask, "Was that a rooster or a hen?" as birds flush wildly ahead of you.

A bird trapped in a patch will either elect to sit tight or try to slip out by some small outlet. The tight sitters will sit amazingly tight. Many of those stories we all know of birds that would hardly flush even when kicked involved patch cover situations where the rooster knew he couldn't escape unseen. Expect the birds to run or fly from patch cover by going as far as possible along any odd corner or projection from the patch.

Hunting Pressure

The most distinctive quality of modern pheasant hunting is that fewer birds are subjected to more pressure. Birds that don't respond to that pressure intelligently end up stuffed with apples on a bed of wild rice. Hunters who do not respond to hunting pressure intelligently end up buying their roosters from commercial game farms.

But what is hunting pressure? Well, you have seen its effects when you hunt hard all day in order to flush nineteen hens with nary a rooster. Or when you find that half the roosters you take in tough cover turn out to be cripples left by other parties. Or when the normally docile hen birds run madly ahead of you to flush a hundred yards ahead of the guns. Or when you see forty cocks in a weekend of heavy hunting, and none of them are in range. I have seen all that and more. This is the result of hunting pressure.

Through the heart of the pheasant season, hunting pressure is the dominant influence on the behavior of pheasants. The benign fall weather puts no pressure on them, and food is more abundant than at any other time in their lives. The only problem a fall pheasant has is the intrusion of hunters. They are free to concentrate totally on keeping out of shotgun range, which they do very nicely. In the most heavily pounded areas, one cock in four survives to enjoy a busy spring love life, and in most areas the harvest is well below that. As pheasants are exposed to more hunting pressure they get smarter, while their ranks are thinned. Soon the law of diminishing returns sends most hunters to their homes to do their "hunting" by the fireside. A typical late season situation might see you hunting when a little more than a third of the opening day rooster population is remaining. That would seem to say you need to hunt three times as hard now as you did on opening day; but the unhappy truth is you will need to hunt six or ten times as hard.

That, again, is because of hunting pressure. After the first two weekends of shooting most of the hunting pressure drops off and relatively few birds are harvested in the following weeks. The real difference between early and late season hunting is not so much how many cocks are alive as how smart the surviving birds are. Any rooster which survives the first week or two of hunting becomes supremely difficult to hunt. Those roosters adapt to hunting pressure far better than most hunters do.

This, I am convinced, is why you hear so much about the "new genetic strain" of ringneck, that superbird which refuses to fly and loves to run embarrassing circles around hunters. People who argue that we have created a damn near unhuntable superbird will tell astonishing stories of how roosters have outsmarted them and their dogs. But listen carefully, and you will soon note that they all deal with late season roosters, birds which have survived their initial trial by gunfire early in the season. If today's pheasant were truly genetically different, we would see astonishingly deceptive behavior on opening day. But we do not. The simple truth is that today's infamous superpheasants are just canny roosters who have learned how to make fools of hunters. Rather than giving false credit to man for having altered the birds' genetic makeup, let's credit the pheasants for their amazing ability to learn how to beat humans at a game humans invented.

Because I have so much respect for the roosters who have managed to survive several encounters with other hunters, my advice on hunt-

This "superbird" is evading a hunter in what might be termed "heavy" cover. (Photo by Minnesota Department of Natural Resources)

ing them is this: do not try it! That is, the best way to get around the difficulty of hunting highly experienced cocks is to not attempt it. Never underestimate the ability of a smart rooster to beat excellent dog work and superior hunting skills. When you hunt in an area which has been pounded by other hunters, even if you can leap buildings at a single bound and walk on water, you are going to be beaten more often than not.

"Popular" Areas and Alternatives

Modern pheasant hunters need to avoid the tendency to flock like sheep into the areas which have earned a special reputation for high bird populations. When a state enjoys a period of high bird numbers, very quickly the names of the three or four towns will become national catchwords for easy pheasant hunting. Soon hunters will be pulled in like moths to a flame. Perhaps some outdoor writer will be treated to an impressively easy hunt (often on opening day, on a farm carefully selected by local contacts eager to publicize their good hunting), and so he will write a glowing report on the marvelous hunting around Birdville. Soon hordes of hunters fill the little town's cafes, big strings of dogs will be staked out behind the local motel each night, and the hardware store will be unable to get enough nonresident hunting licenses.

But there are only so many roads leading from town, and only so many farms with nice looking cover along them. Soon the landowners in the area are weary of saying either yes or no to requests to hunt, and they are far wearier of chasing off trespassers. You can bet that the public lands in the area will be combed several times a day by hunters with dogs. Any rooster left alive in the general area after a week or two of that kind of pressure will be, for all practical purposes, unhuntable.

Thus pheasant hunting meccas are ruined by the tendency (which is natural, for we have all done it) of hunters to flock to the center of the region with the best bird populations. In other words, hunter pressure concentrates on famous areas to a degree which is far out of proportion to any real superiority in preseason bird numbers. When hunting such an area early in the season you may have to fight through crowds to get your birds. Hunt them when the smoke has cleared and you only have the "superbirds" left to hunt. It is a losing proposition!

Unless you have some exclusive land lined up to hunt on, you are wiser to avoid such situations, or get out of them as soon as you find you're in them. You will be far better off hunting in country with marginal pheasant populations where the birds have been left alone after the locals took their easy early season limits. Many states publish maps showing the areas of highest pheasant populations. A smart hunter will often look for action on the fringes of the areas marked as best rather than following the crowds to the regions with the glamorous reputations.

Hunters who live fairly close to the good hunting enjoy the advantage of being able to cultivate relationships with landowners so they can hunt on lands where other hunters are forbidden to go. Even better, they can often learn about small areas where birds are abundant even though they are surrounded by poor hunting country. These small pockets of bird abundance can be created by the vagaries of weather or changing farming practices. A friend of mine used to scout out new areas to hunt by talking to a fellow who did a lot of hay harvesting, and he would often know where a surprising number of pheasants were being seen in a region not known for good hunting. A bonus enjoyed by those who hunt such areas is that few hunters with dogs will have worked them early in the year. That's a great way to surprise those roosters who have learned they can sit tight and watch hunters stride past them.

Midweek hunting is the simplest and one of the most effective adjustments you can make to hunting pressure problems. If you can hunt only on weekends you naturally will find yourself more frequently in competition with other groups. Landowners will be less receptive to requests to hunt if they have been approached recently, and on Sunday you might find it difficult to get permission to hunt on private land since some farmers like to go visiting on that day and some others disapprove of Sunday hunting. But the biggest problem with weekend hunting is the effect of the pressure on the birds. When armies of canvas-clad hunters hit the fields Saturday morning the birds are quick to sense it. Already wild pheasants become paranoid. The very best days to hunt, if you are so lucky as to be able to choose, are Thursday and Friday, when few hunters are afield and the roosters have had a few days to calm down after the last weekend.

If worse comes to worst and you have to hunt the superbirds left after intensive pressure, there is not much to do except hunt smarter and harder. You are in luck if you can find some cover which is so disgusting to walk in that other hunters have avoided it. That will generally be a huge, thick, and very wet marsh. You may not feel very fortunate when hunting there, yet such places offer your best chances when armies of hunters have been prowling all over the easier cover.

As a desperation measure, you can hunt cover which is just the opposite. Select some private lands which look totally devoid of cover and get permission to try them. If they are near wildlife management areas, so much the better. You are apt to hear from the landowner that he has no pheasants on the place, but thank him and say you will take your chances. Farms with "no" cover, since they have not been walked by other parties, will often hold birds during the day which go elsewhere to roost when hunters have retired to the bars and motels. Try walking the shabby fencelines or almost any other little scrap of cover. Since the birds will not have experience with hunters coming at them in these poor farms they are apt to sit for a close flush. Just keep walking and checking out all that cover which appears too insignificant to hold pheasants.

When hunting hard-hit areas it pays to stay afield until shooting hours close. Many parties exhaust themselves before the legal shooting hours are over. Pheasants adjust to that, often making massive movements back into the obviously good cover in the last hour or so of shooting time. Still, your best response if you find yourself in country already walloped by hunting pressure is to move somewhere else. I have hunted where half the roosters I took were gangrenous from the encounters with other hunters' guns. I will take that sort of hunting over no hunting at all, but only if I have no other choice.

Oddly enough, hunting "no" cover works well when you are in an area with high bird populations and excessive pressure.

9

Bagging the Bird

I have read just about everything written by authorities in the past twenty-five years about shooting pheasants, and it has been a troubling experience. What they say seems true enough, with all those precise diagrams about angles and leads and so forth, but all of it is totally irrelevant to the experience as I know it. Here is my problem: the advice is always presented in rational terms; yet the actual experience of shooting a pheasant has nothing to do with conscious thought processes.

The Shooting Experience

In this sense I can say that I have never shot a pheasant. The "I" which is my mind has watched with interest as my body blazed away at a whole lot of birds. And it has been a strange experience for my mind because it is accustomed to being the boss rather than a helpless witness to what my body does. Sometimes my mind has been pleased to cheer the astonishing accomplishments of my body and sometimes (too often, in fact) it has had to shriek with frustration at my body's ineptness. No matter. Whether I hit or miss, I always end up thinking of shooting at pheasants as something which happens to me—not something I do.

All of which is great when you are hitting, and hell when you are not. You see, most of the time when we perform tasks improperly we can improve our performance by thinking things through and trying harder the next time. For better or worse, that is not true of field shooting. You can analyze and cuss and coach yourself, but when the next cock slashes his way through a tangle of horseweed and bobwire, your body is going to step forward and pop away at the bird in its preferred way, no matter what your mind thinks of it.

This is another way of saying that upland wingshooting is almost purely a conditioned reflex. I am coming around to seeing that as a blessing. Think of it: when a rooster pops up, you are presented with a highly complex trigonometric problem. The bird appears from a location you could not have guessed in advance, flies in a direction you could not guess in advance, and flies at a speed you cannot anticipate accurately. In the space of a second or two you must make a set of calculations which will allow the shot swarm to intercept the target. Then you have to execute the proper motions with nearly perfect accuracy. If you consider all these problems rationally, it would seem nearly impossible to hit a pheasant on the wing. Gee, if shooting were a complete mental act, we would never hit a bird! Yet our bodies, amazing machines that they are, do it all the time. It must not be as difficult as it seems.

The way we do "the impossible" so routinely is by building up a set of conditioned reflexes which actually do the shooting for us. By simply acquiring the habit of seeing the right relationship of bird to barrels we learn to do unthinkingly what we could never do through conscious mental processes.

Practice

That leads to a basic but terribly important observation: before you can become a competent wingshot, you must pay your dues by shooting and shooting until hitting becomes easier than missing. And

The hunter's response to a flush should be a conditioned reflex that lines up the bird in one smooth motion, aiming slightly ahead of the bird. (Photo by Jim Layton)

I have always felt it is unfair to your partners and even more unfair to the pheasants to do your practicing in the hunting fields on wild birds.

The only sensible way modern shotgunners can learn their craft is through extensive practice shooting clay targets. When field hunters scoff at clay target games as being artificial, they miss an important point. Sure, they are artificial and limited. Wild birds do not appear obediently when you holler "Pull." But by eliminating some aspects of the field shooting situation, clay target games allow you to concentrate on others and learn them faster. The real beauty of trap and skeet is that they dismiss several complicating factors, and force you to concentrate on developing a sweet swing and the ability to lead moving targets.

We need not debate the relative value of trap versus skeet as practice for pheasant hunters. Both are extremely valuable. Skeet field shots are more like early season shooting, while trap fields duplicate the type of shooting you will often get on later season roosters. You are not a competent wingshot until you master all the shots these games offer. I used to grumble about the coming-right-at-you Station 8 skeet shots because no good hunter would blast a bird that way. One reason for my grousing, of course, was that I could not hit those targets. So I practiced, once or twice shooting an entire round of twenty-five birds from Station 8. Since then I have often blessed those hours of practice, for several times each season I get shots at incoming roosters. Ironically, that is now my favorite shot, and I believe I have missed only one "Station 8" rooster in twenty-five years of hunting.

How much practice is enough? Let's say you should practice both clay target games until you attain a basic level of competence, defined as the ability to consistently hit twenty-two or twenty-three of twenty-five targets thrown. You are a pretty fair shot when you can do that. To get practice mounting your gun you can call for your birds with your gun held at waist level.

Trap and skeet lack the spontaneity and variety of field shooting, so other clay target games should be part of your preparation. I highly recommend practice on "duck tower" fields. If nothing else, that offers a useful lesson in humility. I love friendly sessions of banging away at hand-thrown clay targets. If you try to make your buddies look bad by throwing difficult targets they are sure to return the favor. And everyone will be a better shot for the experience. An advanced form of practice is shooting barnyard pigeons. You even get to practice your skills at asking permission to shoot on someone's private property.

Mental Factors

As important as practice is, it is not the only factor separating good pheasant shots from bum shots. There are some subtle things beyond basic wingshooting competence which we should also mention. They are mostly acquired from actual hunting experience.

The outstanding pheasant shooter always has a highly developed sense of anticipation, so he is rarely caught totally flat-footed when a rooster flushes. You will only start to recognize those critical moments by doing a lot of pheasant hunting, though it also helps if you are exceptionally keen to get some action. For example, experienced hunters automatically know the chance of getting a flush is high when they draw near the end of good cover. Those who hunt with dogs also learn to "read the dog" so they are mentally prepared for action before it breaks.

Beyond anticipation, you should sometimes take some action to be in position to shoot. Have you ever had the experience of hunting with someone who seemed to have all the "luck" because he was always at the right place to get shots on flushing roosters? Chances are he made his own luck by doing a little quick moving just before a flush. For example, you should never let yourself be caught in a low spot when a flush is likely. Get up high as quickly as you can so you can command a wider field of fire. Similarly, never let yourself get trapped in entangling, screening brush at critical moments. If the dogs are birdy, get out of there immediately so you can see what is happening and swing a gun.

The best pheasant shots, in other words, have a certain amount of aggressiveness. While the sport has finesse, particularly in the area of field strategy, there is a certain rough and tumble side to pheasant hunting. The faint of heart and the unsure will not find hunting roosters their natural sport, while the fellow with a little bit of wildness in his soul will be more at home hunting this very wild bird. I am not endorsing unsafe or inconsiderate hunting practices here, just noting that the best pheasant shots I have seen in action all enjoyed those moments when it was important to seize the opportunity and take decisive action. That aggressiveness carries over to the actual shot. You must swing aggressively to shoot well on roosters. Do not ever think in terms of "shooting at" a pheasant: tell yourself you have got to hit the bird as hard as possible.

In spite of the need for aggressiveness just described, there is a critical split second in pheasant shooting during which you should clear your mind and concentrate calmly on the shot. Several great shotgun artists have written about a slight delay in the act of shooting: a tiny moment during which they blotted out everything else from mind and focussed totally on the shot. I hunted for almost twenty years before I gained enough composure during the shot to know what they meant. In this brief moment the mind gets its last chance to tell the body what it must do and assure it that a careful shot will bring the bird down cleanly. In my case it seems as if a little voice were saying, "You've got this bird!" or "Long shot—better lead it!" Wouldn't you know—just when I gained this small bit of conscious control and calmness while shooting, I began to swing the gun tentatively and commenced to fringe-hit some birds. Composure and aggression must be balanced.

Anything which causes you to falter during the mount and swing will cause a miss. Several times I have flushed wet-feathered roosters which thrashed along so laboriously I took them to be cripples who might fall at any second. Such a slow bird would seem to be too easy a shot to miss, yet that flash of doubt is enough to disrupt the fluid motion of the mount and swing. Or if you are in the act of shooting when a ghost of doubt about the sex of the bird crosses your mind, the result is often a weak swing and a miss.

Sex Discrimination

Other writers describe the identifying of the sex of a pheasant as an easier matter than I find it to be. Sure, it is often overwhelmingly apparent that you are looking at a rooster or a hen. But when you jump a bird in dim or flat light; when a bird flies right at the sun; and especially when a bird flushes at the outer edge of shotgun range and flies absolutely straight away; it is damned difficult to identify. I have had more than my share of frustration late in the season when long hours of hiking resulted in long range flushes from birds which flew so directly away from me that I could see neither their profile nor the white ring. Because of this problem you should try to approach key spots of cover with the sun at your back.

Always try to spot that white ring. If you try to judge the sex of a pheasant by looking for long tail feathers you will shoot some long-tailed hens and hold fire on some roosters with shabby tails. More to the point, you will be looking at the wrong end of the bird. Half a rooster's body length in the air is just tail feathers. If you look at tail feathers you will shoot tail feathers, and tail feathers make disappointing table fare. Look for that bright white ring. That is your sex key, and that is your target. I do not care how "slow" a rooster is supposed to be: almost nobody misses them by shooting too far ahead.

When a rooster flushes you must make a quick, terribly important decision. Do you shoot or hold fire? Many factors must be weighed in a split-second, even as your body begins to move into the shot. The most crucial decision is whether or not the shot is safe: whether you might possibly hit people, dogs, or property with the shot. Simultaneously, you must judge whether the bird is in range. That is not as simple as it seems. Experience has taught me I can responsibly shoot at roosters which are quite far away if they are crossing my path, while shots at straight-away flushers at the same ranges would be irresponsible. Straight-away birds present the smallest possible target, and your shot must carry through the greatest amount of feathery armor and body tissue before hitting a vital area. Long range straight-away or gently angling birds account for a high percentage of the gut-shot, broken leg cripples which are not brought to bag.

Before shooting you must also consider the nature of the cover. It will be ethical to attempt some difficult shots if the bird will drop in open country, while the same shots would be irresponsible if you are hunting in a thick marsh where a cripple could easily escape. A fresh snow will make a slightly questionable shot more appropriate. But

It is often impossible to distinguish sex of straight-away birds like this.

never take a tough shot if there's a good chance of it resulting in a running cripple. The birds deserve more consideration than that.

I frankly do not understand how all these complex considerations can be dealt with in the space of a second or two—while cocks are hammering the air with their wings and a hunter's heart is banging at triple-time speed. While I do not enjoy killing pheasants (I actually dislike that part of the hunt, to tell the truth) I always feel privileged to participate in a miracle when a tough shot brings a rooster down cleanly.

Doubles

These difficulties, plus the generally low number of birds these days, make getting an honest double an exceptionally memorable feat for the modern pheasant hunter. To shoot a double you have to maintain fierce concentration and shoot the first bird before you allow yourself to think about any others. In one season I passed by chances on two potential doubles because in each case there was a good chance the second bird would have been a lost cripple. Once, two cocks came up thirty-five yards away from some brushy timber. Since Brandy cannot trail two crippled birds at once in bad cover like that, I settled for shooting one bird. The second situation was more unusual. Two roosters jumped up about thirty yards ahead of me. They came from some high grass on a steep slope that fell away toward a swiftly moving South Dakota river which emptied into the mighty Missouri. I got a solid hit on the first bird and had the second bird covered, when I realized it would drop into the river. With Brandy already chasing the first bird, I did not relish the prospect of watching helplessly as the second rooster floated rapidly off toward Nebraska, so once again I did not shoot.

In my last season I had the rare good fortune of shooting two doubles. The first was that classic and improbable event: a perfect set-up with two cocks up and flying near each other in close range. The second was rather different. I was hunting around a shelter belt which was stiff with pheasants. The shooting was so frenzied that one of my buddies burned his fingers on the hot barrel of his pump. I was standing at the end of the trees when I saw a rooster flying toward me from the back side. He was on a course which would take him past me out of range, yet he was floating along slowly just a few feet over the weeds.

Doubles should not be attempted unless the cover is short as it is here. (Photo by Gene Kroupa)

Suddenly it came to me that, though he surely saw me, I had a chance to get in range if he continued to float along so slowly. So I took off as fast as I could to reduce the distance between us, running mostly parallel with him but cutting the angle a little bit all the time. When he suddenly dropped into the high grass I never slowed up. Just as I hit the spot where he had come down, I heard a bird flushing behind me while my rooster was coming up in front of me. I put my pattern right on the white ring of the first rooster, then turned to see what was behind me. It was another rooster flying directly away from the direction the first had taken; a slightly long shot dropped him too. A hunter remembers such moments as long as he remembers anything.

Cleaning and Freezing

The pheasant is as noble a bird on the table as in the field—which is all the praise any wild game needs. Not too gamey for delicate palates, the pheasant still retains an agreeably wild tang which never lets you forget what sort of bird it was in life. Those who hunt pheasants owe it to this bird to treat it with as much respect after the shot as before.

Fortunately, caring for pheasants after the kill is not difficult; in spite of that fact you will sometimes hear that extreme measures need be taken to avoid spoiling the meat. Some folks will say a bird must be gutted right after being shot. Others regard any cleaning except painstaking plucking as a sacrilege. Under most circumstances you will not find extremely fastidious measures necessary. The delicious taste of pheasant meat is not as easily lost as you might have been told.

Probably the most useful thing you can do, other than quickly gutting the birds, is to cool them down as quickly as possible and keep them cold until they are finally cleaned and prepared for the table or the freezer. This is no problem in the chilly weather that prevails during pheasant season in most places. In warm weather you may want to travel with an ice chest. Pop the birds into plastic garbage bags to keep them dry, then ice them. I have kept pheasants for five days this way with no loss of table quality. When hunting in bitter weather a different problem presents itself. On those occasions I like to gut the birds, but I leave them in their feathers to prevent premature freezing.

Gutting birds quickly also helps to cool them, and it may reduce the chance of intestinal acids tainting the meat. I usually wait until a slow moment in the hunt before gutting birds, and I have not been bothered by tainted meat. If you know you have hit a bird badly in the abdomen, you should clean it as soon as possible. My experience with so-called bird hooks for pulling out intestines has been disappointing. It is no trick to open up the stomach just below the breast and pull the entrails out. As a matter of courtesy, if you pluck or gut your birds in the field you should do it where the remains will not be seen by others.

No hunter should feel like a barbarian if he skins his birds out instead of plucking them. Badly hit roosters are all but impossible to pluck anyway. Either process will yield a superb table bird, and skinning is undeniably more convenient. The easiest time to pluck a bird is in the field shortly after the kill when the feathers are still loose. If you must pluck your birds later it helps to douse them in scalding hot water first. But a skinned pheasant tastes as good as a plucked one to me. The main consideration is that you need the skin on for certain recipes, principally roasting recipes. Compared with domestic chickens or wild ducks, there is relatively little fat near the skin of a pheasant and you consequently lose little taste when you sacrifice the skin. Of course, others disagree. Suit yourself. When I clean a bird which has been lightly shot, I will often decide to pluck it just to permit variety on the table. But I skin most of my birds, and they are delicious.

To clean pheasants you should have a very sharp knife, a shot digging tool, and either a pair of poultry shears or the pruning shears gardeners use for trimming shrubbery. The shears are much faster and more convenient for some operations than a knife.

Put the bird on its back, tail toward you. Rip the skin up toward the head to bare the breast, starting down near the vent. Then catch a fold of skin, and slip it down over first one leg, then the other, turning the skin inside out the way you would take off a dress glove. When the skin is turned down over the legs as far as it will go, snap through the legs right below the skin with the shears. Next, you rotate each leg outward in its socket as if the bird were "doing the split" until the hip joints pop. You can then easily separate the legs from the body with your knife.

Now go back to the breast, pulling skin away from it until the meat is exposed all the way to the wing "shoulder" joints. Using your knife, cut along a sort of seam which joins the breast to the back, starting from the lower breast and continuing up toward the shoulder joints as far as possible. Now the breast is attached to the rest of the body only by a joint on each wing and another joint where the back attaches to the breast on each side. Go after those attachments with the shears. While you could mess around with a knife trying to find the right angle to separate those joints the job goes much quicker with the shears. Next, you pull the breast away from the back (to which the wings, head, and skin are still attached). That process produces a breast and both legs. Very little meat is wasted. The whole process up to this point should not take over ten minutes, whether or not you field dressed the birds. At this time you might want to go after the shot and cut feathers. A nail with a point you have flattened with a hammer is a dandy tool for that.

Fresh birds taste a whole lot better than frozen birds, yet freezing is often the only way to handle the pheasant pieces. When I freeze pheasants, I generally triple-bag them, putting each bird in three bags of heavy mil poly, then wrapping one or two of those packages in a tightly taped layer of heavy freezer paper. Write the date and origin of each bird along with its age ("old" or "young") on the paper before popping them in the freezer. Be sure to mark those birds you pluck so you can thaw out the right pheasant for a roasting recipe. Treated this way, I have found pheasants have kept perfectly well for months.

10

Hunting the Landscape

Basic pheasant hunting strategy must be tailored by all of us to deal with the particular hunting country we are working. The following comments might help you deal with specific ringneck hunting situations.

Draws

Draws are a classic pheasant cover found in most regions of the pheasant range. Draws are common in rolling farm land, being formed where the folds of hills come together. Usually they experience some seasonal rainwater runoff, and that often leads to a little erosion which cuts them deeper. Weeds, shrubs, and even trees are common features of draws. These birdy low areas persist as good pheasant cover in spite of intense agriculture because it is still difficult to get at them with clearing and filling machinery. Because draws typically wind right through cornfields they offer birds that combination of security near food that the birds love so much.

A big draw like this is not easy to hunt, especially if you try to keep a party together.

Small draws are strip cover and should be hunted accordingly. Remember that the birds know they cannot outflank you so they will sit extra tight (especially early in the season), or run ahead of you and flush wildly (especially later on). Place blockers at the ends of draws whenever possible and work the cover painstakingly. When small draws lead away from the main draw they should always be worked out to their very ends. Three or four hunters are an ideal number for working small draws, with a driver on each side and one or two hunters to post the end.

You will also find some whopping big draws, especially in the Dakotas. These need to be worked a little differently. Usually they occur in steeply dropping land. In spite of the natural temptation to walk draws downhill, you should hunt them uphill. The birds work better that way and give you better shots. I have not found it critically important to post the ends of these huge draws.

The large western draws also cross you up all the time with small or even sizable draws running away from the major cut. These need to be worked unless your dogs tell you they are empty. But that makes it all but impossible to keep a party together as you thread around the labyrinth of large and small draws. It generally works best to tell each hunter he is free to do a little freelancing on side draws though he should try to coordinate with the rest of the party as much as possible. Marching up these things in a neat line is just impossible.

Roadsides

Roadsides—"ditches" to many of us—sometimes offer more cover than is found in the surrounding farmlands. Pheasants make extensive use of roadsides for nesting and, early in the season, as cover which is convenient to food. Hunting pressure quickly removes most of the roosters who sit in the ditches. Because of this culling and because hunting ditches is boring, I only hunt them as a last resort. Like many other hunters I rarely set out to hunt the roadsides, though I will go back to try for a cock I've spotted while driving to my hunting grounds. I do not like road hunting, but I usually am hungry enough for a rooster to dislike driving right past one in plain sight.

Serious road hunters have worked out several strategies for getting shots on birds they have spotted, and some of them are not particularly safe or pretty. I would advise against taking the time to prepare an elaborate ambush because roosters are inclined to get bored and walk off while you scheme.

The most sporting roadside hunting involves walking the birds up with no aid from a car. In some areas you will find roadsides provide almost the only cover around. Walking miles and miles of ditches will not tax your brain, but it can be the most productive way to hunt at times. Of course, deeper ditches with heavy vegetation are better than skimpy ditches. Pheasants make much heavier use of roadsides early and late in the day. If the wind is high you will find more birds in the ditches which run at right angles to the wind.

Different states have different laws on roadside hunting, so be sure you know the regulations prevailing in the area you are hunting. Yet there are some unwritten codes you should consider. Road hunting, even when you avoid the obscenity of "ground sluicing" your birds, is a form of hunting which lowers hunters in the eyes of the general public. It looks lazy, and undeniably it tends to be dangerous because the shooting often takes place near passing vehicles and farm homes or outbuildings.

Big Management Areas

Several of the best hunters I have known have counted heavily on big management areas for their birds. You might come to feel a special satisfaction, as they have, when you bag a supersmart rooster in these jungles of heavy cover. It is also a nice feeling to be hunting land that is "yours" where you have a perfect right to hunt. If birds are easy on these areas on opening weekend, they are anything but easy later on.

The first challenge you must meet to hunt well here is handling competition and the effects of extreme pressure. These vary enormously from area to area and one time of year to another. A general pattern, though, is that the wildlife areas get pounded early in the year, with pressure dropping off rapidly as the hunting gets harder. If the birds have any alternative cover or if the weather is mild they will often roost in the management areas and spend their days on private land. Still, they do often return to the management areas at dusk, and smart hunters know that is a key time to hunt them. When cold weather arrives you are also apt to find that the pheasants return to the now quiet management areas.

It is not easy to find a rooster in a huge management area. This is a classic block cover situation. After the first few hours of the season, if you do not have a dog—or two or three—you do not have a chance of putting up a cock. A hard working one-man, one-dog team can do well late in the season because they only need to cross paths with two or three roosters to get a daily limit. Larger parties can run sweeps through the cover, but fewer birds will be seen in relation to the number of hunters.

Finding the birds in these huge areas is rarely easy. Some of the best hunters I know use the simple approach of systematically combing the cover, logging miles until a bird is found. They do not get discouraged by hours of walking with no action, for they believe that means all the birds are in the cover not yet walked. It is one of those situations where finesse is worth less than strong legs. You will often do better by walking the perimeter of the area because that way you intercept some cocks commuting between the heavy cover and the adjacent grain fields. It sometimes helps, too, to check all the distinctive bits of cover in the overall area. Creek beds, willow stands, draws, small pockets of cattails, stands of phragmites, and other different cover types are more likely to hold birds than the ocean of prevailing vegetation surrounding them. But not always.

Some smart hunters do well by hunting private lands lying right around big public hunting areas, particularly in the middle part of the season. They reason that while the birds are driven off the public lands they are reluctant to move very far (pheasants rarely stray more than a mile from their home base). Meanwhile private landowners near public areas often do not get many hunters on their land since the wide-open management areas are so near.

Note that we have not talked about hunting small management areas later in the season. It is not worth it. Small areas quickly lose their birds in the opening day fusillade, and they are not attractive enough to pull the pheasants back.

Cornfields

Pheasants are strongly identified with corn country, and hunters have traditionally keyed much of their efforts on cornfields. Since I was introduced to pheasant hunting in corn, many of my early memories of the sport are set in cornfields.

Yet today I hate to hunt in corn, and I do not generally recommend cornfields as a place for most hunters to work. You are faced with two problems. First, because modern cornfields have unwanted vegetation ruthlessly suppressed with chemical sprays, there will be little in a modern cornfield except cornstalks and bare dirt. Oh, sure, you will find the occasional weedy cornfield, but it is a rare field these days which has enough weeds to tempt a cock to sit for a close flush. When I hunted corn with my father back in the '50s we always looked for the "dirty" fields, the ones with lots of weeds close to the ground. It was common then to hunt in corn where the understory of grass, foxtail, and cocklebur was so thick that roosters would be able to hide in it. Alas, that is rarely the case these days. The second problem with corn is that it is about the worst cover type to work a dog in. The row

Corn as clean as this is rarely worth hunting. Pheasants run in this kind of field and rarely give you a flush.

structure, overall size of the fields, and lack of cover all are against you. Dogs and roosters alike see those long, naked furrows as an open racetrack. Even when most of the cocks are in the corn it might make more sense to hunt elsewhere. And many farmers refuse to let hunters stomp through their valuable unpicked corn.

Yet corn can be hunted. A moderately sized party can drive small cornfields effectively, and even if they do not get flushes in the corn they may push the birds out into areas where they can be better approached. Weedy cornfields can be hunted like any other block cover. Some harvesting methods leave plenty of broken stalks on the fields, and that can make the cut corn huntable if the birds have not been pressured too much. Some big-running pointers work well in these cut cornfields, particularly where birds have been so safe in the corn that they have no experience with hunters or dogs. Other hunters do well by hunting the perimeter of cornfields, often catching roosters in the weeds that still can be found along some fence lines.

The big drive is still the preferred way to hunt cornfields, though it takes a mighty healthy rooster population these days to make it worth while to summon up a small army. About one-half to one-third of the group will "post" or "block" the end of the field while the rest of the party pushes the birds toward them. Drivers and blockers should be spaced carefully so nearby hunters can keep track of each other and so no birds slip between them. Intervals of from ten to twelve yards are common, though clean or dirty corn might call for adjustments either way. If your party is too small to cover the whole field—which is the usual case—you will need to execute a series of sweeps. On these sweeps the idea is to force the birds forward to the blockers or sideways into the unhunted portion of the field where later sweeps will pick them up. You do not want them to squat down to watch the drivers sail by, and you do not want them drifting into the hunted portion of the field where you are not going to see them again. Thus the drivers

A classic large-party drive. Note how the line has sagged in a big "U" to keep the birds from outflanking the drive.

should line up in an angled line so as to push the birds forward and to the side of the field where the last sweep will pick them all up.

No one should make any extraneous noise. The birds will still hear you coming, you can be sure. Blockers should move into position as quietly as possible, going there by a roundabout route which passes through previously hunted parts of the field. Once in place they should hunker down to be as invisible as possible where they should make a noise just like an area of corn on the ground.

Drivers should move slowly, stopping from time to time, occasionally stepping into a different furrow. They should always stay in sight of each other, though in standing corn that will mean staying in sight only of the nearest hunters in the line. Sloppy drives are dangerous drives. No shot should be taken unless the bird is so high that no other hunter could conceivably be hit. Most of the action comes in the last thirty yards of the drive when the roosters realize they are trapped. Some, however, dope out the situation and loop back into the corn even though the drivers are coming. You will get a few of them if, after the two lines have met, the group scrambles to kick through the last stretch of cover again.

Big drives need not be so foxy. The best lineup is a wide, shallow "U" so that sneaking roosters tend to drift toward the center of the drive.

The same principles work almost as well when you drive other types of block cover, though they are most appropriate for cover like corn which is not thick. In thick cover the roosters are too inclined to skulk.

Marshes

My personal pheasant hunting specialty is hunting marshes. My reasons are simple. Most hunters leave marshes alone since they are so beastly to walk in. That means that I, by virtue of my insane zeal, have areas to hunt which are virtually untouched preserves. I also wade marshes because I hunt with an explosive, zippy type of springer who moves too fast in all but the most godawful cover. She works best in the muck and impassible vegetation of marshes, so that is where I do best, too.

For someone who has spent so many sweaty hours floundering around over my boots in the water of marshes, I find I do not have

Throw a flushing dog in a deep marsh like this, and you have a good chance for a close flush. (Photo by Ron Spomer)

much to say about how to hunt them. Brute strength and masochism usually count for more than refined strategy. Hacking around in swamps is just plain hard work. I often hunt in places where it is impossible to fall down. It is easy—too easy—to trip, but the cover is so dense you can only tilt over into it so far.

Just getting around in marshes is a big problem. You should work upwind in choice cover whenever possible, though the density of marsh vegetation may cancel out some effects of wind. Most marshes have a "grain" effect caused by the prevailing wind tipping over all the weeds the same way. It is easy to move with the grain, tough to go against it, and sometimes next to impossible to move sideways to the grain. You will also find pathways in many marshes made, usually, by animals. It is far easier to walk along them than to buck the brush all day in an ill-advised effort to walk a straight line. Because the paths wander drunkenly all over the marsh you will not be able to walk in neat rows with other hunters. When I hunt marshes with friends we all take advantage of the easy walking whenever possible, trying at the same time to keep reasonably coordinated with each other so a cock booted up by one man might fly near one of the other hunters.

Great big wet marshes can become rooster sanctuaries, for many of these areas are impossible to hunt unless you can walk on water. These monster marshes often have water several feet deep with islands of floating vegetation which are dry enough to suit the birds. A small number of rugged hunters jam their legs in hip boots and wade into wet marshes after these tough swamp cocks. They earn their birds. Few hunters want a pheasant that badly. But we all get a special break when cold weather freezes the marshes to the point where the ice will support a man. If you are the first hunter to penetrate the islands of a monster marsh after a cold snap you might get hunting you have only dreamed of.

Right toward dusk you may get a final flurry of shooting when roosters from the surrounding fields fly back into the marshes to roost. The same thing happens on big management areas which do not have marshes, as well. You might take a bird or two by pass shooting as they come sailing in, cackling back and forth to each other as garrulously as a flock of geese. Usually you have to mark them down in the marsh, then hustle to the spot before it is too dark for legal shooting. In your favor is the fact they do not want to run once they have landed to roost for the night.

Marsh hunting has a crazy, crude quality which will not suit many hunters. I love it, especially when going after roosters one-on-one with a wriggling, snorting flushing dog. I even like being down in cover so high that, like the pheasants, I cannot see anything but weeds unless I look up. Marsh hunting is personal, intense and exciting, and it gives more close flushes than any other type of pheasant hunting.

Timber

Roosters have an affinity for timber, just as hens have an affinity for grassy cover. No cover type offers the potential for bagging a long-spurred, long-tailed trophy that timber does. But timber is mean cover to hunt. Even small woodlots are usually big enough to force you to go into them to kick the birds out (as opposed to surrounding them and sending in the dogs). The shade of trees usually discourages the ground level vegetation which encourages roosters to sit for close flushes, so timber hunting readily ends up in wild chases and blown opportunities. Even if you do not have to contend with wild flushes in timber you can face mighty tough shooting. A rooster flushed in timber can juke and dodge his way through branches as neatly as any ruffed grouse. That, incidentally, tells you that roosters flushed in open country fly straight simply because the shortest way from point A to point B is a straight line.

Timber roosters are tough to work. Timber tends to slow a man down, while allowing both pheasants and dogs to run full bore. You may find weedy patches in timber, and these are well worth hitting carefully. Also be sure to check the edges of woodlots where they meet crop fields. If there are weeds there, they will be prime spots.

Pheasants do not generally do well in timber, but those which survive there tend to be giants. My buddy, Jim Layton, used to manage a wildlife area in Iowa which featured lots of timber. The woods held few birds, though they were big. I remember one bird Jim took in there; the spurs were almost an inch and a half long, proportioned like a two-penny nail. There was another rooster which hung out in those woods for a while, a bird so big that two deer hunters on stand saw it and told Jim he had a huge "turkey" in his woods. It was just a pheasant, but quite possibly a world record pheasant (if such records were to be kept). The one time Jim flushed that monster cock he did not get a good shot at it.

Railway Sidings

Railway sidings are important in many parts of the pheasant range. While in some states they are technically private lands which can only be hunted with permission, as a practical fact they are generally treated by hunters and conservation officers as lands open to public hunting.

Thus they get hit with plenty of pressure. The roosters will often be driven away from them after a week or two of hunting pressure, and, unlike big management areas, these railway sidings do not pull birds back late in the year.

Railway sidings are strip cover. I have never seen pheasants try to cross railroad tracks, so you can expect the birds either to run, sit tight, slip out into the adjoining fields, or flush. Which of those tactics they use depends on the quality of the cover and the amount of pressure they have experienced. The best railways are those with such steep sides that they hold a generous growth of weeds.

Working railway sidings is just like working other strip cover except that you do not need to block the end of the cover. If the birds elude you they will do it by sitting tight or ducking into the adjacent fields. They rarely flush wildly. Not all dogs are suited to working railway sidings. Some feel a compulsion to come up to the tracks where you are walking to check on you, while others (primarily Labs and goldens) are entirely comfortable working the cover off to the side of you.

Your best tracks hunting will be found on those stretches which lie far away from crossing roads. In much of the pheasant range the roads are laid out strictly on a mile-long grid system so that tracks are crossed by a road every mile. But you can often find stretches of track which do not have such frequent road crossings, and these are better because they get less pressure. You can work tracks in a "leap-frog" system when roads do cross every mile. Your buddy will drop you off at one crossing then drive to the next crossing and leave the car there. You can work the most promising cover along either side of the tracks until you get to the car. Then you drive to the next crossing off, park, and take off while your friend works up to the car. And so it goes, mile after mile, until you are pooped or you have gotten your limit. The same system works when walking roadside ditches.

Tracks, especially on stretches far from crossing roads, offer some excellent hunting.

Shelterbelts

Shelterbelts may hold more pheasants than any other cover in the area. Often, the biggest problem you will have is getting permission to hunt them, as many lie near farm homes and barns. Since shelterbelts are prime roosting cover it works best to hit them just before evening. They will be more productive if you leave them alone for several days between hunts.

Shelterbelts are usually a form of patch cover. That means you should surround them from a distance and work quietly in toward them before putting men or dogs in the actual cover to roust out the cocks. Really large shelterbelts must be hunted with a blend of driving and surrounding; the party surrounds the cover, then a hunter or two should walk from one end to the other of the cover to push the birds out. Dogs will often be a nuisance in these hunts, though controllable retrievers will save a few running cripples.

Irrigation Systems

Pheasant hunting is often tightly associated with irrigation systems, especially in dry regions.

Center pivot irrigation systems are popular in many of the western areas of the pheasant range. These involve a huge watering machinery which revolves around a central water supply. The area encompassed by the machinery will usually be nothing but clean grainfields, but there will often be a significant fringe of weeds at the perimeter of the irrigated circle. Naturally, that is where the pheasants are.

A more typical situation has water running though a straight irrigation ditch. Since these areas are often the wettest and lowest in the region, they sport the best weeds and pheasant populations. Irrigation ditches are classic strip cover. In no other cover are you and your dogs so likely to run past cocks who choose to sit tight. At the same time, the birds are inclined to run and flush wildly if you hunt them later in the year. The best approach to irrigation ditches is to work them very carefully with a blocker or two at the far end. Watch carefully the little fingers of cover that extend from the sides of these ditches, for they are natural rooster escape routes to other cover.

Fence lines are especially attractive to roosters, and give up more birds than their thin cover would lead you to expect. (Photo by Chuck Wechsler)

Fence Lines

Fence lines would hardly seem to rank with other important cover types mentioned here. They have one surprising qualification: fence lines are rooster cover. Do not ask me why, they just are. If you simply set out to walk miles and miles of fence lines you might not get many birds up each hour, but well more than half of them would be cocks.

Some fence lines are much better than others, of course. These days too many fences are just naked strands of barbed wire with nothing beneath them. Yet one of the surprising things about fence lines is how skimpy they can be and still hold a rooster here and there. One nice thing is that these fence line cocks will not be accustomed to people coming at them. While they are spaced far apart, they are surprisingly huntable.

When walking the fences with a dog you should move downwind whenever possible—just the opposite of the usual tactic. If you work into the wind the dog will get scent from far away and be hard to control. I like to walk fences with Brandy on heel, knowing she will disobey me if she gets close enough to a cock.

Bramble Patches

Bramble patches provide most of the hunting after the opening weekend in areas of Pennsylvania and Ohio. Uneducated pheasants can be found in grassy fields and cornfields early in the season, but hunting pressure quickly sends the survivors right into the most hellish, predator-proof cover the land offers: bramble patches.

A bramble patch is a nasty mix of brush, timber, honeysuckle, laurel, and other scratchy, viney, thorny vegetation types. These pockets of cover generally sit in gullies or hilly corners which many generations of farmers have deemed not worth clearing because the land would be too steep for cultivation. Bramble patches are just the sort of place a rooster will hide to escape hunting pressure.

Hunting bramble patches is dirty work. A season of fighting brambles will leave most hunting clothes looking like they had been put through a paper shredder. Those who hunt bramble patches should protect themselves with the toughest, most briar-proof clothing they can find, including thin gloves and protective glasses. Most shots will be snapped off at close ranges, so fast-handling guns with open chokes are best here.

Bramble patches require a specialized hunting approach. One of their distinctive qualities is that they are terribly difficult to walk in. Birds and dogs can scoot around with relative ease, but human beings (no matter how well armored with nylon clothing) are incapable of moving quickly in bramble patches. Most hunters end up deciding it is better to hunt brambles without a dog, because dogs tend to cause out-of-range flushes. A few hunters take highly disciplined Labs into brambles, keeping them on heel almost all the time and using them mostly to prevent cripple losses.

Small hunting parties of two or three hunters are about right for hunting bramble patches. The birds can often outflank a single hunter, but a carefully coordinated team can conduct mini-drives and trap roosters in places where they will flush. Slow, quiet drives are usually best. That is good, because it is near impossible to move quickly in brambles, anyway.

11

Fine Points of the Game

When you come right down to it, most of the time fancy strategy is not worth as much in the pheasant fields as a good candy bar. If you muck about in good cover near feeding areas long enough you will get your share of pheasants. But it satisfies a need in some hunters to have a higher plan (or at least think they have). For sure, there is no more satisfying rooster than one you think you have bagged through finesse. Here are a few fine points which just might make the difference on a tough day.

Second Flushes

I learned much of my pheasant hunting style from a friend who had done all his hunting in poor pheasant country. Because Gary was not the best shot, a few roosters escaped him on the first flush—but they were far from safe then. Gary never considered the first flush the end of the encounter. If he had any idea of where the bird came down, he would go on hounding it for a second or third flush. Eventually he would get his bird.

Later I took that hunting style into good pheasant country and made all my local hunting pals fall down laughing. They hardly gave a second thought to cocks which flushed wild or were missed. They knew they would get another bird if they just kept hunting the cover. I always broke away to chase the one we had seen, pursuing it with the determination of a Canadian Mountie trailing a lawbreaker. Guess I looked pretty silly.

Yet it often makes sense to try for a second flush on a rooster. We always hope the cover we are hunting holds several cocks, but there is something to be said for hunting where you know a bird is. Experience, however, has convinced me that it rarely pays to disrupt a drive through promising cover just to chase a single bird, especially in good pheasant country. You should continue working out the cover before chasing the one that got away. Give him a few minutes to settle down and spread a little scent around.

To get second flushes on cocks, you must mark them down carefully. When they go into a long glide they are hard to spot down, and usually they have gone farther than you thought, perhaps because birds which land at a gentle angle are likely to start running when they touch down. Those birds which buttonhook before landing are apt to sit where they come down. You can often find a bird that landed out of sight by merely walking out the line of its flight and combing the best cover on that path.

Your best chance for second flushes comes when roosters land in thick cover. Write off those birds that fly to standing corn. The smaller and thicker the cover they land in, the more likely it is you will see them again. I began to get more second flushes when I realized that cocks almost never come down in a randomly chosen spot. They know their territory and usually have a good bit of security cover to fly to. Even if you do not mark a pheasant down, you can often find it by following its general flight and looking for the best security cover along the way.

Hunting Away From the Birds

It is true. You can be cursed by having too many birds to hunt.

One advantage of working lighter cover is the clear line of scent the dog gets.

When pheasants are so numerous that they flock up in big groups, you may end up wishing their spring hatch had not gone so well. Big flocks of birds are harder to hunt than small groups or singles. A pheasant lays down a powerful scent trail, so imagine what happens to a dog that hits a field with thirty or forty birds in it. All that scent seems to overload the scenting circuits in the canine head, a fuse blows, and the dog goes berserk. I do not know what type of dog has a worse time of it then, a pointer or a flusher.

Flocked up pheasants are tough in other ways. If they have experienced pressure, the flocks can become unapproachable. As you come near them, the most nervous bird in the gang will flush and pull the whole flock up out of range. When you find yourself frustrated because you have got too much of a good thing (too many birds) you ought to try hunting away from the flocks. If there are really that many birds around, you can scratch up a rooster here or there by hunting in less appealing bits of cover out away from the big flocks. Or you can try to bust into the flocks to break them up, then hunt singles and pairs. It does not matter where most of the birds are, you have to hunt them where they will be huntable.

Hunting Solo

Yes, it is difficult, but it can be done. If you must hunt without canine or human assistance you can still bag pheasants. The following tips will help, though it also helps to be ecstatic about any success you earn.

You will obviously do better in strip cover, particularly narrow strips like skinny draws, small irrigation ditches, and thin fence lines. The beauty of strip cover is that the birds cannot run around you. But if you are to do well you must hunt in strips which have not been walked through by other parties. So, you simply make a specialty of hunting strips so skimpy that they do not attract the attention of bigger groups.

The second obviously smart tactic is the classic stop-and-go. Your best hope for getting a bird is to move so slowly that the cocks are not panicked into running or flushing wildly. Then, if you stop when you are close to them—and you are lucky—they might lose their cool.

A more desperate measure, useful when you have to hunt patches or blocks of cover, is to simply proceed as if you were driving a flock of imaginary pheasants. Walk in a pattern that would push that flock out toward the margins of the cover where it will have to fly. You might feel foolish while executing an elaborate drive without ever knowing if you are near a bird, but it is the only thing you can do when hunting big cover alone. After shooing your imaginary flock out to the edge of the cover you should do the stop-and-go. That is when you find out if your flock was imaginary or real.

The best advice for the lone wolf, however, is to hunt in country which nobody else hunts. If you live in good pheasant country, get in the car and drive a few hours until you are in a place where everybody regards the ringneck as an endangered species. Then start logging miles through strip cover. You are hoping to cross paths with a rooster who never before had to avoid a hunter with a gun. It will take a minor miracle to flush an experienced bird in hard-hit country, so don't even try. Go find some roosters that do not even know the season has started.

Odd Spots

Past the opener, but before winter weather arrives, you can have fun poking around in odd spots for sneaky roosters. Odd spots are, by definition, unlikely places to find pheasants, so to find these birds you have to take chances.

Examples? Try that huge harvested soybean field with "no" cover? Let's say that right along the fence is a big boulder the farmer has not cleared out yet, and it has a few paltry weeds at its base. There probably is not a pheasant there. On the other hand, if there is a pheasant, I will bet you it is a rooster.

Other examples? A memorable one was the huge rooster a friend found slinking around the gravestones of a small rural cemetery. Then there was the time I impressed my pals by predicting I would find a rooster under an abandoned windmill in the middle of a bare field. A long hike out there was rewarded when a little rooster rocketed out of the grass below the old windmill. And I missed him twice—never cut a feather—which also impressed them.

Plowed fields and similarly barren areas offer a final example of odd cover. Pheasants do use plowed fields, for they find grain out there in the fall-plowed dirt and because no hunters bother them in such open spots. These birds are safe unless someone happens to spot them.

I have noticed a surprising thing about these cocks. When you do spot one, you're apt to write the bird off as unhuntable, since you have to cross open ground in plain sight of him to get in range. But it is worth the effort. These birds act so confident in their strange hiding spot that they often let you walk right up to them.

Many years ago while hunting in corn, my father downed a bird which fell in a plowed field. When he walked out to retrieve it, he found the bird lying there with its tail feathers high; so he grabbed the tail to stuff the bird in his game pouch. That cock came to life with a great ruckus and flew away, leaving part of his tail in my dad's hand. He shot it again and downed it again, but when he went to find it this time he saw two dead roosters lying side by side on the ground. One was the first bird he had shot, and the other was a rooster that was so confident of its safety in the plowed field, it let a man walk up and grab its tail.

Predicting Flushes

I make a little game of predicting which way a rooster will flush. For the most part, roosters make a big game of crossing me. I am right just often enough to keep trying. It is not mere guesswork. Flushing roosters go where they go for good reasons. Sometimes they simply mean to get straight away from trouble—from you, that is. These cocks often fly low and fast. They are hard to identify for sex and hard to hit. Only the most experienced roosters are apt to do this, for which I am glad.

It is more likely that they pick their route by flying straight to the best refuge cover the area provides. Standing corn or milo, swamps, willow stands, densely weeded creek bottoms, and similar places attract birds escaping from trouble. Smart hunters keep track of these places as they walk, anticipating that a flushed bird might go that way. Wind can also dictate the way birds fly. Roosters like to flush into the wind for a quick takeoff. Then they will turn and go with the wind for the quickest exit from danger.

Predicting flushes gets tricky when these influences occur in various combinations, as they so often do. If a stiff breeze is blowing across your path right toward an uncut cornfield, that's very likely where most flushed birds will go. If the wind is going the opposite way from the best cover, you are back to guessing blindly which way they will break. Being able to predict flushes can help you. Most of us shoot better if we have thought out the shot in advance. You can also give more shooting opportunities to less lucky party members by placing them where you think the birds will go.

Sometimes strategy works, and it sure feels good. Once, Brandy and I were hunting alone, looking for the last bird that would let us make the long drive back home. We were working a weedy hillside when a bird flushed wildly before either of us had any idea it was there. It was out of range—about seventy yards out—but the cock was so large I almost lost control and shot. Brandy showed me where the bird flushed, and from there we walked up a hill on the line taken by the rooster. From the top of the hill we looked out on a big valley of cut corn. One weed patch at the far end of the corn stood out. It was the only cover in sight and it lay along the path taken by the bird. When we began working up through the weeds we were at first in a strip cover situation. There was no scent, but I was not discouraged. The

Flushing pheasants almost always try to head for refuge cover like this.

bird would have headed for the greater security of the taller weeds at the top of the patch. Soon the strip became too wide for us to cover well. This bird had already shown itself to be spooky, so I pushed fast uphill rather than zigzagging the cover thoroughly. Where would the rooster fly? I recalled there was a thickly weeded drainage ditch across the picked field to our left, the best security cover I had seen. That was our clue to choose the left side of the cover when we could not hit it all. Still no scent.

My pulse quickened when we were eighty yards from the end of the patch in that dangerous area too far away to cover a panicky flushing cock. Our prospects improved when we covered those critical yards and were in range of the end of the patch. Brandy suddenly struck scent and disappeared completely in the ragweed. If I followed her I would lose mobility and vision. Looking ahead, I saw a little strip of weeds projecting away from the larger strip. It pointed like a finger at the distant drainage ditch. I ducked out of the weeds and took a dozen quick steps toward the finger. Brandy, the rooster, and I all hit the tip of that finger at the same split-second.

Cutting Your Cripple Losses

While anyone who hunts pheasants will inevitably lose some cripples, good sportsmen have always been saddened by this. For selfish reasons and because of the concern he feels for the well-being of all pheasants, the modern pheasant hunter is especially hurt when he leaves a bird to die slowly in the cover. We owe it to ourselves, to the birds, and to the sport of pheasant hunting to reduce cripple losses to the lowest possible level.

The rugged physique and indomitable spirit of the pheasant make cripple losses far more likely compared with other upland game. It takes very little shot to drop a cock; indeed, a single pellet in one wing can do that. It takes a whole lot more to make a rooster give up the ghost. Once, when I was a kid, a friend's father returned from pheasant hunting with a limit of three birds. All of the youngsters in the neighborhood stood around to admire the birds. But when the hunter opened his trunk, not one but all three cocks came to life and tried to escape

Late season roosters like this one stand out because of their well-developed tail feathers, their prominent white neck ring, and their distinctive coloring.

through the crowd of shocked onlookers. It was quite a scene, and it made quite an impression on me. Pheasants will struggle to escape as long as there is the slightest life left in them.

That is not mere rhetoric invented to glorify pheasants. At various times field researchers have kept careful records of pheasant hunters' cripple losses. Hunters with dogs lose about 10 percent of the birds they down; hunters without dogs lose from 20 to 40 percent of their downed birds. As sobering as those numbers are, I fear they do not reflect the full dimension of the problem because they deal only with downed birds. Many other roosters keep flying with broken legs or fatal hits, quite often giving no indication they have been hit.

How can you reduce cripple losses? Start by making a maximum effort to find any bird which has been hit. I will stop the hunt to search for at least fifteen minutes when there is a cripple down, and on more than one occasion I have trailed wounded birds for over an hour.

Teamwork and Marking

The time to start cutting cripple losses is when the bird is still in the air. Carefully observe any bird you have shot at, as well as those shot at by your partners or any other hunters in the area. If another hunter scratch hits a bird which does not fall, you should try to stop that bird even if it means taking a longer shot than you ordinarily consider responsible. Pheasants that flutter or glide down are easy to hit with an anchoring shot. Wing-tipped roosters, however, drop so suddenly that I can rarely get my barrels down fast enough to hit them with a follow-up shot. And they are the friskiest birds on the ground. You sometimes see them working their legs in a running motion before they have landed.

You have a more difficult decision to make when you see a lively cripple on the ground. It is usually best to shoot it again if you think it can still travel, although you must be absolutely sure that your shot will not hit a companion or a dog. Those low angle shots are inherently dangerous. Even good dogs can lose cripples in bad cover, so do not adopt the attitude that cripples are exclusively the responsibility of the dogs to retrieve.

Experienced hunters make a point of watching apparently missed birds until they are out of sight or marked down. This lets you follow up some cocks for a second flush. And every now and then an apparently unscathed rooster will be almost out of sight when it suddenly towers, fails, and drops like a stone. Bill Gallea, my physician friend and frequent hunting partner, once performed an autopsy on a rooster which did that; he found a single pellet had scratched the bird's heart and caused the tough sac surrounding the heart to fill with blood until the heart could no longer pump. I have often heard that birds which tower this way have been struck in the head, but I am more inlined to think they bleed to death or lose heart function. These birds are extremely hard to locate if you do not watch them like a hawk. They invariably die in the air and are apparently washed of scent when they fall, so that a dog can almost step on them without getting their scent.

When a bird towers and collapses this way you should fix your eyes on the spot and make note of some feature in the surroundings. If you see no good landmark, you should keep your eyes on the location while scuffing a large arrow in the dirt with the heel of your boot to point the way to the rooster. All other members of the party should follow the same procedure. Frequently, the help of a buddy is crucial, for it is far easier to find a distant bird if you have got its location marked down from two different angles. The scuffed arrow also lets you try a second time to find a distant fallen bird; it lets you return to the spot you shot from to try once again to walk out the line of the bird's flight.

Towering birds are just a single example of how teamwork reduces cripple losses. Whenever a shot is fired, every hunter should turn to watch the rooster so he can note the effect of the shot and help mark down the bird. Often, one fellow will be in a position to see that a seemingly missed rooster "dropped a leg" after the shot. That is very important knowledge, for it means the bird is a cripple which should be pursued at all costs. Most broken-legged cocks are easy to capture because they cannot run well, and many cannot spring high enough to flush a second time. They may look so healthy in the air that you give up on them, so do not be fooled.

Get to downed birds as quickly as possible, even when they seem to drop stone dead. Remember, wing-tipped roosters fall so suddenly that the average hunter thinks they have been clobbered, until he goes to claim his prize and sees it racing into the next county. Hustle to the spot whether you have a dog or not. Sometimes even lightly hit pheasants will be stunned for a few moments after hitting the ground. The bird is not bagged until it is, indeed, dead and in your bag. In fact, I

Mark a pheasant's fall by aligning yourself with the pheasant and an object beyond the point of the pheasant's fall. Then walk carefully toward it keeping the object in focus until you reach your fallen rooster.

once had a "dead" rooster escape from my game bag. The whole story is too long and humiliating to be repeated here.

Cripple Behavior

You never know for sure what a cripple will do. Often, I've seen them leave good cover and run across open country. I now understand that cripples have their own priorities and cannot be counted on to act like an unhit bird. Hard-hit birds, if they cannot run, will make every effort to get under something. Running cripples often head to low areas. If you have got no better guide to where they have gone, ask yourself where water would run in the area, then hunt for the cripple there. Remember that the bird knows exactly where it is and where the nearest security cover is; it will try to go to that cover.

If you lose a running cripple in spite of your best efforts, you still have a chance of retrieving it. Just because it did not stay near the point where it fell does not mean you have lost it forever. Go on hunting the best cover in the area, and look for new birds, but keep in mind the fact you know there is at least one rooster in the nearby cover. Your dogs may pick up the trail somewhere farther along. It sometimes even works to leave the area where you lost a cripple and return much later to comb through the cover again. Again, you can hunt with the knowledge that there is at least one bird in the area.

When they are hit, crippled roosters display as much resourcefulness avoiding hunters as they do before the guns go off. They have been seen crawling into woodchuck dens, deep into blowdown tangles, and into other impenetrable places. Al Berner, an excellent hunter and progressive pheasant biologist in Minnesota, once saw a cripple come down between two hunting parties near some water. When everyone converged on the spot, the bird had dematerialized, though it clearly could not have escaped. Then Al's Brittany went on point right at the water. There was the rooster completely under water, his head sticking up "just like a periscope."

Dogs

Beyond doubt, the best way to reduce cripple losses is to hunt with a sharp retriever. Since the flushing and retrieving breeds of dogs

To dispatch a cripple, press hard on the heart.

hunt foot scent rather than air scent, and since they have highly developed retrieving instincts, they work better than other breeds when a bird is loose on the ground. In my own hunting I have seen more incredible retrieves made by Labs than by any other breed, though Brandy, a springer spaniel, has a few to her credit which thrilled and amazed me. One research study found that Labs lost only five of 100 downed birds, which is as near perfection as any breed will get. Veteran dogs have it all over puppies when working out a difficult cripple trail, for the young dogs do not trust their noses enough. I have also seen Brandy come up with a few tricky cripples that she located strictly by looking in the sorts of places which she knew through experience were good bets.

It took me a long time to find a satisfactory way of dispatching crippled roosters. As a kid I did as my father did: he spun the birds around while holding them by their heads, then broke their necks with a sharp snap. But that often left a grisly headless corpse. I have tried striking their heads against my gunstock, but I gave that up as a bad way to treat a pheasant or a gun. If you hold a bird across the small of the back and put sustained pressure on the heart for a few moments, the bird quickly dies without a lot of fuss and flutter. Keep the pressure on until the head drops.

Competent hunters spare no effort to find a cripple. Considerate hunting partners are not only patient while you work to find a cripple. They will join in the chase as diligently as if the cripple were their own. Good sportsmanship calls for no less.

12

Pheasants for the Future

Have a little pity for the person who has primary responsibility for managing pheasants in your state. His job title probably promises something he can never deliver. An "office manager" is rightly expected to manage an office; so it would seem that pheasant managers should be accountable for the highs and lows of pheasant populations. Yet is is not so, and for good reason. The pheasant manager has virtually no power or influence over the major factors determining fall populations: weather and the amount of quality habitat. When murderous blizzards slash through regions with marginal quality cover, the wildlife manager is as helpless as you or I to save the birds. When extended droughts result in shabby spring nesting cover, the manager can perform no rain dance to improve the hens' nesting prospects.

Today, as before, pheasant populations are largely an accidental by-product of agricultural operations on privately owned land. Private landowners do most of the important pheasant management in this country, for better or for worse, usually without giving much thought to the consequences of their actions to wildlife. But even when farmers are aware of the ways their actions hurt wildlife, they rarely can afford to put the interests of the pheasants ahead of the interests of their families. Farmers, like pheasants, are fighting for survival in a rough-and-tumble world. Crop prices plummet and soar, interest rates seem only to soar, and tax policies shift maddeningly. Ultimately, it is these factors which determine the way privately owned land is used. So, farmers drain marshes, level shelterbelts, burn ditches, raze woodlots, and take early hay crops. And the pheasant manager watches all this with frustration and has little more power than the birds themselves to alter the course of events.

Harvest Regulations and the Public

The manager would seem to have control of at least one area: the harvest regulations. Yet, closer examination reveals another picture. In the absence of political pressure (an ideal situation which rarely exists), managers decide which daily limits, shooting hours, and open season dates are appropriate for current bird numbers. These regulations are usually announced shortly after the August road counts have been collated and digested. Actually, the whole affair is more a media event than an exercise of wildlife management.

Why? First, the harvest regulations are largely irrelevant to next year's pheasant population. So long as 10 percent of the roosters survive the fall hunt (which they do, no matter how hard hunters pressure them) hunting pressure has no significant impact on bird numbers. Pheasant seasons could be set at twice their length and all bag limits could be doubled without bird numbers in spring showing any difference. Looking at this from the other end of the telescope, extensive research has shown that closed seasons do nothing to boost bird population.

In spite of assurances of scientific calculation, game seasons are usually set with more than ample consideration for public opinion. When Iowa game biologists recently found an unusually strong pheasant population, they recommended a change from three to four roosters in the daily bag. They were shouted down, however, mostly because the three-bird daily limit had the force of tradition behind it—so much for scientific management. Hunters and nonhunters alike continue to believe (in the face of all the evidence) that closed seasons benefit the pheasant population, so managers know that one of the unsavory aftereffects of a killer blizzard is intense public pressure to close the next fall's hunting season.

When you come right down to it, harvest regulations are a way of managing hunters, not pheasants. For one thing, farmers have strong opinions about how seasons are set, for those decisions have impact on how much they will be bothered by hunters at different times of the year. A more legitimate use of bag rules is to spread around the harvest so the more efficient human predators do not get to hog the resource. Oddly enough, daily bag limits are of more importance to hunters than to birds. When daily bag limits have been eradicated, hunters have been the first to complain about being robbed of the satisfaction of "getting a limit." Artificial though it may be, that bench mark of success is attractive to hunters because it offers a more tangible goal than the vague objective of having a nice day afield.

Stocking

If harvest regulations have little prospect for improving the ringneck population, much the same can be said of pheasant stocking programs. Stocking programs, of course, were once wildly successful. Although that time and its special circumstances have passed into history, many hunters continue to believe stocking can restore failed pheasant populations in areas where habitat has been wiped out. Much of the former pheasant range today has as much real cover as you would find on an astroturf football field, and it makes about as much sense to stock birds in the one place as in the other.

Yet stocking programs can be valuable, even today. We should not underestimate the public relations value of stocking programs. They are solid evidence to the general public that a game agency is "doing something," and that is pretty important. The better stocking programs often involve youth groups, like 4-H clubs, which raise pheasant chicks until they are old enough to release. The youngsters learn a great deal about the birds in this process, especially in states where game agencies work closely with the groups to tell them about the real problems with pheasant populations.

Stocking is also a defensible management practice in states where no other means exist to support a huntable fall population of pheasants.

Yes, I have heard about the abuses—the situations where a tiny handful of hunters clean out the stocked birds minutes after they have been put down—sometimes after literally chasing the stocking trucks down country roads. Managers who sanction this put-and-take type of stocking are not deluded about its long range value, which is negligible in terms of establishing a strong bird population. What they are doing is providing a reasonable facsimile of wild pheasant hunting for a large number of hunters who, without the stocking program, would have no pheasant hunting at all. Thanks to the inherent wildness of pheasants, the stocked birds are surprisingly quick to behave like wildbred pheasants.

Stocking programs are not worth much if the birds are put into areas with little habitat. (Photo by Jim Layton)

The most productive stocking programs are those which seek to establish pheasants in areas where they have not caught on before. Managers are often baffled by the invisible barriers that limit the pheasant range. While there are many theories on this point, there are also some mysteries. Pheasants have succeeded in areas as far north as Edmonton, Alberta, and as far south as the border with Mexico. They are found from the Pacific shoreline all the way north and east through Maine and into Nova Scotia. Yet, there are some big gaps in this range, and plenty of areas of spotty populations.

Carefully designed stocking programs are showing some success in piercing these invisible barriers. Modern stocking is a far cry from the old "throw-a-few-birds-in-the-bushes" approach. Managers now recognize there are small but critical differences among apparently identical subspecies of ringnecks, differences which can make for success or failure when birds are placed in a new area. Best results come when the stocked birds are wild-trapped (not pen-raised) or are the offspring of wild birds, especially birds who have succeeded in a region very near the birdless area. When this type of stocking works, it establishes self-sustaining populations in areas where pheasants never occurred before and emulates the success of the original stocking efforts.

Habitat Acquisition

If my comments on stocking have seemed less than enthusiastic it is because stocking is so terribly expensive. The rate of return on stocked birds is notoriously poor, while the cost of raising pheasants has increased sharply. By any accounting system it is difficult to defend the economics of stocking. That would not matter if game agencies had money to burn. But they do not, and too often stocking is equivalent to flushing precious management dollars down the drain.

Habitat acquisition has done more for pheasants than any other single program since the first pheasants were stocked. Temporarily, the old Conservation Reserve and Set-Aside Acres programs were great for pheasants—as long as they lasted. They did have the unfortunate effect of disguising the way lands not set aside in special programs were losing their habitat, and when the programs were withdrawn it was like pulling the rug out from under the pheasant. Meanwhile, however, lands purchased with sportsmen's dollars and held for wildlife now can be seen as some of the greatest bargains in the history of wildlife management. In many parts of the country these publicly owned lands are the only salvation for pheasants and pheasant hunters alike. Unlike other management programs, habitat acquisition costs a lot at first but then pours out a bounty of birds year after year with very little additional expense.

Yet habitat acquisition programs are in trouble in many areas. Wildlife agencies now find they can buy very little land because of inflation and spiraling farmland prices. At a time when sportsmen have less discretionary money to spend, they are being told to dig deeper in their pockets to keep habitat acquisition programs from failing altogether. That hurts, and so does the recent attack on habitat purchasing programs being mounted by certain agricultural interests. The attitude of these groups is that the only good land is land which is in active crop production. Astonishingly enough, they contend it is not the right of a landowner to sell a slough to a wildlife agency without receiving the permission of some third party—usually a county board stacked to favor the interests of major landowners. This antipathy toward public land ownership has hurt wildlife management by bleeding off precious management funds in order to wage court fights to defend the basic right of wildlife agencies to buy lands for the public good.

Habitat acquisition, the most successful pheasant management program since the original stocking efforts, is probably on the wane. Where these programs have been strong in the past they will continue into the future, yet the combination of public opposition and sharply increased land prices is seriously weakening the ability of state and federal agencies to add to the public's land holdings. Wildlife lands, at any price, are a wonderful bargain. Hunters should support habitat acquisition to the fullest extent possible. Sportsmen can reflect with pride on the important purchases made in the past. But they must be vigilant to defend those lands against the insatiable appetite of developers, land speculators, and certain types of agricultural interests.

Increasingly, research programs and management practice subsidy programs will be important to the future of farmland wildlife like the pheasant. Only these programs have much of a chance to halt the systematic destruction of all pheasant cover. The subsidy or support programs include all those state and federal efforts to encourage good soil, water, and marsh conservation. Since farmers realize immediate financial gain by converting every possible square foot of their land to active row crop production, these programs have been established to offer desperately needed incentives to leave marshes undisturbed and to save or even plant shelter belts. Ultimately, good land management is good pheasant management. The problem here is that this point is difficult to make to the farmer who is mortgaged to the hilt and scrambling to improve his crop output in any way possible. If he seems shortsighted, please try to understand his situation. He is beholden to bankers on a far grander scale than ever imagined by the city-dweller. When you force farmers to make a decision between "birds and bucks," bucks are going to win almost all the time.

That is why these programs are so important. When they work well, they make it possible for a farmer to follow good land and water management practices without financing them out of his pocket. But

Without subsidy programs, today's farmer cannot afford to leave cover for wildlife, and cover such as this will soon yield to crop fields. (Photo by South Dakota Game, Fish and Parks Dept.)

sportsmen need to know that these critical programs are severely underfinanced: the farmer who defers draining a marsh is not reimbursed in an amount equivalent to that he would have realized if he had destroyed the marsh and put it into production. These programs have been crunched hard by the recent fiscal problems of state and federal government agencies, and all sportsmen need to support them enthusiastically.

Research programs also offer some hope for the future. A promising effort has identified switchgrass as a vegetation type that favors nesting success and is, at the same time, attractive as a hay crop for livestock farmers. Any time an agricultural crop is economically advantageous to farmers and still good for wildlife, it is something special. A good example is the current effort to improve the potential of roadsides for producing wildlife. Once managers believed that ditches were used by hens for nesting only when more desirable cover was not available. Now, because other cover has been lost and because research has shown nesting success in roadsides can be high, managers see a great deal of promise in properly managed roadsides. For example, in Minnesota only 30 percent of the roadsides are suitable for wildlife production, yet this slim acreage may account for over half of the wildlife production in some areas. If the other 70 percent could be managed for wildlife the benefits would mount up rapidly.

Proper management of roadsides comes down to two things. They must be seeded with vegetation types which are appropriate for nesting pheasants, rabbits, and songbirds. And the cover must not be disturbed—in particular, it must not be mowed—before the young are out of the nests. Obviously, such weed suppression techniques as burning and herbicide spraying should not be allowed. Managing roadsides for wildlife would not be at all expensive. Yet, managers have had difficulty gathering support for the program. Farmers in some areas count heavily on roadside hay for their livestock. Many farmers generally hate the sight of "nonproductive" land of any sort, while others prefer to see the ditches neatly mowed for aesthetic reasons. Where roadsides are publicly owned, managers have had good success improving their potential for producing wildlife. In areas where roadsides are owned by the adjacent landowner or by myriads of local townships, it has been impossible so far to establish any common policy to give wildlife a break. This is a program which still holds good potential, one deserving of the support of all who love wildlife.

A two-day-old chick killed by a mower. Annual losses to mowers can be terribly high.

One State's Answer

Of all the states, South Dakota has the most comprehensive management plan, their "Pheasant Restoration Program." Funds come from a pheasant stamp purchased by all grouse and pheasant hunters. Some of that money is bled off for predator control and stocking (concessions to public opinion), but most of it goes for nesting cover and a fair amount is set aside for shelterbelt management. The importance of wide, thickly vegetated shelterbelts is easy to appreciate in the flat plains of the Dakotas, where often the only thing between a pheasant and a deadly Canadian blizzard is a few strands of barbed wire. But South Dakota managers stress, above all, the need to develop secure nesting cover. That emphasis reflects two stark facts: if no pheasants are born, there will be no more birds; and the pressures of modern agriculture have left pheasants in many areas with virtually no secure areas in which to nest. So far the program has succeeded at putting fewer acres into nesting cover than were hoped for, yet managers proudly point to the positive results.

To understand the need for secure cover, we can look at the matter from a backwards perspective. Let's imagine the pheasant was a pest we wanted to eliminate from the land. How could we do it? Easy. Just wait until reproduction time when all the hens are in a limited amount of cover. We obviously want to kill the hens and chicks before those nuisance chicks are big enough to survive on their own, so we wait until the hens are most firmly intent on staying with the nests—just before or during that period in which the chicks emerge—and then we send a deadly machine through the cover at high speed. It will kill a high percentage of the hens. If we time things properly we will find the hens so reluctant to fly that they will allow themselves to be sliced up rather than desert their young. As a biologist friend sardonically observes, "Dead hens seldom renest." So by killing the hens and disrupting their nests we can keep those pesty pheasants at an acceptably low level.

Agriculture and the Pheasant

Pardon the bitterness of the preceding discussion. It was not meant to assert that anyone deliberately sets out to limit pheasant populations. It was meant to suggest that typical hay cropping practices are very little different from a conscious program to eradicate pheasants as if they were vermin. Farmers commonly try to claim three hay crops from areas where there is appropriate vegetation. All too often, that vegetation is the only available nesting cover for hen pheasants. The first hay cropping is the deadly one. If it comes early enough the hens will desert their nests and attempt to renest in an alternate area. If it comes late enough (with spring weather being the main factor determining when the high speed mowing machines are put into action), the hens might have already brought off their broods and taken them to safer cover. Year by year, it comes down to a gruesome battle against time, with neither the farmers nor the hens knowing the consequences of the exact timing of that first harvest. If it is a little late or a little early, the birds have a chance for normal reproductive success. If the

The nesting hen's coloring would seem to keep her safe from most predators, but is useless against a mower. (Photo by Minnesota Department of Natural Resources)

harvest comes at the time when the hens are most tightly bonded to their nests, the birds lose badly. Dead hens seldom do renest.

When all is said and done, what does the future hold for the pheasant? Well, if you believe the future can be predicted by straight line projection of trends in the present, there is no doubt that pheasants and all farmland wildlife face a grim future. But simple projection of trends is not a very sound way to predict the future. Oddly enough, the energy shortage and the general increase in ecological awareness may emerge as the two most important factors in the future of the pheasant in America.

To see how that can be we need to understand that modern American agriculture is enormously wasteful of energy and extremely harsh on the land. The modern farmer is "hooked" on a system of agriculture heavily dependent on dangerous chemicals and profligate expenditures of energy. It is a style of agriculture which seemed to make sense in the 1960s, which was accepted as the only workable way to farm in the 1970s, but which may be repudiated as environmentally and economically wasteful in the 1980s. Energy and chemicals are no longer as cheap as they once were. Meanwhile, evidence mounts to show that contemporary agricultural practices are destroying precious topsoil and are not really cost effective. Some observers feel already that current farming styles are no better than an even match for more natural farming methods. The problem seems to be that a farmer has to endure a difficult two-year transition when switching over to more sensible farming procedures (while the chemicals leach out of the soil). Artificial farming will continue to appear superior in terms of yield per acre, but only by disregarding the costs—all the long- and short- range costs—of farming that way. As the habitat base withers it is hard to feel optimistic about the prospects for farmland wildlife. And still I take heart from the conviction that what is good for the land is good for the pheasant.

Preserves: Hunting versus Shooting

More and more you are apt to hear that shooting preserves represent the best hope for the future of American pheasant hunting. That is a sad outlook for the dedicated hunter, inasmuch as the preserve experience is at best a good imitation of the real thing. Preserves vary in quality. Some offer only the poorest copy of a wild hunt, with poorly conditioned birds stuck in scruffy cover just moments before the guns are brought up to "hunt" them. Other preserves take great pride in their fast flying birds, and these birds will be released long enough before the hunt to make finding them again less than a dead certainty. Better preserves also take pains to see that their dogs, handlers, and associated facilities contribute to a quality experience. What high- and low- quality preserves have in common is that they eliminate the problem of finding pheasants—the most important aspect of wild bird hunting—while still providing the challenges of shooting.

From that perspective, what can we say about the value and role of preserves in the future of pheasant hunting? To my mind, the preserve experience is so different from true hunting that I hardly see them as related sports. Yet I know hunters who accept preserve shooting totally as a satisfying substitute for hunting wild birds. One friend, a fellow who long ago became frustrated with the problems of asking for permission to hunt on private land, is ready to deliver a ringing endorsement of preserve shooting. He especially likes the arrangement whereby he is allowed to hunt on the grounds for birds other parties have passed by: he pays only for birds he shoots. Some hunters like to "tune up" on a preserve before starting the season. But most of the clientele of preserves do not perceive major differences between hunting there or anywhere else, except for the significant difference that they enjoy more success on preserves. I am not interested in criticizing

Pen-raised birds such as these may seem tame but are surprisingly quick to adopt wild ways. (Photo by Wisconsin Department of Natural Resources)

them. They have found an easy answer to the challenges of hunting that I work so hard to meet. I might find myself hunting thin populations of spooky birds just miles from where those hunters walk easily among the grass cut in strips shooting bird after bird. If they are happy, I am happy for them.

This is not to say that preserve shooting will replace wild bird hunting. It is a good thing preserves exist to serve those who simply do not see a big difference between trying to find and outmaneuver a wild cock, and shooting pen-raised birds in a controlled environment. Preserves offer the only pheasant hunting in some states. Moreover, preserves are changing in response to a changing clientele. Once patronized mostly by wealthy shooters who wanted to buy guaranteed success, preserves are now seeing more serious, hard-working hunters who turn to preserves to escape the frustrations and expense of hunting wild birds. Preserves are accommodating these folks by becoming more and more reflective of wild bird hunting. In spite of the artificiality of the preserve situation, the untameable heart of the pheasant always lends an element of wildness to the experience.

The pheasant has come a long way to be with us. Once here, it stormed across the land to establish itself almost instantly as the most popular gamebird and the king of the uplands. Now, as the screws of the economy tighten relentlessly, it sustains its race in spite of terrible pressures and uneven odds. Whenever I am tempted to give up on the pheasant I remind myself that the pheasants have not given up. Each fall they display the great reserves or courage and resourcefulness which have always obliged men like myself to love and admire them. Each winter they claw their way through snowy drifts to snatch a little nourishment from their hostile adopted homeland. Each spring the cocks and hens gather in what is left of the nesting cover, to once again introduce new pheasants into a world which increasingly seems to be too grimly devoted to profit-making to give them a place to live. The birds obviously do not know that their long range prospects are not terribly encouraging. If they did know that, however, I have a hunch they would go on kicking and fighting for survival here just as heroically as they always have.

I still hear them each spring when I walk my dogs near the small patches of cover which have so far escaped urban and rural development. Out in the weeds somewhere a cock grips the soil with his wickedly spurred feet, thrusts his glowing chest outward, hammers his wings, and lets loose a brazen challenge. A sharp, raspy sound pierces the sweet April air: "Cawww Cawk!" He is crying, "This land is mine! Anyone who thinks otherwise can go to hell or, better, come out and fight me for it!"

No, the pheasant hasn't given up yet. Not by a damn sight.

13

Trophies and Mementos

It is too easy to bemoan the passing of the "good old days" of pheasant hunting, in which it was a routine matter to knock off a quick limit of cocks. Today, in many regions, a man might hunt hard all day to get a shot at a single bird. Should the modern pheasant hunter, then, feel sorry for himself? I wonder. I have listened carefully to the old timers telling stories about their hunts, without hearing anything to suggest they got more genuine pleasure from their easy hunting than today's hunter gets from his difficult hunting. When success is routine, after all, it does not count for much.

And so, while all the advice of the preceding pages was offered in the hope it might help you bag more birds, the advice which follows is intended to help you get as much satisfaction as possible from the birds you get.

Any rooster you kill past the opening weekend is, to one degree or another, a "trophy" to be valued. Now, the bird you call a trophy and the bird I honor that way are not necessarily the same, which is as it should be. Any bird you take which means a great deal to you is a true trophy, and I do not care if it is a shrimpy little late-hatch rooster with half a tail. If it means something special to you, it *is* a trophy.

The Mounted Trophy

You can commemorate a trophy pheasant in many ways. The most traditional of these is to have the bird mounted by a taxidermist. It is not very expensive. A full mount—either standing or flying—is a handsome addition to any sportsman's den. Smaller head mounts or head-and-tail mounts will please some hunters just as well. Or you might simply choose to save a tail feather and attach to it a tag which notes the reasons the bird is special to you.

At this time I have only one mounted pheasant in my home. He is an exceptionally big and brightly colored rooster which I took with a difficult shot on an early morning hunt I will always remember. I wish now I had saved a few other birds the same way. Kathe's first pheasant would have been a wonderful bird to mount. She shot it on her very first pheasant hunt, and it was in every respect a rooster that deserved to be honored. Kathe and I were hunting with our close friends, Gary and Jan Crawford. Rip, Jan's excellent yellow Lab, jumped the cock in some corn. Kathe and I were blocking the far end of the field. The bird sailed down the cornfield quite a distance from Kathe. At her shot, though, the rooster seemed to flip and then dropped. It took two good dogs several minutes to find the still-lively rooster where it came down in some tall grass. This would have been a rooster to celebrate even if it had not been Kathe's first. The bird had lived for at least a year with only one foot, the other having been shot or broken off so long ago that the protruding leg bone was polished smooth. Although forced to maneuver on only one leg, that rooster almost eluded us. Kathe's long shot had broken the tip of one wing, leaving the gallant bird with neither the ability to run nor the power to fly. If ever I felt remorse when dispatching a pheasant, I did then.

How Big Is Big?

Though we should remember that any rooster can qualify as a trophy, we can indicate here some measurements which are indicative

Any bird with a tail over two feet long is a trophy. This handsome rooster went to the taxidermist.

of exceptionally big birds. The largest pheasant I ever shot had a tail feather which, when plucked, measured twenty-seven inches. That is big. He was memorable for more than his size, for I found out right after shooting him that I was hunting well inside the city limits of a major metropolitan area where hunting was strictly forbidden. The bird I have mounted has spurs five-eighths of an inch long and a tail which extends twenty-three inches from his body. Any rooster with a tail feather two feet long is a trophy. In some towns in the pheasant range they have tail feather contests. The winning feathers are usually twenty-six to twenty-eight inches long.

While I do not know anyone who makes a sport of pursuing trophy pheasants, it can be done. Of course, almost all our bigger birds come to us in the normal course of hunting. Yet, if you want a particularly large bird, try hunting in woodlots or possibly on brushy islands in large rivers or wet marshes where a wise old rooster has learned hunters never go. But do not forget, a "trophy" pheasant must be defined by each hunter in a personal way. As an example, the first fish my daughter caught was a perch barely six inches long. Kathe and I had that fish mounted. For Molly, then two years old, to have caught that fish was a greater accomplishment than that of most adults who bring a lunker to net. I am committed to making sure Molly never becomes ashamed of her little mounted fish. It is a trophy.

Captured on Film

Many of us find the best way to honor our memory of a good hunt is with photographs. Elsewhere in this text I have suggested carrying a camera in the field in order to catch excitingly authentic pictures of hunting action. The kind of photo you will get that way will be at the opposite end of the spectrum from the usual "kill shot" most of us have lying around in our photo drawers. You know the picture—several feathery masses are lined up in neat rows in the grass with the hunters (and usually the hind end of the car) posing behind them. If that sort of picture satisfies you, fine. I find such pictures very poor representations of the joy, beauty, and action of pheasant hunting.

If you are not happy with the pictures you have taken of your hunts, the problem is less likely with your camera than with your use of it. Still, it does not hurt to work with good equipment. You will get excellent pictures from any modern 35-mm camera. Serious photog-

This picture is very special to me. I was able to snap this staunch point of Tom Huggler's setter, Brinka, because I always hunt with a small camera in my game bag.

raphers work with the more costly single-lens reflex models. Casual snapshooters will be just as happy—perhaps happier—with the compact rangefinder models with automatic exposure and focusing devices. Recently introduced models have made quick point-and-shoot photography possible for any of us.

To get more pleasing photos you should take a few moments to think about what pictures you want to take on your next hunt. Study magazines and books to find pictures you especially admire, then try to duplicate them. At the same time, do not neglect to take a few candid shots which capture those moments of silliness that add smiles to a hunt. You will get nicer pictures if you feature a single bird or two instead of a whole party limit. Move in close with the camera—cropping off part of your subject's body—so you can let the pheasant be larger in the picture. Much of the pleasure of pheasant hunting is drawn from the beauty of the natural surroundings, so take pictures in the field rather than in your basement when you are about to clean the birds. That means you should at least have a camera in the car, if not in the field. You will be glad you did.

The Journal

You can also enrich your satisfaction by keeping a hunting diary or log. Right after a hunt we always think we will never forget what happened; yet the passing years will fuzz up memory until most unrecorded hunts will be lost as though they never happened. Your hunting log does not need to be elaborate. My own crude notes on my hunts are hardly an example I would wish to hold up for emulation; yet they are far better than nothing.

I recently reviewed my notes on hunts I took in 1974 and 1975. What I enjoy most in them is the list I kept of my reasons—"excuses," if you insist—for missing roosters. Here they are: "was working with a new gun and could not find the safety in time"; "bird was probably out of range"; "missed first shot but would surely have hit with second shot if wife had not beaten me to it"; "bird really surprised me"; "damn dog got in the way"; "another bird really surprised me"; and "tried to shoot bird while I was falling down."

Ah, I remember that last one quite well. I was hunting in a marsh with cattails so high I only had a small window of sky visible over head. I had lost track of where Brandy was until I heard the rooster erupt from the cover cackling furiously. It crossed right into the little piece of sky I could see, calling my dog names we will not repeat here. As I brought my gun up, I could feel my heels sinking into the slimy softness of the bottom of the marsh. I fired three desperate shots while trying to calculate two types of "lead" simultaneously: the ordinary forward allowance needed to hit a moving target; and the extraordinary horizontal allowance needed to compensate for the fact I was falling over backwards quite rapidly. Well, that was a bird I did not get to put on the table next to a casserole of wild rice and glasses of wine. But I have placed him prominently in the trophy room with my most cherished hunting memories.

Pheasants I Remember

I can remember most of the pheasants I have shot. With the other upland birds and waterfowl I have hunted, unfortunately, the passing of time has blurred their individuality. But not pheasants. They are special to me. I naturally remember them one by one, just as many people remember the finest books they have read. Sometimes a particular bird is memorable because of the dog work which led to the flush. Some birds are easy to recall because of their distinctive appearance or behavior. Others are unforgettable because there was something remarkable about where I found them or, perhaps, the weather I hunted them in. In some cases I remember birds because I encountered them at special moments in my life, and many are memorable because of companions who shared the hunt with me. Indeed, not only do I remember the birds bagged, I also recall many of those which outmaneuvered my party and flushed wildly as they sent their derisive cackles ringing across the prairie to us.

And it has always been a great pleasure to call up their ghosts on long winter evenings by the fire, letting memory browse through the past as though it were paging through a dog-eared family photo album. My former hunting partner, Gary Crawford, had the same near-total recall of the pheasants he had met. Gary and I could sit and reflect on our hunts by the hour. For a few moments, as we retold the tales of our favorite exploits, each bird would live again, would flush again, would attack the air again with stubby wings and pumping tail, and would thrill us again, whether it had fallen to the guns or made good its escape. Perhaps it was those fireside sessions with Gary that started my habit of assigning names to the most remarkable roosters I have encountered. These are some of them.

First Blood

I was 12. Parts of my memory of that day are crisp and clear. Others are hazy. For some reason my father and I approached the cornfield we were to hunt by walking through a pigpen. I remember being terrified of the huge sows. The cornfield swept north toward a weedy railway bed. To the east there were some giant powerline towers. My father and I walked abreast a few yards apart from each other through unpicked corn which seemed at least as high as an elephant's eye. But I was pretty short back then. After a while I was astonished to see several animals running down the corn row ahead of me. They looked like turtles. What would turtles be doing in a cornfield?

Suddenly my turtles turned into pheasants—several of them—all beating their wings furiously to rise above the corn. I saw one rooster duck into the row I was walking in, squat for a moment, then leap skyward with a frenzy of hammering wings. As if by magic the gun floated up into view, and for a second I could see the bird and the barrel together. There was a bang, and the cock exploded into a kaleidoscope of brightly colored feathers. I seemed to hear my father booming away at a different bird.

It was my first shot with a shotgun, my first shot at a moving target, and my first pheasant. The gun was a borrowed .410 bolt action—certainly not a gun I could hit anything with today. But the red gods had chosen to smile on a boy that day. I found the rooster piled up under a small blizzard of lazily drifting feathers. He was spectacular. A pheasant hunter was born.

Butch's Bird

It was the last pheasant hunt I had with Butch. Neither of us said anything about it at the time, but I suspected he was dying and I think he knew it too. Butch had already lost the use of his legs a year earlier when he suddenly fell in a pheasant marsh and had to crawl out on his belly using his arms. It was fairly clear to his friends that the rare

This was Butch's bird, along with another I got that day. (Photo by Butch Goplin)

disease which had taken his legs was continuing to throttle off his spinal cord, killing him slowly. He was in his early twenties.

Butch had been the most gifted athlete and dedicated outdoorsman I had met. Until the disease struck he was legendary for his magical command of shotguns and fly rods alike. Even when he could no longer walk, he had friends pull him in a child's wagon up to the one hole on a local trout stream which he could fish from a single position. For as long as he possibly could, Butch warred against his continuing debilitation by fishing and hunting from a canoe. Finally, the loss of strength in his arms made that impossible too; yet, even then, he got a special permit to hunt from his four-wheel-drive vehicle. I am told he shot his last pheasant by firing his heavy double-barrel one-handed, like a pistol, at a bird that flushed toward his parked Blazer. But when Butch called me this day, he said he was not strong enough to hold a gun. He wanted to go out just to watch me hunt. His love of outdoor sports was so strong that he would struggle to go afield, even just as a spectator.

Our last hunt took place late in a season which was poor because a blizzard the previous winter had knocked bird numbers down badly. Brandy was not much more than a pup that year. Butch parked the Blazer in a marshy wildlife management area, and Brandy and I began working our way around it. We had circled the marsh and were pushing through an old apple orchard when Brandy struck scent. At first it was faint. Then the little springer began to sprint. She lost the trail several times in the gusty November winds. Each time she lost it, though, she would cast about until she found the line the bird had taken. Suddenly Brandy spun around and began to look frantically for the bird. I guessed the wind was whipping the scent downwind to her, so I jumped into the grass upwind of her. The rooster spiralled up, seized the wind with his wings, and was making good time when my shot folded him. Only then did I realize that the chase had taken us quite close to where Butch sat in the parked Blazer. The cock dropped twenty yards from him, so he had been able to watch the whole thing. When I came back to him, holding the bird aloft, he was grinning just as he had in the days before the disease.

The Buck Bird

Brandy and I needed one bird to fill out our opening day limit, and she was telling me we were close to it. We were hunting a small but dense triangular patch of weeds which lay near a big management area. Brandy was definitely birdy. Suddenly the weeds shook and parted, and the "bird" got up—a tremendous whitetail buck. My mouth dropped open as the buck bounded away, flashing enough antler to supply half the heads in a taxidermist's shop. As I remained standing, jaw ajar, the buck's third bound brought it down right on top of a rooster skulking in the grass, and it flushed with a storm of flapping and scolding. I finally recovered and managed to toss off a shot with one eye on the buck and the other on the rooster. It is not possible to hit a pheasant more weakly than I hit that one. Brandy, however, was able to dig the cripple out after a long search. As I put that bird in my game bag, I told myself such a sequence of events would not occur again in a lifetime of hunting.

The Coyote Cock

Exactly one week later, while hunting along a weedy waterway in southern Iowa, I was startled to see an odd-looking animal loping right at me. Brandy was behind in pursuit, although something about her expression made me doubt she really wanted to catch up with this thing. It looked like a fat farm collie. Then I realized I was confronting a coyote. As I threw my gun up the coyote wheeled sharply and cut out of the far side of the waterway. Its violent turn startled a huge cock pheasant into flushing out of my side of the weeds. Thoroughly rattled, I jerked off two shots, and then lowered my empty double to watch the cock fly on. It was just a speck in the sky when it suddenly towered and then dropped dead as a stone somewhere in the middle of a featureless cut cornfield. Five men and three dogs combed that field for the better part of an hour before we finally found the rooster.

The Keystone Cops Bird

I think this was the last hunt I took before having my own hunting dog. My wife Kathe and I were hunting with two friends and the owner of the farm we had permission to work. After five miserable hours of slogging through muddy fields we had not even seen a hen. But we did meet up with another party of hunters, a motley crew made up of three adults, two teen-aged boys, a younger kid, a beagle, a collie-shepherd cross, and a very gun-shy springer. They had not seen a pheasant either. So we all took a breather while we tried to scrape pounds of gumbo off our boots. Then the eleven hunters and three dogs heard an electrifying sound—the nearby crowing of a cock pheasant. We stared at each other in disbelief, not moving, until the rooster crowed defiantly a second time. Then, bedlam.

The pheasant was apparently in some weeds along a cornfield, but between us and that cornfield lay a steep ditch. The ditch was thoroughly overgrown with weeds, vines, and spikey thornapple trees. And, right in the middle of the ditch, there stood a loosely strung barbed wire fence. Everyone—all eleven hunters and three dogs —broke at once. Pell-mell down the ditch we went, through the thornapples, up the fence and down again, and then up the bank at the far side. I have often wished I could have witnessed that made stampede from a vantage point high in the sky. It was straight out of a Keystone Cops film.

Two roosters flushed when we straggled up toward the corn, and I was lucky enough to scratch one down with a long shot. It was truly a rooster who had chosen to assert his territorial dominance at an unfortunate moment.

The 200-Yard Bird

I was working the top edge of a deeply cut rail bed when Pawnee, Gary Crawford's wonderful little black Lab, suddenly turned up the side of the bed and lit out straight away from me. "Go with her, Steve!" Gary cried. I began to run as fast as I could, trying to keep in gun range of Pawnee's busy caboose. Oh, was she birdy!

Nothing happened for several long moments, except that I learned again that I cannot run as fast as a dog on a hot trail. Then Pawnee stopped to fuss around with a clump of weeds, and I panted my way up to her, expecting the bird to pop at any moment. Instead, she took off again. Far behind me I could hear Gary shouting encouragement. After another stop and another tense moment, Pawnee went bounding away again on a line at right angles to the tracks. I careened along behind her, losing ground with each stride. When Pawnee got to a barbed wire fence she seemed to lose scent for a few seconds, which gave me time to lurch up closer to her. Then she shot away again and left me to flounder under the fence, gasping for air.

When Pawnee hit the patch of high ragweed, my heart just left me.

She was going too fast and I was going too slow. By now I was blowing so hard I could not hear a thing. I was just ready to say "to hell with it" when the little dog looped and came back on a course which would take her slightly nearer to me. I made a few wild marines-storming-the-beachhead type leaps through the weeds, cutting the angle between us, and I was barely in range when the large old cock went up. Somehow I got the gun up, and somehow the bird tumbled at the shot. I let Pawnee make the retrieve on her own while I fell back into the weeds to wheeze. It was definitely not a routine bird, but then I do not find many pheasants routine.

After the Hunt

I treasure each chance to hunt pheasants and regard the end of every hunt with a bittersweet mixture of gratitude and regret. A man only has the health and opportunity to hunt pheasants for a limited number of seasons. Each season has only a small number of weekends, some of which will be lost from hunting time due to bad weather or business and family obligations. With luck, perseverance, and good health, you and I may be granted the chance to walk the fields in pursuit of roosters for many years to come. And yet we may not. It is not for us to know the future, so we do well if we draw the full measure of joy from the hunts we are privileged to take.

Thus, it is fitting to end each hunt with some sense of the importance of the occasion. I am not criticizing hunters who want only to cram their birds in a plastic bag and quickly seek out a noisy tavern with a television tuned to the game of the week. It just does not feel right to me. I would rather take a few moments to admire the birds, praise the dogs, and relive the highlights of the hunt. There is no more pleasant time to savor the warmth of friendship than when floating in that unique atmosphere of happy exhaustion which follows a good hard hunt.

After taking care of the birds there is nothing more appropriate than seeing to the comfort of your dogs. Too often, hunters forget all about the dogs as soon as the hunt is over and canine assistance is no longer needed. While the men treat themselves to good food and drink, the hungry, thirsty, bur-afflicted dogs are left to shiver in the car. Better rewards are in order for dogs who have hunted their hearts out for you all day. Plenty of fresh water and a full bowl of chow laced with some special doggy treat should come first. Then it is only fair to get down on the floor with your dog and check him over for injuries while you remove any burs. My buddy Brandy is so stoic I cannot count on her to tell me when she has been hurt while hunting. On a hunt late last year she suffered a nasty gash on her chest but gave no indication of it during or after the hunt. If I do not discover her injuries, she will sleep the exhausted sleep of a tired dog, then get up and go right back to hunting the next day, no matter how dangerously hurt she is.

You might also pause at the end of the hunt to remind yourself of exactly what it was that you were hunting for all day. In the afterglow of a hunt most of us think only about how well we shot or how many birds we bagged. Yet that, of course, is not why we hunted. Meat was not the goal. Hell, you can buy game farm pheasants already cleaned for far less than the cost to hunt them. Crude concepts of "success" or "challenge" do not help explain the matter either, for if we merely seek to triumph over an opponent there are many more convenient ways of doing that.

No, something else is supposed to happen when we hunt. In order to justify all the expense and effort of pheasant hunting I have to point to a more valuable end result than a pile of roosters. Simply put: if there is not a spiritual reward in each hunt the whole endeavor does not make much sense. What constitutes that spiritual element is not easy to define. Sometimes I think the most important things that happen in hunting are the surprises, the sights, the smells, and the turns of events that no one could have expected or planned for: like seeing three whitetail bucks rising suddenly from the cover, bounding away with the grace of dancers, then floating over a fence as if levitated by some gifted magician; like urging your dog into a clump of weeds to bounce out a rooster and having a twenty-five-pound coon come scrambling out while the dog looks on with wide-eyed astonishment; and like stopping to stand on the prairie while a majestic flock of sandhill cranes sweeps southward overhead, sending their mysterious flute-like trilling miles ahead of them.

Yet, there is a spiritual element in the hunting itself which keeps me in love with the sport. At no other time am I quite as fully alive as when caught up in the thrill of the hunt. It is as if all my other hours, pleasant though they might be, are less valuable because I am not totally focused on and involved in what I am doing. I think that in all of us there is another person, a sensual and primitive being, who is ignored or suppressed while we do the things we normally do. We get back in touch with that hot-blooded person in us only at isolated moments in our lives. Yet he or she is always there, a part of us we miss much of the time without knowing what we are missing. When I hunt pheasants I believe I am hunting for that wild part of myself, and for a few heady moments, I can live with an intensity and a completeness that are missing from the rest of my life.

Appendix I

Age and Effects on Population

While there are said to be other ways to tell youngsters from oldsters, the simplest technique is to separate them by examining their spurs. If the spur length is three-fourths of an inch or less (measured from the tip to the back of the bird's leg), the bird is one of this year's crop. Young roosters can be surprisingly large and fully feathered. Then, too, some late-hatching cock birds are so underdeveloped that you would never be able to tell them from hens. First year cocks have soft, grey, conical spurs. You can scratch them with a fingernail. Older birds will have spurs that are harder and more polished looking, in addition to being longer.

While it is always interesting to know the age of a bird you bag there are two reasons in particular for aging your birds. Old birds are significantly tougher if not cooked properly, so you will want to be sure to keep track of them before choosing a way of preparing them. I am always eager to age the birds my group takes on opening day

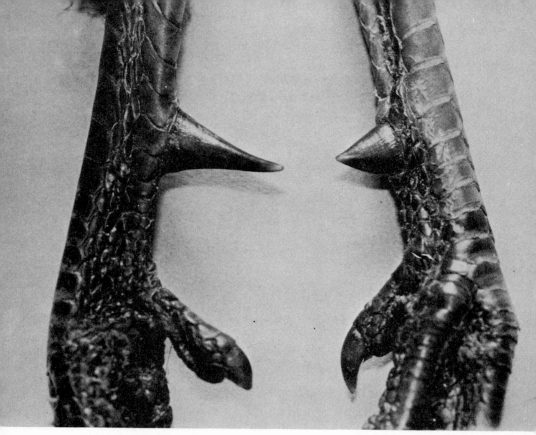

Spur length is the best way to age roosters. Older birds have long, hard, pointed spurs. The spurs of young birds are soft, short, and conical.

because it will tell me what sort of season we have got to look forward to. If short-spurred cocks comprise five-sixths of the bag, the birds probably had a fairly normal spring hatch. That means that overall bird numbers will be typical for the area. If there are more youngsters proportionately than that, I know the season will be exceptionally good. Opening day bags with equal numbers of youngsters and old birds bode ill for the rest of the year. One interesting age ratio study showed that the opening day ratio of young to old birds was five to one, but at the end of the season it stood at a little more than one youngster to one old cock. What that says to me—as if I needed more proof—is that those roosters that defy the odds by surviving a fall season and a winter are so rugged and shrewd that they will not easily make a fatal mistake in their second hunting season.

Age ratios fluctuate wildly this way because pheasant populations typically rise and plummet dramatically. Hunters have always had trouble understanding these swings of bird abundance; I fear they always will. At bottom, the problem may lie with the fact that small game populations go up and down in response to entirely different principles than human populations. The average American family has about two children these days, and their survival prospects are excellent. Pheasant families often start with a dozen or so youngsters, and they are successful if six or seven of them make it from spring to fall.

So when bird numbers plummet, hunters tend to ask "what killed all our pheasants?" They will accuse the foxes of having eaten too well, or they even might decide a closed season will help. These are false answers, though, which follow from asking the wrong question. No single agent kills unacceptable numbers of pheasants over a long period of time. The truth is that many things kill pheasants: feral cats, automobiles, winter storms, owls, mowing equipment, and spring rains all kill pheasants. And the birds have accidents. I saw a hen fly into a telephone wire and break her neck. You would never want to underwrite life insurance policies for a flock of pheasants, for the birds die with disheartening frequency.

High mortality rates are part of nature's plan for small game populations. The other part of the plan is high reproduction rates, so the birds annually recoup their losses with strong nesting success. And here is the true answer to the question "what killed all the birds." If, for any reason, the hens fail to have a good spring nesting season, the fall population will look puny. Pheasant populations certainly are based upon the number of birds surviving the winter, and they are influenced powerfully by the relative nesting success of the surviving hens. Even a relatively weak population of hens can amaze us with their ability to repopulate an area, if they have good cover and ideal spring nesting conditions. Conversely, an exceptionally good population of birds can produce a disappointing fall population when circumstances are against them. The key to excellent populations, then, is not limiting pheasant deaths but assuring that the survivors will enjoy the kind of nesting success which allows them to outproduce their losses.

This basic idea is worth repeating because it is so hard to grasp. Even the seasoned wildlife biologist must struggle with himself to keep things in perspective. Looking back on a fall season in which adverse weather caused few roosters to be harvested, he is apt to think: "Next year is going to be a barn-burner because we have got all those roosters left over!'' That is just the way we naturally view population levels. But experienced managers know that the availability of good cover and favorable spring weather will count for far more in the long run. Pheasant populations are the result of a dynamic tension between losses and additions. Put all the negative factors on one side—losses to hunting, predation, storms, farming activities, and accidents—and they will usually be balanced by that single, potent force: natural reproduction.

This is not to say that all other factors are insignificant. The more hens you have alive at springtime, the less critically important the nesting success of each one is. Winter is an especially dangerous time for pheasants in much of the pheasant range. That is true in spite of the fact that pheasants handle normal or even adverse winters surprisingly well. Numbing cold and deep snowdrifts often cause hunters to wring their hands with concern for the birds, but pheasants just reach back for reserves of their impressive will to live. Pheasants have survived a whole month of winter with no food at all. A flock of birds which has been denied food a long time by winter may be in poor condition, but let a single break in the weather come and those birds will pounce on the nearest food and almost instantly regain their vigor.

Blizzards are another story. There is little in a pheasant's survival kit which arms it against the threats of killer blizzards. The combination of wet snow, howling gales, and plummeting temperatures is so deadly that one Minnesota blizzard came close to wiping out the pheasants in the affected area; 90 percent of the birds were killed. When you see charts of pheasant populations, quite often the drastic dips are explained by blizzards. Strong climbs upward usually correspond to periods not cursed with blizzards.

While the grey partridge from Hungary has an instinctive response to winter storms which allows it to survive, the pheasant is not so lucky. Pheasants, unlike partridge, offer each other no protection in a blizzard. Each bird is on his own. The feathery armor which protects pheasants so well at other times of their lives is of little use when winds whip snow at them. Some birds turn away from the storm only to have the wind drive snow up under their feathers: they usually freeze to death. Others turn to face the blizzard, with the frequent result that snow encases their beaks or blows into them until the birds suffocate. Spring thaws reveal the frozen carcasses of those which do not make

A blizzard-killed rooster. Wind-blown snow has packed into the bird's mouth. (Photo by South Dakota Game, Fish and Parks Dept.)

it to secure cover, grim statues standing as monuments to winter's cruelty.

Let's return to that phrase, "secure cover." Given some shelter, pheasants can survive the worst that winter dishes up. Six years ago a killer blizzard swept through the pheasant country I most liked to hunt, and killed 80 percent of the bird life in its path. I went elsewhere to open the season the next year, but friends took easy limits of birds from a big brushy wildlife management area right in the center of the blizzard's devastation. That just demonstrates again the critical importance of good habitat.

Today's pheasant hunters seem, at last, to appreciate the value of good habitat. That appreciation did not develop easily. Not long ago, pheasant populations were declining steeply, and I recall all the long and heated debates that attended that sad spectacle. Many hunters blamed foxes or avian predators, perhaps because hunters, being predators themselves, can more easily understand the effects of predation than failed reproduction. Other hunters cursed pesticides, sunspots, and excessive hunting pressure. Bounties were placed on foxes in some areas, and in other areas hunters forced wildlife agencies to close hunting seasons. Although wildlife managers kept pointing toward habitat losses as the fundamental problem, hunters seemed to look desperately for scapegoats. Yet, that era appears to be behind us. Hunters now largely appreciate the vital role habitat plays in pheasant populations.

Thus, as habitat goes, so goes the pheasant. We see that now. Ah, but we can still wish it were not so, for the inescapable fact is that both habitat and birds are going, going steadily out of the farmland landscape. Modern drainage and clearing technology is capable of turning the funkiest swamps into clean, flat soil bearing row upon row of neatly planted crops. I would rather believe that today's weak bird populations could be blamed on great horned owls or foxes. Those are enemies we could do battle with, unlike such abstractions as U.S. Department of Agriculture policies or the international balance of trade. I would rather find some scapegoat than to believe the persistent eradication of cover—a process which moves with the terrible inevitability of a glacier—was really to blame.

Yet, it is far too soon to write epitaphs for the pheasant. After all, this is the bird which came to us through the hands of Jason and his Argonauts and Julius Caesar, not to mention George Washington. I cannot believe the ringneck has come this far only to fade away. In

A photo showing a shelterbelt in "the good old days" of pheasant abundance. When you have habitat, you will have pheasants. It is that simple. (Photo by South Dakota Game, Fish and Parks Dept.)

some regions, the birds cling resolutely to the remaining shreds of their habitat, while in others they are responding lustily to sound management efforts. The pheasant is still with us, still savagely asserting his claim to his new homeland. God bless his sassy heart. May he long prosper.

Appendix II

Favorite Pheasant Recipes

It is always hard to know what to say to people who ask you why you hunt pheasants. Why, indeed? I suspect those people would generally not understand the reasons I have given elsewhere in this book. Perhaps, if they had enjoyed the recipes listed below, they would understand that. Over the years I have found my taste in pheasant recipes growing steadily more simple and basic. Complex recipes featuring pheasant almost always taste good, but they would probably be just as delicious with chicken. Some seem to have been concocted by cooks who simply do not like the taste of wild game and who struggle to disguise it with herbs and sauces. What a waste!

Aside from abusing the meat before it gets to the table, there are only two ways you can actually ruin a pheasant dish. The first and most common mistake most cooks make is to overcook the meat. Overcooked pheasant is tough and objectionably strong-tasting. The other frequent error is to let the meat get dry. Pheasants have little fat,

Good friends, good wine, and some darn good eating. The perfect end to a hunt.

even in fall, and any cooking technique which dries the flesh out will result in dangerous-to-dentures rawhide. This is especially a problem with old roosters, which is why you want to determine the age of each bird and mark it on the package. If you let an old rooster get freezer-burned, and then bake it dry, please serve it with little power saws for cutting and copious amounts of bourbon for washing it down.

Speaking of which, let's say a word about wines. More Americans every year are enjoying wine with dinner, and nothing adds a nicer festive touch and complimentary taste than a good wine served with your pheasant. But many of us still are buffaloed by the mystique of what wine "goes" with what meat. It is not such a big deal. The basic principle is that light meats are overpowered by heavy wines just as strong meat dishes will overwhelm light wines. You are supposed to balance the weight of the wine and the meat.

Many of us have heard that white wine is supposed to be served with poultry. It is, unless you are talking about wild-grown poultry, in which case wild birds, like pheasants and grouse, are strong enough in flavor to push a delicate white wine all over the table. The most appropriate pheasant wines are the lighter reds. Of French wines, that might be a Beaujolais or one of the lighter Bordeaux wines. Of the more attractively priced California wines, a light Cabernet, a Gamay, a Zinfandel, or a Barbera would be an excellent choice. A nice Rosé or Chianti won't go wrong either. A final word about wines: suit yourself, but I have found that cheap wines taste cheap even when used in cooking, and "cooking wines" taste worst of all.

The following recipe is the one I will use four times out of five. It is simple, quick, and scrumptious.

HURRY-UP PHEASANT
1 pheasant (skin on or off)
approx. ½ stick butter
approx. 1 C liquid (part water, broth, wine, or sherry, chosen and
    combined to suit your taste and mood)
4 T flour
pinch sage or poultry seasoning
salt and pepper

Bone the pheasant, then cut the meat into bite-size pieces. Melt butter in a skillet; when it bubbles add meat and brown quickly. Sprinkle in flour, toss lightly, and brown a moment more. Stir in liquid, add seasonings, bring to a boil to thicken sauce. Cover and simmer gently, adding liquid if needed, until the meat is tender (about 15 minutes, depending on the size of the pieces). Serve on a bed of rice.

If you wish, you can add a dozen or so halved fresh mushrooms just before simmering the dish. They extend the dish and end up tasting very much like the pheasant.

Is that too basic? Then try this fabulous dish, modified slightly from a recipe I got from Dan Brennan, a novelist and inveterate plains grouse and pheasant hunter.

PHEASANT DUMPLING PIE

2 pheasants cut up
4½ C water
6 carrots, sliced
4 onions, quartered
6 peppercorns
1 bay leaf
water or chicken stock
1 onion, chopped
½ C butter
2 pods pimento, chopped
8 T flour
½ C whipping cream
1 pkg. frozen broccoli spears
1 pkg. refrigerated biscuit dough
1 or 2 sticks pie crust mix

Bring pheasant, water, carrots, quartered onions, peppercorns and bay leaf to a boil and simmer covered for about 30 minutes or until pheasant is tender. Bone the pheasant and cut the meat into bite-size pieces. Strain the broth, reserving 4 C (add chicken stock or water if necessary), and mix the pheasant with the vegetables. Brown the chopped onion in butter and add the pimento. Stir in the flour, then add the reserved broth plus the cream to make a medium white sauce, stirring until thickened. Season to taste with salt and pepper. Grease a 3-quart casserole. On the bottom put the thawed broccoli spears cut into bite-size pieces, then the pheasant and the vegetables. Cut the biscuit dough circles into quarters and place them on top. Add the white sauce over all. Make the pie crust according to directions and roll it out to cover the casserole. One stick of mix will cover the casserole, but two give a thicker crust. Press crust to the rim and slash generously. Bake at 400° until the crust is golden and the sauce bubbly, about 40 minutes.

The following is an absolutely un-original recipe used in kitchens across the country wherever grouse or pheasant are found. It is quick and sure to please, and a fine way to cook old birds.

PHEASANTS IN MUSHROOM SAUCE

1 or 2 pheasants
1 can condensed cream of mushroom soup
½ can sherry or dry wine
½ can water or chicken bouillon
pinch sage or poultry seasoning
salt and pepper
1 T chopped (or dried) parsley
1 lb. fresh mushrooms, cleaned and sliced thick

Disjoint birds and brown quickly in butter. Meanwhile mix the remaining ingredients in a greased 2-quart casserole. Stir in the meat and pan drippings, cover, and bake in a 350° oven for an hour. Serve over rice or stuffing.

The following is my own invention. If you have a fondue pot and a little patience it is loads of fun.

FONDUE PHEASANT

1 pheasant
either peanut oil or chicken stock to fondue in
sauces

Simply bone and cut up the bird until the pieces are small enough to cook quickly in a fondue pot. Set up the fondue pot with the stovetop-heated liquid over the fondue flame; put it in the center of the table with an assortment of sauces. Some of the sauces I like with pheasant are soy sauce, Lord Grey Chutney sauce, Chinese duck-orange sauce, sparkling sauce, Chinese plum sauce mixed with sharp mustard, sweet-sour sauce, burgundy sauce, and currant jelly. You can probably think of others that would appeal to you and your friends. I enjoy moving around from sauce to sauce, getting a full mix of flavors.

Here is a festive but easily prepared recipe. Your guests are sure to rave about this dish.

FLAMED PHEASANT

1 pheasant
2 T butter
salt and pepper
2 oz. brandy
4 green onions, chopped
1 carrot, minced
1 T chopped (or dried) parsley
1 pinch each thyme, marjoram
2 T flour
1 C chicken bouillon
½ C dry white wine
2 C sliced mushrooms

Disjoint meat and rub with salt and pepper. Brown in butter for 5 minutes. Pour brandy over meat and light it; allow it to burn out. Add onions, carrot, parsley, thyme and marjoram; brown 2 to 3 minutes. Sprinkle flour over all, stir to blend well, and then stir in the bouillon, wine and mushrooms. Cover and simmer 30 to 40 minutes (until tender). Tip: reserve a teaspoonful of brandy when you pour the rest on the meat, let the brandy warm in the pan for a moment, and then light the reserved spirits in the spoon. Lower the flaming spoon into the pan, and lean back!

This recipe is offered by a friend who grew up in pheasant country. It will make a treat of the oldest rooster.

LAURA'S CHEESE PHEASANT CASSEROLE

1 pheasant, sectioned
paprika
4–6 C white sauce
¾ C Swiss cheese, grated
½ C parmesan cheese, grated
1 C chopped mushrooms
3 T diced onion

Prepare 4–6 cups of medium white sauce, diluting the mixture with chicken bouillion instead of milk. In a separate pan, sauté mushroom bits in butter and diced onion. Do not overcook. Add mushrooms, onions and half of the grated Swiss and parmesan cheese to the white sauce and stir until the cheese is melted. Arrange the cut-up pieces of pheasant in a 9″ by 12″ covered pan and pour white sauce over. Garnish with paprika for color and bake for 1½ hours at 350°, checking for tenderness. Large birds might take longer. During last 20 minutes of baking, sprinkle remaining parmesan cheese over top. Remove cover so cheese will brown. Served over rice with broccoli and cold fruit salad for color, this is an excellent large group meal.

The next dish is a tangy sauce Kathe and I always serve with pheasant which has not been cooked in a sauce. I cannot praise it enough. One of my favorite ways to eat pheasant simply involves cutting the bird into nuggets of meat, browning the pieces quickly in butter, then putting them on a plate with a big dollop of Sparkling Sauce. You just cannot do better than that.

SPARKLING SAUCE
1 jar (approx. 1 C) currant jelly
1 jar (approx. 1 C) orange marmalade
4 t lemon juice
2 t grated lemon rind
1 t vinegar
½ t dry mustard

Melt all ingredients over low heat while stirring. Cool and return to washed jelly jars and store in refrigerator. Served with any baked or roasted game birds.

One of the compensations for living in Minnesota, where pheasants are hard to find, is that it is easy to find economically priced wild rice. The difference between wild rice and "tame" white rice is, to my taste, analogous to the difference between mass-processed chickens and wild pheasants. The recipe offered here is delightful in texture as well as taste.

NUTTY WILD RICE
1 C wild rice (or half wild and half brown rice)
2 C chicken bouillon
1 t butter
salt and pepper
1 pinch oregano
1 T chopped (or dried) parsley
2 T chopped onion
½ to 1 C chopped walnuts

Wash the rice thoroughly in cold water. Bring the rest of the ingredients (except nuts) to a boil and add the rice. Cover, reduce heat to very low, and cook 45 minutes, or until tender. Mix in nuts and serve. Or, alternatively, bring bouillon and seasonings to a boil in a pressure cooker. Add washed rice, cover, and bring to full pressure. Cook on medium heat for 15 minutes and turn heat off. When pressure returns to normal, remove cover, heat quickly to drive off any remaining liquid. Add nuts and serve.

Index

Other Outdoor Books From Stackpole

Hunting Ducks & Geese
by Steve Smith
Hard facts, good bets, and serious advice from a duck hunter you can trust.

How to Carve Wildfowl
by Roger Schroeder
Nine North American masters share the carving and painting techniques that earn them blue ribbons.

Modern Falconry
by Jack Samson
Your illustrated guide to the art and sport of hunting with North American hawks.

Complete Book of the Wild Turkey
by Roger Latham
"Best general purpose volume on the wild turkey available."

Wildlife Management Institute

Grouse & Woodcock
by Nick Sisley
Filled with woodland savvy about two of nature's finest upland game species.

Drummer in the Woods
by Burton L. Spiller
Twenty-one wonderful stories on grouse shooting by the "Poet Laureate of Grouse."

AVAILABLE AT YOUR LOCAL BOOKSTORE or
STACKPOLE BOOKS
P.O. Box 1831
Dept. MP
Harrisburg, PA 17105

EAU CLAIRE DISTRICT LIBRARY